The
Surrogate
Assassin

A Sherlock Holmes Mystery
Based on the characters created by
Sir Conan Doyle

by
Christopher Leppek

A Write Way Publishing Book

Dedication
For Lisa, who lived this story by my side, and kept
the faith.

Write Way Publishing
10555 E. Dartmouth, Ste 210
Aurora, CO 80014

First Edition; 1998

ISBN 1-885173-54-7
1 2 3 4 5 6 7 8 9

All the world's a stage,
And all the men and women merely players:
They have their exits and their entrances;
And one man in his time plays many parts.
—William Shakespeare

Foreword

Who has never dreamed, at least once in their lifetime, of stumbling across a wondrous treasure? Who has not coveted the experience of those lucky few whose eyes first, before all others, gazed upon something rare, precious and beautiful?

I have dreamed this, and I have been one of those fortunate few. That which I found (or which, more accurately, found me) is without doubt rare and precious, even though this treasure held no gold doubloons, no silver pieces of eight. This was no weatherbeaten seachest from which diamonds, sapphires, rubies, emeralds and topaz overflowed in burlesque profusion.

This particular treasure, rather, is a fortune in words and of facts, a long-sleeping revelation waiting for the right moment in which to make itself known. It is, to be precise, a Sherlock Holmes adventure from more than a century ago—one which deals with one of the most dramatic events of American history, and does so in a way that shall change a great many long-held beliefs. It documents the unravelling of a mystery most of us never even knew existed. It is, as its narrator, the deathless Dr. John H. Watson writes, the telling of a colossal secret. Rare indeed!

Even so, I can't say that it was beautiful, at least not in its physical form. I haven't the slightest idea, in fact, why I did not reject the manuscript out of hand when it arrived, unannounced and unexpected, aboard a lumbering UPS van and was placed unceremoniously upon my doorstep earlier this year. I am a newspaperman, after all, trained to suspect the origin of all things unrequested which come in plain brown wrappers. There are few reporters with more than a few deadlines under their belts who have not been the recipients of such parcels or letters. More often than not, the senders are odd folk— bothersome gadflies of one stripe or another, harmless but deluded eccentrics or, perhaps, considerably worse—who feel that the writer in question might be able to somehow bring to light their stories, their ideas, their expressions or their visions through whatever publication they happen to represent. And journalists, of course, are in turn a fearfully suspicious and cynical lot. They shed no tears and bat no eyelids as they throw such epistles into the circular file. It is a strange and common ritual.

I've done it myself, plenty of times, but on that cloudy Saturday in early March, for some reason, I declined to treat this particular parcel with the usual heartlessness. Perhaps it was the return address, from a place called Polk City in Iowa, that made me hesitate. I'd never heard of the place, but I could well imagine it as a pleasant and sleepy little town, the sort of place about which Garrison Keillor might wax poetic. I could not imagine it, however, as the hometown of anyone with questionable motives or lunatic aspirations. Strange parcels simply do not come from places like Polk City.

Enclosed within a simple box was the complete manuscript of *The Surrogate Assassin*, handwritten on elegant, slightly translucent paper of heavy stock. The hand was crude and masculine, but displayed the craft common among the educated classes of a century past. The fountain ink had apparently once been black or blue, but with the progression of years had turned a rusty, reddish brown. Along with it came an efficient letter of explanation from its sender, written in a crude hand with a Bic fine point.

The sender gave me his name but demanded total anonymity. He identified himself as a farmer (corn and oats) who had once read, and had not forgotten, an article of mine in one of the so-called "farm weeklies" so popular across the Great Plains. The article had dealt with some of the many fascinating legends and ghost stories which have long surrounded the tragic assassination of Abraham Lincoln, long a topic of great personal interest to me. The article, he explained, bore more than a few striking similarities to claims made by the alleged Dr. Watson of *The Surrogate Assassin*, and since it was the only article he'd ever read which delved into such esoteric matters, he decided to forward the manuscript to me.

It had come into his possession not long before, with as little forewarning as he'd given me. It had been hand-delivered to him by a representative of a venerable and respected law firm in nearby Des Moines. The representative informed him that the firm had been holding the manuscript, totally sealed, for more than 50 years under a detailed agreement into which it had entered with two English gentlemen in the year 1935. As the heir of a certain individual mentioned in the account, the Iowa farmer was to be the legally designated recipient for the writings, whether he liked it or not.

I gather that after reading the long-hidden work, he didn't much like it. The certain individual mentioned in the story turned out to be his grandfather, long ago deceased, and, as it developed, appears to have been a strikingly different individual from the one his grandson (or virtually anyone else who had known him) imagined him to be. If I am able to gauge his feelings from his letter to me, I'd have to say the unsuspecting farmer from Iowa was mightily jarred by a couple of revelations concerning the kindly grandfather he remembered from his own early youth.

At any rate, he wanted nothing to do with the manuscript, even though I think that he fully believed in its claims. "I know nothing about such things," he wrote, "and I'd just as soon be done with it all." He had sufficient foresight, however, and enough concern for history, that he didn't relegate it to the ash pit nor to a forgotten shelf in his house near sleepy Polk City. He went ahead and sent it to somebody he "reckoned to be an expert in such things" (meaning, I assume, me) and thereafter wished to "wash my hands of the whole affair."

Before I even began reading the treasure that had been left to my care, however, my skepticism asserted itself. I know enough about Sherlock Holmes to realize that a goodly number of supposedly "lost" cases have recently come into view. There are some, I admit, which I find quite credible. It is not so shocking to consider the possibility that Holmes might have worked with Freud, with Roosevelt, even with Houdini. It is just as reasonably logical to speculate that Holmes might have lent his talents to the case of Jack the Ripper. His dreadful crimes took place, after all, in the London of the mid-1880s. Why in the world shouldn't Holmes have been involved?

All the same, I have three or more books on my shelf at this moment which purport to tell three utterly different tales of Holmes' activities in the Ripper case. And next to them sit books which pit Holmes against Count Dracula, against Mr. Hyde, against a Professor Moriarty who more resembles Batman than the Napoleon of Crime. More than a grain of salt should be taken, obviously, with such "lost" cases.

Nevertheless, time and time again Watson did inform us, from the depths of the sacred Canon itself, that many if not most of Holmes' cases have never been publicly revealed. The lost or unpublished cases "grow as thick as blackberries among the stories and actually outnumber them," wrote the eminent Sherlockian H.W. Bell, of such enticingly invisible adventures as the Giant Rat of Sumatra, the Bishopsgate Jewel Case or the Colossal Schemes of Baron Maupertuis. Watson told us further that many of these cases were dutifully chronicled by him and stored in a dispatch box in the vaults of Cox & Company bankers in Charing Cross. *The Surrogate Assassin*, if one can believe its own Prologue, once reposed in this box as well, and was fortuitously removed by Watson a few years before Luftwaffe bombs fairly demolished the stately old place during the Blitz.

Watson's plentiful allusions to hidden or secreted cases, however, no more establishes the authenticity of this particular manuscript than the existence of obviously bogus cases discredits it. I decided that the credibility of the case would have to be established on its own merits or not at all, and I have spent much of the past seven months engaged in this pursuit.

My final report, greatly summarized, is that I believe fully not only in the authenticity of the manuscript and its authorship, but in the many striking, even outrageous, claims which it boldly makes. I have forwarded copies of the manuscript to several highly knowledgeable Sherlockians (or Holmesians, as some of them prefer to call themselves) and have, without exception, received the opinion that the manuscript is likely an authentic one. They have found its penmanship to bear a remarkable likeness to the surviving specimens of

Watson's hand; they have cited its writing style and syntax as highly similar to the early canonical writings; they have found its chronology to be well in line with the known history of Holmes' casebooks; they have found the methodology ascribed to the Great Detective to be credible.

Based on my own research, I find its accuracy in the realm of detail to be remarkable. The various characters who roam through the account were, in historical terms, in the right places at the right times for the events of this case to have taken place. Such minutiae as street names, ship crossings, building descriptions, weather reports, news events, addresses, ad infinitum, correspond without fail to the references within the manuscript. Its adherence to the known facts, great and small, of its central mystery—the Lincoln assassination—is utterly faithful.

Admittedly, there are several blank spots. Holmes, Watson and other parties wished for this case to remain secret until now, and for this reason certain leads simply cannot be followed. The identities of certain important individuals were changed, for example, and no post-case correspondence of the case was preserved by any of the participants. I had hoped to find the names of Holmes and Watson in one of the registers of the three hotels where they stayed in America, to put forth another example—New York's Windsor, Washington's National and Baltimore's Carrollton. Alas, not only have the hotels themselves long ago disappeared, their guest books were somehow lost within the rubble. There is, in short, no hard proof, no "smoking gun" with which to firmly establish the case.

I am not daunted by this. On the whole, the manuscript has stood up very well to careful and critical scrutiny, and there are less forensic components to my faith as well. I believe I was no further along than the third or fourth page when I became utterly convinced that I was in Watson's storytelling hands. Somehow I could simply feel it. There is not only the historically credible notion that Holmes, without doubt the world's greatest consulting detective, would likely have somehow involved himself in one of the greatest crimes of the 19th century. There is also the conviction that the peculiar oddities, the profusion of paradoxes, which are interwoven into the Lincoln assassination would have been far too much for Holmes to totally resist. Somehow, the very premise of this case seems right. It would never stand up in a court of law, of course, but then many true things could not.

Interestingly, Watson seemed not to have given a second thought to the skepticism which might greet the remarkable tale he arranged to preserve for posterity. In his Prologue (which, along with an Epilogue and a few notations, was apparently written many years after the adventure itself had been put into writing) Watson worries only about whether future generations might find the story a bit too quaint, or a tad tame for their tastes. Despite his otherwise insightful ruminations about the people who would one day read his story, I fear that Watson misunderstood us on that one point. On the question of modern-day interest in such a case as this, I think the good doctor need hardly have worried.

On that note, and without further ado, I turn the forum over to those whose story this is. It has come a long way indeed since being written, and I can only hope that the good Dr. Watson and the legendary Sherlock Holmes, wherever their adventurous spirits may now reside, will somehow be able to witness its telling at last. I am honoured to be of service to them.

Respectfully,
Christopher Leppek
October 7, 1997
Denver

Prologue

I have just completed reading the account which follows, the adventure of *The Surrogate Assassin*, which I put into words more than half a century ago. In reading, for the first time since its composition, the long-secreted chronicle of my exploits during one remarkable summer with Sherlock Holmes, I experience a curious sensation of alienation, or of distance, from my very own words. It is markedly unlike the familiar sense of *déjà vu* I had expected to encounter. Although I recollect the events as if they happened yesterday, and remember just as well writing them down, it nevertheless feels as if another writer entirely, from a place and time utterly alien to the man I am today, had written the account, and not I.

There is, of course, the undeniable difference in my own chronology. When the events of this story took place, I was a hale and hearty young man of less than 30 years, yet to experience my first marriage, yet to experience a great many things in life. I am today a white-haired, rather feeble and occasionally forgetful old fellow of 80 years who has gained, at least I hope, an ounce or two of wisdom in the interim. Still, it is not the simple arithmetic of years that jars me. Something considerably more profound than the mere passage of time has taken place since I wrote down those words.

Yes, there are many striking outward differences between now and then. From where I sit today in my London study, I can clearly see through the window a steady stream of rushing automobiles and lorries. Above my rooftop is plainly visible the winged profile of an aeroplane, heading for some distant destination. I own a telephone with which to communicate with those far away, and a phonograph and radio by which to be entertained by those far away. It is said that soon a device will become available which will allow moving images to be glimpsed within a box in my very own living room.

If someone had told me 50 years ago that such ideas would eventually become reality I would surely have laughed at them to their face. And who could blame me then for scoffing at the sort of ideas that authors like H.G. Wells were using for sensational novels? I laugh at such talk no longer, dear readers, for today such advances seem hardly remarkable at all. If someone were to tell me—as indeed one or two people already have—that human beings will travel into space before the end of this mind-boggling 20th century, I would have no reason to doubt them and every reason in the world to believe them fully. What was once impossible has now become quite possible indeed, and the horizons, it seems to me, are without limit.

Yet it is still not this that strikes me. It is not the changes in and of themselves that are disturbing, but the effect of these changes upon mankind. I refer to changes within man's heart and soul, a far more elusive essence to describe than industrial advancements. Such progress as mankind has witnessed within the past 75 years is without any precedent in human history, and has come far swifter than any human ability to evolve in tandem with it. I sense a certain fear in the humanity which surrounds me now, a sense of anomie, that gives me trepidation for a future I shall never see.

When Holmes and I traveled to America to pursue the case of the surrogate (for this is very much an American tale) the world seemed an infinitely slower, more graceful—and honourable—place. I readily admit that war was a feature of that time as well, and in a form as ugly as any war has ever been. This story, in fact, took place at a time when America was still reeling from the blows it had dealt itself during its Civil War. Those who had fought beneath the Stars and Stripes still held hatred in their hearts for those whose banner was the Southern Cross, and vice-versa. Much more central to the case of the surrogate, the assassination of Abraham Lincoln—truly one of the darkest, most catastrophic single acts committed in history—was something discussed only with pain, with regret and, yes, with bitter hatred by the Americans of that time. It was a tragedy whose wounds had yet to heal and whose pain had yet to fade.

No, the past was certainly no Eden, and it is my hope that your generation does not misunderstand it as such. But behold the present!

Today's banners are the swastika, raised over Germany, and the hammer and sickle, which flies over Soviet Russia. The storm clouds now gathering upon the world's horizon are far greater, and far blacker, than any that have come and gone before. I sense no honour nor restraint within these forces, no belief that warfare, as horrible as it must be, should itself have limits placed upon it lest utter chaos prevail. As hypocritical or paradoxical as it may seem to you, such restraints, such a notion as honour, once did govern man's behavior, even during times of war. I remain convinced that these social controls, which seem so badly shaken today, did much to pull the human race from out of the worst disasters it managed to bring down upon itself.

This concern, mind you, makes me neither bitter about the present day nor foolishly nostalgic about times gone by. The evolution within the span of my own lifetime is not something I dwell upon or, for that matter, even bother to give much thought to on a regular basis. The changes we have witnessed and are daily witnessing are dramatic surely, but I do not feel them to be beyond the human ability for adaptation. Without question, there are great benefits to be had if caution and prudence prevail in the long run, and I believe they ultimately will.

As I read *The Surrogate Assassin* from this point in time, however, these differences seem to jump at me from the very pages. It makes me realize just how long a time these 54 years have really been, and how far mankind has come in that time. Although this case dealt with a very real tragedy, and while its ultimate solution itself necessitated tragedy and grief, it now seems almost civilized to me. I remember well that as I wrote the story, I often envisioned a future generation reading it, and experiencing the same sense of breathless surprise that I felt as Holmes unerringly forged his way through the case's many twists and turns. I can only wonder today whether a generation that has already seen so very much that is shocking and surprising—perhaps too much—and which is anticipating the vision of a great deal more within the near future, may still be interested in a case as prosaic and, for lack of a better term, as genteel, as this one might seem.

Only you, can be the judge of that. For my part, reading my account of the case brought back to me many rich and potent memories of one of the most fascinating cases with which Holmes was ever involved. I have spoken of it with him dozens of times over the years, and he agrees with that assessment, rest assured. Holmes, like myself, would have loved to be able to discuss this adventure publicly. He was never so modest nor so free of vanity that he wouldn't have enjoyed the celebrity which the disclosure of this case would surely have brought him, over and above the fame he continues to enjoy to this day.

Such a disclosure, however, has been declared an impossibility by Holmes, by myself and by certain other individuals who play an important role in the events of this account. As long as any of us shall live, and for 50 years more than that, *The Surrogate Assassin* must remain hidden from public view, for reasons that will become clear as the story progresses.

I am addressing you therefore from the grave itself. While obviously I live as these words are written (as does Holmes, incidentally, in his country residence on the Sussex Downs) by the time they are read, I shall be at least a half-century dead. I find it a fascinating perspective from which to address a reading audience, a time capsule of sorts, in which only I am allowed to speak.

Last week, I opened my tin dispatch-box deep within the vaults of Cox & Co. in Charing Cross, and removed the manuscript of *The Surrogate Assassin* from among a goodly number of other case histories which, for various reasons, Holmes wishes to remain untold. Soon I shall mail the only copy to an attorney in Des Moines, an American city I have never seen, along with instructions to see that it is delivered to the descendants of an individual portrayed in the narrative, only after 50 years have passed since the death of Sherlock Holmes or myself, whichever is later. I have sealed its box in wax to insure that this attorney (or, quite probably, his professional successors) follows these instructions faithfully and does not read the manuscript himself. I have also made arrangements to inform the law firm in question of the death of myself and that of Holmes shortly after their occurrences. In this elaborate and admittedly rather cabalistic manner, I feel confident that the story will eventually be told in line with the conditions of a secret pact of which Holmes and I are the only living participants.

I know nothing of the time you will know, dear readers of the 1980s, the 1990s or well beyond. I know not how successfully, or unsuccessfully, your immediate forbears will have managed to deal with the storm clouds I am seeing today. I know nothing of your losses or your gains, your despairs or your glories, and this is how it must be. It is the unbendable nature of Father Time that one's vision be limited to the present and to the past, and that we must remain blind to the events of the future.

This gives you the distinct advantage of knowing not only the answers to most questions I may ask, but of questions that my generation has yet to conceive of. Were I, or any of my contemporaries, to somehow journey to visit your time (perhaps aboard the good Mr. Wells' time machine!) we would be hopelessly out of place, anachronistic antiques from an era of quaintness.

In light of this hard fact, you will perhaps forgive an old veteran of such quaint times if he feels a touch of selfish glee for possessing at least one advantage over you.

And that is a secret.

It is a secret which will shatter a number of widely-held, historically accepted—and utterly false—beliefs. At the same time, it will confirm a number of much-denied rumours which, despite their ill-repute, have at least of this writing stubbornly refused to fade away. It will, in short, force the publishing houses to revise their very history books.

I understand that this in itself is a rather risky exercise. Beliefs that have been held, even cherished, for generations, seldom die easily. There may, in fact, be a hostile response to the individual who manages to pull down, or even threaten, such beliefs. As one of those involved in this case was astute enough to say to Holmes: "The world doesn't always react kindly to those who take it upon themselves to rewrite history."

Obviously, I cannot judge whether this will be your reaction. Nor can I predict whether the events which make up *The Surrogate Assassin* will still hold any interest at all after the passage of so many years. Once again, dear readers, only you can be the judge of these things. My task is to get the story into your hands. If indeed, these words are being read, then I have done so. My work is finished.

Yours in word and spirit,
John H. Watson, M.D.
6 May, 1935
London

—1—
ⅅr. Sherlock Holmes

"It is surely the greatest irony of my profession," remarked Mr. Sherlock Holmes with some agitation, "that my work is devoted to the very eradication of crime, yet the absence of it drives me to absolute distraction."

Holmes stood in his dressing gown at the window of our sitting room at 221-B Baker St., holding the curtain aside so as to gaze at the scene below. His angular features stood out dimly in the weak gaslight emanating from the street.

"Surely, Holmes," I said, looking up from the newspaper which had consumed my interest for the past half hour, "you're not saying that you'd prefer more crime, more criminals?"

He shot me a glance which seemed almost malevolent at the moment, letting the curtain fall back against the pane. "Not necessarily more, Watson, but better," he said, returning to his chair in a typically rapid and restless motion. "The more able, the more daring, the prey, the better the hunt, but until the game is afoot, of course, there is no hunt. The hunter remains trapped uselessly in his lodge waiting and as I'm sure you've discovered by now, waiting is not among my preferred occupations." Holmes grasped his Stradivarius and began carelessly scratching the melancholy and enchanting notes of Saint-Saens' "Danse Macabre."

Throughout the entire evening, Holmes had stalked our quarters in a state of restless impatience, alternately sitting down to his violin, leafing through his formidable collection of clippings and notes or gazing disconsolately through the windows as a fierce equinoctial storm held London in its cold and rainy grasp.

"Well, Holmes," I ventured almost timidly, "it's not as though you haven't had cases. Just last week there was the incident of Nehemiah Lane and his beads. Surely that—"

"That," Holmes interrupted, looking up from his instrument, "was a case of ponderous banality. In replacing the Brazilian topaz with Baltic amber, our good Mr. Lane demonstrated only that he ranks with the most uncreative of contraband smugglers. Really, I'm surprised that Lestrade didn't put that one together himself. Or Gregson. It is sad but true that one mustn't over-estimate Scotland Yard these days." He resumed the lilting air he had been playing earlier.

I considered myself unvanguished. "Very well," I remarked, "but it was only last month you solved the mystery of the Brixton Road murder. No matter what the tabloids had to say, I found the mystery completely baffling, as did Scotland Yard, and your solution was nothing short of brilliant."

For the first time in what seemed like a week, Sherlock Holmes smiled. "I thank you, Watson," he said, looking at the ceiling in reflection. "You're right about the case, of course. Jefferson Hope's crime was highly unusual in that it was not committed by a genuine criminal at all. It was the work, rather, of a magnificently patient man whose motive of revenge bore very little resemblance to the simple greed or mindless aggression that motivate the common criminal. Hope didn't behave like a dishonest man, so yes, he did present an unusual challenge indeed."

Holmes' faint smile was soon replaced, however, with a frown. "But don't you see, Watson? Cases such as this only make it harder to endure the boredom which inevitably follows. A good chase is much like a drug; it satisfies and exhilarates, yet leaves its user with a terrible void after its departure, and a longing for more." He strolled to the window for yet another anxious look at the stormy night. "Neither am I encouraged by the fact that the only substantial case I've seen in months was imported, as it were. Hope and the circumstances of his crime were products of the American culture. I'm beginning to despair, honestly, as to whether the British population has lost its penchant for creative malfeasance."

The manner in which Holmes then poked the logs in the fire signalled clearly to me that he wasn't eager for further conversation.

He sank back into his chair and retreated into the violin without another word. It was not a surprise for me. In the short time that he and I had been sharing our Baker Street lodgings, I had already learned something of these blacker moods. While I was becoming increasingly adept at anticipating these anxious periods, and in steering clear of him during these times, I had yet to fully learn that his apparent anger was never directed personally toward me. Frequently during those early days we seemed to avoid one another entirely—he relentlessly pacing and I quietly sulking. I strongly suspect, however, that I was the only one detecting such tension.

In May of 1881, when the events described in this narrative properly began, Holmes and I had known one another for only six weeks. While I would not venture to determine what opinions regarding me Holmes may have held at that point, I can safely describe my own regarding him. For one thing, I must admit that my initial fascination with his many eccentricities had already faded to a significant degree. His maloderous chemical experiments, often conducted in the very depths of the night, had awakened and offended me more than once. No more pleasant was his habit of filling our apartment with the acrid stench of his exotic brand of shag, usually burned in a greasy cherrywood pipe. His untidiness had proven to be nothing short of profound.

I must say though, that already then I realized that such sundry discomforts would well be worth the privilege of living with a person of such a remarkably keen intellect, to say nothing of the chance to observe, and hopefully to occasionally share in, the sort of work he performed as the world's only consulting detective. Holmes had invited, or permitted, rather, my participation in only one of his cases to date—the Jefferson Hope affair, which would soon become known to the world through my account entitled *A Study in Scarlet*. I'd witnessed enough in that single case, however, to become convinced that Sherlock Holmes was the sort of person very few would have the opportunity of knowing.

As the storm intensified, I haphazardly perused my *Telegraph* as Holmes continued to play languidly on the violin. I finally landed on something of interest in the theater section.

"Holmes," I said, looking up, "listen to this . . ."

"The answer is no," Holmes interrupted without waiting to hear what I'd planned to say. "The performance of Othello at the Lyceum this week is definitely not among my plans."

I was dumbfounded. "Holmes! I blurted. "Surely this is witchcraft! How in blazes could you possibly have realized that I was about to ask you to attend the performance with me?"

He smiled. "Really, Watson, I would have imagined that your knowledge of my methods thus far would have blunted your sense of surprise when I demonstrate them for you. I reached my conclusion as to your question after a short but illuminating series of gestures on your part. They told a clearer story than any school primer ever could."

"Impossible! For mercy's sake, I was doing nothing more than reading the newspaper. There was absolute silence in the room."

"Silence, yes, but your statement about doing nothing more than reading is quite inaccurate, I'm afraid. Let me explain. While you scoured the theater page, the banner of which is clearly visible from where I sit, I detected in your eyes sudden concentration, obviously indicating that you'd located an item of interest. After apparently absorbing its contents, your gaze immediately switched to the portrait of Abraham Lincoln which, for reasons I confess myself unable to fathom, adorns this tin of excellent Virginian cigars preferred by a grateful client of late. Now I could determine no logical connection between today's theatrical notices and the subject of cigars, so therefore your gaze must have been seeking Lincoln's solemn visage. There the link was plain as day. I knew that today's theatricals note the coming performance of Othello with the great American tragedian Edwin Booth, whose very name, of course, conjures memories of his infamous brother, John Wilkes Booth, the arch-assassin of Abraham Lincoln. Your decision to ask me to attend with you was revealed by your careful scrutiny of the calendar tacked to the bookshelf, followed by a furtive glance in my direction. Clearly you were considering the availability of free time, and then considered me as your companion."

"Stupendous Holmes!" I exclaimed. "It's all as plain as day!"

"Plain it is, Watson, and clearly visible to the physical eye, but simply seeing, of course, is not quite the same exercise as observing.

Our eyes see a virtual infinity of things, most apparently meaningless to us by and large, but our mind seldom observes what the eyes see. When I refer to a trained eye as a vital component of my work, I'm referring to observation—the logical path of reasoning which must follow that initial act of seeing."

"It certainly seems simple enough, but I must admit that I'd have stumbled somewhere along the line."

"That," countered Holmes with the trace of a twinkle in his sharp grey eyes, "is why the science of deduction is able to provide me with a living."

"There's still one thing that mystifies me, Holmes."

He merely raised his eyebrows in response.

"Why do you spurn my offer? The chance to witness the opening of *Othello*, one of Shakespeare's finest tragedies, with Booth in the lead and Henry Irving as Iago is a rare gem, I'd say. The greatest of the American stage and the greatest of the British—nothing less than historic."

"I fail to share your enthusiasm."

"But why?"

The detective sighed in exasperation. "I could think of perhaps a dozen feasible excuses, Watson," he finally said. "I might just be occupied on the night of the play, perhaps, or the fact that Othello is among my least favored works of the Bard, or I'd rather avoid the shallow display of wealth and social posturing which such extravaganzas inevitably attract. All would be true enough, and they will have to suffice."

"Still, Holmes," I began.

"Watson," he said sharply, bringing his foot loudly to the floor and straightening himself in the chair.

It was a subtle warning from my new friend Mr. Sherlock Holmes that further conversation on the topic would be useless. The warning was duly heeded.

—2—
Mr. Edwin Booth

If the truth be known, I was slightly offended by Holmes' decision not to attend the Booth-Irving spectacle with me, and perhaps a little baffled, but neither to the extent that I would deprive myself of the pleasure of going. I managed the difficult task of procuring tickets through the good offices of an acquaintance with contacts in the theater and, even though I was placed in the farthest, most dismal reaches of the mezzanine section, considered myself fortunate indeed.

Holmes was correct in one sense at least. The performance had become a social extravaganza, an event considered mandatory in the most elite quarters of London society. The American community in London must have considered it at least as significant, for they came in great numbers as well. I arrived a full forty-five minutes before the curtain rose and entertained myself watching the exquisitely-tailored, elegant gentlemen in their gleaming top hats and their splendid, silken-robed ladies in glittering gems of every hue. There was a festive air within the spacious theater, and a sense of restless anticipation.

It was not, by any means, Booth's first performance in London; he'd done quite splendidly, I was told, during his earlier engagements over the past several months at the Princess, even though the press treated him savagely. And Irving, of course, was easily the most popular and visible actor in London at the time. To see the two of them together on the same stage, however—to witness the drama as Irving's polished discipline squared off against Booth's legendary impassioned fire—that was the rare attraction.

The din of chattering quickly became a subdued hush as the house lamps went dim, heralding the play's commencement. The appearance of Irving in the opening scene was greeted immediately with the warmest applause a friendly audience can muster, but the master's sheer physical command upon the stage soon won over its complete attention. Irving's Iago commenced his treachery with Roderigo at once, reawakening for the audience that strange and paradoxical attraction for beloved actors portraying villainous characters.

As rapt as our attention for Irving was, in truth, most of the spectators, including myself, waited impatiently for Scene II to arrive. We did not have long to wait. As Edwin Booth in the role of Othello, the Moor of Venice, entered the stage, the applause was instantly thunderous. Booth took a barely perceptible bow to his audience, and faced Irving.

The first line was Irving's. "Though in the trade of war I have slain men," he began before the hushed theater, "yet do I hold it very stuff o' th' conscience to do no continued murder, I lack iniquity, sometime, to do me service. Nine or ten times I had thought to've yerked him here, under the ribs."

Then, with the simplest of opening lines, Booth's Othello responded: "Tis better as it is."

Although from my obscure position in the theater the figure of Booth was but a distant sight, that voice sounded as if the words had been spoken in the next row. The tone was deep and sonorous, the words empowered with dramatic conviction. Booth's gestures as the play unfolded were graceful and strong, almost of a dancer's control and design. I saw and heard for myself, in the space of time it took him to utter that first line, why Edwin Booth was considered one of the very best—perhaps the best—tragedian of his time. The play went on for hours, and not once did the attention of the audience wane. All of us found ourselves utterly under the spell of these masters.

It was for me a decidedly enjoyable experience. I remain convinced to this day that the performance of Othello was the finest bit of theater I have ever witnessed. I found myself completely disappointed when the curtain at last fell for good. I stood applauding and shouting "Bravo!" with the rest as the cast went through their curtain calls.

On the ride back to Baker Street I traveled with the feeling of contented fulfillment one experiences only after seeing art realized and presented with utter success. The feeling remained the following morning as London awoke under the first sunny, pleasant day of what had been up to then a stormy and dreary spring. I rushed to the street to gather the morning newspapers in order to compare their reviews with my own, and returned to our rooms to find that Holmes had arisen. He was pecking with scant interest at the bacon and eggs Mrs. Hudson had laid out for us and stirring his coffee cup in an endless circular motion.

"Curious as to the Othello reviews, I see," he said without looking up.

"Really, Holmes," I replied with a casual indignation that was already becoming customary between us.

"Of course, I'm usually the one who brings in the morning papers. That you did so today could mean only one thing, considering your activities last night. But never mind. Now you've saved me the trouble of making the run myself and if you would be so kind, the agony columns of each would liven up my breakfast considerably."

I handed Holmes his requested pages and searched for my reviews. He scrutinized his advertisements, suddenly attacking his meal with renewed vigor. The *Chronicle*, the *Gazette* and the *Telegraph*, I was soon happy to learn, agreed with me perfectly, all holding both Irving and Booth up for the highest praise. The *Times* alone quibbled in its acclaim, calling Irving's Iago "too playful," and Booth's Othello "indifferent as to a whole." His American dialect resulted in the reviewer taking issue with an "occasional jar of accent," but otherwise even the *Times* man was highly impressed.

I soon passed from the reviews to other sections of the papers, taking full advantage of the leisure this period of idleness afforded me. I was still collecting the eleven shillings and sixpence a day from the government, compensation for my having caught a Jezail bullet in the shoulder some months before in the Afghan war, and my associate at Bart's, Stamford, was occasionally able to find relief work for me at that venerable institution. Generally, however, my time was as free as my pocketbook was empty, as I had yet to establish anything remotely resembling a functioning medical practice in those days.

Holmes, who found himself in a similarly free condition this sunny morning, contented himself with perusing the trivial and common regions of the newspaper's varying streets and alleys of words.

Occasionally he would murmur in some vague and private reference to a particular item, or utter a single word such as "Indeed!" or "Obviously." I knew well that he was absorbing the tiniest details of the most base and sordid crimes in London, and storing away the information somewhere in that magnificent brain of his.

Not long after Mrs. Hudson cleared the breakfast dishes, the sound of wheels and hooves clattered up from the street. Holmes sped to the window, as was his custom, and drew the curtains aside. I expected perhaps an expression of pleasure at the prospect of a long-awaited client, or a hasty, but deadly accurate, detailing of a stranger ascending the stairs. I was, rather, quite surprised at his reaction.

"Oh, my!" he said with some agitation. "I was afraid this might happen."

"What is it, Holmes?" I demanded.

He seemed not to have heard me as he looked at the floor in perplexity. "I would have preferred avoiding this meeting entirely, Watson," he muttered. "As it is, I haven't had time to prepare for it properly at all." His demeanor seemed strange to me.

There was no time for further discussion. Mrs. Hudson immediately knocked and opened the door. She bore a flushed, excited expression on her face. "Forgive the intrusion, gentlemen," she said, "but I'm sure you'll understand that I couldn't keep such a visitor as this waiting." She opened the door wider to admit our mysterious guest.

The man who stood before us was Edwin Booth.

Holmes and I stood speechless in the presence of the actor. He stood of normal height, dressed somberly in black broadcloth and a dramatic cloak. The hair was long and flowing, deeply brown, interrupted here and there with strands of silver. The eyes were large and luminous, with a focused gaze that seemed almost mesmerizing. His face was of the classical mold—slender, pale and aquiline, in the very form of a marble statue from some great and forgotten civilization of old.

I forced my gaze from Booth toward Holmes. He and Booth stared at each other intently, almost knowingly, it seemed. Neither spoke at first. The strange silence finally grew unbearable for me, however. In the clumsy and boyish manner of a commoner addressing a person of great stature and renown, I eagerly shook his hand.

"Mr. Booth!" I exclaimed. "This is a wonderful honour indeed!

I'm Dr. John Watson, a great admirer of yours and a member of your audience only last night. I'm very pleased to meet you face-to-face."

Booth received me warmly. "The pleasure is mine, Dr. Watson," he said in the resonant voice I remembered from the Lyceum stage, made only more impressive within the confines of the tiny room. "I'm gratified that you found the Othello to your liking. I'll freely admit I was nervous as a cat under those circumstances."

He paused and returned his gaze to Holmes. "And this," he said to Holmes more than to me, "must be the celebrated Mr. Sherlock Holmes."

"Forgive me!" I blurted. "Of course, this is Holmes! Holmes, this is none other than the great Edwin Booth!"

Holmes moved at last toward the actor and took his hand. "Thank you, Watson," he said quietly, "but I rather suspected that to be the case."

As they shook hands, their almost mystical stare resumed itself. Holmes grinned slightly at last, and said, "Yes, indeed. I see it clearly. It's quite astonishing, actually."

He regarded Booth with his chin slightly raised, a posture I took to be cautiously defensive. "Mr. Booth," he said simply. "Or is such an address terribly formal under the circumstances?"

"Terribly formal, I'd say," Booth said. "Just 'Edwin' would do fine. Even 'Cousin Edwin' sounds a bit stiff, doesn't it?"

I was astounded, but held my tongue.

"Then Edwin it shall be," Holmes said firmly. "And you may call me Holmes, as that seems to be the custom even among those who know me well."

"I honestly felt this moment would never come about," Booth said.

"Nor I," replied Holmes, "although now that it has, I can see my foolish reluctance for what it was."

"Reluctance?"

"I'm afraid there's really no diplomatic way to say it," Holmes said. "Ever since that day—you know which day I refer to—I've come to dread your surname, the name of Booth. To grow ashamed of my connection with it. It's unfair, I realize, and unjustified and . . ."

"And understandable," Booth interrupted quietly. "My brother's crime was one of infamy. The crime of the century, Holmes. My curse is much the same as yours, only a great deal closer to its source. It's a cross I'll have to bear for the rest of my days but I'll be damned before I surrender to it. I rather expected you to go a bit white in the gills to see me. Many people do, at first. They overcome it, eventually."

"As shall I," said Holmes. He turned toward me. "Perhaps now, Watson, you'll better understand my reluctance to see Othello with you?"

I could contain myself no longer. "Of course, Holmes," I said, "but please excuse my intrusion into private matters. Am I in the presence of . . ."

"Yes, Watson," Holmes interjected. "Cousins. First cousins in fact. The man whose performance you so appreciated at the theater last evening, and whose glowing reviews this morning so clearly pleased you, happens to be the cousin of the man with whom you are presently sharing quarters."

"And, to boot," Booth added, "cousins who have never seen each other before this day."

"It's an interesting family history," Holmes said, "and Edwin and I must undoubtedly bring one another up to date on our respective families' fates, but I'm afraid such niceties will have to wait. I'm quite sure that Edwin's call is not merely that of a long-lost kinsman seeking a meeting with a distant member of his family."

"What in the world told you that?" Booth asked with curiosity.

"I'll explain," Holmes answered, "but please, give me your cloak, take a chair and share a glass of brandy with us. In the face of surprise, I fear, all traces of civility tend to disappear."

Booth took the seat offered to him, sipped his brandy and seemed to relax. Holmes stayed on his feet as he so often preferred to do in the presence of a client, and steadily paced the floor to and fro.

"You are here," he said to his cousin, "because you're frightened. You've been threatened a number of times in recent months, the last coming as recently as last night. Your outward calm belies the fact that you're in dread of your very life."

Booth's outward calm seemed utterly unaffected by this dreadful prognosis. "Bravo!" he cried, raising his glass. "You're right on the money, Holmes. You're quite as sharp as they say. Tell me how you knew all that."

"The timing of your visit struck me as curious. That your visit comes on the very morning after a bravura performance suggests the importance you attach to it. Is it not the custom for actors to receive the congratulations of well-wishers and admirers on the morning following an opening night?"

"Indeed it is."

"And yet, here you are. One would also have expected a man of your station to have hired a hansom for the trek across the city, but from my window I observed that you were riding on an ordinary dairy wagon. The manner in which you concealed your face with the collar of your cloak furthered my conviction that your travel was intended to pass unobserved. You are wary of followers, are you not?"

"I am indeed," Booth said, "but what gave away the previous threats?"

"Your watch-chain, Edwin, is adorned with a most unusual token. It's a bullet slug unless I'm very much mistaken. You've had it plated with gold, an unusual degree of attention to pay to a spent pistol slug. I know enough about you to realize that you couldn't have won that bullet in war, hence it must be a memento of another sort of attack. An attempt on your life perhaps?"

"Well, bravo again!" cried Booth, clapping his hands. "You've got it all just as straight as crow's flight! You're quite a marvel, Holmes. I'd heard that my cousin was an ace, but I never expected him to know my own story before I'd even told it."

"You're very kind," Holmes replied, casually touching the tips of his fingers together in a narrow triangular shape. "But we digress. Why not give us the full story?"

"Very well," said Booth, fingering the shiny misshapen lump on his watch-chain. "This bullet, as you correctly suggest, was intended for none other than myself. It was almost exactly three years ago. I was in Chicago, at the theater of my father-in-law, in *Richard II*. I was delivering a last act soliloquy when I made a slightly unbalanced step. I leaned, very gently, to steady myself, when I felt and heard this very bullet whistling past, just inches over my head. I heard another report from the darkness within the theater, and then I saw him, for he was the only one standing. He was in the gallery, aiming a pistol directly at me and looking for all the world like he was about to fire once again. By that time, I'm happy to say, several nearby members of the audience seized him and held him down. I assumed the very edge of the stage and ordered the man's arrest, which was done within seconds.

"It turned out to be a young fellow from St. Louis, Mark Gray Lyon by name, although he generally went simply by Mark Gray. A dry-goods clerk, they told me, who informed the Chicago police that he had what he called a 'good, oh a very good, reason' for trying to cut me down. He had somehow gotten the idea that I had dishonoured his sister in some way and was bent on avenging this imagined offense. I swear now as I swore then that I had never met this cracker in my life, not to mention his supposedly dishonoured sister. As was expected, Mr. Gray was soon found to be mildly insane, suffering from one or another form of brain fever, and within weeks found himself transferred from a prison in Chicago to an asylum in Elgin, Illinois. He wrote me a letter, rather apologetic in tone, some months later, with the preposterous request that I forward him funds."

"And the so nearly successful bullet," Holmes asked, "do you keep it as a reminder of mortality?"

"Of survival rather," Booth replied with a smile. "You see, I've had it engraved 'From Mark Gray to Edwin Booth.' A touch of morbid gallows humour one might say. When I dug it out of one of the stage timbers I thought it a rare prize."

"Rare indeed," Holmes rejoined. "Pray continue."

"Two years passed before I was next attacked. Since November, in fact, I've been assailed twice and, quite frankly, very nearly killed both times. The first was in Oberammergau, the quaint German village we'd visited during our brief Continental tour in order to see the Passion Play. My wife and I, and my daughter Edwina, had taken rooms in a tiny hotel near the ampitheater and it was in the crowded lobby of this inn that the attack occurred.

"Mary and I had just descended the staircase, and were making our way through the busy room toward the street, when we heard the sharp report of a small pistol, fired quite close to us. There was a scream and a brief moment of confusion, but whoever fired the shot apparently found it quite simple to disappear into the throng. Neither did anybody know who had been the shooter's intended target. That is, mind you, until later that evening, after the play, when I was back in our rooms with Mary. I removed my coat and was horrified to find a neat bullet hole within the lining, on the left side breast, as if the shot had traveled from the inside of the coat toward the outside. My attacker came within an inch of what I think was his bullseye and that, my friends, was my heart.

"I didn't mention the bullet hole to Mary. She is now a very sick woman, a fact which causes me considerable dismay, but even then she was terribly fragile and excitable. Nor did I allow word of this to leak to the press. Their fascination with my name would have caused only a repeat of the miserable circus in Chicago, after Mark Gray's fool's revenge. Some of those scavengers went so far as to suggest I was engaging in some sort of self promotion trick."

"Ah yes, the fourth estate," said Holmes, rubbing his hands together knowingly. "The newspaper can be a terrific ally if properly manipulated, but woe to the man who excites the bloodlust of hungry reporters. I assume you have maintained similar discretion with regards to your most recent misadventure?"

"Yes," said Booth. "Neither the press nor the police have been contacted. Dr. Watson and yourself will be the first to hear of both the attempt on my life in Germany and the one last night."

"Last night!" I exclaimed.

"Yes. Just moments before the curtain rose on the first act, in fact. I was making final adjustments to my costume in a narrow passageway leading to the wings when I heard the door open behind me. I turned to see a man of medium height, dressed in a heavy greatcoat and a wide-brimmed slouch hat over his eyes, making it impossible to see whose face it concealed. The man drew a gloved hand from within the folds of his coat and pointed a small pistol toward me.

"He spoke these words: 'From tiny acorns mighty oaks are grown, Mr. Booth. And with tiny axes mighty oaks are fallen.' He then fired, but I had anticipated his action, flattening myself against the wall of the passageway. The shot missed me, once again, by mere inches. I was lucky enough to be in full costume, in Othello's elaborate garb, which includes a handsome, even fearsome, sabre. Without thinking, I drew the weapon and advanced quickly on the man, swinging the sabre in the most menacing fashion I could muster. It was surely the finest and most valuable performance of my career, gentlemen, for the reward was not applause but my very life. My attacker was sufficiently convinced, apparently, of my prowess with the antique sabre that he turned away without attempting another shot. He slammed the passageway door in my face and when I reached the handle I found it locked. I considered another route in order to reach him before he escaped the theater, but at that very moment the curtain rose. I heard the applause greeting Irving and I knew I'd have to be on the stage in minutes. I resumed my way toward the wings."

"And went through your entire performance after an episode like that!" I exclaimed. "Where did you find the courage?"

"As much as I'd like to believe it was courage, Dr. Watson, I rather feel my actions were purely instinctual. As for taking the stage just moments after being shot at, well, to be honest there's no place on earth as natural to me as a stage. The incident was already in the back of my mind by the time I'd spoken my first line."

"Did nobody else witness the shooting in the passageway?" Holmes demanded.

"Only the attacker and myself."

"Was there anything familiar in your visitor's voice?"

"I'm quite sure I've never heard that voice before last night."

"And the accent—was it British? American perhaps?"

"Now there's a good question. You know, I never gave it a thought before this moment. I have a feeling the accent was a French one."

"Did the phrase about acorns and oaks make any special sense to you?"

"I assume," Booth replied, "that the comment was somehow related to these." He took a folded envelope from his breast pocket and handed it over to Holmes. Holmes opened it and allowed its contents, three small acorns, to roll out into his hand.

"This little present was left for me at my message box in the theater, Holmes, apparently on the very afternoon, yesterday, of the attack. I received them this morning. There was no note, no explanation. Just the envelope with three acorns."

Holmes examined the woody objects closely, holding them up one by one toward the light coming in from the window. "Did the clerk give you a description of the man who left them?" he asked.

"Yes, and from all appearances it was the same fellow who paid me the visit in the passageway. Tall, greatcoat, slouch hat. Said 'this is to be delivered to Mr. Booth' and nothing more. But that's really not the most interesting part, Holmes."

The detective looked up from the acorns with interest.

"I received these," said Booth, taking yet another envelope from his coat, "at my hotel in Oberammergau on the day immediately following the close call I had there." He opened the envelope to display three acorns identical to the first three.

"And, the day after Mr. Gray came so close to ending my days in Chicago, I received my very first acorn delivery, in the mail. Three, just like these, no return address of course."

"And what," said Holmes, "did our friend Mr. Gray later have to say about that?"

"It was mentioned to the police investigators, who later told me that they'd asked him about it. Gray told them he didn't have the slightest idea what they were talking about."

"Interesting," Holmes muttered. "And we can safely assume that Gray remains to this day within his cell at the Elgin asylum?"

"To the best of my knowledge, yes," Booth responded.

"We will send a cable to Chicago to be sure," Holmes said, finally taking his seat and filling his amber-stemmed cherrywood with shag. The pipe was soon sending great clouds of smoke through the sunlit room.

"When Gray corresponded with you, and asked for funds, did he mention anything else of particular interest?"

"Let's see," said Booth, rubbing his chin thoughtfully. "He wanted nine hundred dollars, he wrote, or he would surely die—something crazy like that—and he claimed to have absolved me of whatever offense I was supposed to have committed against his sister. And he asked, unsuccessfully I might add, for my signature on a petition which he felt would get him released."

"Did he shed no further light on his reasons for making an attempt on your life?"

"Only the strange phrase that I had 'got the wrong pig by the ear,' or some such thing. It sounded almost as if he were denying the shooting, which was preposterous, considering his earlier confession and all the witnesses, myself included, of course. I took it as another one of his ravings."

Holmes leaned back in his chair and puffed a great cloud of grey smoke. "This should be enough to get things started, Edwin," he said. "I will need one favor immediately. Inform the proper people at the Lyceum that Dr. Watson and myself will be paying a visit soon and that we'll need complete access to the theater. You needn't provide them with any reason."

"That will be easy enough," said Booth. "I guess you'll take the case then."

"But of course!" said Holmes, rising to shake Booth's hand. "It's the least I can do for a cousin, not to mention the fact that the case seems to offer any number of intriguing elements already."

"I'm gratified to hear you say that. I'm beginning to feel better already. My only regret is that our first meeting should take place under circumstances as bizarre and dire as this."

"Me, no less," responded Holmes warmly, "but I'm glad for the meeting in any case. Let's first clear out of the way these present dangers so that we may later speak at length as cousins, in a spirit of relaxation, and bring our sadly distant families a bit closer. For now, take care of yourself, Edwin, by which I mean take every precaution during the remainder of your stay in London. Bodyguards would be an excellent idea, I should think. Do not stray out into the streets alone in any case. Dr. Watson and I will inform you as to any developments in the case."

With that, Booth swung on his cloak and headed for the door, but not before I shamelessly asked him to autograph my program from Othello. He did so graciously and seemed to depart in much higher spirits than when he had arrived.

"I think you hardly needed to have bothered with the autograph, Watson," said Holmes when the door was closed. "Something tells me you'll be having plenty of opportunities in the near future. I think we will both be seeing a great deal of Mr. Edwin Booth."

—3—
The Lyceum

So fascinated did Holmes immediately become with the Booth affair, and so impatient was he at the prospect of challenging work, that we left Baker Street within the noon hour of the very day we had received our celebrated visitor. Our hansom weaved and twisted its way through the heavy mid-day traffic on New Bond Street and Picadilly Circus on the long ride to the Lyceum.

Holmes was enthusiastic and cheery during the trip. "Is it my imagination," he remarked with a subtle twinkle in his eyes, "or do I sense on your part a new respect, a trace of awe perhaps, toward me?"

"I don't have the faintest idea what you're talking about, Holmes," I rejoined.

"Yes, I'm quite sure of it. Now that you know of my relationship to Edwin Booth, to the entire Booth family for that matter, you no longer view me merely as an eccentric roommate working in an unusual field. Suddenly I am seen to have connections with the famous, the infamous, the mysterious. Is it not so?"

I thought about it for a moment. "Maybe you have a point after all," I said at last. "Perhaps you do seem the slightest bit different to me now. There is to the Booths an undeniable sense of adventure and destiny, and perhaps a certain mystique, that frankly fascinates me."

"You and many, many others Watson, including myself. Although my family has virtually forbidden any and all conversation relating to our American relations, and though I myself felt an irrational but consuming sense of guilt over a certain Booth's tragic act, I was fascinated nonetheless. I've kept up with them, Watson, occasionally asking certain relatives of mine for bits and pieces of information about them. I've read and collected many a newspaper article, from Britain as well as the States, containing various developments in their careers and lives."

"Were you aware of them as a child?" I asked.

"Yes, but we never spoke of them at home, even before the assassination. I first learned of them, in fact, when I was a lad of ten, in April of eighteen sixty-five. I overheard my parents speak of John Wilkes Booth—the only time the name was ever mentioned within our household."

"Upon hearing of Lincoln's murder?"

"Exactly. My father actually wept when the reports of the murder were made known here. I heard him shouting before my mother quieted him down, so that Mycroft and I would not hear him. But it was too late. 'Damn the Booths!' he cried. 'Now we see the bitter harvest our wretched Mary Ann has sown!' It was a scene impossible to forget, Watson."

"Mary Ann, I take it, would have been your aunt?"

"That she was. My father's sister, Mary Ann Holmes, some ten years older than he, mother of John Wilkes, Edwin and assorted other Booths. She left her mother, my grandmother, for reasons that remain unknown, forsaking the country life to seek work in London. She had little success as an actress, so the story goes, and wound up selling flowers in Bow Street Market, near the Covent Theater. It was there that she met the young English actor, Junius Brutus Booth, already then beloved and celebrated as a tragedian. She fell in love with him and was soon seeing him regularly.

"Whether Aunt Mary Ann knew then that Junius had already been married some five years, and already had a young son, both wife and child living in London, nobody seems to know. What is known is that the two of them, my aunt and Booth, abruptly left together in eighteen twenty-one, I think it was, and eloped, if you will, to Maderia in Portugal. They soon made their way to America. Both of them had left their kinsfolk without further word. Junius abandoned, for all practical purposes, his wife Adelaide and little son Richard, returning to London only twice in the next two decades or so, falsely promising that they would soon be sent for. They never were, of course, and spent the years living in London and Belgium, living off the pitiful pittance Booth infrequently forwarded, and the charity of friends. Mary Ann never so much as left a note of parting for her poor mother, not to mention my father, before she left."

"Forgive me, Holmes," I interjected, clearing my throat, "but very simply put, that's a terribly sordid tale."

He grimaced and nodded. "What deeds the heart compels one to perform," he said. "Now you know why dear Aunt Mary Ann was regarded as persona non grata in our home. But wait, the tale grows more sordid as the years progress, Watson. Junius and Mary Ann set themselves up in remote farm country in northern Maryland, near Baltimore, where they stayed throughout most of the year. After a period, they also kept a home in the city, primarily for winter occupancy. The elder Booth alternated between the farm and an acting career that grew even more celebrated and respected than it had been here. He was very literally the unchallenged actor of his day. His idyllic life was eventually chilled, however, when he was greeted one day on a Baltimore street by his abandoned son who had, after twenty long years, finally scratched together the funds needed for a trip to America.

"There followed a most uncomfortable period in the life of Junius Brutus Booth. Richard, the son, was able to bring his mother to America in fairly short order, but the effort was utterly in vain. Junius made no effort at reconciliation with Adelaide, and hardly a gesture to support her, save for the few dollars he occasionally threw her way to help her maintain a bleak existence in a poor section of Baltimore. He tried briefly to apprentice Richard as an actor, in an apparent attempt to stave off scandal, and is said to have taken him along on a few tours. The effort was unsuccessful, it seems; the young man returned to his mother disillusioned.

"It all ended, not surprisingly, quite bitterly. Adelaide eventually forced the public scandal her wayward husband had so feared, initiating an ugly divorce trial that finally resulted in their formal separation in April of eighteen fifty-one. Three weeks later he finally took Aunt Mary Ann's hand in belated wedlock.

"Junius, of course, had sired a whole new family with her well before that time. There was Junius Jr., born soon after their arrival in America, who is today a respected theater operator in Cincinatti; several babies who died in infancy or early childhood; Rosalie, who remains a spinster to this day; Edwin, the actor, whom we met only this morning; Asia, who married the well-known American comedian John Sleeper Clarke and who resides currently within London itself; John Wilkes, the late actor and assassin; and Joseph, now a doctor in New York, if my facts are current.

"Except for Junius Jr.'s brief try at acting, only Edwin and John Wilkes would follow their father's footsteps onto the stage, and both would eventually gain renown to rival his. Some still say that John could have surpassed his father and brother had it not been for his crime. You saw the greatness Edwin has achieved just last night. Imagine what John Wilkes could have been."

"Quite a formidable family," I said.

"As brilliant in its triumphs," Holmes returned, "as it was tragic in its failures. The genius of the Booths was all too often tempered with disaster. There is in America a saying and a belief about the 'mad Booths of Maryland,' based on the very probable suspicion that Junius Brutus Booth was, at least partially, a madman. He was given to bouts of highly erratic, sometimes lunatic, behavior which explains, perhaps, his treatment of the first wife."

"But what of Edwin," I ventured. "I don't see the slightest trace of instability in him."

"Nor do I, Watson. In all likelihood, Edwin is perfectly sound in all ways, but I've studied the family well. I know of their tendency toward melancholia, and outright tragedy at times, as well as their penchant for intensity. The trouble Edwin is having in London right now is but another example of this. Strange things tend to happen to these people."

"Whatever became of the first wife, Holmes?" I asked, seeking to hear the complete story.

"Adelaide Booth died miserable and penniless a few years after her bitter divorce. Of their son Richard, the eldest, little is known. He is believed to have lived in Boston, Baltimore or Philadelphia, either as an instructor of languages or as an attorney. Maybe he lived in all three cities; possibly he worked in both professions. All traces of him, and a wife called Sarah, disappear at about the time of the American Civil War, save one. I've located Richard Booth's death certificate here in London. He obviously returned here at some point, and here he seems to have died."

"What was the fate of Junius Brutus Booth?"

"Dead, after less than two years of marriage to my aunt, of fever while upon a Mississippi River boat after his final stage tour to California and New Orleans."

"And Mary Ann Booth, your aunt. What became of her?"

"She lives still, Watson, a frail old grandmother who must forever endure the curse of her favored son's crime. She is well into her eighties now, living with her youngest son Joseph, and spinster daughter, Rosalie, in New York."

We both fell silent for a while and listened to the varied sounds of London as we drove on. I reflected on the strange and dramatic history of the notorious Booth clan. I suspected that Holmes grew silent out of discomfort at his own frankness, and of the pain those memories obviously still caused him. I had never before heard him speak with such openness of his own family and background, nor have I since. It was a subject one seldom broached, if at all, with Holmes.

"For all its sadness," I finally said, "it certainly is an intriguing story."

"I couldn't agree more, Watson, and something tells me that we may soon find ourselves in the middle of a new chapter in it for, unless I'm very much mistaken, I see the portals of the Lyceum through the window at this moment."

Holmes was right, and in no time at all we found ourselves at the ticket window of the great edifice asking for entrance. We were greeted at a small door by a dour, sullen man who announced himself as the head usher. He seemed singularly unimpressed at the mention of Holmes' name but nodded in recognition when the detective mentioned that Booth had given us clearance to inspect the premises. Almost reluctantly, it seemed, the man bade us enter.

He immediately began to leave, apparently content to let us have the run of the empty hall, but Holmes caught him by the elbow. "A moment of your time," he said, placing what appeared to be a silver coin into the man's hand. "Just a question or two."

The head usher smiled warmly. "Happy to be of service, sir," he said.

"If someone desired entry into the backstage area of the theater, just moments before an evening performance were scheduled to commence," Holmes queried, "how might such a person go about doing that?"

A look of sudden concern crossed the man's face. "Oh, I couldn't permit anything like that, sir," he said. "I'll be giving back your sovereign if that's what you had in mind."

"Nothing of the sort. The deed I refer to has already been done. My interest lies purely in determining precisely how it was done."

"You mean, how could some person have made his way backstage?"

"Quite."

"Well, let me think," said the head usher, thoughtfully scratching his narrow forehead. "If the person were a member of the crew it would pose no problem, of course. They'd be expected backstage anyways, some of them at least. If it were someone from the audience, he would have to approach the stage doors in the orchestra section. I keep ushers posted at both such doors whenever the theater is open to the public. To keep them away from the actors, of course."

"Of course. And what if the person were neither of the crew nor of the audience," Holmes pressed. "How might he or she gain entrance to the wings?"

"Now that would be fairly difficult. They would have to pass through these offices here." He gestured to a cramped administrative area adjacent to the lobby where we stood. "In the evening they are usually well locked up. But once in, it would be a matter of taking one of the hallways that lead either to the dressing rooms or to the wings. There remains but one other means. It's possible, I suppose, they might use the back entrance, the one we use for shipping and the stagehands and so forth."

"And is the back entrance kept secured?"

"Well, now that you mention it, it seems that door is usually kept open during the performances. The stagehands like to sit and smoke near the door between scene changes."

"Ah!' said Holmes, rubbing his hands together. "And might one of the stagehands who was on duty for last night's Othello happen to be in the theater at this moment?"

"There's Yockey," the usher said immediately. "I can summon him if you like."

"You're very kind," Holmes said. "Yes, summon him at once. I promise not to keep him away from his duties for long."

A smiling lad of less than fifteen years was soon brought before us and introduced as Charlie Yockey. He readily acknowledged that he had worked the previous night's performance.

"In the minutes before the curtain rose last evening," Holmes asked the boy, "did you spend any time near the rear entrance, the one which leads, I believe, into the alley?"

He glanced nervously at the head usher who listened attentively. "I was there for ten or fifteen minutes, sir. Before we were called to raise the opening curtain."

"While you were there, did anyone not familiar to you, not connected to the theater staff or company, gain entrance through that door?"

The lad hesitated. "Yes!" he finally cried. "There was one rather queer fellow, about ten minutes before curtain time. He asked whether he might see the crew manager, to ask about employment, I think. I told him where to find the boss and let him in."

"Please describe that man, Yockey."

"Not very tall, sir. Five foot six, seven maybe. He was wearing a long coat and a large hat over his head which made it tough to get much of a look at his face. Spoke with an accent, French I'd guess. He was carrying a fairly large suitcase, bound up as if ready to be loaded, and he left it by the door as he came in, saying that he'd be back to claim it just as soon as he was finished with the boss."

Holmes clapped his hands together in delight. "Splendid!" he said. "You've already been of great assistance, Yockey. Thank you. That will be all."

He turned once more to the head usher. "Now, if I might ask one more favor. Would you be so kind as to direct us to the small passageway which leads from the dressing rooms to the wings?"

The usher nodded and gestured for us to follow. We passed through the series of small offices into the general maze of the backstage area. "I probably shouldn't be asking this," the usher said tentatively, "but just what is all this about?" Holmes merely smiled and raised his finger to his lips. "Both silence and discretion are noble virtues," he said.

We came to a narrow door. "There aren't too many who use this passage anymore," the usher said, opening the door. "Most of the cast simply walk around the sets to reach the wings. Mr. Booth, it seems, found this route more convenient. Will there be anything further, Mr. Holmes?"

Holmes shook his head, thanked the man, and said we would leave when our inspection was complete. Alone in the dim and narrow hallway, Holmes immediately dropped to his hands and knees. Taking his magnifying lens from his coat, he began a slow and methodical search of the floor, the baseboards and the two doors at opposite ends of the hall, taking pains not to miss an inch of their surfaces. He ran his hands over the plaster of the walls and the wooden slats of the wainscoting with keen attention. Finally, near the opposite door, he cried out.

"Aha!" he exclaimed, taking a small penknife from his pocket. He scratched briefly at a tiny dimple in the plaster that I would scarcely have noticed, and soon produced a small lump of grey metal. "The slug intended for Cousin Edwin," he said triumphantly.

He resumed his minute scrutiny of the hall but seemed to lose interest rather quickly. "Watson," he said, straightening himself, "we've seen everything the Lyceum has to offer us with relevance to the case. I come away better informed than when we arrived, but no closer, I'm afraid, to our mysterious stranger. Shall we go?"

On our way out of the building, Holmes led me on a brief detour into the dim vastness of the great auditorium itself. He whispered, almost in reverence, it seemed, at the stately performance hall. "Is there anything in the world more haunting than an empty theater?" he asked. "A place of brilliant lights, glorious music and great throngs of people—shrouded in silence and darkness. A hall of life itself, seemingly within the very shadows of death. One senses its power all the more through its emptiness."

I shuddered at the emptiness myself, remembering all too well how vibrant and full of life it had seemed last evening. I was relieved when we finally regained the street.

During our tour of the theater, a thick afternoon fog had suddenly enveloped the city, utterly replacing the morning's brilliance. So opaque was the weather that the gaslights were already being lit. The air had grown damp and close and I immediately reached for my gloves. Holmes produced his hunting cap from within the folds of his Inverness.

I raised my arm to hail a cab but Holmes stopped me. "Let's walk instead, Watson," he said. "At least for a while. I need some time to think and nothing stimulates good thinking like a brisk stroll through London. What do you say?"

I assented, realizing that Holmes would have his walk whether I accompanied him or not. We strolled in silence through the gloomy streets for what seemed like an hour. Holmes buried his chin deeply into the upturned lapels of his coat and sent up occasional plumes of smoke from his calabash. The monotonous sound of our bootheels on the cobbles was interrupted at last when Holmes stopped at a kiosk and asked for yesterday's edition of the *Times*. He resumed the walk with the newspaper spread out before him.

After some minutes Holmes crumpled up the newspaper and, angrily it seemed, cast it into a rubbish heap. "That settles that," he said with disgust.

"What, Holmes?" I asked.

"Our would-be murderer, Watson, is, I'm quite sure, well beyond our grasp at the moment. He was, in fact, well clear by the time we first heard of the case at all."

"I don't understand."

"If the play commenced last night at seven o'clock sharp, then the attempt on Edwin's life must have taken place at five minutes to the hour, or less. Am I correct?"

I nodded in response.

"Assume that the stranger had five minutes to make his escape from the Lyceum, including a stop at the office to leave the envelope for Edwin, and he would have been on the street by seven. That would have given him time aplenty to reach Waterloo Station by seven-thirty, even if he chose to travel by foot, and to board the evening train for Dover. From there he may have boarded the late ferry for Calais—I have just learned from the *Times* that last night's ferry was scheduled to shove off around ten in the evening. He would have made it quite nicely. By the time Edwin paid us a visit this morning, his assailant was surely well out of England, perhaps into the French interior."

"It all certainly sounds plausible," I rejoined, "but still it seems a rather large leap to make such assumptions of the man's escape route simply because the train and ferry schedules happen to coincide."

Through the mist I thought I saw the slightest of grins cross Holmes's face. "I'll admit," he said, "that assumption does play a role, but I assure you that coincidence does not. That the schedules happen to coincide merely strengthens my theory. Let's not forget that both Edwin and the stagehand identified the stranger's accent as French. France would therefore provide a logical refuge. More significant by far is that he had with him, at the very scene of the attempted murder, a large, bound suitcase. That's hardly the sort of thing one lugs through the streets of London, unless of course the intention is to embark upon some sort of trip in very short order."

"Fine, Holmes, but how can you be sure that he didn't head for Liverpool, perhaps, or Scotland, or Ireland . . ."

"That's entirely possible, but I doubt it. Either the attacker would have stayed in London, with the intent perhaps to have another try at his target, in which case there would have been no suitcase, or he planned to flee to safety, likely to await another opportunity elsewhere. We have learned through Edwin, who has already faced him in at least two countries, that the man has quite a penchant for overseas travel. A foreign country would logically offer a far safer refuge than any domestic hiding place and, of course, he knows that Edwin has been alerted anew to the threat, and that the actor's time in England is growing short. Both facts diminish his present prospects for success in this country. It would be far better for him to lay low for a period, probably in France, and await another chance."

I couldn't dispute my friend's logic as we walked through the deepening afternoon. By Oxford Circus, Holmes had apparently had enough of walking. He hailed a cab and we rode in comfort for the remainder of the trip. The detective retreated into a state of studious silence.

As we left the cab in foggy Baker Street I turned to Holmes. "If the attacker has indeed fled England as you suggest, what shall we tell Edwin?"

"Only that the danger has yet to pass," Holmes said grimly, "and that there's very little we can do to help him now."

—4—

A Proposal

For the second time in as many days, Holmes and I found ourselves within the cavernous space of the Lyceum. This time, however, the hall was not entirely vacant, although we were the only two souls constituting any sort of audience. Upon the stage stood Edwin Booth, Henry Irving and several actors whose names I did not know. Since the Booth-Irving stand had been such a satisfactory success in terms of attendance, further performances had been scheduled. We had arranged to meet Booth after rehearsals.

The cast was rehearsing the final scene from Hamlet, even though the Lyceum shows would continue to feature Othello. Booth had declined public stagings of Hamlet with Irving, in order to graciously prevent direct comparisons with his British colleague, so intimately identified with the play had the latter become. Still the two thespians couldn't resist the temptation to give Hamlet a try together, if only partially and in rehearsal.

Although the lighting was dim and the company attired in the loose and casual clothing preferred for routine rehearsal, the stage fairly crackled with their informal performance. Amidst a stage quite littered with the bodies of those portraying the Queen, the King and Laer, Booth as Hamlet—already fatally poisoned—finally dropped his rapier and collapsed to his knees. Booth raised his head nobly toward the empty seats and delivered his final lines with eloquence.

"O, I die Horatio; the potent poison quite o'er crows my spirit; I cannot live to hear the news from England; But I do prophesy th' election lights on Fortinbras. He has my dying voice; so tell him, with th' occurrents, more and less which have solicited." His voice lowered into a powerful whisper. "The rest is silence." He collapsed gracefully.

The rest of the cast quickly finished up the few lines remaining to the play as Booth lay motionless upon the stage. A director in the orchestra section, previously unseen to us, clapped his hands along with the cast members themselves, now all restored to proper life. "Excellent dear people, excellent!" he said to them. "If we convey just that spirit with Othello we'll have to turn them away at the door for the rest of the run."

The cast, looking relaxed but tired, all headed for the wings, except for Booth, who leapt from the stage and made his way to where we sat. We shook hands.

"Greetings once again, gentlemen," he said. "Follow me round to my dressing room. I have a bottle of properly aged Tennessee corn whiskey, no brandy I'm afraid, and we'll drink as civilized men before we discuss dreadful business. Come along!"

We did as we were told and soon found ourselves in Booth's tiny dressing room, huddled on folding canvas chairs around a table covered with jars and bottles of stage cosmetics. The whiskey was brutal on the first sip but mellowed considerably with each succeeding taste. "I quite like it," I said to our host who, I noticed, had not taken a glass himself. He was looking rather dejectedly at the floor.

Booth's expression betrayed profound fatigue and sadness, a considerable contrast from our first meeting. "I sense you've come with discouraging news regarding the lunatic who wishes me dead," he began. "I sense also that you're both quite unaware—your skills notwithstanding, Holmes—that I have other woes to plague me as well, no more pleasant than the one you're helping me with.

"At this moment," he continued, "my wife Mary lies in her bed at the Brunswick Hotel, not far from here. She is dying of consumption, and suffering more than she has any right to. There is so much pain and confusion in her eyes that she no longer knows who I am. Doesn't recognize me at all, after twelve years of marriage, gentlemen. At times, she orders me angrily out of our rooms! The doctors have hope for her to live no longer than the summer. There is nothing to do but wait for the inevitable. Nothing at all that I can do."

"I'm sorry Edwin," Holmes said quietly. "I had no idea . . ."

"Thank you, Holmes," Booth responded with a wan smile. "I'll probably finish this run with Irving and then take the poor creature home, to her parents I guess, where she can spend her last days with the people she loves. The people she recognizes."

"I'm sure your presence is of great comfort to her all the same," I said, trying to mollify, at least a little, Booth's dejected spirits.

"One hopes so," he said, "but it's a task I find daunting to undertake, having gone through this grief once before. I lost my first wife, my first Mary I call her, for that was her name too, after but four short years together. My God, how I loved that woman, and how ill I treated her with my drinking and my absences. My damnable absence on the day of her death, gentlemen! And here I am once more, about to become a widower twice, and still younger than half a century." Booth sighed laboriously.

"And if that weren't enough, my friends, Mary's parents, the McVickers, have come to London upon hearing of the severity of her illness. They hate me, to be perfectly frank, as much as I regret having to admit it. They have continued here that wretched art they have perfected in America—slyly and inconspicuously spreading the vilest imaginable slander about me, often to the press itself. All behind my back, of course. It's enough to drive a soul to distraction!"

Booth shook his head in obvious disgust and depression. "Such misfortune," he said, "for somebody who was supposedly born to be lucky."

"Lucky?" asked Holmes, raising his eyebrows slightly.

"Born with a caul, Holmes," Booth replied. "Arrived in the cold cruel world in the very sack in which I had grown in the womb. Among the country folk I grew up with in Maryland, this was believed a sure sign of good fortune. I have contemplated that fortune, believe me, in places like California, with my father, may he rest in peace, and I had to track him through the streets of San Francisco or some God-forsaken gold camp. Would he be drunk tonight? Had he once again gone mad, perhaps? Hurt himself, or gotten himself arrested? Well, I'd always find him somehow, and drag him back to the room. Never once did the poor old man remember a thing in the morning.

"I've contemplated that fortunate caul, my friends, when they told me that my brother had put a bullet into Abe Lincoln's brain, and I had to rush to my mother's side. When they hunted John down in that horrible swamp somewhere, and shot him dead like a dog; when I stayed away from the stage for months because of what he did—during all this time I contemplated the cruel mockery of that caul. Misfortune! That's been my true calling! And now Mary, my poor Mary."

Booth lowered his head and wept softly. I glanced nervously at Holmes, who put a finger to his lips. We both remained silent for several minutes.

It was Holmes who finally broke the silence. "Let us not forget, cousin Edwin, that your life has indeed seen a share of fortune, too. There has been luck." Booth looked up with faint curiosity.

"Look at your successes," Holmes said. "Despite everything you have encountered, despite every obstacle thrown in your path, you have persevered to become one of the greatest actors of your time. You have had to work hard, I realize, to overcome it all, but you have prevailed. Don't forget that."

Booth smiled slightly. His mood appeared to be lifting slowly but surely, like a morning mist rises steadily away from a lake. "That's true enough, I suppose," he said, "although difficult to believe sometimes. It all depends on how you look at things, and what you're looking for. In some ways I have done all right. I saved the life of Abe Lincoln's son for example. Did you know that?"

Holmes and I shook our heads in amazement.

"Just a few weeks before my brother murdered his father, I pulled Robert Lincoln from the railway tracks in Jersey City, just seconds before he would have been crushed by the cars. I had no idea who he was, had never seen the man before. He had been pushed off the platform by the press of the crowd. He thanked me profusely, of course, but my real reward would come later."

A glum look returned to Booth's face. "I'd tried for years to get the United States government to release the body of my brother John after they'd hidden it away somewhere. Finally, after telling President Johnson of my service to young Mr. Lincoln, I persuaded them to give it to me. It did my poor mother's soul a great deal of good when we had John back, or at least a body for a grave to decorate with a flower every now and then. If looked at from the proper angle, I'd say that could be seen as a twist of good fortune, wouldn't you?"

"I suppose so," I replied, "although the coincidence of those two events, and their utterly opposite natures, is nothing less than chilling."

"I agree," said Booth. "Still, I choose to see it as fortunate, and not only for Robert Lincoln. You're right Holmes, I should give proper credit to the fortunate caul when it is due. What of these attacks, for another example? Don't they prove it even further? Three times now somebody has done their level best to do me in. Each attempt has come pretty close, too, but each ended in failure. Now if that isn't luck . . ."

As if suddenly reminded of the purpose of our visit, Booth immediately straightened himself in his chair. "I beg your pardon gentlemen," he said. "I've been boring the trousers off the two of you, wallowing in sordid self-pity, burdening you with my private worries. There have been so many difficult things lately, and so few with whom I can converse. So forgive me. You must have news to tell and I've not given you the chance to tell it."

Holmes rose from his chair and walked to the wall where he seemed to study an old and fading theatrical poster bearing the likeness of Edmund Kean. Lighting a cigarette, he leaned casually over a cold radiator. "We'll have the good news first," he said. "During the remainder of your stay in London, Edwin, I'm fairly certain that your assailant will not be paying you any further calls. He fled the city in great haste after his encounter with you in the passageway and is now, I'm confident, out of the country."

Holmes explained his logic to Booth, as he had done for me, and seemed to have similar success in persuading him of it. Booth sighed in relief. "That surely takes a weight from my shoulders," he said. "It hasn't been easy watching every corner in every hallway, searching the countless faces in the audience, all the while thinking that maybe he's out there. Maybe he's preparing for another try."

"That's where the bad news comes in, I'm afraid," said Holmes, grimacing at the flavor of the American whiskey. "The stranger obviously remains free of our grasp, firstly. Secondly, there's nothing in the world to indicate that he won't, in fact, strike again. Indeed, everything observed so far indicates to me that he will do precisely that. In time."

Booth seemed unsurprised. "I figured as much. But tell me Holmes, how did you come to that conclusion? Tell me everything you've learned to date."

"I can't paint you a detailed portrait," Holmes responded, "but I can make a pretty fair sketch. Your assailant stands roughly five foot seven, a fact ascertained by the location of the bullet hole at the Lyceum, as well as the footprints left in the collected dust on the passageway floor." Holmes paused momentarily, handing Booth a small object. "Incidentally, here is the infamous Lyceum bullet, Edwin. An additional charm of survival for your watch chain."

"Further," said Holmes, resuming his monologue, "he walks with the slightest of limps on his left leg, the result surely of an old injury or deformity. It wouldn't be perceived as more than the favoring of one leg to the casual observer, but the footprints in the dust revealed a pronounced imbalance of stature. He is also a horseman, or at least once was. The footprints revealed that his boots were doubtlessly those of a horseman, a cavalryman in fact, as they are of a military cut."

"Remarkable, Holmes," said Booth, warming to the detective's analysis. "What else do you know about him?"

"That he speaks with a French accent, of course, a point of yours we have since corroborated with a stagehand at the theater. Which may or may not mean that he is, in fact, a Frenchman, but hints strongly at the possibility. Assuming so for the moment, it would be probable that his place of hiding after his latest attack lies in France. I cannot yet be sure of that, but I am positive about something else, and that is where he has already been. And that, Edwin, is in America."

"You're suggesting then, that Mark Gray, the man who shot at me in Chicago, has followed me to Europe?"

"No, in fact, I learned only this morning that the opposite is true. I wired the asylum in Elgin yesterday and just this morning received their reply that Mr. Gray remains safely and soundly locked up behind their bars. But I strongly suspect that Mr. Gray, while indeed the man who fired the shot, was acting on another's orders or instructions. He is, as you've said, a lunatic, and would likely be an easy mark for a clever manipulator who preferred not taking the personal risk himself."

"A manipulator?"

"Yes. The manipulator, who is, I'm convinced, our current attacker, merely used Mark Gray in his first attempt on your life. You said that all three attacks were accompanied by the mysterious gift of acorns, did you not?"

"Yes, of course, Holmes. I've always felt that the attacks were somehow connected, but I've been totally baffled as to how they could have been, with Gray locked up and all. Your manipulator idea makes sense."

"In addition to proving the connection between the attacks, the acorns also prove that the man behind the attacks has been spending considerable time in America. All of them are of the same species of tree, the southern red oak of the three-lobed leaf variety, a tree virtually exclusive to the south-central United States. They're likely taken from the very same tree, to judge by their similarity, which suggests that your attacker has something of a permanent base in the States. The ones left for you so recently at the Lyceum, in fact, still bear signs of freshness. Almost certainly they were plucked from the tree only last autumn."

Booth looked grim. "I'm not enjoying the implications of all this," he said.

"Nor do I blame you," Holmes rejoined, stubbing out his cigarette. "The man is following you, Edwin, with remarkable patience and persistence, and his intent is clearly deadly. I'm convinced he hired Mark Gray to do the job in Chicago and when that failed, he took the responsibility onto himself. I warn you that he's growing either more bold or more desperate. His first attempt was carried out by a deranged hireling. The second was by his own hand, in a crowded hotel in Germany. The third and latest attempt saw yet another escalation—he faced you alone, backstage in a theater, which he must have known would greatly enhance the chances of his being seen and identified. I fear his determination has only grown with each successive failure."

"Meaning that the attacks aren't likely to stop."

"Unfortunately, that appears to be the case," said Holmes. "His behavior indicates that he too will return to America, if he hasn't already set out, to await your return. I'm afraid the danger simply has not passed."

"Damn him!" Booth cried out suddenly, smashing his fist onto the table. "I'm stalked by a cowardly killer whose grudge I don't even know!" He rose and stalked the room angrily, his expression and gestures assuming the fiercely dramatic quality of his stage persona. At length he returned to his chair, but the anger remained fixed on his expression.

"What does he want with me, Holmes?" he asked. "What is this man's purpose?"

"As to that," Holmes replied, "we will have to remain in the dark, unless an obvious possibility occurs to you. I hope you will forgive my boldness, cousin, but I must ask whether there is in fact any potentially significant motive for vengeance upon you. Unpaid debts, for example, or a competitor upon the stage?"

"No, my debts are all paid in full, except those to my dreaded in-laws, and I cannot imagine another actor jealous enough to devote his life to my destruction."

Holmes voice grew quiet as he approached a sensitive question. "A lover's triangle, then? A romantic indiscretion gone bad?"

"Holmes!" I blurted. "Really, this . . ."

"Watson, Watson, forgive me, but in matters as dire as this the most painful questions are justified, as are the embarassing ones. I assure both of you I don't relish asking it." He turned toward his cousin. "Edwin?"

"No. Rest assured that no such indiscretion has ever taken place. There are no jealous husbands on my trail."

"Then we are left without an answer," said Holmes.

"Unless, of course, the vengeance isn't really for anything I've done, but for what John did to Lincoln," said Booth. "The sins of the brother shall be visited upon the brother, to paraphrase Scriptures a bit. Sixteen years, you know, is really not such a long time."

I joined the conversation. "But Edwin, the man has practically devoted his life to your destruction. Surely there must be a greater motive than your brother's crime."

"Don't forget, Dr. Watson, who my brother's victim was. Mind you, I supported Abe Lincoln myself, voted for him, stood by the Union, recognized his greatness, but since his death I've witnessed his legacy grow into amazing proportions. He is today viewed in almost god-like terms in America. His portrait is regularly beside that of

George Washington. History may vindicate such lionization, I suppose, or it will deflate it, but what's important now is that old Honest Abe is still very much beloved in the States. There may indeed still be people whose outrage at his fate has yet to subside."

"An interesting theory," Holmes mused. "And just as Lincoln was the Christ, so was your brother the Judas or, if you prefer a less religious analogy, the Brutus to Lincoln's Caesar. Remember the words he spoke to you before firing in the passageway: 'From tiny acorns, mighty oaks are grown, and with tiny axes mighty oaks are fallen.' It's a twisting of the old Latin saying *parvis e glandibus quercus*, tall oaks from little acorns grow. Who better than Abraham Lincoln, the rugged and kind father of a pioneer nation, to personify the mighty oak?"

"It does make a bizarre sort of sense, I suppose," said Booth, "although I can't imagine who the 'tiny axe' might represent."

"Either your brother, the assassin who slew the oak," said Holmes, "or your assailant himself, in which case one would assume that you represent the oak."

"It's all so queer. If I wasn't sure of his deadly intentions, I'd be tempted to have a good laugh over it. Still, what does it really matter what his motives are? That he is determined to finish me off presents me with a rather more immediate problem."

Holmes paced the tiny dressing room. "When do you plan to return to America?"

"Within two weeks," said Booth. "I've already booked passage for Mary, Edwina, the McVickers and myself for New York."

"And once you arrive in New York," asked Holmes, "what will be your living arrangements?"

"I plan to allow Mary to be taken to her parents' house on Fifty-Third Street. It will be easier on her, quieter and all, and I'm not so selfless as to deny that it will be easier on me, too. As for myself, I'll probably take rooms with Edwina at the Windsor Hotel. Perhaps, as the summer progresses, I'll do some traveling, visit some friends in the vicinity whom I've not seen in too long a time."

"Do you plan to work upon your return?"

"Not at least until, well, until I know more about Mary's condition. Surely not before the autumn. My funds are sufficient and I'm finding it more difficult to perform by the day with Mary so ill and this lunatic lurking around some corner for me. I'm unable to concentrate. It's time for a little hiatus."

"That will make protection considerably easier," said Holmes.

"Protection?"

"You'll have to have it. You will need someone near you at all times, someone capable of handling the next attack. So long as you avoid the stage, that task will be infinitely easier."

"So," Edwin asked dismally, "we have finally come down to bodyguards?"

"I see no effective alternative. Until there's another attack, it will be difficult, if not impossible, for the local police to do anything for you. Considering the likelihood of that attack, it's strongly advisable to be prepared for it. The attack itself may, in fact, be the only way to clear up the problem—so long as you're prepared for it when it comes. With good bodyguards, you might collar the scoundrel himself. I recommend the Pinkerton Agency, for whose investigative skills I cannot vouch, but whose expertise in personal protection is unchallenged anywhere."

Booth sighed loudly. "I guess that sums it all up," he said. "Holmes, I cannot thank you enough for what you've done."

"What I've done," muttered Holmes, "is precisely nothing. I haven't moved the problem one iota closer to its solution, I'm afraid."

"But you have! Don't you see, now I have a pretty good picture of this character. Knowing something of him makes me feel like I have a few cards of my own, as well. I'll take your advice. I'll provide myself with protection. On his next visit, our dark stranger is bound to have a tougher time."

There being little else on the subject left to say, the three of us rose and prepared to part. At Booth's suggestion, however, we agreed to meet a final time for dinner and brandy, so as to give the cousins at least one chance to converse at ease. We set the date for a week hence, just before Booth's scheduled return to America.

The period passed quickly for Holmes and myself, and fortunately without incident for Edwin. Holmes busied himself with a couple of mundane cases—"amusing trivialities," he called them—and spent a great deal of time consumed within the vast depths of his tomes. As for me, a minor outbreak of influenza in the city resulted in my being called to St. Bartholomew's where my services contributed to that hospital's efforts for 10 hours a day for nearly a week. We discussed the Booth affair once or twice, but I suspected Holmes was still unhappy over his inability to help further and I brought it up no more.

On the appointed day our supper with Booth took place, the three of us enjoying a sumptuous roast beef dinner at a restaurant along the Strand. There Booth and Holmes successfully updated one another on the fortunes of two families separated by an ocean for a full 60 years. They laughed at some stories the other told, and grew solemn at others, as their discussion followed the crests and valleys of their parents', and their own, lives. At length they agreed that it was regretful that the familial separation ever took place, and that Holmes and Booth themselves should have been deprived of each other's company during the days of their youth. They agreed further that their contacts during the past several weeks had been a meager, but still fortunate, opportunity to bridge the families closer together.

"To which notion," announced Holmes at the conclusion of our dinner, "we must have a proper toast. Let us repair forthright to Baker Street where we may do so."

We soon found ourselves gathered before a warm and cheery fire at 221-B, slowly sipping the French brandy Holmes had procured for the occasion. Booth finally broke what had been a long silence.

"Well, I'll be!" he exclaimed, pointing at the wall. "Now there's a touch of home." He pointed to an unframed portrait of Henry Ward Beecher I had tacked to the wall.

"He hated Lincoln with a passion," Booth said, "but he hated the Confederates even more. What in the world is a picture of that old firebreathing preacher doing in faraway London?"

"He was highly regarded in England during your Civil War," I said. "I've always admired the ethical quality of his work, especially his efforts to keep Britain from siding with the Confederacy. It was largely Beecher, you know, who convinced Victoria that aligning herself with the Southern cause and its slavery was too high a moral price for England to pay in return for the economic benefits of the cotton trade."

Booth smiled. "I gather, had you been an American in those days, that you'd have made a fine abolitionist."

I nodded.

"And what of you, Holmes?" Booth asked, turning to him. "Which side would you have chosen?"

Holmes snorted and sipped his brandy. "Political matters have never held the slightest interest for me," he replied, "other than the fact that they occasionally bring me cases of interest. Politics, it seems to me, is the dangerous art of power, often practiced by those who have no business wielding it. And wars, I remind you, are inevitably political matters."

I could tell that Booth wanted to challenge Holmes, as did I, but the seeming conviction of the detective's cynical contention kept both of us quiet.

"Have either of you ever been to America?" Booth asked at last.

I shook my head. Holmes did not respond.

"It's an exciting country," he said. "Growing and anxious, exuberant and a little drunk with its own successes. A dangerous place sometimes, yes, but a fascinating one."

"I've long been fascinated with it myself," Holmes said graciously, "and readily confess that I've stood in admiration of many an American, including yourself, Edwin."

Booth lowered his head, as if taking a bow, and smiled. "In that case gentlemen, perhaps you'll consider the proposal I'm about to make."

We looked at him with interest.

"Within this," Booth said, holding up a narrow manila envelope, "is a substantial amount of money, enough to pay easily for the passage from England to New York for the two of you, provide adequate living expenses for a stay of several weeks duration, and provide a rather handsome royalty on top of it all."

Holmes and I stared at him in surprised silence.

"In other words, gentlemen, I would much prefer not saying goodbye to you at all. Instead, I would like you to come to New York with me, just for as long as it takes you to track down this fiend, or at least to give it a good try. I've not the slightest doubt that you're up to it Holmes."

I stared at Holmes in expectant silence. He folded his fingers together and stared impassively at the wall for a moment, causing both myself and, I'm sure, Booth as well, to believe that he frowned on the very idea.

He suddenly started from his chair and clapped his hands. "Excellent Edwin!" he cried. "That is precisely the proposition I was hoping you'd make! There is nothing worse in this world than leaving a case unresolved, especially when it offers as many features of interest as does yours. I wouldn't miss the opportunity for the world. What do you say, Watson? In for a little overseas adventure?" His eyes sparked with interest.

The whole thing had caught me utterly by surprise. "I don't quite know," I began, "I—"

"Why, of course you'll come, Watson!" Holmes interrupted. "The season is perfect for travel and you're practically free as far as medical responsibilities go. There may never be a better chance."

"Well then, I suppose so," I finally agreed. "Yes, yes. I believe I will come!"

"Wonderful!" Booth exclaimed. "Then we're a team. Our ship sets sail in two days. The *Bothnia* from Liverpool. I'll expect to see the two of you aboard."

"That you will," said Holmes, shaking his hand. "That you will."

—5—
Tales of an American Cousin

We set sail from Liverpool amidst one of that port city's legendary fogs, far cleaner than the deadly vapors for which London is rightly infamous, but no less pervasive for the comparative lack of smoke. The *Bothnia* was towed out of the harbour to the mournful accompaniment of foghorns sounding calls of warning.

It is, actually, incorrect to use the phrase "set sail," for the *Bothnia*, being a bright new steamship, hadn't a sail to her name. It was a well-appointed and comfortable, if not luxurious vessel, far less susceptible to the vagaries of wind and climate than her stately sisters, the schooners, sloops, barks and brigs that lay at anchor in Liverpool harbour.

Holmes and I took separate berths while Booth, his ailing wife and his daughter Edwina had quarters on another deck. Booth's dreaded in-laws, the McVickers (or McDevils as he'd caustically taken to calling them) traveled in their own suite, and seemed fastidious in avoiding Booth. In order to avoid sensational publicity (which Booth believed his in-laws were not above feeding) he had told no-one about his plight and the nature of our association with him. As far as his wife, his in-laws or his sister Asia were concerned, Holmes and I were to be regarded as nothing more than British acquaintances for the duration of the passage. Only his daughter Edwina knew otherwise. The fact that Holmes and Booth were cousins was likewise concealed, in Booth's belief that knowledge of this would only lead to natural suspicions on the question of our traveling with him.

For most of the ten days it took the steamship to traverse the Atlantic, Booth maintained a lonely vigil at his wife's bedside, only occasionally coming out onto the deck for meals or fresh air. From his drawn and pale appearance, it was evident that he slept little during his wife's sufferings. Making it infinitely more difficult for him was the fact that Mrs. Booth was apparently still unable to recognize her husband. She usually displayed nothing but hostility toward him. As her illness appeared to lead her into dreadful periods of delirium, she took to angrily ordering him out of their berth, insisting that as a stranger he was unwanted in her presence. These incidents, added to Booth's already depressed state about her prospects for recovery, made the journey a frightful one for the actor.

Sometimes, during the evenings, once he was assured that his wife was resting at last, Booth would join us on deck or in one of the ship's parlors. Despite his condition, these visits seemed to animate him considerably, never seeming to fail in lifting his spirits. He joined us on the second night of the passage as Holmes and I were irritably discussing the pros and cons of Edgar Allan Poe's fictional detective C. Auguste Dupin.

"As I've already made plain, Watson," said Holmes, blowing carefully formed rings of smoke across the parlor, "I have nothing but praise for Poe's work in poetry and the macabre prose for which he is so highly regarded, but his so-called tales of ratiocination leave a great deal to be desired. Dupin displayed some skill and insight in *The Purloined Letter*, true enough, but on the whole he was a showy pretender to the mantle of true detective."

Booth then took charge of the conversation. "I met him, you know," he said with a tired smile. "Poe that is, not Dupin. My father knew him. They were fairly notorious for a time in Baltimore as drinking partners and, if I may be so irreverent, as occasional ruffians, too. I've been told they terrorized their share of passers-by."

Holmes seemed fascinated. "Tell me," he asked, "when did you meet him?"

"When I was a boy of twelve years. Father brought him to the farm one morning for breakfast, rather the worse for wear the two of them, after what had doubtlessly been a night of hard drinking on the docks. I found him a terribly somber and spectral fellow, not

unlike some of the characters from those stories of his. All dark and
serious, dressed in a long black cloak. But John . . . John was absolutely thrilled with him. He begged Poe to recite something for us and
the poet obliged, selecting 'The Raven' which was then quite new. We
were all dumbfounded at the performance, so brilliant was the poem
and so impassioned and forceful its recitation. I was convinced, and
still am, that Poe would have made an absolutely sterling actor had he
chosen that pursuit. And John . . ." Here Booth seemed to grow
suddenly quiet, as if his remembrance of pleasant memories had suddenly been interrupted. "John kept a book of his poems near his
bedside up to the very end." The actor looked somberly at the floor.

"I read somewhere," said Holmes, "that Poe was sometimes compared in physical appearance to your brother John, and in the power of
his poetry reading to your own dramatic skills."

"Yes," said Booth, looking up. "That has been said. In my case at
least, having seen him that one morning in our sitting room, I can
but consider it a compliment."

On another night, the three of us spent considerable time discussing Charles Dickens' last, and unfinished, novel, *The Mystery of Edwin
Drood*, which I'd brought along to help while away the hours. Holmes
had never read the book, naturally enough, but after seeing the word
mystery in its title, insisted on borrowing it from me.

"I have the solution," he said triumphantly that evening in the
parlor, handing the book back to me. "And I daresay, were the good Mr.
Dickens here to discuss it with us tonight, and not eleven years in his
grave, he would utterly agree with me."

It was a characteristically confident and arrogant statement from
Holmes, one of many which in the early days of my association with
him never failed to irritate me.

"And so," said Booth, with just a trace of dubious sarcasm in his
voice, "what was the fate of poor young Drood?"

"His fate was one of narrow survival of attempted murder. He
survived, just barely, the poison administered by his uncle Jasper.
Neville Landless was but a clever red herring on Dickens' part."

"But Jasper," said Booth, "was the very picture of a caring and
devoted uncle. What would have been his motive?"

"Lust," Holmes said casually. "Simple, base lust, focused in this incidence on Miss Rosa Bud, Drood's fiancée. That Jasper was indeed depicted as caring and devoted only heightened my suspicions about him, knowing a little of Dickens' storytelling methods. Those methods, combined with the subtle clues provided in the text, led me inexorably toward my conclusion. It's a clever mystery, I must say, made alluring by the fact that the author died before its completion, thus forever leaving a question mark at the end."

We spent several evenings aboard the *Bothnia* engaged in similar idle conversations, interspersed with relaxed play at cards. I rarely saw Booth during the days, and usually contented myself with reading. Holmes, however, seemed restless and impatient, as if frustrated that the long grey days at sea were keeping him from the case he craved. He consumed himself, therefore, with frenetic activity.

The man who not more than two months before had told me that he neither knew nor cared whether the planets circled the sun or if it were the other way around, suddenly developed a keen passion for celestial navigation. He trailed the poor quartermaster everywhere aboard the vessel, asking him pointed questions about the constellations and their movements, and trying his hand at the sextant. He even guiled his way onto the bridge somehow and convinced the captain to give him a turn at the helm. With his rare powers of perception and absorption, I've no doubt that Holmes was a top-notch navigator by the time our journey was over.

As we neared New York one cool and cloudy day, however, I found him leaning on the rail, apparently uninterested in his usual nautical pursuits. He stared thoughtfully at the low clouds overhead and the oily monotonous seas that stretched in all directions into eternity.

"Greetings," he said to me. "I see you're getting your sea-legs at last. I haven't seen you looking so rosy since Liverpool." He was referring to a persistent case of seasickness which had haunted me since our departure. It wasn't nearly as terrible as my first bout less than a year ago, on the Royal Navy hospital ship that carried me back from Afghanistan, through a ghastly gale off the Cape of Good Hope, no less. Still it had kept me in my bunk for longer than I care to admit.

I was less concerned on that morning with my own discomforts than with those of Booth. His pallid and weak appearance only seemed to worsen as we steamed westward. I mentioned this to Holmes who merely shrugged it off, predicting that once we reached land Booth would be better able to deal with his many problems.

"All the same Holmes," I said, "I'm worried about your American cousin."

He gave me a strange look. "How interesting that you should use that phrase," he said.

"In what sense?"

"Don't you remember? The play. It was entitled *Our American Cousin*. It was a Friday night performance at Ford's Theater in Washington. April the fourteenth. Harry Hawke was in the leading role, along with Laura Keene, but the true starring role that night belonged to another actor."

He was referring, of course, to John Wilkes Booth, who would only depart the stage that night after committing the worst crime in American history.

"It's difficult to imagine," I said, "that such a fiend was the brother of Edwin Booth. I've never seen a more striking or terrible contrast between brothers."

"So it seems now Watson, sixteen long years after his crime and his own death. But from every account I've ever seen or heard, Wilkes Booth seemed a rational and pleasant enough fellow for the most part, up until the time of the crime, of course. It's said he was lazy in comparison to his older brothers, and disliked the discipline demanded of his theatrical studies, and so his early performances were abysmal. He was hissed off his share of stages for forgetting lines, or for uttering them so unconvincingly that the audience would suffer no such fool gladly. Still, he learned. Slowly and patiently, he learned, so that by the time he was but twenty-two years old, his star was already posing a challenge to Edwin's, and his houses were rarely less than full."

I pulled my overcoat up closer against the sea's chill. "Yes, of course, Holmes," I said, "that's all well known, but the man must nevertheless have been utterly mad to have done what he did."

Holmes smiled faintly and carefully tamped shag into an old briar. "Madness is usually far too subjective a concept to be of much use in serious analysis of a problem," he said. "That he was a fervent and outspoken supporter of the Southern cause is beyond doubt, of course, even though he was never known to wear the uniform of the Confederate States Army. He was an insufferable libertine, it's well known, quite literally a practicing Romeo; he was said to have been highly vain, but vanity is common enough among actors. He had a quick temper when the issue was slavery or the Secession, but there really is no evidence to indicate that he acted in a deranged manner until that fateful day, Watson. Perhaps he was insane on that one point. Perhaps not."

"Then how do you explain his motive in murdering Lincoln?"

Holmes put a lit match to his pipe and soon had it billowing in the deck's salty air. "Quite frankly, Watson, I make no effort to explain it. People sometimes do things for reasons that make absolutely no sense to others, yet seem perfectly logical to themselves. Perhaps Booth had such a reason. Then, of course, one cannot totally discount the possibility of a conspiracy whose branches reached higher than the assassin himself. Historians and journalists, for some reason, seem to have rejected these ideas in totality, but much of the American public still embraces many of them."

"Well, I have heard of the Confederate conspiracy idea, that the recently vanquished South felt it best to strike one final and terrible blow of vengeance against the hated North. It always made some sense to me."

"It makes no sense whatever to me, Watson," Holmes said between puffs. "Of all people, the Southerners realized that their best hope in the wake of their surrender at Appomatox lay in Lincoln's hands. His plan for the postwar period was a relatively merciful one, calling for the speedy return of Southern representatives to Congress, for an expedited resumption of citizenship, for a slow and gradual elevation of the black man's state, so as not to shake the Southern social fabric too drastically. No, Watson, the defeated South had no motive in murdering Lincoln. Quite the opposite, in fact."

"And yet you find the idea of a conspiracy plausible."

"I find the possibility of a Northern conspiracy immensely more likely. Lincoln's political opponents in Washington, the Radical wing of his own Republican Party, had far harsher intentions regarding the Southern states than Lincoln had. They felt the powerful allure of easy profits as well, but Lincoln's plans conflicted with all of these ambitions. Any number of Radical leaders in the House or Senate, or more likely, Lincoln's own Secretary of War, the Radical Edwin Stanton, had far greater motives in removing the president than Jefferson Davis may have had."

"Stanton?" I said in surprise. "But he was Lincoln's staunch ally, his right hand man. He stood by his deathbed and placed the coins over his eyes on the morning after the shooting. In fact, he led and coordinated the entire investigation into the murder conspiracy, and the trial of Booth's assistants."

"All of which," said Holmes, "lead me closer to my thesis, much in the manner of suspecting Jasper of guilt in the Drood mystery. Consider the possibility that Stanton only appeared to be Lincoln's staunch ally. That much is arguable at least. All the while, then, he was plotting with his fellow Radicals behind the president's back. As for his role in the investigation, well Watson, this casts gravely suspicious light over Mr. Stanton's actions. He demanded and was given a military tribunal for the conspirators, a court martial in reality, when the legal circumstances of the case clearly called for a civilian trial. Witnesses were routinely harassed, evidence was occasionally doctored or, in one case at least, conveniently lost. I refer, of course, to Booth's diary, the desperate and rambling journal penned in the Maryland swamps before his capture and death. Its very existence was only discovered more than a year after Stanton's tribunal had done its harsh work with the conspiracy suspects. When it was accidentally found at the War Department in eighteen sixty-seven, Stanton found himself in big political trouble with President Johnson, and the discovery of his silence on the diary two years before only hastened Stanton's political downfall. He never gave a satisfactory explanation at the time and is now dead himself, unable to explain the long disappearance of such a fundamental piece of evidence. You see, Watson, there's an additional intrigue: When it was found, eighteen pages of the diary were missing. If one assumes that Edwin Stanton, as chief investigator and guardian of evidence, read those eighteen pages in eighteen sixty-five, one can only speculate as to whether he tore them from the diary, and for what reasons."

"Then John Wilkes Booth," I said, "would have been nothing but Stanton's tool."

"Possibly. Mind you, I'm merely reciting one of the more persistent theories still maintained in certain American quarters. It might just as well have been Andrew Johnson, Lincoln's vice president, who was, in eighteen sixty-five at least, still firmly within the Radical camp himself, and under Stanton's influence. His motive would have been nothing less than the assumption of the nation's presidency, which must surely have seemed a tempting prize. There is one tantalyzing piece of evidence to support this theory—the fact that Booth left his calling card for Johnson at the vice president's hotel on the very day of the assassination. What a marvelous puzzle that is."

We stood at the rail in silence for several minutes, mulling over the vague and complex possibilities of conspiracy, and contemplating the sheer density and mystery of the Lincoln case.

I finally broke the silence. "For someone who professes to be above politics, Holmes, you certainly seem to have mastered a good piece of the American political picture, at least as it existed sixteen years ago."

"You're right, Watson. I have been doing my homework, but rest assured, it's not out of any fascination with politics or politicians. My interest, rather, lies in a full understanding of the case at hand, Edwin's case, that is. I cannot help but consider the possibility of a connection between his current troubles and his brother's crime. If that should turn out to be the case, prudence dictates that I be sufficiently knowledgeable to deal with it."

Holmes relit his pipe and returned his restless gaze to the grey seascape. "In fact, my dear fellow, I've spent the last few weeks engrossed in lengthy and esoteric materials dealing with the Lincoln murder. I now qualify as something of an expert on the subject, I daresay. Here's a suggestion: Let's return to my cabin before this chill puts the two of us in the sick bay with pneumonia, and then, with a glass of claret to warm our bones, I'll tell you a story for my own review and for your edification—the story of John Wilkes Booth and how Abraham Lincoln met his unfortunate end."

In the dimly lit cabin, Holmes and I spent the afternoon going over the old case, he displaying a yeoman's familiarity with the myriad details, fully in character with his rapid ability to grasp information, and I listening in rapt attention to a story that had already started to grow dim within my own memory.

In the autumn of 1864 (Holmes told me) John Wilkes Booth began a deliberate reduction in the number of his theatrical appearances, despite the fact of his gaining popularity and rising reputation as an actor. In November of that year, he performed *Julius Caesar* in New York with his brothers Junius Jr., who had yet to relinquish his own acting career, and Edwin. It was to be the only performance ever shared by these three sons of the celebrated Junius Brutus Booth. At about the same time, young Booth apparently hatched the beginnings of a Quixotic plan whose dreadful end would culminate with the Lincoln assassination six months later.

In its earliest form, the idea was to kidnap the president and spirit him behind Confederate lines to Richmond where, Booth reasoned, the Southern authorities could hold him for ransom—either for the return of Confederate prisoners-of-war held in Union camps or for some form of armistice. It was the very twilight of the great rebellion and Booth must have believed that desperate times called for desperate actions. No evidence had ever been found that the Confederate government ever approved, or even knew of, such a plan.

After unsuccessfully trying to enlist two fellow actors in a plot, Booth soon surrounded himself with a crew of helpers, dull and unambitious fellows for the most part, attracted to Booth because of his celebrity or, perhaps, by the air of danger and intrigue that his plot manifested. John Surratt, a clerk, had been introduced to Booth shortly before. Both were engaged in certain smuggling tasks for the

Confederates, operating out of southern Maryland. Booth is said to have worked in the smuggling of quinine, a scarce medical commodity in the desperate South.

Sam Arnold and Michael O'Laughlin, both veterans of the rebel army, had been boyhood friends of Booth's. George Atzerodt, a native of Germany, was a carriage-maker from the Potomac River town of Port Tobacco. A drunken, fawning man, Atzerodt was probably brought into the circle by Surratt, who recognized that his knowledge of the territory might prove valuable in ferrying the kidnapped and kidnappers southward from Washington. David Herold, a young ne'er-do-well, had failed at pharmaceutical work repeatedly—he is said to have had, at most, the intellect of an eleven- or twelve-year-old boy.

Certainly the most imposing of Booth's gathered characters was Lewis Payne, also known as Lewis Powell, a giant of a man whose smallness of brain was rivaled only by the sheer immensity of his size. A veteran of some of the Civil War's bloodiest campaigns, fought from the southern lines, Payne was first a Union prisoner and later an escapee. Apparently familiar with Booth through some previous meeting, he was called into the circle at a late date to provide the muscle and capacity for action they felt would be needed in order to succeed.

The conspiracy was based in Washington from the beginning. They met only rarely at Booth's rooms in the National Hotel and much more frequently in the boarding house owned by Mary Surratt, John Surratt's widowed mother. As conspiracies go, it seemed to have more of a romantic genesis than a practical one; its earliest plan called for kidnapping Lincoln in an intentionally darkened theater, tying the president up, and furtively whisking him out of the theater in the darkness. That Lincoln was almost surely a man of fearsome physical strength, not to mention courage, seems not to have occurred to the plotters at all. Wisely, this ridiculous notion was never attempted.

A later plan, however, featured more realistic ambitions. The group hoped to waylay the president's carriage on a lonely road leading to the Soldier's Home outside Washington, where Lincoln was known to have been fond of taking occasional relaxation from the pressures of the capital. This plan came quite close to success, but when the highwaymen had halted their prey in the presidential carriage, they found instead Samuel Chase, the Chief Justice of the U.S. Supreme Court, who had taken Lincoln's place on this particular day. They allowed the jurist to pass unmolested and returned to the city cursing their dimming prospects.

The conspiracy began to unravel at this point, with O'Laughlin and Arnold leaving Booth in disgust and Surratt returning to his smuggling and spying work for the dying Confederacy. Booth was left with the towering Payne, the simian Atzerodt and the imbecilic Herold. It was by this time March of 1865, and the rebellion's doom was a foregone conclusion.

It was probably during this immediate period that the plan changed from kidnapping into murdering Lincoln. If Booth's few, rather jumbled, correspondences are to be believed, his only motive was one of deranged vengeance operating under the guise of justice.

The preparations were simple enough. Booth would reserve for himself the historic role of presidential assassin, taking pains to ensure that the country would know all too well who had committed the crime. Payne would be assigned the murder of Secretary of State Seward, aided by Herold, who probably knew Washington's streets much better than he. And Atzerodt, the last conspirator, was instructed to kill Vice President Andrew Johnson.

History has recorded, of course, that Payne came close to success, very nearly killing Seward as he lay in his bed at home, injured in a recent carriage accident. A special brace, fitted for his broken jaw, was all that kept Payne's brutal knife thrusts from killing him. Atzerodt characteristically drank himself into a stupor and shied away from his part of the plot, leaving Johnson unbothered and unhurt.

Only Booth himself, the star of this terrible tragedy, would achieve his aims on the night of April 14, 1865. As Abraham Lincoln, his wife Mary and two guests sat in a specially prepared box at Ford's Theater—awash in the glory and relief of a weary nation just released from the grip of a bloody war—Booth stole in through a narrow passageway. His presence caused no suspicion in a theater where his face was highly familiar. Securing the door of the box against intrusion, using a plank and chipped groove in the plaster of the jam which he'd improvised earlier, he silently approached Abraham Lincoln from the rear. No guard was present at that crucial moment to guard the nation's chief.

Booth fired a small derringer directly into the back of the president's skull, timing the report perfectly to coincide with audience laughter. With a knife, the assassin then bloodied the arm of Lincoln's guest, a Major Rathbone, who tried to stop him. Booth stood upon the edge of the box and jumped the ten or so feet to the stage itself, catching his spur on a flag which was used to decorate the presidential box. The fall broke Booth's leg as he reached the stage, but did not prevent him from rising to his feet and facing an audience that knew his face well. He dramatically raised his knife into the air and cried "*Sic Semper Tyrannis!*" before rushing past the actor Harry Hawke, the stage's lone occupant other than he. He rapidly disappeared into the wings and out the theater's rear door where in the dark alley a horse awaited him. In a fury of hoofbeats, with the horrified cries finally shrieking out in the theater behind him, Booth escaped into the April night.

Within the theater, all was chaos at first. The crowd managed to reach Lincoln after some minutes, and succeeded in carrying the stricken man across the street to a private dwelling. The audience was quick to realize the terrible import of the incident that had just taken place in their presence, and just as quick to recognize its perpetrator. Within minutes, the name of John Wilkes Booth, along with a curse, seemed on every lip.

The president, never regaining a moment of consciousness, lingered through a seemingly endless night until finally, under the chill of a rainy grey morning, he breathed his last, plunging his nation into a grief from which it may never fully recover.

The life of his assassin would last but 12 days longer than his victim's. Of Booth's fellow conspirators, only Herold would manage to make a planned rendezvous with him; Payne found himself hopelessly lost soon after his attack on Seward and was easily captured within a few days when he stupidly returned to Mrs. Surratt's boarding house, which the authorities had already linked to the plot.

Atzerodt, who never fulfilled his murderous assignment, was tracked down with similar ease.

Booth and Herold, however, proved more canny prey. They convinced a sentry at the Navy Yard Bridge at the city's limits to let them pass into Maryland, despite wartime rules which closed the city to travelers nightly. Foolishly, however, Booth told the sentry his real name when asked, thus giving his pursuers a helpful, and ultimately fatal, headstart. The pair rode through southern Maryland, halting briefly at the small inn at Surrattsville owned by Mary Surratt, where Booth drank whiskey to ease the pain in his leg and picked up a carbine. He also took a telescope and other equipment which Mrs. Surratt had taken there earlier that day, at his request.

Near dawn, they stopped at the lonely house of one Dr. Samuel Mudd, a physician and Southern sympathizer with whom Booth had previously had business dealings, and requested treatment for Booth's broken leg. Booth made a half-hearted attempt to disguise himself from the doctor, wearing whiskers and inventing a story. After his medical services were rendered, the pair rode off again into the woods and swamps.

Had his leg not been injured in the fall, Booth might have made good his escape, taking advantage of a disorganized and frenzied army pursuit. One band of Union troops however, found themselves on the right track early on, but were still well behind their prey on the morning after the crime. Booth's broken leg made travel slow and painful and the troops steadily gained on the pair. Much to Booth's disappointment and surprise, they received little help or sympathy from the rural folk they encountered, Southern sympathizers though most of them were. They spent most of their days hiding in the brush and their nights moving slowly and painfully toward the South. They eventually reached the Rappahannock, which separates Maryland from Virginia, and persuaded a group of returning rebel cavalrymen to help ferry them across the mighty river. They would eventually inform the veterans who they were and what they had done.

A few miles into Virginia, Booth and Herold took temporary refuge at a remote farm near the town of Bowling Green, belonging to the Garrett family. They told the Garretts that they were Confederates themselves, returning after the fighting, and persuaded them to provide a place to stay. The end came here.

In short order the Federals learned of the rebel horsemen helping two strangers across the river. They soon tracked down one of the Confederates, Captain Willie Jett, and threatened him with summary execution, rapidly convincing him to reveal the fugitives' hiding place. The Union cavalry detachment raced north once again, and within the wee hours of the night, arrived at the Garrett farm. Once there they fiercely confronted the family, who wasted little time in revealing where their guests were staying. They told the soldiers, in fact, that they too had suspected the pair, having sensed that they were horse thieves. Thus wary, they allowed them to stay, but only in an old tobacco barn on the property, which they had later surreptitiously locked. Booth and Herold were, without their own knowledge of it, utterly trapped.

Once awakened and aware of their peril, however, Booth grew defiant in his desperation. Herold surrendered quickly and meekly, but Booth remained in the barn, asking for a chance to fight for his escape, even suggesting that he fight each and every member of the detachment. Lieutenant L.B. Baker, who was more or less in charge, would suffer no such nonsense, and insisted on Booth's unconditional surrender. In order to hasten it, he set fire to the outbuilding, and then a shot rang out.

Some say that one of Baker's men, Sergeant Boston Corbett, fired at Booth against orders not to shoot. Others insist that Booth fired the shot himself. In any case, Booth took a bullet near the base of his neck and was soon dragged prone out of the burning barn.

The assassin would manage to linger for but a couple of pain-filled and largely delirious hours upon the porch of the Garrett house. He muttered a few seemingly incoherent sentences, such as "useless, useless," most of which seem overly dramatic, perhaps in line with his temperament. Finally, just before sunrise, after the vainglorious words "Tell mother I died for my country," Booth did indeed expire.

His body was promptly hauled back to Washington by the soldiers, duly identified as being the remains of John Wilkes Booth, and then buried beneath the floorboards of an old shed at the Capitol Prison. Stanton considered it a fittingly humiliating resting place for such a villain, and felt confident that it would help forestall any Southern effort to lionize Booth's deed or, worse, to serve as some sort of morbid rallying symbol for the rebellion's revival. There, the tragic story comes to its end.

Holmes leaned back on his bunk and blew smoke from his smoldering cherrywood. "I find Booth's words—'useless, useless'—among the most fascinating features of the case, Watson," he said. "How could he mean useless in terms of Lincoln's death? On that score, he had been entirely successful. Did the phrase perhaps denote a much-too-late change of heart on the killer's part? We'll never know the answer, of course, as it continues to lie unspoken with the assassin in his grave."

"Of course," I said, "it didn't all end with Booth's death."

"By no means, Watson. The crime's aftermath was dreadful in itself. Lewis Payne, George Atzerodt and David Herold all swung from the gallows before that summer was out. Considering their involvement in the case, the executions were understandable. But the fourth person to hang—Mary Surratt—now that might not have been so neatly justified."

"Don't many Americans believe that she was innocent, at least as far as the assassination goes?"

"Quite, and she's also considered so by myself, I might add. She kept the boarding house, the 'nest that hatched the egg,' as Stanton so aptly described it. And yes, she did indeed deliver Booth's articles to the tavern at Surrattsville on the afternoon of April fourteenth, but claimed it was without knowledge of their eventual purpose. She was certainly "Secesh," a Southern sympathizer, but it seems doubtful that she knew of, or assisted in any knowing way, the murder itself. There was a tremendous lust for vengeance in the assassination's wake, Watson, and a pervasive fear that the whole business had been engineered and carried out by the Confederacy. Maybe, and I emphasize the tentative quality of that word, maybe that's why Stanton was so careless in his administration of justice."

"Weren't there other innocent victims, too?" I asked. "Didn't Dr. Mudd come close to sharing Mrs. Surratt's fate?"

"Indeed, and the evidence against him seems even weaker than in Mrs. Surratt's case. He helped set Booth's broken leg, that's beyond dispute, and he may well have recognized Booth from his earlier meetings with him, despite the paltry efforts at disguise. Still, there was no way he could have heard news of an assassination that took place scarcely two hours before. No solid evidence was ever found that he plotted anything with Booth. He did, however, make the very unfortunate mistake of denying that he had seen Booth before, an understandable if foolish result of his fear of Stanton's retributions."

"And it cost him dearly, that mistake. Having narrowly escaped the rope, he soon found himself in irons aboard a U.S. Navy gunboat bound for the Fort Jefferson prison, in the hellish climate of the Dry Tortugas. I'm sure you've heard the story of how he nearly died there, after a deadly outbreak of yellow fever struck prisoners and prison-keepers alike. If it weren't for Mudd's courageous medical work, the whole island might have died of it. His service earned him a pardon in eighteen sixty-nine, that and the fact that forgiveness and fairness were a bit more in fashion in Washington by then."

"And among those saved by Mudd," I said, searching my memory, "were two other conspirators, correct?"

"Excellent Watson," Holmes said. "Samuel Arnold, one of the original conspirators from the kidnapping days, was treated by Mudd and pardoned along with him. He served as the doctor's nurse and aide during the epidemic. A certain Ned Spangler, a stagehand at Ford's whose link with the plot seems dubious at best, was also released. Michael O'Laughlin, however, was not so fortunate. He was among the earliest victims of the yellow fever. That leaves, of course, only one conspirator unaccounted for—John Surratt, who quit the conspiracy early on and was quite adept in eluding the authorities for some time. They finally ran him down in Alexandria, after a frustrating and dramatic chase through Canada, Italy and Vatican City. It might interest you to know, Watson, that the name he assumed during his two-year flight from justice was none other than John Watson!"

I winced at the unfortunate coincidence.

"When he was brought back to America, in 'sixty-seven I think, the fevers of vengeance had subsided considerably. He was summarily freed by a jury that found itself unable to hang a conviction on him, making Surratt the only conspirator to make it through the whole maze relatively unscathed. I understand he works the lecture circuit these days, regaling his audiences with tales of Booth and the early conspiracy."

I sighed deeply and shook my head. "A tragedy all around, Holmes. So many lives lost or ruined. Such a terribly sad affair."

Holmes drew the curtain aside and gazed out the porthole at the deepening Atlantic dusk. "Yes, of course, Watson, terribly sad," he said coldly. "But from the purely analytical eye of a consulting detective, the case remains infinitely fascinating nonetheless."

"What's so fascinating about it?" I scoffed. "The whole affair is a matter for the historians by now, all solved, resolved and neatly written up in texts already growing dusty."

Holmes smiled patiently and stretched out fully on the comfortable bunk. "As to history I can but agree with you, my dear fellow. The crime shall not be forgotten for a great many years. Who knows what impact it may have on America's future, or the world's future for that matter? But as to its being, how did you say it, solved and resolved, well, I'd hesitate before making any judgment as rash as that."

I leaned closer. "You fascinate me, Holmes. What do you know about the case that you haven't told me?"

"In sweeping terms, Watson, what I've just completed telling you is what might be termed the official version of what took place sixteen years ago, and for the most part, the popular version as well. As I've already said, there are any number of alternative theories in addition to this one. The various scenarios range in credibility from comprehensive to absurd, but all of them contain certain illogical bridges of thought in various places. A number of fundamental and important aspects of the assassination are, to this day, misunderstood by those who profess expertise on the subject. The case is, believe me, far more complex than the journalists and pamphleteers would have you believe."

"Are you satisfied that Booth was indeed the assassin?" I asked.

"Oh yes, that much at least is clear as crystal."

"Then your doubts are as to the nature of his conspiracy."

"Actually no, Watson. I'm quite satisfied that Booth and his merry band of crooks acted pretty much on their own authority, misguided and bizarre though that authority may have been."

"Well then," I said, relaxing back into my chair, "tell me all about it. How has posterity gone so vividly wrong?"

Holmes placed his hands behind his head and closed his eyes. "We are scheduled to make landfall in New York on the morrow. I can speak but for myself, but I expect a rather jolting cultural shock, even rude perhaps, as I understand the city to be a fairly raw place. Instinct and judgment compel me to absorb as much rest as possible before disembarking and that is precisely how I plan to invest my evening. Besides which, I think we've quite exhausted the Lincoln matter for the present, don't you think? Good-night, Watson. The rest will do you good, too."

I knew, of course, that protests were useless once Holmes grew tired of a subject. I left him to his slumber, which commenced even before I left the cabin, to breathe again the salty Atlantic air.

—6—
New York

I was awakened in the early dawn by a loud and insistent knocking on my cabin door. Holmes stood there in the grey half-light, fully dressed and obviously excited.

"Rise and shine, my good man!" he cried. "The New World itself awaits us on the western horizon!"

I began to protest at the early hour but agreed, begrudgingly at first, to rise nonetheless. In all frankness, I was myself eager to glimpse the approach of the American shore. Within minutes I had joined Holmes on the forward deck of the *Bothnia*, populated at this hour by a few crewmen far too busy with their work to show any interest in the scene before us.

The great American continent appeared but a greyish line on the horizon as we gazed from the ship's prow, the gaining daylight to our backs slowly illuminating the endless landmass. We could discern through the distance but a few lights twinkling in faint welcome, beacons perhaps.

"What Englishman does not keep a fond spot in his heart for America," Holmes asked, "and a parent's sense of pride in a child that has done well indeed?"

"None that I know of," I acknowledged, "but many of our countrymen entertain a trace of resentment too, don't you think? After all, it's only been a century since the Revolution."

Holmes casually waved this suggestion aside. "Any parent feels a touch of resentment, more a sense of abandonment really, when the fledgling finally takes wing and flys away by itself, Watson, and isn't that precisely what the colonies did? But look at her now—a strong, strapping youth already past the pains of adolescence, ready to become a powerful adult. Ready to become, I believe, the very empire that shall succeed our own, in fact."

I'm not ashamed to say that I found this proposition quite offensive. "Holmes," I said, "are you suggesting—"

"I'm not suggesting, Watson, I'm predicting. I'm predicting that the child Columbia shall eclipse the parent Britannia in the next century, yes. As well it should. Empires come and go according to the brutish tides of history. They gain strength according to historical circumstances and lose it, either swiftly or gradually, according to other historical circumstances. It's inevitable, despite the nationalism of the moment, dear fellow, and really nothing to fear. I'll tell you this: We could do a lot worse than to be succeeded by America. To be represented in the future by one's own offspring, one's very legacy, is an enviable destiny for any old empire."

I took the topic no further, realizing well that the soundness and dispassionate logic of Holmes' argument would inevitably overcome my impassioned, and slightly wounded, sense of patriotism. Besides, I thought, it was far too early in the morning for anything so strenuous as a debate with Holmes on any topic. We spent the remainder of the dawn, therefore, silently regarding the approach of our destination.

Our reverie was broken by a familiar voice behind us. "Well, well," said Booth, "I see my co-travelers are up before the sun. A fellow might get the impression you were anxious to be somewhere."

We turned to face the actor, and were gratified that he'd thoughtfully brought two steaming mugs of coffee for our benefit. "Waylaid the steward for these," he said cheerily. "Thought you might appreciate it."

"We do indeed," I said, taking a cup and shaking his hand. "Thank you, Edwin. And what brings you out so early?"

"The same thing as the two of you, I suspect. Anxiety. I'm always this way when I'm about to come home. There's really no other sensation like it, as far as I'm concerned. It makes me nervous and glad at the same time, both happy and sad." Booth pointed to the shoreline. "I can only imagine what it's like seeing that for the first time."

"Frankly, it's quite exciting," I rejoined. "It reminds me about being a boy and dreaming about sea voyages, visiting strange and exotic places far away. I felt that way when I sailed with my regiment for Afghanistan, not so very long ago. Thankfully, of course, the level of danger shall be far less a concern on this trip."

"Don't be thankful yet, Watson," Holmes said suddenly. "About the lack of danger, that is. Let's not forget why we've come, and who we may shortly find ourselves having to contend with."

"Actually, Holmes," Booth broke in, "that's really what I wanted to talk about this morning. I want to speak with you now, privately, before the nosy McDevils get up on deck. It's about our arrival. There will likely be reporters at the dock, looking for me, and they're the last people who should know that I'm in any sort of danger. The same goes for my in-laws. If they have any inkling of trouble, or if they infer that the two of you are accompanying me for some suspicious and unknown reason, God alone knows what sort of misinformation they might feed to the press. We'll have to be highly discreet today, especially as we disembark. We'll act as complete strangers to one another."

"I should think that wouldn't be difficult," Holmes said.

"The McVickers will be taking poor Mary to their home shortly after we arrive. We'll wait for them to leave the docks before we reunite. I wired my younger brother Joseph from Liverpool; he'll meet us there. He knows everything, about the attacks, as well as our being cousins, Holmes. He can be trusted completely. Hopefully, he will have already arranged to have a Pinkerton man in my employ so that protection shouldn't be a problem."

"So all is in readiness then," said Holmes. "Your preparations appear superb, Edwin. Hello? What's this?" The detective glanced quickly behind Booth's shoulder. "You must run along now, Edwin. Your in-laws have just come onto the main deck. We'll talk later."

Booth walked away without another word and joined the increasing number of passengers milling about the deck in the brilliant sunshine. They all seemed intent on viewing the shore as the ship's crew frantically handled pallets of bags and steamer trunks, worked on a multitude of ropes and winches, and re-adjusted the colourful signal flags in anticipation of our docking.

Before long the harbour of New York was close enough for us to read the painted signs on the squat red brick buildings crowding the shore. As the sea narrowed gradually into the Narrows, the Upper Bay and finally the East River, the Bothnia came under the power of a handful of dirty-looking tugboats. Here the maritime traffic quickly grew heavy with dozens of other tugs, freighters propelled both by steam and by sail, and smaller craft perilously sharing the rights-of-way. Although we were the only passenger ship in view, the *Bothnia* seemed to attract scarce attention from the many seamen in the busy harbour.

New York itself seemed bustling and huge from our perspective on deck and, while harbours traditionally offer travelers the ugliest possible view of their cities, I was impressed with the sheer scope of the place. Holmes was right: The city we were now entering was clearly the pride of a young empire. Under the sunny skies of a balmly summer morning, it seemed a city filled with hope and bright prospects.

We docked on the southeastern shore of Manhattan, where a substantial crowd waited for the ship. It was a colourful and gay scene. Many of those on shore waved white handkerchiefs or flags—the Stars and Stripes as well as the Union Jack—in warm welcome. They cheered and applauded when the *Bothnia*'s captain sounded the ship's mighty whistle. Crewmen on shore caught ropes thrown from their fellows on board and rapidly tied them onto the heavy stanchions upon the dock. At last the great anchor was dropped into the water. We had arrived.

Almost immediately, it seemed, passengers began a hurried but orderly rush to gain the gangplank and leave the ship. Holmes and I fell into line just a few yards behind Booth and his family. He looked tired from the difficult voyage but still beamed in the sunlight. He placed one arm around his lovely daughter Edwina, radiant in the bloom of early womanhood, and the other around his wheelchair-bound wife Mary, pale and wan in what seemed the shadow of imminent death. Mrs. Booth blinked against the harsh light but her face displayed no other emotion or awareness of her surroundings. They stood with the McVickers, both of them rather harsh and unhappy-looking people dressed in heavy coats, almost in stubborn defiance, it seemed, to the warm June weather in New York.

Booth had been correct about the reporters. A small cluster of them waited patiently near the end of the gangplank, notebooks and pens in hand. They weren't alone in their attention to him. This was America, after all, and the face of Booth was obviously a familiar one to many of these people. I heard several in the crowd whispering to one another such phrases as "That's him!" or "Look, it's Edwin Booth!" With characteristic grace, he acknowledged their attention with a subtle smile and nod of his head. Once upon the dock, he handled the journalists with courteous dispatch, answering one or two questions briefly and telling them how he had loved his trip to Europe but was happy to find himself back in his native land. He excused himself from their company in short order, telling them that he had personal matters to attend to.

As Holmes and I—as unnoticed as Booth had been the center of attention—stood quietly off to the side of the crowd, we saw Booth's departure from his wife. He embraced the stricken woman warmly, and whispered something privately into her ear, but offered only a cursory farewell to the McVickers. He regarded them coolly, nodded his head for a moment, and turned away from them. They quickly wheeled Mrs. Booth into a waiting landau which wasted little time finding its way out of the crowd and onto the street.

Booth walked in our direction at last, Edwina's hand in his. He made no comment about his in-laws but the expression on his face showed his obvious relief at their exit. "Look, Edwina!" he cried to his daughter. "There's Maggie, over by our rickety old carriage!" He pointed toward an elegant black surrey which was waiting for our party. A kindly-looking elderly woman stood by the curb with open arms. "Why don't you go see her, darling, and leave me alone with these gentlemen for just a few moments?" The young woman smiled prettily and rushed off to see her caretaker.

"Well, Holmes, Watson," he said, turning to us with a smile, "here we are. Welcome to America! The land of the free and the home of the brave and all that poetic stuff!" Booth took off his silk top hat and spread his arms widely around us. "It might not look like much to Londoners like yourselves, but it's home, and it's fine for us Yanks."

While I was amused by Booth's exuberance, Holmes was in a nervous and businesslike mood. "Edwin," he said quietly, looking rather furtively around the crowd, "didn't you say that your brother was to greet us here?"

"Ah," said Booth with a sudden awareness, "you're worried, Holmes. Yes, of course, Joseph should be here. And here he is. Hello, Joseph."

Two men came from out of the throng toward us. Booth embraced one of the two and quickly introduced him as his younger brother, Joseph Booth. He was a slender man, and appeared even more so by the long black frock coat he wore. He had a narrow, rather solemn, face and a receding hairline. He was, in fact, as unlike the celebrated handsome Booths as one could expect a brother to be. He took each of our hands in turn and said to Holmes: "A pleasure. Eddie tells me that we're cousins." The statement was made matter-of-factly, I thought, with no real emotion or interest apparent.

"This fellow," said the younger brother, turning to the other man, "is Titus Oglesby of the Pinkerton Agency." We regarded a rather rotund man with a demeanor as jovial as Joseph Booth's was somber. He wore a brown derby, a bright suit of green-and-yellow checks and a watch-chain of heavy gold which highlighted his ample girth.

"Nice to meet you gentlemen," he said loudly through a bushy handlebar moustache. "Especially you, Mr. Booth. You'll be in good hands from now on. You just rest easy about that."

Holmes addressed the Pinkerton man directly. "Tell me, Mr. Oglesby, just exactly what are the details of your assignment?"

The man's pleasant demeanor suddenly darkened. "And just who might be wanting to know those details?" he asked with a trace of suspicion in his voice.

"Sherlock Holmes," replied the detective. "I'll be handling the investigation into this matter. I assume you have some knowledge of the circumstances regarding Mr. Edwin Booth here?"

"I know what I need to know, considering the fact that my role is limited to that of bodyguard. The agency told me that there would be another detective, an outsider, working on the case. I don't much like that arrangement, to be frank with you sir, but I can live with it if I must."

Holmes grinned widely at the mention of the word "outsider." I knew that his experience with such Scotland Yard detectives as Lestrade and Gregson had already made him accustomed to, and quite fond of, the outsider's role. "Good," he said to the man. "May I repeat my question then? What exactly are the details of your assignment?"

The Pinkerton detective shrugged. "I'll be in the company of Mr. Booth, his virtual shadow, for as long as it takes you to complete the case, Mr. Holmes. By that I mean I'll be within arm's reach of him by day and by night, whether he stays in New York or travels anywhere else." He turned to face Booth. "And as I said, Mr. Booth, you can rest easy from now on. Any fella means to do you harm will have to contend with me first, and that'll be a right difficult chore." He pulled his coat slightly aside to reveal the handle of a large revolver tucked into his waistcoat.

"I'm sure I'll be grateful for your service," said Booth rather uncomfortably.

"As will I," said Holmes, "and rest assured Mr. Oglesby, I hope to solve this case and put an end to the danger as soon as possible. Dr. Watson and I will waste precious little time getting down to business."

"And all of us," interjected Booth, "should waste precious little time in getting to the hotel. I, for one, am utterly exhausted and I see that Edwina is growing impatient in the carriage. The driver has secured the baggage, I see. Let's take a drive, shall we?"

Nobody protested. Joseph took leave of us at the dock, wishing us luck in removing the danger from his brother and accepting Edwin's thanks with saturnine grace. Shortly, the six of us were crammed tightly into the surrey, rattling our way through the streets of Manhattan. New York City was a beehive of activity on this summer morning. Though it was well before noon, the traffic was already heavy as we pulled onto South Street. Oglesby, his spirits apparently back in good order, cheerily took on the unofficial role of tourguide as we traveled.

"This, my British friends," he said eloquently as we pulled away from the docks, "is the pride of our fair city." He swept his arms grandly toward an architectural spectacle of marvelous proportions. The Brooklyn Bridge, quite near to its completion, towered to our right, a massive, beautifully-wrought structure. "Within two years it will be ready to take on traffic bound for Brooklyn and vice versa, gentlemen. Truly a wonderful prospect for the city in all respects."

We barely had time to nod in agreement before Oglesby pointed out Printing House Square, a congested and terribly busy spot farther inland from the river. Its streets were neatly lined with endless rows of imposing commercial buildings boasting handsome stone or cast fronts and crowned with intricate stamped-tin cornices. Its sidewalks were jammed with pedestrians of all stripes, from jaunty, well-dressed young dandies to raggedy beggars to blue-clad police constables very similar in appearance to their British cousins. Filling the cobbled streets were wagons and carriages in endless succession, jockeying for position with rather odd-looking omnibuses, the prevalent mode of public transportation. Even the sky above Park Row and Broadway seemed busy, with an amazing web of cables and wires, serving the railcars, telegraph lines and brand-new telephone system. The whole effect was quite a surprise for me. Like many of my British countrymen, I suspect, I'd always regarded America in somewhat provincial terms. This city was nothing if not cosmopolitan.

Our driver headed north on the great thoroughfare known as Broadway, struggling against the traffic as we passed by a series of business districts, all paying noisy tribute to New York's penchant for commerce. Oglesby described various areas with relish, telling us of the Garment District's burgeoning importance and Greenwich Village's increasingly fashionable status among the city's neighborhoods. From the seat of the carriage we could detect other changes by listening to the languages and dialects being spoken by the people in the street. I had never before seen such a mixture, from swarthy Negroes to slender Chinese to burly Irishmen to bearded Hebrews.

As we passed by Greenwich Village, I noticed that the congestion had eased considerably, both on the street and the sidewalks. There was an increasing number of shade trees and the clustered storefronts had been mostly replaced by large and solemn-faced apartment buildings, known locally as brownstones, Oglesby told us. "The gentry is developing a fondness for the neighborhoods in this area," he said, glancing in Booth's direction. "Between here and Central Park one will find the society's cream of the crop, and I should know, as the agency is called upon often enough in these neighborhoods."

"There is nothing so distinctive about New York, in fact, as its neighborhoods," said Booth. "The variety of them boggles the mind. Should you go tromping about the city, Holmes and Watson, I strongly suggest you take pains to be careful. Not all of the areas are as civilized as this. Some of them, I fear, might rival the Black Hole of Calcutta."

Holmes had been preoccupied with studying the streets and traffic as we rambled on and didn't seem to have heard a word anyone was saying. As we approached the intersection of 22nd Street he blurted to the driver: "Stop here please!" He turned to us with a glance and said he'd be back in a moment. He rushed across the street to a squat, triangular building and stepped inside. He was out again in a moment, a small bundle in his hand, and hurried back to the carriage.

"Photographs!" he cried jubilantly. "Current views of the fair city of New York from the Continent Stereoscopic Company over there." He began to unwrap his parcel, removing a heavy stack of photos of buildings, parks and places of interest. "With these, and a comprehensive map of streets, I'll know my way around the city in a matter of days. I won't have the sort of knowledge I can claim of London, mind you, but enough to traverse the city with some degree of skill."

Booth looked a trifle concerned. "Holmes, as strange as it might seem, I'd never given a thought to the nature, or the approach, of your investigation. Do you think you'll be concentrating on New York?"

Not taking his gaze away from his photographs, Holmes answered casually. "You are here, Edwin," he said. "That automatically increases the likelihood that your pursuer is here as well, or soon shall be. Therefore, New York shall serve as the very seat of our investigation, at least for the present."

When we reached Fifth Avenue we turned onto that handsome street, traversing steadily more attractive districts. At last, at 47th Street, we reached our destination. The Windsor Hotel, in all its stately splendor, stood before us. "Home for Edwina and I," Booth said, "and home away from home for all the rest of you."

Only eight years old, the Windsor was obviously one of the city's most prestigious places of lodging. It filled the whole block between 46th and 47th Streets and stood a full seven stories tall with hundreds of rooms. Its roof was adorned with attractive ironwork and gaily-striped awnings covered each window against the increasing summer heat. A handful of hansom cabs waited patiently at curbside.

We strolled into the spacious and opulent lobby, furnished with smooth marble and fine woods, and approached the reception clerk.

"Mr. Booth!" the clerk exclaimed immediately. "How wonderful to have you home again! You will find your rooms ready and prepared for your return."

"Hello, Masterson," Booth said warmly. "You received my cable then?"

The clerk nodded.

"Then you're also ready for the additional guests. This is Sherlock Holmes and Dr. Watson, my friends from London. They'll be taking the suite of rooms immediately adjacent to my own. And this is Mr. Oglesby. He'll be staying in the extra bedroom in my own quarters for a time. Mrs. Booth, well, Mrs. Booth will be joining us later, I hope."

"I understand, Mr. Booth," the clerk said solemnly. "And as to your guests, all preparations have been made for them as well. The bellboy will have your bags up shortly. Welcome home, sir."

Booth tipped his hat as we ascended the sweeping stairway which rose gracefully above the lobby. Our rooms were nearby, on the second floor, and Booth wasted no time in entering his. He was clearly tired from his many sleepless nights on the sea voyage and anxious to gain some rest at last. Edwina, and their new bodyguard-houseguest Oglesby, followed him behind the rosewood door.

Our suite was just next door. Both of us must have gasped as we gazed within it. It was huge and luxurious beyond our wildest dreams. All was velvet and silk and shiny brass. The walls were beautifully papered and decorated with splendid paintings of the Hudson River School. The large, lace-curtained window faced on the peaceful quiet of 47th Street below us.

"Quite a cut above Baker Street, wouldn't you say, Watson," Holmes said, throwing his jacket onto the long couch. "I get the distinct impression that we're moving up in the world." He laughed and began filling his cherrywood.

"Absolutely wonderful, Holmes," I said, "but we'll have plenty of time to enjoy it. Why don't we step outside and have a stroll about the streets? I'm anxious to feel my legs working on solid ground once again."

"Not just now, Watson," he said distractedly. "You go on without me." Already Holmes had spread a huge street map over the desk and was arranging his newly-acquired collection of stereoscopic views around it.

"I have a lot of work to do. The city will wait until tomorrow for my forays into it, I'm sure. As for now, I wish to gain every possible advantage over our invisible opponent."

—7—
A Nocturnal Visitor

I ended up taking Holmes' suggestion that afternoon to take my walk alone, as it turned out, and it seemed I spent the better part of the following week doing exactly the same thing. If there was any progress in Holmes' investigation into Booth's unfortunate situation, he certainly made no mention of it to me. He seemed constantly preoccupied with rather intense studies, whose details he likewise kept to himself. And with Booth apparently resting and lying low in his apartment, faithfully guarded by Oglesby of course, I found myself with a bountiful surplus of time.

I took advantage of it by acquainting myself with the American metropolis, becoming fairly adept in a few days at masterminding the routes of the curious, stage-like omnibuses, and even using the various trains and trolleys that criss-crossed the city. I was amazed at the elevated portions of the railways and found their height useful in catching long-range views of New York.

There was, to my surprise, an abundance of cultural opportunity. Drama, opera, music and art could be had nightly in any number of institutions, much of it of a quality that compared well with the European versions. The city's library was massive, the bookstores plentiful and well-stocked.

Most of my time, to be truthful, was spent walking about the streets, usually until fatigue or hunger would draw me back to the Windsor. I'd already explored a wide range of neighborhoods within a mile's radius or so of the hotel, most of them fashionable and well-to-do. I also discovered early on that Central Park was but a few blocks to the north, and found this tract of wilderness within the city a welcome escape from the rush and commotion of the streets. Its oaks, ash and maples were tall and full, offering plentiful shade against the heat and its graceful rustic arbors offered idyllic places of rest. The evenings here were enough to inspire poetry, with the coolness of twilight carrying the fading scent of lilac and the emerging scent of summer rose as ladies and their escorts, dressed in their finery, walked along the long, covered promenades.

As for the Americans themselves, I was getting along famously with the lot of them. They seemed a casual and friendly people for the most part, and most of the passers-by I'd spoken with had regarded England with some warmth. I was growing adept at grasping the nuances of the American accent, especially the many New York dialects which changed from borough to borough.

It had been some time since I had spoken to Holmes at any length at all, and I continued to have no idea of the status of his investigation, if indeed there was a status at all. He spent most of his time in our rooms, going over maps, photographs and odd texts, and regularly going out alone into the city itself. I presumed his only strategy at the moment was to await another attack on Booth's life, in the hopes of putting an immediate end to the matter, or at least gaining a valuable clue.

I had seen no more of Booth in the week since our arrival than Holmes. I had spoken to Oglesby once or twice outside the actor's door and was told by him that Booth was not only resting, but seemed a trifle unhappy. I remembered Booth telling us how prone he could be to melancholia, and asked the guard to inform me if he thought Booth's lethargy was becoming excessive. Oglesby agreed.

When I finally did see Booth, early one warm morning, he was the exact opposite of lethargic. He rushed into our rooms, still in his dressing gown, clutching a crumpled newspaper with a look of absolute shock on his face. He approached our breakfast table, where Holmes and I had been lazily drinking coffee for the past hour, and threw the paper down before us.

"Dear God!" he cried. "History repeats itself! The president! It's happened again!"

We scrambled to read the words on the front page, learning in horror that James Garfield, who had been president for just over a year, had been shot at the Washington railway station the day before. His attacker was a deranged man by the name of Charles J. Guiteau, apparently a frustrated office-seeker. President Garfield had been badly wounded, the paper reported, but was clinging to life in hospital.

Booth seemed to be slightly swooning as he stood watching us read, his hand covering his eyes. I rushed to him and helped him into a chair, asking Holmes to bring brandy. The actor took but a tiny sip and replaced his hand over his eyes.

"The same nightmare," he muttered. "It's the same thing. They're down in the lobby now, gentlemen. Reporters, asking to see me. Me!"

"But why, Edwin?" I asked.

"God alone knows! Here we have another assassin, a second Lucifer to follow my brother's bloody footprints. I'm the brother of the first, of course. That's why they seek me. They suppose me some sort of sage, some sort of expert on the subject of assassination. The heartless fools!"

"Edwin," said Holmes, "try to relax, try—"

"Damn it all!" Booth cried. "I won't do it! I won't be their sage! What can I tell them, anyway? What wisdom can I offer fools vain enough to seek answers to a madman's deed?"

"You need tell them nothing," Holmes said quietly. "Watson and I will take care of them. Try to relax, cousin. Drink your brandy." Holmes looked up to our open door where Edwina stood cautiously looking in, an expression of deep concern on her face. "Here's Edwina," he said. "Come in miss, see to your father. He's distraught. He needs your comfort."

The young woman thanked Holmes and rushed to her father, putting her arms around him. "Come, Daddy," she said soothingly, leading him slowly toward the door where Oglesby patiently waited. She turned to us. "He'll be all right, Mr. Holmes. It's just been too much for him, with my stepmother so ill, and that terrible man in London, and now President Garfield."

"Far too much," Holmes agreed. "He's fortunate to have so loving a daughter as yourself. We'll look in on him later."

As they returned to their rooms, Holmes beckoned for me to join him in following them out the door. He led me down the

Windsor's grand staircase into the lobby where six or seven impatient-looking reporters were arguing loudly with Masterson the clerk. He was dutifully telling them, in tones of increasing anger, that Booth was indisposed and unavailable to answer their questions. The newspapermen, in turn, were having none of it and pleaded all the more fervently for the right to see the actor.

Holmes casually walked up to the small group and asked, in sufficiently loud tones for all of them to hear, what the fuss was all about. "Booth!" said one gangly fellow impatiently. "We want to see Booth, and this doorman refuses to get out of the way!"

"Booth?" said Holmes, appearing interested. "Why, what's he done?"

"Well, nothing exactly," said another reporter. "It's just that with the Garfield shooting, our editors want comments from him, you know, since he is the other Booth's brother and all."

"Of course," said Holmes. "But I'm afraid you're out of luck, gentlemen. I just saw Booth ducking out the north door into a waiting carriage."

"Drat!" said the impatient gangly one. "How long ago, then?"

"Not more than one minute, I'm sure."

This triggered the pack of reporters into action. They headed *en masse* for the northern doors, leaving us suddenly alone in the lobby with the clerk. Holmes winked at him slyly and said to both of us: "A little white lie could be seen as justified if the cause were good, could it not?" We both nodded and smiled. Holmes then took me quietly aside, walking slowly toward the main door.

"I'll be out again today," he said.

"To where, Holmes?"

"Not important at the moment, old fellow. I'm afraid it will be best for me to go alone, and I think you may be of assistance to Oglesby today. Look in on Booth once or twice, will you? In your physician's capacity? I'm growing worried as to his health. Today's news certainly hasn't helped."

"Of course, Holmes, but if I may be so frank, I'm growing impatient for developments in the case. What can you tell me?"

"Nothing more than you can clearly see, Watson, which is precisely nothing. There's no direction in which to turn with the evidence we now have in hand. We'll either have to wait for our mysterious stranger to make a move or hope for some unforseen development. Or, as the last resort, if absolutely nothing happens, we'll have to return home. We can't stay here at Edwin's expense forever, after all, and the tiny chance does exist that the London attack might have been the final one."

We parted on that note. I soon headed out for another of my restless walks about the city, strolling rather aimlessly along Fifth Avenue until the mid-day heat drove me back to the shade of the hotel suite. The heat grew rapidly more intense from that point on, climbing to well over 90 degrees by mid-afternoon. It was a heavy, oppressive heat, considerably enhanced by a swampy humidity and unchallenged by the slightest breeze. It was terribly uncomfortable from my temperate Englishman's perspective, unlike anything I had seen away from India itself.

Until well into the evening I sweltered in the room, gradually removing my coat, waistcoat, collar and shirt in succession. My morning's copy of the *New York Times* had become a makeshift fan. I finally drifted off to an uncomfortable and troubled sleep by nine o'clock.

I had no idea what time it was when I was later awakened. I started up from the bed when I heard it—a loud thump, followed immediately by what sounded like a struggle. It came from the other side of the wall directly next to me—Booth's apartment.

Without bothering for the light, and totally forgetting my service revolver, I rushed out of our suite into the carpeted hallway, softly lit by the dimmed gaslights. All was silent now, but I saw immediately that Booth's door was ajar. I walked quickly but quietly toward it.

It was pitch dark within the apartment. I entered it cautiously, quietly calling "Oglesby . . . Edwin . . ."

The blow struck me utterly by surprise, and set me reeling violently against the wall and onto the floor. I had not a second to worry about my jaw, however, for I immediately felt the heavy weight of a grown man crashing down onto me. The figure struck me in the face once more and then raised both his arms high over his head. In the dim light from the hall I saw the glint from a long dagger clutched in those hands, poised directly above my neck.

Our struggle couldn't have lasted but a moment but it seemed like an eternity. He was of considerable strength and agility, and I had difficulty finding his hands when my own became entangled in what seemed to be a heavy cloak. At last I grasped his clenched fists and held them with all my might, shaking with the force of his effort to drive the knife into my throat. I believe that he weakened momentarily, allowing me to divert the thrust of his arms. He veered off to the side and the dagger skidded silently across the rug. The man struck me once more, in a sweeping motion with the back of his hand. The movement caused a ring to fly off his hand and strike the wall behind me. I heard it strike the floor just as I fell utterly unconscious from the blow.

The attacker must have fled at that moment, taking his weapon with him, as Booth came out of his room. It was Booth who I saw when I came to moments later. He was shaking me vigorously. His face was ashen, and he was still attired in his long silk robe. "Dr. Watson!" he cried. "Are you hurt? What has happened?"

I told him groggily what little I knew, rubbing my already swollen jaw. "Where's Oglesby?" I asked, suddenly thinking of the bodyguard. Booth regarded me with silent fear.

As if in answer to my question, we heard a soft moan from the other side of the room. We rushed to the sound, Booth carrying a flickering chamberstick for light, and saw the unfortunate agent. He lay on his back beside a large davenport where he had apparently been sleeping. Oglesby's blanket was still lying crumpled upon it.

I took Oglesby's hand and saw at once the large stain of blood upon his chest. The man was pale as a sheet and felt cold to the touch.

"Never saw him coming," the agent whispered. "Never heard . . ."

"Be still, Oglesby," I told him. "Edwin, get me some brandy quickly."

But Oglesby refused to be still. He lifted his head weakly and continued to whisper hoarsely. "Booth is all right then?" he asked. "Then I've done my job okay, I guess. Do you . . . do . . . you know what the man said before he stabbed me, Dr. Watson? Do you . . ." Oglesby gasped, and a bright flow of blood came from his lips.

He somehow mustered the strength to croak the attacker's words, just as Booth knelt down beside us on the floor.

"*Sic semper tyrannis!*"

They were the last words ever uttered by Titus Oglesby. He died at that very moment.

—8—
Afoot at Last

Allan Pinkerton was obviously enraged but was managing some-how to keep his temper under control. The legendary detective stalked Booth's apartment angrily, occasionally barking curt orders to two of his agents who had accompanied him here on short notice. Booth and I had hurriedly sent him a message an hour before. A third agent, faithful Oglesby, lay dead on the floor under a sheet.

With the arrival of dawn, a strong thunderstorm had moved over New York, obliterating the sunrise and dropping the temperatures dramatically. A sullen rain now fell constantly as Booth, myself, and the Pinkerton men viewed the scene of the recent murder. Holmes had still not returned from his previous day's foray into the city.

"No man murders an agent of mine and gets away with it," mut-tered the elderly but obviously energetic Pinkerton. "I'll track him down 'til the Judgment Day if I must, but I'll corner him sooner or later. And when I do . . ." He didn't bother to complete the sentence.

"What about the police?" I asked him. "Shouldn't they be called?"

Pinkerton turned to me. "There's plenty of time for that," he said curtly. "They'll have their chance to destroy what little evidence there is here, but not until I've had my look, I assure you." Even as he spoke, his agents probed the floors and furniture of the apartment.

"That sounds like something my colleague would say," I ventured. "He's always complaining about Scotland Yard's clumsy methods—"

"Yes," interrupted Pinkerton. "I've been meaning to ask you about this colleague of yours. He's the independent detective hired by Mr. Booth to look into this matter, I understand."

I nodded.

"And just who is this fellow?"

The familiar voice came from the doorway. "Sherlock Holmes," said Holmes himself, walking inside. "At your service, Mr. Pinkerton."

Pinkerton regarded Holmes closely. "Indeed?" he said with some interest. "Well, I've heard a few things about you, young man, most of them good, I must admit."

Holmes bowed ceremoniously and thanked him.

"Of course you realize that the situation has changed, don't you, Mr. Holmes?" Pinkerton said. "After I inform the police of this incident, I'll be launching my own investigation into the matter. I'll be taking over the case."

Holmes sat down and calmly lit a pipe. "Understandable," he said, "but of course I'll be involved as well. My client, as you know, is Edwin Booth and from what I just overheard in the hall about last night's incident, it seems clear that the danger to my client is far from over."

Pinkerton regained some of his earlier anger. "Now look here, young man, this is New York City—my turf, if you understand what I'm saying—and that body over there belonged to one of my best agents. I'll be damned if I'll let some British greenhorn try to edge in on a case as important—"

"What if I guarantee you a complete solution to the case?" Holmes asked casually. "What if I promise to have the culprit by the collar before the summer is out?"

Pinkerton looked at Holmes aghast. "Now if that isn't the cockiest, most—"

"Allow me but a moment of your time," Holmes said graciously, rising and taking Pinkerton by the arm. "As we converse semi-privately, allow me also to view the scene of poor Oglesby's murder, will you? Just as a courtesy between colleagues, of course."

The elder detective seemed taken aback at the audacity of the younger, and in his surprise allowed him without protest to join his two agents in scrutinizing Booth's parlor. Holmes spoke with him in an inaudible whisper.

Booth took me aside. We spoke quietly as we peered out of the window at the rainy streets below. "Thank God I'd sent Edwina away last night to stay with her cousins, Dr. Watson," he said. "I can only imagine how all this would affect her." I nodded in reply. "I'll be forced to send her away until this business is completed, I'm afraid. I have no right to expose her to danger such as this. I've been selfish. She's really all I have left, you know."

"I understand, Edwin. Her safety is the main concern."

"Do you think Holmes means it? About completing the case within the summer?"

"I've never known Holmes to lie, Edwin, nor to brag beyond the real extent of his skills. If he says so, I can only believe that he means it."

"Let's hope your instincts are right."

Meanwhile, in the parlor, Holmes and Pinkerton seemed to have fallen into friendlier spirits. They stood smoking over the covered body of Oglesby, seeming to match their impressions.

"From what your friend Watson tells me," Pinkerton said, "the man stood four or five inches under six feet."

"A observation supported by his bootprints in the carpeting," Holmes rejoined.

"I believe he must figure that he's gotten the right man."

"Quite likely," Holmes said. "Oglesby was obviously attacked in his sleep, or just a second or two after awakening. He was stabbed with utterly murderous, and not defensive intentions."

"In the mistaken belief that the sleeping man was Booth."

"Of course. I can also confirm by our visitor's footprints that he is, beyond doubt, the same man who tried so determinedly to kill Edwin in Europe. The footprints show the identical favored gait I noticed in London."

"Then your theory is sound," said Pinkerton with conviction. "I see the train of your investigation very clearly now. Very good, Holmes! Quite impressive. I could use a few agents like you, believe me."

"Tell me, Pinkerton," Holmes queried, having grown noticeably more informal with his colleague, "what do you make of the attacker's words, as related to us by Oglesby? You're familiar with *Sic semper tyrannis*, of course."

"Well I should say so. It's the Virginia state motto—'thus always to tyrants'—uttered by John Wilkes . . ." Pinkerton paused and regarded

Booth directly. "Excuse me, Mr. Booth, I know that you prefer his name not be mentioned in your presence. All the same, those were the words uttered by Lincoln's assassin at the moment of his deed."

"It's a trifle odd, don't you think, that those words should have been repeated in this very room, just last night?" Holmes asked.

"Not particularly," Pinkerton rejoined. "It's obvious, at least to me, Holmes, that last night's attacker is a madman bent on vengeance for the Lincoln murder. In some twisted way, he feels that he can avenge Abraham Lincoln by murdering Edwin. The fact that we're dealing with a violent person under the spell of dementia convinces me more than anything else of the difficulty of the case."

Holmes rubbed his chin as he pondered Pinkerton's theory. "At any rate, Pinkerton," he finally said, "you are quite an expert on the assassination, if my sources are sound."

"I know as much as anyone else, Holmes. It's a personal matter for me, of course. Abe Lincoln was a close friend of mine. I provided for his security and protection during his early days in Washington. I'm convinced that I saved his life on more than one occasion and, had I been in Washington instead of New Orleans sixteen years ago, there's no doubt in my mind that Abraham Lincoln would never have been shot in Ford's that night."

"I cannot but agree with you," Holmes said. "You are also an acknowledged expert, are you not, in the area of the secret intelligence and underground warfare practiced by the Confederacy?"

"I spent the entire war working on nothing else, Holmes. There's not a man alive who knows more about the rebel spies than I."

"Excellent," Holmes said, rubbing his hands together. "You will serve as an invaluable ally, I'm sure."

To our surprise, Pinkerton's men then began rolling Oglesby's body firmly within the sheet. They tied the gruesome bundle securely with twine and headed laboriously for the door. "Carefully and unobtrusively, men," Pinkerton said to them as they left. "Make absolutely sure that nobody sees you taking that out."

"What's this?" asked Booth with sudden apprehension. "You're taking the body yourselves? Isn't there supposed to be a police investigation?"

Holmes cleared his throat. "Mr. Pinkerton and I discussed that detail, Edwin. We agreed it would be best for you personally, in terms of avoiding scandalous publicity, and best for the Pinkerton Agency, in terms of preventing publicity that could be disastrous for the firm's reputation, to keep the police out of it for the present."

"Isn't that illegal?" Booth asked sharply. "Isn't that considered concealing a crime?"

"Only in technical terms, Mr. Booth," Pinkerton answered. "Oglesby's death will simply be recorded as accidental for now. I'm owed enough favors by the New York Police Department to have that much influence, believe me. That will prevent the filing of an official case, and keep the press unaware of the incident. The police trust me to pursue the matter at least as diligently as they themselves would pursue it, Mr. Booth. They know I do not rest until I have my man."

"Or, in this case," Holmes interjected, "until I have your man."

"Of course, Holmes," Pinkerton said, turning to Booth. "I've decided not to launch my own investigation, Mr. Booth. I'm going to let Holmes try to tackle this case alone, at least for the moment."

"But you seemed so adamant about it a moment ago," Booth said, suspicion still evident in his voice.

"When the victim is one of my agents, Mr. Booth, I tend to take such cases quite personally. Holmes enlightened me on his own personal involvement in the case, however, by informing me that you are blood relations with him. How can I believe that my own desire for vengeance and justice are stronger than his desire to protect his kin? Besides, I've read of his work. I think he's up to it."

"I shall do my best," Holmes said.

"Do better than that, young man," Pinkerton said, rising to get his coat and hat. "And don't worry about your promise to complete the case by the end of the summer. I know perfectly well that you have no way of reaching that goal without considerable luck. This is going to be a tough and nasty case, Holmes; I can smell it already. Take it a step at a time. Keep me updated weekly on your progress and I'll keep my nose out of it. Deal?"

"Deal," Holmes replied with a smile.

Before leaving, Pinkerton presented each of us with one of his calling cards. It read PINKERTON'S NATIONAL DETECTIVE AGENCY in elaborate script which enclosed the emblem of a staring, vigilant eye. Silently, we all noted the grim irony of the motto WE NEVER SLEEP, as we contemplated poor Oglesby's fate.

"They call that the Private Eye here in New York," Pinkerton told us, pointing at the staring orb. "Short for private investigator."

"Catchy term," Holmes mused.

As Pinkerton walked out the door he was passed by the hotel clerk, who smiled as he entered the apartment. The clerk was clearly unaware of the entire dreadful incident only recently concluded here. He walked directly to Booth, hardly glancing at anyone else in the room, and handed him a small brown envelope. "This was left for you at the front desk last night, Mr. Booth," he said. Masterson left as quickly as he came.

Booth looked apprehensive as he ripped open the envelope. A groan escaped from his lips as he shook its contents into his palm—three acorns.

"As if we needed further confirmation," Holmes muttered angrily. "The fiend is playing games with us, taunting us as a cat would taunt a mouse."

"With the rather important exception that we're no longer quite playing the role of mouse, are we, Dr. Watson?" Booth said.

"I don't understand, Edwin," I said.

"You just saved my life, Dr. Watson, at the very real risk of your own. You stopped the killer in his tracks. It's emboldened me to no small degree, I assure you. I'll never be able to repay you for that."

"Oh, really Edwin, it . . ."

"Never mind the modesty. I think your face could use a few dabs of iodine tincture. It's an absolute mess, to be honest, doctor."

I looked in the mirror and saw that he was right. The attacker had left two large bluish bruises which were now covered with dried blood. Booth washed the wounds over my protests and began daubing painfully at them with cotton soaked in iodine.

"I'm glad I asked you to stay here yesterday, Watson," Holmes said, watching Booth's clumsy attempt at nursing. "You're as stout as they come, old fellow. I owe you no less than Edwin does."

I was about to demand that they cease from their embarassing praise for what I saw as a basic animalistic instinct when there came a knock at the door. Holmes admitted two burly, well-dressed young men.

"Ah, the new Pinkerton men," he said, showing them in. "I neglected to tell you, Edwin, that while the celebrated agency has graciously bowed out of the investigative aspects of the case, it very much remains a part of the protective aspects. Bodyguards, two of them this time, until we bag our catch. Hand-picked by Allan Pinkerton himself. What do you say?"

"How could I possibly protest, Holmes?" Booth said, putting the finishing touches on my battered face.

Holmes quickly showed the bodyguards to their stations and returned to us. "I wasn't altogether boasting in vain, gentlemen, when I promised that I'd have the culprit collared in fairly short order," he said. "As gruesome as last night's attack was, and as tragic as it proved to be for Oglesby, it was just what I was waiting for. Now that he's made his move, I have every reason to believe that the trail will soon grow warmer. I sense progress around the next corner."

Holmes rose. "Come, Watson, back to our rooms with you. You've had quite a night. I think a good long rest has been earned. Edwin, we'll keep you informed." When I shook Booth's hand it was with the new awareness that a powerful, and unbreakable, bond had just been formed.

I took Holmes' advice and tried to rest upon returning to our suite, but to no avail. The night's excitement had apparently ruled that out—I was utterly unable to sleep. I reclined on our luxurious davenport instead, smoking a Havana as Holmes paced thoughtfully through the sitting room. He decided to take full advantage of my wakefulness.

"You say the attack took place at about three?" he asked.

"It was a quarter past three when Edwin shook me awake," I said. "I checked my watch at that moment."

"Good, good. I heard you telling Pinkerton that the man sprang at you from out of the darkness."

"Yes, from my left side as I entered the apartment."

"And you saw absolutely nothing of his face?"

"Nothing. He was wearing some sort of cloak or heavy coat, and he may have had a hat of some sort. I cannot be sure. But I saw no details of his face in the darkness, and heard nothing from his lips save for the sounds of exertion he made as he tried to force the knife into my throat."

"He took the knife along with him, it seems."

"There wasn't a trace of it when I awoke."

It was at that moment that the realization struck me like a thunderbolt. The ring! In the chaos and confusion of the past few hours I had forgotten it entirely.

"My God, Holmes!" I exclaimed. "I've told you nothing of the ring! It fell from his hand as I thrust his arm aside during the struggle. I saw it on the floor and picked it up afterwards. I've absolutely no excuse for such a transgression, but it slipped my mind until this very moment!"

I reached into my pocket and was immediately relieved to feel its presence there. I handed it over to Holmes, who took the object with obvious enthusiasm.

"Watson, my friend, you've done it again!" the detective said. "This is indeed a stroke of good fortune! And please, Watson, don't be absurd. You forgot about it because you received a violent blow or two to the head. If that isn't an adequate excuse I can hardly imagine what is."

He took the ring and held it up to the weak light, turning it so as to view it from different angles. He placed it at last upon the table and put it under the glass of his most powerful magnifying lens. He spent at least five minutes closely and silently scrutinizing the ring before handing it back to me.

"Take a look," he said, handing me his lens. "Tell me what you make of it."

The ring was large, cast in yellow gold, and bore a striking heraldic escutcheon of some kind upon its face. Beneath the lens I could discern its many tiny details. The emblem itself was composed of gold, silver and copper inlays with enameled portions. There was a Maltese cross within a circle, in the center of which appeared the miniscule word "Bickley." Around the outer edge of the circle were the enigmatic words "American Legion, Power, Union." The entire emblem was enclosed within a gold, eight-pointed star which formed the shape of the ring's face. I glanced inside the band and saw that no monograms or other engravings marred the smooth surface there.

"The ring apparently denotes membership in some sort of patriotic fraternity, Holmes," I theorized, "perhaps one which dates from the time of the Civil War. I can imagine no other reason for the word 'Union' to appear. It might also be the insignia of a secret society, since the ring bears no initial or other sign of its owner, despite the fact of its obvious value. I doubt the word 'Bickley' denotes ownership of the ring itself because it's such a prominent part of the design. Perhaps it's a secret word, or code of passage."

"Excellent, Watson!" Holmes cried, clapping his hands. "You've struck more than one valid point there. You're wrong, however, about the order being patriotic. The members of this group, which you correctly described as secret, were anything but patriotic in their intent. They did try hard, however, to appear that way, which explains the rather jingoistic mottos thereon."

"Then you know the design?" I asked, rising from the davenport with deepening interest.

"I do. Do you remember Enoch Drebber, Jefferson Hope's rather deserving victim from several months ago in London?"

I nodded, remembering all too well the murder victim from the Brixton Road murder case, completed only weeks before our American trip.

"He was, as you know, active in certain Masonic orders in his native Utah. It had little to do with that particular case, of course, but the subject interested me all the same. I've since made a study of a number of American secret societies, including those which identify to some degree with Freemasonry."

"Then we're holding the ring of a Mason?" I asked, studying the ring with renewed interest.

"Only indirectly, Watson. The fraternity in question based much of its structure and ritual upon the Masonic model, and may well have consisted of Masons for the most part, but it stood as a distinct and unique entity with an utterly separate agenda and purpose. And that purpose, simply stated, was to work against the Union war effort during the War Between the States. It was called the Knights of the

Golden Circle, or Order of the Golden Circle. It was highly secretive and quite active in supporting the Secessionists. I don't know that it cared a whit for the issue of slavery, but as a tentacle of the infamous Know-Nothing movement it held the issue of states' rights as supreme. Its supporters were both Confederates and Copperhead Northerners as well. As I recall it took several forms and varied names, of which the Golden Circle was only one. As far as I know, the order has been inactive for years."

"Fascinating, Holmes. But what about 'Bickley'? What does that signify?"

"It was the name of the order's president, a certain George S.P. Bickley, who was rumored to have held the rank of Brigadier General in the Confederate Secret Service. He was eventually arrested and imprisoned, by the men working for Allan Pinkerton, no less, and spent some time in a Northern prison. He denied any involvement in the order throughout his ordeals."

I handed the elaborate ring back to Holmes. "Well then," I said, "this could prove a valuable clue indeed. Our attacker is obviously a former Knight of the Golden Circle. That should narrow things down considerably."

"Oh it shall prove valuable, Watson," Holmes replied, "but not quite in the way you envision. The Golden Circle, and such related secret societies as the Sons of Liberty, the American Knights and others, boasted some three hundred thousand members during the war years. That hardly narrows anything down. No, dear fellow, the ring's value lies in a far more specific direction."

"And that direction is—"

"John Wilkes Booth," said an unsmiling Holmes. "There is firm evidence to link the assassin with the Knights of the Golden Circle, and some reason to believe that his smuggling work for the Confederacy was done at the order's bequest. There is said to be a badge denoting membership in the Knights among Booth's personal effects still in the possession of the War Department."

"But Booth has been dead for sixteen years," I protested.

"Of course, but that doesn't necessarily mean that the order does not continue to maintain some sort of twilight existence. Note that the attacker's target is the assassin's brother. Note also the words spoken last night as Oglesby was murdered—the very oath uttered by the assassin at the moment of his crime. I also find it interesting, Watson, that the Knights' official motto happened to be 'Resistance to Tyrants is Obedience to God.' Rather familiar, is it not? Taken together with this ring, the elements begin to weave an intriguing pattern, don't you think?"

"It suggests a multitude of possibilities, Holmes."

"Well expressed, old fellow. It suggests, for one thing, the possibility of Golden Circle involvement in the Lincoln murder. It also hints at some form of unfinished business involving Edwin, although what that might be I have yet to gain an inkling."

"Certainly you cannot imagine that Edwin had anything to do with something as seditious as this society?"

"No, not at all. I'm confident that he did not, Watson, but consider the possibility—remembering that it remains only that—that Edwin might be aware of some fact, some seemingly insignificant detail about his brother, that could, in ways unknown to us, link certain Knights still living with the president's death. Chances are that Edwin is quite unaware of the importance of this information himself. I've already discussed with him at some length his knowledge of the assassination, and his brother's conspiracy, and am convinced that he knows no more than the average American who read of the tragic news in the newspaper."

"The terrible irony in all this is that he's being persecuted not for having done anything, but simply for possessing information in innocence."

"Yes, but let us not jump to hasty conclusions, Watson," the detective cautioned. "This theory has occurred to me only in the last quarter of an hour, and is inspired in totality by this fascinating ring of yours. It might establish a motive for the attacks on Edwin, but then again it might not. I suspect we'll have a great deal more learning to do as the case develops."

We were startled at that moment by an angry-sounding commotion in the hallway. Holmes strode rapidly toward the door and opened it. We saw standing there Masterson, the harried hotel clerk, looking more flustered now than ever. He was holding a boy of nine or ten years roughly by the collar. The lad was filthy and clad in ill-fitting, baggy kneepants with suspenders, a tattered plaid shirt and a large floppy cap on his shaggy head. He was giving the poor clerk a stout resistance and looked relieved to see Holmes standing inside the doorway.

"A thousand pardons, Mr. Holmes," gasped the clerk between his panting. "I told this little ragamuffin that you'd be the last man on earth who'd care to see the likes of him! I caught him sneaking up the service stairs, didn't I, you little—"

"Let me go!" the boy shouted impudently. "Mr. Holmes, would you tell this clod we had an appointment?"

The clerk regarded the detective with surprise. "Is that so, Mr. Holmes?"

"I'm afraid so, my good man," Holmes said with a mischievous smile. "This is young Billy McPheeters, and I do indeed have an appointment with him at this very hour. I should have informed you earlier, I realize, but his presence is needed here nonetheless. Here's a half-dollar for your troubles."

The clerk took the coin and reluctantly released the street Arab. "If you say so, Mr. Holmes," he muttered in resignation, shaking his head and leaving the boy to us.

"Now," said Holmes, drawing McPheeters into the suite and shutting the door, "I should like you to meet Dr. Watson, my good friend and colleague." The boy approached me tentatively and shook my hand, looking rather fascinated at the bruises upon my visage.

"Watson, you're familiar of course with my corps of assistants in London—the Baker Street Irregulars? Well, I am finding the same sort of strategy of great value here. And what do we call the platoon of detectives led so intrepidly by yourself, Master McPheeters?"

"The Fifth Avenue Irregulars, sir," McPheeters replied with considerable pride.

"Precisely. Now McPheeters, tell me whether your watch witnessed anything of particular interest at around three o'clock last night, here at the hotel."

"Well, Mr. Holmes," said the lad, fairly glowing with anticipation, "that was my own watch, it was. I did just what you said. I hid in the bushes by the fence of Mr. Gould's mansion across the street. And I didn't nod off to sleep once. There was a visitor at about that time, sir, and he acted mighty strange, he did."

"Tell me about this visitor."

"He was a tall thin fellow, with a heavy coat on, which ain't usual for summertime, and a big hat on top, like a soldier's hat or a cowboy's, if you know what I mean. I didn't see much of his face but his hair looked to be grey, or white maybe."

"How did he travel? Was he on foot?"

"Well he was at first, sir. He came up Forty-seventh Street, from the east, and went into the hotel door on that side, not through the lobby."

"Wasn't that door locked?"

"It surely was, but this man, I think he picked the lock. He had some tool in his hand and he messed with the knob for a minute before it opened up."

"How long did he stay in the hotel, McPheeters?"

"Maybe five minutes at the outside, Mr. Holmes. He came out the same way he went in, and he was a'runnin' somethin' fierce. He saw a cab parked up near the front and just jumped into it. It was off in a flash, it was. Turned onto Fifth Avenue heading downtown."

"Excellent work!" Holmes said, patting the lad on the back. "Now, this is very important, McPheeters: Do you know the cabman who was driving that particular cab?"

McPheeters smiled widely and puffed up his chest. "I surely do! It was the driver named Jarvis. Big, fat fellow with whiskers down to here. He works the Windsor most every day."

Holmes sighed in obvious relief. "You've proven yourself a superb detective, Master McPheeters," he said warmly, shaking the boy's hand. "Here's your wages for a good night's work." Holmes held up a half-eagle.

"A fiver!" cried the boy, caressing the golden coin in awe. "Wow!"

"That will be all for now," Holmes said, opening the door, "but keep yourself available as we may need to work together again. And think hard, McPheeters, before you spend that five dollars. Think of your mother and sisters first, will you?"

"I surely will, Mr. Holmes! Thank you!"

The lad had hardly left the suite before Holmes donned his deerstalker, obviously preparing for a trip into the rainy streets. "A beginning at last!" he cried. "I knew that McPheeters would come through for me. Watson, get your day's rest as best you can. I've a bit of work to do today but I'll return as soon as possible. When I do, we'll have plenty to keep us busy, I assure you." He smiled widely as he paused for a moment at the door.

"The case, Watson," he said, "is afoot at last."

—9—
Mulberry Bend

On the evening following poor Oglesby's dreadful fate, I received a telegram from Holmes. The arrival of the Western Union boy was a welcome reprieve from a thoroughly dreary, if peaceful, day in which I managed to obtain some rest and help my bruises along in their healing.

The message was brief and succinct: "Watson, come at nine tonight," it read. "Be standing beneath the light at the corner of Hester and Baxter Streets at that hour. By all means, bring your service revolver."

Exhilarated to have a chance for action at last, I immediately felt my pulse quicken. I followed the detective's instructions to the letter, hiring a cab outside the Windsor at precisely eight o'clock for the trip downtown. The driver raised his eyebrows when I mentioned the desired destination but motioned me inside nonetheless. The steady rain had by now dwindled to a soft and cool mist that cast the city in a pleasantly gentle atmosphere, not unlike the unfocused charm of the Expressionist art so much in vogue.

We drove over the rain-slickened streets for most of an hour, traversing Fifth Avenue until Broadway intersected, and then turned onto the Bowery. Through the windows I witnessed a gradual change in the cityscape speeding by. The spacious houses and wide avenues near our hotel had been replaced here on the Bowery by close and cramped structures of obvious ill repute. The pianos of raucous saloons were joined in the busy street by the sounds of drunken laughter and fisticuffs. I'd heard of the Bowery's reputation, even in far-away London, and found the real thing capable of living up to that reputation quite adequately.

The driver pulled the cab alongside the curb at last. "Here's Hester Street," he announced.

"But we're still on the Bowery," I protested. "I told you to go to Hester and Baxter."

The driver eyed me closely from his perch. "Baxter Street's four blocks up that way," he said, pointing to the west. "In case you don't know it, mister, that happens to be Five Points. I've got a policy about driving into Five Points. I don't do it, and if you've got any sense in your head you won't do it, either. It's no place for a gentlemen such as you. Even the cops don't go sticking their noses in the Five Points, mister."

I thanked the driver gruffly, paid him, and ventured into the street on foot. The cabman wasted no time turning his rig around and heading back uptown.

Hester Street grew rapidly darker and more quiet as I walked away from the noisy hustle-bustle of the Bowery. In the damp gloom of the late twilight, I could discern a few obscure figures huddling in the shadowy doorways of the empty-looking warehouses and brick commercial buildings. The place had a sinister and malicious air about it, a sense that outsiders were far from welcome here. Instinctively, I gripped the handle of the revolver in my coat pocket.

At one corner I was approached by a scruffy and unshaven man with a battered porkpie hat upon his head. "Hey, buddy," he said to me in an accent I identified as that of lower Manhattan, "how about a penny or two for a fella down on his luck."

I handed the man a copper coin and he thanked me with a hoarse "God bless you, sir." I quickened my gait, noticing other such men moving from out of their shadows toward me. Clearly any man such as myself, who displayed any signs of even modest means, would be regarded as a mark in such a district as this.

Soon I saw the engraved curbstone which announced Baxter Street. A heavy wrought-iron lamp-post, sending a weak yellow glow into the filthy street, was the only light at the intersection. I stepped beneath it as I'd been directed to do.

In the next five minutes I must have been accosted by at least five more beggars, each telling me pleadingly how difficult times had been for him. I dispatched them all with a penny apiece and continued to wait impatiently. One of them, however, was not so easily put off. "I'll be needing a dime," he demanded rudely after I held out a penny. "A penny just won't do, sir." He was a thin, bearded fellow wearing the sort of blue denim coat preferred by railroad engineers. He held a cloth bag in his hands.

Not wanting a scene, I offered the stranger another penny. "What's the matter with you?" the beggar asked in a Brooklyn dialect. "What are you, a limey or somethin'? A dime is what I'll be needing. A dime. Ten cents, you know, with Liberty, not a lousy Indian head!"

"Listen here," I said, growing ruffled, "you can take the two cents or the devil with you!"

"In that case," came an unexpectedly familiar voice, "I suppose I'll be taking the two cents." I gaped in shocked surprise at the beggar as he lifted his false beard to reveal the smiling face of Sherlock Holmes!

"Holmes!" I blurted, "this is—"

"Hush, Watson, hush," Holmes admonished, holding a narrow finger to his lips. "The idea is not to attract undue attention. You've surely noticed that the neighborhood isn't accustomed to such fashionable pedestrians as yourself. We must try to blend in with the surroundings. Here, follow me."

Holmes quickly entered the rear of a brewery wagon parked at the corner, lifting its canvas door to allow me inside. I joined him in the rear of the wagon, among the cases of empty bottles and the odor of stale beer. He threw down the bag and told me to place its contents— a long, soiled white coat—over my own clothing. I did so with considerable disgust.

"Holmes," I asked, struggling with the coat, "where in the world have you led me?"

"Welcome to Five Points," he said cheerily through his beard, "one of New York's most notorious and perilous neighborhoods—the sort of place where signposts warning the wanderer to turn back, or to abandon all hope before entering, would not at all be out of place. More importantly, I've led you to a spot very close to the center of the spider's web, Watson."

"You mean the attacker?"

"No less than he. I spoke with Jarvis, the cabman at the Windsor, just a few hours ago. It took me most of the day just to track the man down. It seems he ranges rather widely through the city. Jarvis graciously informed me that after our visitor's bloody call last night, he was taken here in the cab. I don't have an exact address, of course, as exact addresses really don't exist in Five Points, but I have a sufficient description of the murderer's lair to find it. I wanted your strong arm and sharp eye before I made my sally against him, however. Are you quite ready?"

I nodded yes, buttoning the repulsive coat.

"Then let's be off." Holmes drew the canvas aside and glanced furtively around. He motioned for me to follow him when the coast seemed clear. Outside the wagon, the pair of us looked perfectly at home in the desolate streets of Five Points.

Despite the fact that there was still a goodly number of questionable characters lurking about, not a soul gave us a second glance as we walked toward the south. The district grew steadily more threatening and close as we progressed. At one point we passed a massive brick building. Holmes told me that it had once served as a brewery and that it had now become the common home of desperate people by the dozens, if not hundreds. It was that very place, so forboding and dangerous-looking in the darkness, that Charles Dickens once named the Den of Thieves, Holmes said.

The streets grew ever more narrow, not unlike some of the twisting passageways that mark the older sections of London. In fact, the whole feeling of Five Points was markedly like that of Whitechapel or Camden Town, or any number of other bloody districts in our own hometown. The buildings began to appear crooked, as if leaning awry from bad foundations. Second stories seemed to have been nailed upon lower ones with careless abandon. Windows were blank and empty, with weak candles appearing in but a scattered few. Multitudes of dark tunnel-like passageways vented away from the street to destinations one preferred not to ponder.

"The attacker could not possibly have selected a more inconspicuous place for his hideaway," Holmes said quietly. "I've heard it said that the New York police themselves rarely venture into this maze for fear of the threat of violence against them. Ordinary citizens avoid it like the plague. Under normal circumstances, he could base himself here for an indefinite period, planning and executing his attacks on Edwin in leisure. Nary a soul would venture here to find him."

"Although," I said, "he appears not to have taken you into consideration."

"We shall see," Holmes replied.

We didn't have very far to travel. After but a few minutes we came to yet another narrow street. "So," Holmes said, rubbing his hands, "this is the infamous Mulberry Bend. This is the evil heart of Five Points, Watson, the Black Hole of New York. It is like a casbah in its complexity and density and it is precisely here that our prey has kept his lair. Jarvis said that the man lives within an old tower of some sort, an elevator perhaps. We shall see if I remember his directions correctly."

We came to a compact square, surrounded by a handful of buildings that looked very deserted. Holmes eyed the buildings carefully and spied a well-hidden passageway which ran between two of them. "The driver said that our man left the cab here and walked through that passage," he said pointing to the spot. "And that," he added, looking up above the false-front building before us, "is the tower." A tall, thin structure loomed into the night sky, of a square shape and gabled roof. It had but a few windows along its steep ascent. It appeared to be a long-abandoned grain silo, dating from a time when this district actually handled aboveboard commerce.

We entered the narrow tunnel, quietly making progress despite the tiny space, the utter darkness around us and the stale, dank air which filled it. Feeling our way along the splintered walls, we saw at last the dim light of an exit ahead. When we stepped out we found ourselves in a small, litter-strewn yard of hardened dirt. The tower-like building stood directly before us, forming the fourth wall of a squalid courtyard whose only ingress was the passage we had just traversed.

We had absolutely no time to prepare for the figure who suddenly took a stance before us. He was a large, corpulent man with a dirty undershirt and battered derby. His leer showed clearly through a mottled beard.

"Looking for something, friends?" he asked in a gravelly voice.

"As a matter of fact, we are," Holmes replied, again assuming the Brooklyn accent I'd heard before.

"I don't believe I know you fellows," the leering man said. "What brings you to my humble doorstep?" I saw at that moment that the man was clutching a narrow knife. I grasped my revolver.

"Only this," said Holmes, holding out his hand as if to show the stranger something within it. The man peered closely into the palm and hardly changed his expression as Holmes clenched it tightly into a fist. The blow was sudden and fierce, sending the man several steps back. He stared in stupid surprise at both of us as Holmes landed another punch, considerably harder than the first, into the man's jaw. He collapsed immediately this time, knocked utterly unconscious, and his knife slid harmlessly from his hand.

"Nice show, old fellow," I said. "Holmes, is this—"

"No," Holmes replied. "This is not our man, I'm sure of it. Hurry, into the building! We've not a second to lose!"

We raced into the darkened tower, not bothering any longer about being quiet. The building seemed to be comprised entirely of stairs ascending within an empty space. The old wooden steps creaked loudly as we passed the landings, climbing a full three stories at a quick run. Finally, at the top, we entered a large and mostly empty room. We entered the room carefully, my revolver fully drawn and at the ready.

"It's too late," muttered Holmes after but a moment. He sighed deeply as he found a candle and put it to a match. He was right. The room was indeed bereft of any persons save ourselves, although it showed numerous signs of fairly recent occupancy.

"It hasn't been very long, Watson," Holmes said in resignation, peering about the place. "I'd say he left within the past few minutes, surely."

"Then your precautions were justified. He was warned of our approach, probably by the rascal downstairs."

"Almost surely, although it's unlikely that eminently unpleasant fellow will be of any help in identifying the man. His services as a vidette of warning were likely to be had for enough coin to purchase a bottle of cheap sherry." He impatiently removed his false whiskers and threw them to the floor in disgust.

Holmes walked quickly toward a window on the side of the building opposite from the side on which we'd entered. He pointed out a narrow metal ladder leading to the ground. "A handy back door, as it were," Holmes mused. "The man is nothing if not careful in his selection of domiciles." Beyond the window sprawled an immense and impenetrable slum, as squalid and congested as that through which we'd just passed. Even if we'd seen him running from the building, we would never have captured him in that maze of streets and alleys.

"The attacker had likely planned to leave regardless, and our present intrusion, while obviously not entirely unexpected, caught him sufficiently by surprise to force him to rush things a bit. Your altercation with him last night, Watson, might well have put a good scare into him. He knows now that Edwin had somebody else, two persons in fact, within his apartment. Such a discovery might just have made him feel insecure about his present hiding place and plans. More's the shame, old fellow. We have come maddeningly close, but again, not close enough. Tut! Let's have a look and see if he's left anything of interest."

We began a methodical search of the square room. Against one wall, the recent occupant had devised a fireplace, forming a circle of old paving stones atop a layer of similar material. Both of us could feel the weakening warmth still emanating from the embers within it. A few cooking utensils were scattered around the firepit. Leaning adjacent to it was a walking stick of obviously fine make. It was carved of heavy ebony with an elaborate gold knob which, unlike most other such sticks, bore no emblem or inscription. Holmes grasped the stick and walked with it, tapping the wooden floors of the miserable room as he continued his search.

"Our man has a fondness for excellent cigars," Holmes said, brushing at a tobacco ash upon the windowsill. "This is a high quality corona from Havana. It cost him at least twenty-five cents."

We then came to a shaky table, much scratched and stained, which seemed to have served the occupant as an informal desk. A number of items had been abandoned on its top. Beneath an empty small wooden box were a number of newspaper clippings, carelessly torn from their pages. One noted Edwin Booth's recent return to the city, written apparently by one of the journalists we had seen at the docks. Another was a front-page account of the recent shooting of President Garfield.

"Aha!" whispered Holmes as he slid open the table's solitary drawer. "Our attacker left a few articles in his haste." He pulled from the drawer a small cloth bag and held it open above the table. At least a dozen acorns tumbled out. "We can eliminate any doubt that we're in the right man's room, Watson," he said. "Here is our indisputable proof of that."

Next he pulled out a small book, which appeared to be a romantic novel written in French, and another publication, a slender and yellowed pamphlet. "Hello, what have were here?" Holmes asked with obvious interest.

The pamphlet carried the ponderous title: "The Life, Crime and Capture of John Wilkes Booth, and the Pursuit, Trial and Execution of his Accomplices." On its cover was a woodcut of the assassin himself, John Wilkes Booth, in a characteristically noble and arrogant stance, chest puffed out cockily, one hand held behind his back in a Napoleonic pose. Holmes began to leaf through its aged pages.

"A fairly common journal, Watson, one of dozens hurried into print in eighteen sixty-five to capitalize on Lincoln's murder. I've read a number of them myself and have been amazed at the gross inaccuracies and exaggerations they tend to contain. This is an original, dating from the time of the crime, but you'll notice that it was purchased only recently, probably at a secondhand book dealer's. See the price—ten cents—written on the cover in pencil? The graphite figures are obviously fresh. The attacker bought it within the last few weeks surely."

"Whatever for, Holmes?"

"That, my friend, is an infinitely intriguing question," the detective replied, "and here is perhaps our first clue as to the answer." He held the pamphlet open to reveal the page describing the assassination itself. Across a printed diagram of Ford's Theater was written in violet ink, and with exquisite penmanship:

I love thee brotherly; but envy much
Thou hast robbed me of this deed: I would revenges,

that possible strength might meet would seek us
through. And put us to our answer.

"Does the message ring any bells for you, Watson?"

I shook my head. "I've never heard those words before."

"The play, I believe, is *Cymbeline*, one of Shakespeare's most forgotten and thoroughly forgettable efforts. The lines are spoken by Arviragus, a supposed son of Belarius, and the genuine son of Cymbeline. I find it interesting that he would quote as obscure a line as this, and inscribe it on this particular page. Interesting too that the passage directly relates to the questions of vengeance and fraternal love."

"What in the world does it point to, Holmes?"

"It's too early to tell, Watson. It will require considerable pondering before any useful theories can be drawn, but even without the potentially valuable tidbits left behind for us here, we can assume one or two things about the attacker at this point."

"Such as?"

"We can assume firstly that he returned here after having killed Oglesby last night, with the probable intention of leaving soon, confident that his work was done."

"But his work wasn't done, Holmes. He killed the wrong man."

"Obviously, but how could he have known that at the time? You said yourself that the room was pitch dark in Edwin's apartment. It's unlikely that he would have gotten a good look at his victim's face. It couldn't have been until sometime in the late afternoon today, after the evening papers were available on the streets, that he realized that he'd missed his target. If he had succeeded in killing Edwin, in other words, the evening papers would surely be carrying the first news of it."

"Which means that by now he knows of his own failure."

"Yes, and also that his work remains unfinished. He neither read of Edwin's death nor Oglesby's, of course, since Pinkerton and I have managed to keep the incident quiet. That may work in our favor as it's sure to confuse and disorient him, to keep him guessing as to our moves and methods in Edwin's defense. It will diminish his confidence significantly, I should think."

I strolled to the window and gazed at the tawdriness below. "It doesn't, however, settle the matter. He remains free of capture and I have seen nothing in this room that could tell us where he might be now."

"Nor do I, Watson, but all the same I feel I know the fellow considerably better now. He is more careful and more cautious than I expected. That indicates intelligence above and beyond that of the ordinary criminal. We see further proof of his determination, which is considerable. This expensive stick, the excellent cigar, the French novel—all suggest a man of substantial means and culture. Yet he's willing to make this bleak hovel his very home in order to help him reach his bloody ambition. He is a very determined, very driven, individual where that ambition is concerned. Nothing suggests that he won't repeat the pattern once more. He'll go back to his headquarters, wherever that may be, lie low for awhile, and begin planning for his next assault on Edwin."

"And all we can do," I said, feeling a creeping sense of pessimism sweep over me, "is go back to the Windsor and wait for him to have another try."

Holmes chuckled lightly. "Don't despair, Watson. It's far too early for that. We have tried waiting and it has not resulted in his capture, but we have gained tools with which to proceed. No, the waiting period of our investigation is over. It's time now for an entirely new strategy."

"And what shall this new strategy be?"

"We shall start with a new investigation, Watson, into an infamous, and very old crime."

—10—
Washington

It was rare indeed to see Sherlock Holmes in a genuine state of anger, but there was not the slightest doubt that he was angry at this moment.

"Your refusal to accept reality, Edwin, is nothing short of petulant!" he shouted at his cousin. "I know you don't wish to speak of it. I know perfectly well how hard it is for you, but you must remember that I'm not a reporter. I have no interest whatsoever in any sensational scandal. Watson and I are here to preserve your very life and you're not making that considerable responsibility any easier by refusing to talk about it."

It was the morning after our near encounter with Booth's determined assailant deep within the shadows of Mulberry Bend. After a thorough examination of the stranger's bleak quarters, we had made our way to the small yard below. There we found the corpulent man in a derby who had tried to impede our progress earlier. He was groggy, just coming to from Holmes' powerful blow to the head, but managed to relate how he had been hired, for twenty-five cents a day, to keep watch over the attacker's lair. He told us that he had been at his post at the elevator building for a week and that he never knew his master's name. He gave us a description of the man that closely fit that given by young McPheeters. Thereafter, we left the district with no further trouble.

This morning, in Booth's apartment, Holmes had been trying to drive home the point to the actor that the assassination of Abraham

Lincoln was somehow connected to the attacks on himself. Booth toyed, rather ghoulishly I thought, with a human skull he used when performing Hamlet. The ghostly object had been willed to him by its very owner, a condemned horse thief who fancied himself a great admirer of Booth's, and found a novel way to express that admiration. The actor, however, was paying scant attention to Holmes' entreaties. He was making it eminently clear that he loathed the subject and wasn't interested in discussing it at all. "I have no brother named John," he said at one point when the assassin's name came up. "Come, let us speak of other matters."

It was fairly obvious to me that Booth was still within the grip of some form of melancholic depression, and that his sense of the urgency of his present situation was rather blunted by it. The news of Garfield's shooting had affected him more profoundly than I would have expected. It seemed the incident brought back to him all sorts of horrible memories of 1865. At that moment it seemed he hardly cared about the fact that he had come within mere inches of his own violent death only two nights before.

"The fact is, cousin Edwin," said Holmes, in a slightly milder tone, "there simply are no other matters where you are concerned. It is my duty to keep you abreast of my progress on the case to date, and that progress has led me to the strong conclusion that the attacker is somehow inspired, or is compelled into his acts against you, by the assassination sixteen years ago. Behold this, Edwin."

Holmes threw onto the table, directly before Booth, the yellowed assassination pamphlet we had found the night before. The actor started and drew back as he saw the likeness of his long-dead brother staring out at him from the cover. The sight of it seemed to stir something within him.

"Where did you find this?" Booth asked shakily, placing the Hamlet skull back onto its shelf.

"It was in his room in Mulberry Bend," Holmes said. "Read the passage written on the page I have marked, would you? I suspect you are familiar with the lines."

Booth read them aloud, his voice seeming to unconsciously assume the stentorian tones used by seasoned actors working Shakespeare. He looked up sharply when he was finished. "Why this passage?" he asked Holmes, growing visibly more alert. "What is this man trying to say?"

"Firstly," said Holmes, assuming the deductive line of questioning he was after from the start, "do you recognize the hand?"

"Not at all. It's unfamiliar to me, although it obviously comes from an experienced and talented penman."

"That's just as I suspected. Now, as to his meaning, who can say? He writes of loving somebody in a 'brotherly' way. Does he mean you, or does he wish to indicate your own brother? He writes that somebody has robbed him of some deed. Which deed? The attempt to kill you, perhaps? Or does he feel in some way that he was robbed of something through the assassination? And envy. We have no way of knowing what he might envy you for. He mentions revenge as well. You see, the passage is ponderously enigmatic when taken out of its context. It surely means one thing, but defining that is like finding the proverbial needle in a haystack. It contains too many elements for us to narrow its meaning down with what we presently know."

"It's confusing, yes," Booth replied, "but no more confusing than his speaking of oaks and acorns in London. It's written in a pamphlet that purports to tell the story of the assassination, but that hardly proves that he's connected with that crime, does it?

"Perhaps not," Holmes said, rising and filling his cherrywood. "But this ring lends a certain weight to that very contention." Holmes placed the Golden Circle ring into Booth's palm. "It came from the attacker's hand while he struggled with Watson two nights ago in this very room. Do you recognize it at all?"

Booth groaned as he examined the object and placed his hand on his forehead. "Yes," he said quietly. "The Knights. John was a member, as I'm sure you've discovered, Holmes. He used to go on about the Knights endlessly when the war was just starting. He was so enamored of them, so proud that they made him a member. I warned him that the order might be considered traitorous."

"That was sound advice," Holmes said, "as they were indeed traitorous. More important than their well-known past, however, are the motivations of the unknown present. The question this ring poses for us is this: What possible connection do former Knights of the Golden Circle think they have with Edwin Booth? Without doubt, Edwin, any such link has to do with your brother, one of their members, and any discussion of your brother, of course, raises the spectre of the assassination."

Booth threw up his arms in resignation and rose from his chair. He walked to the window and stared into the street. "All right, then," he said purposefully. "You've convinced me. There is probably some sort of link, although in my wildest imagination I cannot determine what that might be. I've made it painfully obvious that I wish this were not so, and I ask your forgiveness for my stubborn resistance to your logic, but if we're to work together, Holmes, you must understand this about me: There are some scars which never heal and which remain eternally painful. Despite that, I shall cooperate to the best of my ability."

"I could hardly ask for more," Holmes said. "Now, to get down to business. As I see it, there are two approaches to take in trying to find our way out of this fog. The first would be to examine the Knights of the Golden Circle themselves, seeking out their erstwhile members and trying to identify some bridge between the order and yourself. It is a daunting proposition at best. The society was highly insular and likely required some form of sacred oath of secrecy from its members. Even today it could be difficult to get them to talk, assuming that one could still find them. It would be terribly time-consuming and un-likely to produce satisfactory results."

"Well then, Holmes," I asked, "what is the remaining option?"

"To investigate the Lincoln assassination itself. To approach the case, if you will, as if the crime happened only yesterday instead of sixteen years ago."

Booth and I stared at Holmes in silence. Neither of us could think of a thing to say.

"Don't be alarmed, gentlemen. I have specific directions into which I shall set out, certain vague and premature theories with which to work. I trust fully that somewhere along the line, one of those threads will lead us somewhere. I feel much like a hunter who has pursued the fox into a large and dense copse of woods. He knows the fox is some-where within that particular wood, yet he cannot see where. He must enter it, clear the underbrush, and look closely for the trail. The attacker, gentlemen, is my fox, and the Lincoln assassination is my wood. Somewhere within that vast and confusing thicket, I'll find him."

Booth approached Holmes and smiled. "You do fascinate me, Holmes," he said. "I have no doubt that you believe your instincts to be correct, and how could I dispute them? They've proven flawless up to this point. But I sense something else here, too. I think you see an opportunity. I'd bet a sawbuck that you've been itching to get onto this case for years."

Holmes smiled back at him, and then at me. "I confess," he said, bowing his head slightly, "the Lincoln case has intrigued me from boyhood, and not merely because I have, shall we say, a family connection. I have never been content with many of the official findings. There have always been features of the case that mystified me. Yes, it's a challenge of the most monumental sort to me."

"Where will you begin?" I asked.

"Why, at the scene of the crime, of course, Watson. In Washington. I suggest we leave on the morrow."

"And what of me?" Booth asked. "Am I condemned to wait here at the hotel forever?"

"Not at all," replied Holmes. "Where would you like to go?"

"Well, to see my mother in Long Branch, for one thing. It's been quite some time since I've seen her and I'm worried about her health. I would like to take Edwina there, both for her safety as well as my mother's welfare. And then I have invitations to visit my friend Benedict in Connecticut and J. Henry Magonigle, my first wife's brother-in-law, in Mount Vernon. Mostly I just wish to be free of this hotel and this infernal idleness."

"Then go, by all means," Holmes said. "The rest and change of pace will do wonders for your mind and spirit. Take your Pinkerton men with you, of course, but be quite secretive about your destinations. Certainly, you would be no safer staying here in New York."

Booth looked tremendously relieved at this unexpected freedom. "You will keep me informed as to what you find in Washington?" he asked.

"Watson and I shall maintain contact via telegraph, and I can but hope that we will have a great deal to report."

***

After a hasty packing, Holmes and I left New York later that very morning, boarding a fast southbound express on the Pennsylvania Railroad.

It seemed like but a few minutes before our train sped past the long platform in Jersey City—the scene of Booth's dramatic rescue of Robert Lincoln so long ago—before heading out into open country.

It was a bright, sunny day and the green expanses of the country-side did much to lift my spirits after our stay in the city. The land was verdant and obviously rich, with miles upon miles of ripening corn-fields, vast seas of golden wheat and great pastures for dairy cattle. It was more settled and tilled, somehow, than I had expected. It had an established and even old quality about it that I hadn't associated with the frontier history of America. The groves of trees which separated the fields or served as windbreaks were tall and ancient-looking, giv-ing much of the land the feeling of certain fertile regions of England. The sheer size of everything, however, from the acreages to the white farmhouses to the scarlet barns, seemed unique to this country.

We fled past picturesque small towns by the dozens, each marked with a quaint depot and a sleepy little main street, and paused but briefly in such bustling metropolitan cities as Newark, Philadelphia and Baltimore.

More than once I attempted to engage Holmes in conversation about the panorama passing outside our window, but with little suc-cess. He stared at the changing locales with an expressionless face, blowing great clouds of tobacco smoke into the summer air outside, and said little. It was clear to me that he was utterly immersed in the case at hand, pondering the perplexities of the formidable investiga-tion he was undertaking. I ceased trying to distract him from his reveries after a few tries.

Our locomotive finally pulled into Washington station by late af-ternoon, after having entered the capital city from the shantytowns on its northeast side. By then the day had grown dull and overcast, with an oppressive, muggy heat that hung motionless over the city. I thought it a rather inauspicious introduction to the seat of a great empire.

After Holmes had purposefully instructed our cabbie to take us to the National Hotel, we clattered over the few paved streets and slogged through the mostly muddy ones that lined Washington in bizarre diagonal directions and chaotic traffic circles. From the cab I managed to glimpse briefly the white splendor of the Capitol building with its bright new dome, and the stately grandeur of the White House. For the most part, however, I found the city to be rather drab and dreary, a quite malodorous place, with a great many hungry-looking people, both white and black, lounging about in the streets, apparently with nothing better to do.

The National Hotel was similarly unimpressive at first glance. At Sixth Street and Pennsylvania Avenue, it was no great distance from either the Capitol or the White House. It occupied the better part of its block at the busy intersection, its massive brick bulk of five stories totally dominating, yet not gracing, the area. Inside, however, I was relieved to see furnishings far more comfortable and luxurious than the rectangular exterior might have suggested.

Holmes approached the clerk directly. "A room for two gentlemen, please," he said, "and if Room Two Twenty-eight should be available we would very much like to be boarded there."

The clerk, a thin and nervous looking fellow, peered over the top of his spectacles. "Room Two Twenty-eight, you say. Is there any particular reason?"

"There is indeed," Holmes replied curtly, without explanation.

"Very well then. You shall have Two Twenty-eight, as it is open. Here is your key, sir."

Within a few minutes we entered the room in question. It was a fairly small place, with two standard metal-framed beds, a couple of washstands and a pair of overstuffed chairs. I glanced through the window; the view there seemed quite ordinary. I surveyed the papered walls; the only adornment upon any of them was a scenic print of a moonlit lake in a wood, of the sort the galleries were calling luminescent.

"I don't understand, Holmes," I said, throwing my portmanteau onto the quilt-covered bed. "Why this room?"

"History, Watson," he said, splashing water onto his face from the basin. "This is a room with eminently historical associations."

"Historical?"

"John Wilkes Booth, to be specific. When he journeyed to Washington, remember, he unfailingly stayed here at the National. In the period immediately preceding the assassination, this room—Two Twenty-eight—was his."

I took another look at the humble room, trying to picture its infamous tenant of sixteen years ago. I imagined the assassin here quite easily, but still could not conceive of any value in occupying his room now.

"So what do you hope to find here?" I asked. "Some sort of clue? Ghosts perhaps?"

Holmes laughed and dried his face with a towel. "Neither," he said, loosening his tie. "Sixteen years is much too long a time to expect any clues to survive in a place used as frequently as a hotel. As to ghosts, well Watson, you know my feelings regarding the supernatural realm. I expect we'll have no spectral visitations from the late Mr. Booth during our stay, but I do entertain a notion or two about the significance of environment on an individual's actions."

"I'm not quite catching you there, Holmes."

He patted the bed and sat down. "Perhaps Booth made his decision to murder Abraham Lincoln while spending his hours in this room," he said, "perhaps while lying down on this very bed. He might have gazed out that window as he pondered the consequences of such an action. There's nothing supernatural or spiritualist about any of that, of course. You see, what I'm attempting to do is put myself into John Wilkes Booth's shoes to the greatest degree possible; to view the world from his vantage point. That vantage is composed not only of time and circumstance, but of place as well. I feel I can see through his eyes much more effectively if I can glimpse the actual scenes he once glimpsed."

"A perfectly fascinating notion, Holmes," I said, lying down, "but if you don't mind, I'd rather make use of this bed for its intended purpose, mundane as it is—napping."

"Tut, tut," he said, rising. "There will be none of that. Spruce yourself up for dinner, Dr. Watson. We're entertaining a guest tonight."

"A guest? Already? Who in the world is it?"

"A certain Samuel Arnold. Perhaps you remember the name. I wired him from New York just yesterday. Fortuitously, he happens to be in Washington today. He lives not far from here."

"Arnold," I said. "I can't say that I do remember the name."

"A minor player in the great drama of eighteen sixty-five, Watson. He was one of Booth's original cohorts in the early months of the plot, when kidnapping the president was still the extent of the conspiracy. He happens to be one of only two genuine conspirators still alive, and I've a question or two I'd like to put to him, just to get things going."

So, within the half hour, Holmes and I entered the spacious and glittering dining room downstairs, already busy with the evening clientele. The place was grand in its scale and elegant in the quiet dignity of its decor and service. We saw that Arnold had arrived before us and was occupying a table in one of the darker corners of the hall. He rose as we approached him and we introduced ourselves.

He was of medium height and build, not unhandsome in his overall appearance, although his eyes appeared profoundly sad and distrustful all at once. He was clean shaven, and most of his plentiful hair was silvery grey, which befit a man of his approximate age of 50 years. There was also a certain frailty about his appearance which I took to be the lingering after-effects of his near fatal bout with yellow fever during his imprisonment not so long ago. His clothing was neat and presentable, but humble and slightly worn, as if he were a man of rather modest means.

"First of all, Mr. Arnold," said Holmes, taking his seat, "you may be assured of the utter confidentiality of our conversation this evening, and please feel free to speak before Dr. Watson with the same openness with which you speak to me."

"I have nothing to hide any longer, Mr. Holmes," Arnold said with a weak smile. "I've made my mistakes and paid the price for them. I've been honest about my associations with Wilkes Booth from the beginning and I shan't change that tactic with you."

"I appreciate your candor, as well as your agreement to meet with us tonight on short notice. I promised you twenty-five dollars for the trouble, Mr. Arnold. Here it is." Holmes held out a number of banknotes.

"Not necessary," Arnold replied, shaking his head. "I shan't profit from my past any more than I'll bear false witness about it. Believe me sir, it's no trouble. I farm a small plot in Anne Arundel County, about halfway betwixt here and Baltimore. I travel to Washington every month or so to visit my suppliers, so it's convenient enough to meet with you."

"Very good then," said Holmes after ordering wine from the waiter. "Allow me to explain, if somewhat obliquely, what our business is. As I stated in my telegram to you, Dr. Watson and I are here on behalf of Edwin Booth. The circumstances of the moment prevent me from being specific as to the nature of the dangers now facing him, but I assure you it is a genuine threat indeed. The source of that threat, I am convinced, bears some connection to the plot to assassinate Abraham Lincoln, and to his late brother John Wilkes. It is my present strategy to go over the details of that crime, Mr. Arnold, in hopes of finding a point of genesis for the danger of today. It is your knowledge of that plot's early stages, and your acquaintance with the assassin, that prompted me to seek you out."

"I understand," Arnold said, "and if Edwin is to benefit from any knowledge of mine, then I am all for it. I have always admired the man, from my boyhood. All the boys in the vicinity looked up to him. He was so hard-working, so honest, so unlike his little brother. I think Wilkes' crime stung Edwin more than any other member of the family."

The wine arrived and Holmes waited until the glasses were filled before he resumed. "You were friendly with Wilkes from boyhood then?" he asked.

Arnold took a tiny sip of the Bordeaux. "We lived in the same area, the country around Bel Air, Maryland. The Booths lived at Tudor Hall, a noble name for a rather humble farm. Wilkes and I spent our school days together at St. Timothy's Hall and Mike—Michael O'Laughlin, that is—lived across the street from the Booths' winter house in Baltimore. The three of us were the best of friends until Wilkes went away to pursue his acting."

Holmes seemed to give serious consideration to his next question. "Mr. Arnold," he said at last, "as someone who knew him so well, can you say now with honesty that John Wilkes Booth was mad?"

The former conspirator smiled weakly once again and swirled the wine around in his glass. "You know, after he shot Lincoln, the newspapers came up with all sorts of stories about Wilkes as a boy. They said he liked to kill cats, just to spite the old man—Junius the senior—because the elder Booth was horrified at the thought of death. He used to hold funerals for the animals that died on the farm. Now the old man might have been well off his nut, Mr. Holmes, I think a good case might be made for that, but I never felt that Wilkes himself was. I don't know where they came up with such stories. I never knew him to hurt a cat or anything else at Tudor Hall. He was not a cruel boy, surely. Now, a dreamy boy he was. He dreamed a lot about the days of knights and kings and such, and used to pretend a great deal. He liked to play games of make-believe, all involving glory and adventure in the olden days. I'd say that Wilkes was a great daydreamer, and a man who sometimes thought of queer things to do, but a lunatic? Never."

"And that was true even when you knew him later, when the conspiracy was underway?"

"Oh yes, then too. He'd changed by then, of course. He was a famous actor and a rich man to boot. He didn't entertain such childish notions by then. He'd gotten new ones aplenty."

"Tell me about them," Holmes said.

"They all had to do with the Southern cause, Mr. Holmes. Wilkes lived for the Southern cause. He was a fervent man when the issue of slavery came up, and the right of the South to maintain it. We all were, really, but Wilkes took it a step further than patriotism. He was often angry about it. You see, he felt the Union was raping Dixie, that's how he liked to put it. It was all bound up with honour in Wilkes' mind, and eventually he brought his notions of adventure and glory into it as well, just as he used to do when he was a boy."

"How so?"

"Well, that's how he got Mike and me to go along with him at first. He believed so strongly that a small band of Confederate agents—meaning us—could affect the outcome of the entire war; he believed so fiercely that we could become heroes for all time by saving the Confederacy, that it became contagious. Now I look back on the idea of kidnapping Lincoln in order to ransom him for prisoners or a ceasefire and it strikes me as ridiculous, but back then it all seemed possible somehow. You gentlemen are younger, and you're British, so you can't really know what things were like in those days. Things were crazy in eighteen sixty-five, believe me. Things were happening very fast then. Feelings were strong and judgments were often faulty. Our judgments were certainly faulty."

Holmes quietly ordered a dinner of curried chicken for the three of us and once again addressed Arnold. "I'm curious," he said, "as to why you and O'Laughlin agreed to go along with the kidnapping scheme."

"There were many reasons, Mr. Holmes. We were young and foolish, first of all, and attracted by the idea of being welcomed as heroes in Richmond. The kidnappers of Abraham Lincoln! Imagine it! And we were both Confederates, don't forget. Both Mike and I served with the CSA. It was something we believed in. And then we were flattered. It's true. Wilkes was a star of the stage, a celebrated figure, and here he'd remembered his common old buddies from Maryland. Finally, there was money in it. Wilkes told us that he made twenty thousand dollars per year. He threw money around as if it had no worth. At the time I was working on my brother's farm near Hookstown for bed and board alone. The money was very tempting."

I entered the conversation. "And so, Mr. Arnold," I said, "how did you and O'Laughlin actually get involved in the plot?"

"When Wilkes asked us to, Dr. Watson. He contacted the two of us in September of 'sixty-four. That's when he told us of the plan to take Lincoln from a theater after we'd dimmed the lights. The others began joining up soon afterward—Surratt, Atzerodt, Herold, Payne. There was quite a momentum at first."

"Were you at all familiar with the other conspirators?" Holmes asked.

Arnold shook his head, an unmistakable expression of disgust on his face. "Not a one of them, Mr. Holmes. Except for Mike, I'd never seen any of them before. Herold was a foolish sort, an idle boy really, whose only real occupation had been to go bird hunting in the swamps around Washington. He'd been pampered by his sisters—I think he was a touch soft in the head. Atzerodt was a drunk, a liar and a coward. I've never seen a lesser man. Surratt seemed a decent enough fellow, but I didn't trust him. He was always off to Virginia or to Montreal on some sort of errand for the Confederacy. He had a secretive air about him. And then, of course, there was Payne. He was a dark, eerie man, gentlemen. Very violent, very quiet and very strong. Despite all that, there was a certain cunning, a sort of wisdom about him. I distrusted him more than the rest, and I don't mind telling you I feared him as well. I never feared Wilkes himself, but I surely feared that dark giant of his."

"Your doubts about the chances for success surfaced quite soon, did they not?" Holmes asked.

"Well, they did. It didn't take me very long to realize that the theater plan would be a farce. I never really believed that we could manage it. There were a couple of false starts. We'd get ready to make our move on a certain night and something would happen. Once there was a storm and the roads got too muddy to chance any sort of escape. On another night, Lincoln simply decided not to show up at the theater. I grew fed up with it at last, and told Wilkes that unless he came up with something realistic that I was out of the whole thing."

"Which must have angered him considerably."

"He said to the lot of us that anyone who spoke of getting out was fit to be shot. I looked him in the eye and told him that two could play at such a game. That cooled him off greatly. He came up with a new plan in a few days—the one about waylaying Lincoln on the open road. It seemed a far safer way to go."

"That was in March of 'sixty-five, I understand."

"Yes. Wilkes had learned that Lincoln was supposed to attend a play called *Still Waters Run Deep* at the Campbell Hospital theater, out by the Soldiers' Home. We were all ready to go that day: Wilkes and Surratt were to take the reins of the president's horses; Payne would enter the carriage and restrain Lincoln himself; Mike and I were to take care of any cavalry escorts and Atzerodt—coward that he was—was to hold back in the rear, and offer help if any was needed. We had routes charted for southern Maryland, plans to cut the telegraph wires, arrangements made for the ferry over the Potomac—everything. It might have worked, Mr. Holmes, it really might have."

"Except for the fact," Holmes said, "that fortune persisted in frowning on you."

Arnold sighed deeply and drank from his glass. "We waited for the longest time. When a carriage finally passed our hideout, Wilkes and Surratt rode close enough to get a look inside. It was the wrong man! Perhaps, as Surratt says today, it was Samuel Chase. We waited longer, but no more carriages came. The plan was a bust."

"And that," Holmes said, "was the end of the conspiracy for O'Laughlin and yourself."

"It was. We'd finally had enough. When we rode away from the party that day, it was the end of our role in the venture. I learned that Surratt quit a day or two later. I was convinced at the time that the Secret Service had gotten wind of the plot, and that they'd diverted Lincoln's carriage because of that. I believed that they would be running us down any day. I suddenly saw the danger in it. I wrote a final letter to Wilkes, telling him how I felt he had betrayed the lot of us with his foolish plans, and how I didn't think he'd been totally honest with us. It was a fatal letter, Mr. Holmes. Despite the fact that I'd asked him to burn it, he left it in the trunk in his rooms in this very hotel. That's how they tracked me down after the assassination, you know. I'll never know if he preserved the letter to spite me for abandoning him or not."

"At the time of your departure from the conspiracy," Holmes asked, "was there any intimation from Booth that assassination might be his next step?"

"Wilkes made no mention of murder, Mr. Holmes, nor did any of the others. There seemed so little sense in it that I don't believe it was ever seriously considered by the rest of us, although Wilkes must have already been thinking about it by then."

We were interrupted by the waiter, who brought steaming trays of food to our table. As we had our dinner, Arnold told us of the hardships he was forced to endure after the assassination. He spoke of the agony of wearing chains and a hood over his head during the heat of the 1865 summer as the conspirators underwent trial. He told us of the torture of imprisonment at Fort Jefferson, and of the pervasive epidemic of yellow fever that took the life of his friend O'Laughlin. He praised Dr. Samuel Mudd in glowing terms, relating the heroic story of helping the selfless and courageous physician as he tried to pull as many people, both inmates and guards alike, from the epidemic's deadly jaws. Had he not served as Mudd's assistant, Arnold told us, he may never have earned the pardon that resulted in his present freedom. He shuddered when he considered the prospect that he might still be roasting in the dungeons of America's Devil's Island.

At the conclusion of dinner we retired to the lobby for cigars. Holmes had obviously not exhausted the subject of the assassination to his satisfaction.

"I don't wish to rob you of your entire evening," he said, "but I remain puzzled on a few points concerning John Wilkes Booth."

"Then ask me questions, Mr. Holmes. That's why I'm here."

"You said you didn't completely trust him. Why is that?"

"Mike and I had the feeling that he wasn't telling us everything about the plans for Lincoln. We knew that he was doing something for the Confederate intelligence. He was often traveling to Montreal to meet others involved in espionage, and Surratt had such activities as well. Yet neither of them told the rest of us about these dealings. And he was involved in some sort of secret society, one of the Know-Nothing groups. I forget the name . . ."

"The Knights of the Golden Circle."

"Yes, that's the one. He kept that business under wraps at all times, too. We began to get suspicious that perhaps Mike and I, and maybe some of the others, were in the plan merely to serve as decoys, or to take the blame if things went wrong. That belief did a lot to discourage us from staying with Wilkes."

"I see," said Holmes, rubbing his hands together. "And what of Wilkes' courage, Mr. Arnold. Did you feel him to be a brave man?"

"Now there's a question," Arnold said with interest, pausing to consider his reply. "I'd have to be honest and say no. Wilkes struck me as a man of great words and intentions, but little action—proud words on a dusty shelf, that was Wilkes. When I had my disagreement with him I was amazed at how quickly he backed down from me. The only occasion where I saw him actually intending to do something was that useless day on the road to the Soldiers' Home and, of course, nothing happened that day. Then there was the army. He believed so strongly in the South, and spouted off about it daily, but he never enlisted, never saw a single moment of battle. Now, mind you, Mike and I were no war heroes, Mr. Holmes, but at least we served. So in all honesty, I cannot say that Wilkes was a courageous man. At least I saw no proof of it."

"A final question, Mr. Arnold," Holmes said. "Based on your experience with Booth and the others during the kidnapping plot, do you have any reason to believe that Confederate intelligence was involved?"

Arnold shook his head as I helped him with his coat. "It wouldn't surprise me if it was, Mr. Holmes, at least as far as the kidnapping goes. As I said, those were desperate days, for the Confederacy more than anyone else. With Wilkes and Surratt up in Canada so often, it just might have been a Confederate plan. All the same, I have no evidence, no proof, to back that up. I'm convinced, though, that Richmond had absolutely nothing to do with the killing. That would have amounted to a form of suicide, and the South knew that better than anyone."

Holmes snuffed out his cigar in the ashtray. "And so we find ourselves at a difficult crossroads of logic, gentlemen. Mr. Arnold, you seem convinced that Booth was no madman—that he had full possession of his senses. And yet you do not see him as a courageous man. If he was not mad, if he was not extremely courageous, and if, so far as we know, he was not on assignment from the Confederacy, how then, or why, did he assassinate Abraham Lincoln, an act which surely must have required at least one of those ingredients?"

"I've agonized over that question ever since the morning when I heard the news of Lincoln's death, Mr. Holmes. I've never known how—or why—John Wilkes Booth did what he did."

—11—
A House of Infamy

It was with a pervasive sense of dread that I approached the forsaken-looking structure that once housed Ford's Theater. Although Tenth Street was quite empty on this leaden Washington morning, and although the windows of the once gay theater were all shuttered now, and silent, I could not help but picture in my mind the scene that had once transpired here.

I saw images of the frenzied mob crowding around the doors, and the frantic cries of the policemen and soldiers as they tried to part the throng to make a pathway across the street. I heard the gasps of the onlookers, dressed for an evening's entertainment of light comedy, as they viewed instead the long thin body of Abraham Lincoln being carried still and prone, and with agonizing slowness, to the humble house across the street. I heard them utter "My God!" and "It was that damned actor Booth!" as the dying president disappeared behind the door of the Patterson House. I felt in my bones the fear and shock that filled this street, and wondered if the bricks and stones around me might not have absorbed the terrible atmosphere on that April night.

It was the voice of Holmes that brought me sharply back to reality. "The scene of the crime, Watson," he said, appraising the former theater's now drab facade. "Strange that so unimposing a building should carry such a ghastly air about it, don't you think?"

We had walked the seven blocks from the National Hotel immediately after breakfast, and had found ourselves gazing silently at the place when we arrived.

"You were imagining the horrors of April fourteenth, weren't you?"

"Yes, of course. Were you reading my mind again, Holmes?"

"I knew it only because I was doing precisely the same thing. How could anyone who knows the history of Ford's possibly think otherwise when seeing the place for the first time? Here, Watson, let us take this bench for a moment or two before going inside. Let me try to fill in some of the spaces and borders of the picture we were so busy imagining a moment ago."

As we sat on a wooden bench, Holmes carefully tamped his pipe and gazed at the simple four-story theater building before us. It was built of a dull red brick with an unadorned sloping cornice, faced with a series of five semi-circular arches which once served for the access and egress of theater-goers. Its marquee windows had long ago been taken down and in their place we saw a plain sign announcing the building's present use as an Army storage center.

"On that immortal day, the fourteenth of April, John Wilkes Booth awakened in his room—the very room in which we slumbered last night, Watson. His first act was to go for a trim and a shave at Charles Wood's barbershop near Grover's Theater. He was especially well-dressed that day, attired in a dark suit, light overcoat, silk hat and gloves. The meticulousness of his toilet suggests that Booth imparted some importance to the day ahead of him. He returned to his room at nine a.m. where he chanced to meet his former conspirator Michael O'Laughlin who, despite his Confederate loyalties, had come to Washington to join in the war's-end celebrations just then reaching their peak. O'Laughlin would later testify that Booth made no mention of Lincoln, nor did he try to draw him back into the conspiracy.

"He came in mid-morning to this very spot, Ford's Theater, where he was accustomed to receiving his mail. There were a few pieces of mail for Booth. He read them while at Ford's, but shared their contents with no-one. It was while he was here that John T. Ford, son of the theater owner, made his famous remark about Booth being 'the handsomest man in Washington.' It was also here, significantly, that Booth learned that Lincoln was expected at the theater that night to see *Our American Cousin*. This was apparently Booth's first knowledge of this crucial fact.

He also heard that General U.S. Grant, the Union war hero, would be at Ford's that night along with President and Mrs. Lincoln. That event, of course, never came to pass, much to the general's good fortune."

Holmes paused to relight his smoldering pipe and tossed his match into the gutter. "From here, the assassin visited a livery stable a few blocks distant, where he asked the caretaker to take a particular one-eyed mare, a horse he'd ridden before, to a makeshift stable that Ford's stagehand Ned Spangler kept in the alley behind the theater. It seems likely now, Watson, that this horse—a particularly sturdy mount—was intended for Payne. It is my contention that Booth's original plan that day called for Payne to murder Grant while Booth took care of Lincoln. As we shall see, those plans had to change as Grant opted not to attend the theater. At any rate, from this stable, Booth traveled to another— that of James W. Pumphrey on C Street. Here he arranged to have a bay mare ready for him by four that afternoon. This would be the horse that would speed the assassin along his route of escape that night.

"Historians have tried to reconstruct that day with painful exactness, Watson, and it seems they've managed to get much of the morning correct. The activities of Booth in the afternoon and evening, however, have proven more elusive to confirm. Still, we know a number of things. It's likely that during the lunch hour at Willard's Hotel, Booth was the fearsome moustached fellow who so annoyed Julia Dent Grant, wife of the general, that she took leave of the place. The stranger, she said later, stared at her fearfully and with great malice. We can only guess as to his purposes there. By two-thirty in the afternoon he paid a visit to the Surratt boardinghouse on H Street. While there, he asked the landlady, the unfortunate Mary Surratt, to take a wrapped parcel to her other property, the inn at Surrattsville, well into Maryland, where he would retrieve it later. The parcel, wrapped in twine and brown paper, contained materials which would aid Booth in his escape. Mrs. Surratt, of course, would go to the gallows for doing him this favor, probably unaware of the parcel's contents."

Holmes leaned back on the bench and squinted his eyes tightly, as if he were actually seeing the events of that fateful day with his own eyes. "Soon thereafter, Booth visited Payne at the Herndon House, apparently assigning him the task of murdering General Grant. It was at another hotel, the Kirkwood House, that he then left in the box of Vice President Johnson's secretary, a card reading 'Don't wish to disturb you. Are you at home? J. Wilkes Booth.' Again, Watson, we cannot be sure of this visit's purpose. My feeling is that it was but a simple gambit to confirm the Vice President's presence in the city, the better to send a murderer after him. Booth was spotted again at Ford's, entering the theater this time from the rear. It seems likely that he wanted to reconnoiter the house while dress rehearsals were underway. Later, back in the street, he met a fellow actor, John Matthews, who had refused to join the kidnapping conspiracy a few months before. On this meeting, Booth handed Matthews a sealed letter with the instructions to deliver it to the *National Intelligencer*, a prominent Washington newspaper, on the following day. Matthews, in fact, read the letter later that very night, and for reasons intriguingly unknown, destroyed it without ever showing it to another soul. He claimed, however, that the letter clearly implicated Booth and his fellows in the assassination.

"But I digress from the activities of the day. Booth would later be spotted by General and Mrs. Grant as they rode in their carriage toward the railway depot. They claim that Booth, who had apparently picked up his horse by then, rode alongside and peered within their conveyance in order to get a good look at the occupants. Somehow, probably soon afterwards, Booth would learn that the Grants were heading out to New Jersey that very afternoon in order to visit their children. The assassin's plot would therefore have to be rearranged.

"As the afternoon wore on, Booth returned, once more, to Ford's. This time he offered drinks on the house to a small handful of stage employees, buying drinks at Taltavul's Star Saloon—you can see it there, Watson, just to the right of the theater's doors—and in fact, leaving an entire bottle for the crew. He left them and returned to the now-empty playhouse. This must have been when he tampered with the presidential box, placing a wooden plank within the shadows of the box itself and carving a niche in the plaster besides the box's outer doorway. He probably did this with a common penknife, and perhaps a handkerchief to catch the plaster filings. I hope to see the evidence of this handiwork when we go inside.

"From there, the actor probably returned to the National Hotel where he took a quiet meal. More likely than not, this is where he picked up his weapons—a hunting knife and a small but deadly forty-four caliber derringer. He also dressed himself in riding gear. Upon leaving the National, Booth told the desk clerk that 'rare fine acting' would be had at Ford's that night.

"At around eight o'clock or so, Booth had his last meeting with his co-conspirators, quite probably at the Herndon House, where Atzerodt was staying. The details of this meeting are sketchy, based on the recollections of the conspirators, all of whom were later hung. In attendance were Payne, Atzerodt and Herold. Payne had been told to kill Grant earlier in the day; it is likely that now he was reassigned to the target of Secretary of State Seward. The testimony of George Atzerodt seems clearly to indicate that this was the first they'd heard of any assassination plot. If they were shocked, however, it was not to the degree that they refused their assignments, at least not in Booth's presence. Booth tried to win over Atzerodt's reluctance with intimidation, by telling him that they'd all hang if captured, no matter whether he followed his orders to murder Vice President Johnson or not.

"Payne, as history tells us, performed his task with great alacrity, although he didn't quite succeed in killing Seward. Herold's job, which was simply to help guide Payne to the residence of Seward, was performed correctly, with the exception that he did not linger at the house to await Payne's exit. Instead he bolted early, managing to join up with Booth at some point along the escape route, and leaving Payne to try making good his escape unaided. As for Atzerodt, no evidence exists that he ever made the first move to assault the Vice President. He apparently wandered the city throughout the night, learning of Lincoln's shooting at some point, and fled the city by morning.

"The conspiratorial conclave probably lasted no more than thirty minutes before the party split up. If we assume this took place at half past eight, Booth would have been aware that Lincoln and his guests were already in their seats at Ford's, enjoying the performance. That was surely Booth's next destination. He left his mount at the rear of the theater, ordering a boy named Peanut John, one of the Ford's stagehands, to hold it for him until he called. Before entering the theater, however, Booth visited the Star Saloon once more. For some reason, he drank whiskey this night instead of his usual brandy and spent a few moments conversing with his fellow drinkers. One rather inebriated fellow is said to have challenged Booth there, saying that he'd never attain his father's stature as an actor. Booth's apparent reply was that by the time he left the stage, he would be the most famous man in America, a chillingly prophetic truth.

"He entered the theater at last, through those doors before us. The usher recognized him and permitted his free entry after Booth casually mentioned that he should not be expected to purchase a ticket. Witnesses say he appeared restless for some minutes after entering the lobby. He paced back and forth between the lobby and the street at least five times. On each trip he appeared to be closely checking the clock in the lobby. Doubtlessly, he had timed the moment of his attack with precision and wanted to be sure that his pacing was accurate. Finally, he entered Ford's for the last time. And this, my good fellow, is the portion of the story where I'd much prefer to trace the assassin's precise footsteps through this place of infamy, the house which a grieving and hysterical Mary Todd Lincoln would aptly describe as 'that horrible place.'"

We rose from the bench at last and stretched our legs. "Our assassin seems to have had himself a busy day," I remarked. "There seems to have been a frantic, almost fanatical pace to his movements."

"Indeed, and John Wilkes Booth would never gain for himself another moment's rest, Watson. In studying his activities and actions on April fourteenth, however, I find another significant fact. All signs point to his having made his decision to murder Lincoln on the very day of the deed, or at least very shortly before it. At any rate, his hirelings almost certainly had not heard of it before then."

"Is there some significance in that?" I asked.

"We'll see one way or the other, I'm sure, but for now Watson, I think it's time we took a closer look, don't you?" We walked to the main door and let ourselves in.

It was cold and dimly-lit inside the old hall. We were greeted by a youthful corporal who sat near the door behind a partially-closed Dutch door. "May I help you?" the soldier asked, looking up from the paperwork he was doing.

"Yes, I believe you can," Holmes answered in a friendly manner. "We are interested in having a brief look at the building, out of purely historical interest, of course."

The corporal adjusted his blue kepi and came to the half-door. "I suppose you gentlemen aren't aware of it, but this is an Army post now. The building is no longer used as a theater, and I'm afraid it's no longer a public place. I'm sorry, but we do not allow tourists."

Holmes quickly lost the smile he'd been holding on his face. "In that case, corporal, I must insist on speaking with your commanding officer."

The soldier appeared offended that his authority would be so challenged, but he consented nonetheless, sending a subordinate to bring the commanding officer to us. He was there in a moment, a bearded, greying major by the name of Caldwell.

"As I'm sure Corporal Jones informed you," he said firmly, "the building is closed to the public. I'm sorry—"

Holmes held up his hand in polite interruption of the major. "Major Caldwell, please. I assure you my interest is not one of morbid curiosity. Neither am I here on official business, to be honest, but I do arrive on your doorstep with a good reference." He handed the major a folded letter from his coat pocket.

The officer opened it with suspicion in his eyes, and then read it aloud: "To whom it may concern: This is to vouch for the good intentions and character of Mr. Sherlock Holmes, a consulting detective from London, England, and whomever may be accompanying him in the United States. The cooperation and gracious assistance of all official U.S. personnel in dealing with Mr. Holmes shall be noted and appreciated by this office. Signed, James G. Blaine, Secretary of State."

Major Caldwell handed the letter back to Holmes with an impressed expression on his face. "A good reference, indeed," he said. "You can prove that you're this Sherlock Holmes?"

"My passport, sir," said Holmes, holding up the document.

"Then I can't see why it would do any harm to let you have a look around."

"You're really most kind, major," the detective replied diplomatically.

"I'll send Lieutenant Devereaux, my adjutant, down to show you the building. My apologies if I may have seemed a bit rude with you, Mr. Holmes. It's just that we receive an awful lot of requests to see the theater, er, the facility."

"Not at all, major. Your help is of great value to us."

The officer walked crisply away, leaving Holmes and me alone in a long and narrow room, adorned with a portrait of President Garfield and filled with a drab row of oaken filing cabinets. I leaned over to Holmes and whispered in his ear.

"Where on earth did you get that letter, Holmes?"

"My brother Mycroft, remember, is a man of some influence in Her Majesty's Foreign Service," he whispered back, "of sufficient influence, in fact, to have procured this valuable document on my behalf from a powerful American official indeed. Good references are of supreme value in dealing with governments, Watson, and I obtained this one in the event that I might have such dealings on this trip."

A cheerful-looking young man, with long sideburns and an impeccable uniform then approached us with an outstretched hand. "I'm Lieutenant Devereaux," he said. "The major says you fellows want a look around the old barn."

"Indeed we do," Holmes replied.

"Well, fine then," the lieutenant said. "It'll get me away from my inventory for a few moments. I hope the old man wasn't too rough on you. He's a bit defensive about the theater, or as he calls it, the facility. It's something none of us are really too proud to be spending our days in, if you know what I mean."

"I understand completely," Holmes said. "Just what is the building's present purpose?"

"We store records, Mr. Holmes, by the thousands, if not millions. Most of them are Army—medical records, service records and so forth. But there are things in here from the Surgeon General, the Attorney General, you name it. It's really just a warehouse."

"And how long has the government owned the building?"

"Oh, since the assassination, of course. Secretary of War Stanton took possession of it by fiat, not long after the murder. *Our American Cousin* was the last performance ever held here. There was nothing

Mr. Ford could do about it. He won a settlement in court a few years later, a hundred thousand dollars, I think it was, but old Stanton would never allow another instant of tragedy or comedy to appear here. He was most ardent about it."

"How informed are you, lieutenant," Holmes asked the youthful officer, "as to the details of the crime committed here?"

The lieutenant looked momentarily uncomfortable. "As an officer assigned to my place of duty," he says, "my official responsibilities must come before any personal interests. However, since my duties frequently have me wandering throughout the building, I've become quite familiar with the layout. I have read histories of the event, yes, and I'll admit that I know quite a lot about what happened here."

"Good then," said Holmes, rubbing his hands together, "because I would like to trace the assassin's very steps through this place, beginning at the spot on which we stand. You can certainly tell us, Lieutenant Devereaux, what Booth did upon gaining this lobby."

Devereaux pointed to a weathered, curving staircase at the far side of the lobby. "He headed straight for those steps, sir. They lead to the old theater's second level, the area known as the dress circle. Come, follow me."

We ascended the creaky old staircase after the officer's lead. It led to a wide, open room which jutted out over the main floor in the fashion of a balcony. There was an additional balcony, a smaller one, above our heads. We walked to the end of the dress circle and viewed the interior of the old theater as we gripped a rather shaky old balustrade.

Below us, the erstwhile stage offered a dolorous and melancholy scene. There was no sign of its curtain or props. All that remained to bear testimony to its former use were a few lines for lifting scenery, now hanging limply from the ceiling, and the elevation and curved apron of the stage platform. Like the dress circle where we stood, the main floor and the rear of the stage itself were fairly filled with tall stacks of boxes and filing drawers in neat military rows.

"That's where it happened," Devereaux said, pointing to the right side of the theater. There we saw the once-ornate presidential box, now looking shabby and neglected without its draperies and flags. Despite the dim light, however, signs of its former beauty could still be seen in the delicate carvings and fretwork which enriched its wooden frame, and the huge twin arches which spanned high above the box. Within the gloom of the box I saw but shadows, and realized with a shudder that this was the very spot where Lincoln met his doom.

"Sixteen years ago," Devereaux said, "this floor would have sloped downward toward this balustrade in order for the audience to gain a better view of the stage. The floor has since been levelled out so that these crates can be safely stored here. It would also have been filled with seats, of course."

"And on the night of the crime," Holmes said, "this dress circle would have been packed with members of the audience. I understand that Ford's had a full house that night, with barely a place to stand, because of the presidential appearance."

"That is my understanding also," Devereaux said.

"It would have been quite dark when Booth entered this floor some minutes after ten p.m.," Holmes said. "The lights would have been dimmed and most of the audience would have had their eyes on Laura Keene and Harry Hawke upon the stage. Despite that, as Booth made his way down a narrow aisle running behind the last row of seats, a number of people saw and recognized him."

Holmes pointed to a closed door at the far right side of the dress circle. "And that, of course, was the assassin's destination."

"It leads to the hallway, which in turn leads to the two boxes which were combined on the night of the murder," Devereaux said. "The aisle terminated there. It was the only means of entering them."

"Now on his way to that fatal door, Booth did something rather curious," Holmes continued. "He paused and spoke briefly with a member of the audience who was sitting approximately here." With a circular motion of his hands, Holmes indicated a particular spot on the floor. "That person happened to be President Lincoln's footman and messenger, a Charles Forbes, who was watching the play. Booth interrupted him, and presented his calling card in fact, before proceeding toward the door. Now Watson, why do you think he would go to that potentially risky trouble, when in all likelihood he could have passed behind Mr. Forbes' back without being seen?"

"I should suppose it was a means of gaining entrance into the box," I said.

"I respectfully disagree, old fellow. I propose that Booth presented his card to Lincoln's footman for one reason alone, and that was to make absolutely sure his identity would be established. Just in case the audience would fail to recognize the face of John Wilkes Booth, in other words, he took pains to leave documentary and eyewitness evidence that it was indeed he who entered the presidential box."

Holmes took a step closer to the door. "You see, Forbes was sitting very near to this door, only a few feet away. By the time Booth reached him, the assassin must surely have seen that the door itself had been left literally unguarded. He must have known that he needed no clearance from Forbes, whose back would have been turned to him anyway. His path was clear, was it not Lieutenant Devereaux?"

"You're absolutely right, Mr. Holmes. The bodyguard had indeed abandoned his post."

"He was a District of Columbia policeman by the name of John Parker. He had been posted here at the beginning of the performance that evening. Yet by the time Booth made his appearance, the guard was gone. Do you find that curious, lieutenant?"

"Not only curious, Mr. Holmes, but horribly shameful."

"No sign of Parker was seen until the following morning when he showed up at his precinct headquarters, apparently intoxicated, having arrested a prostitute sometime during the night."

"Probably because he felt he needed to show something for his shameful absence on the previous night," Devereaux added. "It must have been a pitiful sight."

"I have no doubt it was, lieutenant," Holmes said, "but all the same, I feel far too much has been made of Parker's absence. I hardly think it had conspiratorial overtones. I don't believe he left his post at the assassin's instructions. Rather, if you look toward the stage, you can see that it was hardly visible from where we stand, the place where Parker was supposed to be. Consider this: The evening droned on for Parker, he grew bored with his sentinel's monotony, and finally he moved closer to the edge of the balcony, so that he could watch the play. Perhaps Lincoln himself gave him leave to have a look—it would not have been an uncharacteristic gesture."

"Yes," I countered, "but Booth would have had no way of knowing that the door might well be left without security."

"Quite right, Watson, but Booth, you will recall, was armed not only with his pistol—which surely was his weapon of choice for the president—but with a hunting knife as well, which he'd tucked into his belt. The knife was probably intended for the guard at this door, in case Booth was denied entry into the box. Any commotion caused by such a stabbing would have had minimal effects. Booth had prepared the inside of this door with an improvised lock, remember. If he had to, he could still move quickly enough in order to effect the murder with success."

"Of course, he never had to take such action," Devereaux said.

"Exactly. When Booth arrived at this spot, he found the door exactly as we find it today—unguarded and unlocked. I see that the lock is broken to this day. It was broken sixteen years ago, you know, another fact of which Booth must have been cognizant."

Holmes began slowly turning the knob.

"Mr. Holmes," Devereaux said quickly, placing his hand on Holmes' arm, "before you open that door, you should know that we have a policy about going in there. It's an unofficial policy, but we pretty much avoid the box itself. We tend to leave it be, if you know what I mean."

The detective hesitated, smiled and placed a friendly hand on the lieutenant's shoulder. "Lieutenant, are you telling me that the United States Army has a superstitious streak? Come now."

"It has nothing to do with superstition, Mr. Holmes. It's just that—"

"Lieutenant, how can I understand a crime unless I see the scene of the crime? Look around you. The building is virtually deserted save for ourselves. Nobody need know."

"The others are all in the basement with the inventory, sir, but—"

"Tut, lieutenant! I'm sure you've wanted to see the box for yourself. Am I wrong?"

The poor soldier looked quite distraught over his indecision but he finally relented, giving in to Holmes' friendly persistence as so many others had. "All right," he said, lowering his voice to a near whisper, "but for God's sake we must be quiet. Go ahead, open the door."

It opened easily and quietly, despite the fact that it had obviously remained closed for some time. A musty odor of old carpeting and dusty wood emanated from within. We stepped inside, with Devereaux nervously bringing up the rear.

We found ourselves in a narrow vestibule, of perhaps ten feet in length, with walls papered in a floral print of dusty rose. There were two inner doors within this vestibule, both closed. One lay directly before us, at the end of the corridor. The other was immediately to our left.

"More likely than not, Booth used that door simply to view the box itself," Devereaux said softly, pointing at the door to our left. "There is a hole in the wood, made with a gimlet, which would have allowed him to view the scene within before he made his entry. The door at the end of the hall is the one by which he made that entry."

"Yes, yes," said Holmes, obviously fascinated with the details of our surroundings. "But before he did that he secured this outer door first. Do you see? The chipped plaster, where he inserted the plank to prevent anyone from hindering him during the commission of his crime, is clearly visible here." The detective carefully studied a jagged groove in the wall, running his fingers along its dusty surfaces. "A crude but effective means of securing the door, cut laboriously with a small pen-knife, probably during the afternoon before the murder," Holmes mused. "Booth probably spent no more than ten minutes on the job."

Holmes turned on his heel abruptly and headed for the door at the end of the hall. He turned the tarnished knob, causing the door to open with a mournful groan. The three of us walked carefully, almost reverently, into the small room where the act of assassination had taken place.

With a moth-eaten crimson carpet I suspected dated from the time of the crime, and the tattered lace remnants which served only to remind one of the once elegant draperies, the box looked ghostly and forlorn. It was bereft of any furniture or other objects.

Holmes walked purposefully to a spot on the left side of the box, only a few feet from the doorway which once served to permit John Wilkes Booth. "What do you say, lieutenant?" he said. "Would Lincoln's rocking chair have been placed right about here?"

Devereaux gulped loudly and said in a rather shaky voice, "Yes, Mr. Holmes, I would think it sat right about there."

The detective took a step back away from the spot, held out his right arm as if he were leveling a gun, and raised it to the approximate height of the head of a tall man who would have been sitting there.

"Here is where the fatal sequence began," he said in an eerily quiet but charged voice. "Booth entered without being noticed by anyone in the box. Here sat Lincoln. To his right, in another chair, sat his wife. To her right, on the far end of a small sofa, sat Major Harry Rathbone, the Lincolns' guest for the evening. At the far right, in a chair immediately next to the rail, sat Miss Clara Harris, Major Rathbone's fiancée."

He continued, still holding his arm at that terrible angle. "A man from one of the boxes on the other side of the theater, over there"— Holmes pointed to a similar box across the house—"saw the dark figure of Booth as he silently approached Lincoln from behind. He also saw the president's head move sharply to his left, as if he'd heard or felt something behind him.

"And that was the moment of history, gentlemen, the point of no return for victim and assassin alike. Booth fired the derringer into Lincoln's head just as the laughter from the audience was at a loud pitch—Booth knew the play well, remember—and hardly a soul heard the gun's report. As the president slumped suddenly in his chair, even his wife, sitting only inches away, didn't immediately realize what had taken place. She heard something loud, surely she smelled the acrid smoke of the gunpowder, she certainly saw the stranger standing be-hind her husband, but she thought that Lincoln had merely fallen asleep. That is how suddenly and surely the assassin struck."

Holmes lowered his arm at last. "Booth dropped his derringer here, well aware, obviously, that it was but a single-ball weapon, and took his knife into his right hand. He may have said the word 'free-dom' in a soft voice. He made for the railing, but Major Rathbone, who was beginning to realize what had taken place, moved to block the assassin's way. Booth reacted swiftly, slashing the major frightfully upon his forearm. Rathbone made for him again but Booth managed to thrust him aside, and gained the railing at last."

At this point, I must admit, both Devereaux and myself were astonished at Holmes' next move. He grasped the none-to-sturdy railing and lifted himself onto it with both feet, steadying himself by clutching the vertical beam between the towering arches which enclosed the box.

"Holmes, wait a minute," I said.

"Mr. Holmes, really, I think you shouldn't be up there—" Devereaux began.

The detective waved both of us off.

"Booth stood here but for a moment, made a move to steady himself, and then leapt to the stage below." Holmes said these words at the very moment he made the historical leap himself.

As Devereaux and I rushed to the railing we heard Holmes land loudly on the wooden stage some ten feet below. He paused for a second and then slowly raised himself back to a full stance. There was an intense, almost dreamy look in Holmes' eyes as he looked back up at us.

"In Booth's case," he said, "that fall broke a small bone in his lower left leg, the result of his boot-spur having caught the folds of a flag used to decorate the box. It caused the assassin to make his way clumsily and perilously across the stage." Holmes rose his right hand high into the air, as if he himself were clutching Booth's bloody knife. "He looked directly at the audience and shouted *Sic Semper Tyrannis!* and 'The South is avenged!' before heading for the wings there, at stage right, to the left side of the stage from the audience's perspective. The only person upon the stage at that moment was the actor Harry Hawke, who wisely stepped back from this madman he recognized all too well."

Holmes began to imitate the clumsy motions Booth must have made as he struggled diagonally across the stage, dragging his left leg stiffly behind him as he went. It was an eerie, frightening sight.

"The creeping fingers of pandemonium were only now beginning to grip the audience in Ford's Theater," he said. "Mrs. Lincoln, realizing the tragedy at last, finally screamed. Major Rathbone cried out loudly 'Stop that man!' but nobody from the audience was fast enough to do so; Booth's margin of escape was miniscule, but it was sufficient, gentlemen. It was sufficient."

As Holmes suddenly and nonchalantly sat upon the dusty stage,

Devereaux and I seemed to awaken from the spell of his powerful reenactment of the deed. "Holmes!" I shouted to him from the box. "Are you quite all right? You took quite a fall there. I can't believe you actually—"

"Quite well, thank you, Watson. Lieutenant Devereaux, I apologize for abusing your facility thusly, but thank you for indulging my curiosity on that particular point. Come on down, gentlemen. The most dramatic part is over, but we've still a few feet of theater to walk through."

I glanced at Devereaux, who appeared to have grown rather pale, and suggested we take Holmes' advice. He merely shrugged, and the two of us made our way back down to the main floor where we joined Holmes on the stage. Fortunately for Devereaux, it appeared that the commotion caused by Holmes' melodramatic leap seemed to have attracted the attention of no-one else in the building.

"The story is almost complete," said Holmes, who was now puffing away contentedly on his cherrywood. "The final portion involves Booth's rapid rush through the wings. He encountered the leading lady, Laura Keene, within that passageway, and thrust her roughly aside. He also ran into the orchestra conductor, and injured the man with his knife. When he reached the alley, he found the boy Peanut John faithfully holding his horse. With a savage kick, he got the boy out of the way and mounted his steed. It was then, of course, that the real escape of Booth can be said to have started. For the sake of thoroughness, lieutenant, shall we follow those steps as well?"

We made a rapid inspection of the cluttered and dark backstage area, traversing the narrow passageway Booth used to gain the alley behind the theater. When we reached the door, the three of us went outside and blinked against the sudden light.

"This is Baptist Alley," Holmes said, tapping his foot upon the worn bricks of the pavement. "It is, as you can see, Watson, an L-shaped alley, with its terminus here at the rear of Ford's and its open end on F Street. To reach the street from here, Booth would have headed straight back from the theater, turned sharply left with the alley, and then onto F Street. It is an ideal passage for escape for any number of reasons, not the least of which is the fact that Booth's direction once on F Street would have been invisible to anyone pursuing him from the theater on foot."

Holmes folded his arms together and smiled. He was obviously pleased with his examination of the old theater, as he tended to be whenever he was closely inspecting the scene of a crime. He turned to Devereaux with an outstretched hand. "Lieutenant," he said, "I must thank you for being such an affable and patient host. I appreciate your trouble."

Devereaux smiled weakly and nodded. "Glad to be of service, Mr. Holmes," he said, "but I've got to admit that you've made me more than a little uncomfortable with the old barn."

"Why is that?"

"I've been working here every day for two years, sir, and obviously I've been aware of what happened here, but it never really bothered me. Until today, that is. When you jumped from the box and stood on the stage, well, I guess I just saw everything a bit too clearly. I guess it's the first time I've ever really understood what happened here."

"I know exactly how you feel, Lieutenant Devereaux," Holmes said, "for I think I am finally beginning to understand it myself."

—12—
The Road to Garrett's Farm

In the long years of my association and friendship with Sherlock Holmes, I would come to know well indeed the various symptoms which indicated without fail the onset of one of his obsessions. There sometimes came a point in his investigation of a particular case where his devotion to that case transcended mere professional interest and personal curiosity, and was replaced with an almost fanatical determination to find the answer.

Such was now the case, although during our trip to Washington that summer I was not yet clear as to the precise clues which announced the obsessive state. They were all present nonetheless—the reluctance to engage in any activity outside the parameters of the investigation itself, including the function of eating; the long sleepless nights spent pondering possibilities from within a thick plume of tobacco smoke; the virtually endless discussion of the case and its different facets, often as if speaking to himself and oblivious to all others.

Immediately upon leaving Ford's Theater the day before, Holmes had insisted that we cross the street to the plain and humble four-story house where the president had died. Holmes somehow prevailed upon the landlady of the house to permit us entrance; to allow us to view the small bedroom to which Lincoln had been taken, with its metal-framed bed that had proven much too small for his frontiersman's frame; to take from a cedar chest the ghastly blood-stained pillow slip upon which the president's head had rested; even to show us the tiny dooryard where the timeless lilacs were said to have been in bloom on that April night.

We'd rushed from there back to our rooms at the National where

I, glad for a chance at rest, immediately partook of an afternoon nap. Holmes, however, sat himself Indian fashion upon the davenport, poured a large pile of shag onto a newspaper before him, and proceeded to contemplate whatever findings he had been able to gather thus far. He forewent his dinner that evening and, so far as I know, spent the entire night in much the same position.

He rose, however, even before the pale Washington dawn and roused me from my sleep. I was informed that we would be taking a trip this day and that Holmes should like to gain an early start.

"Where to?" I grumbled dreamily.

"Why to Garrett's farm, of course, Watson."

"And where in blazes is that?"

"Northern Virginia, don't you remember? It is where Booth's luck finally ran out, where the Union troops caught up with him. It just occurred to me last night that while we are in Washington the opportunity to trace Booth's route of escape shouldn't be missed. We'll track his movements as if he and Davey Herold were still out there in the swamps."

I rose to a sitting position. "Isn't that route a trifle rustic?" I asked.

"Quite," said Holmes. "That's precisely why I selected good riding horses for the two of us, old fellow. The man at the stable tried to sell me an old Conestoga wagon, canvas cover and all, which had obviously seen much hard service out West. I knew it couldn't handle the terrain through southern Maryland."

"Horses? Really, Holmes—"

"Tut, Watson. We're both young and fit, suitably familiar with the equestrian art. Besides, it's really the only mode of travel available to us. Come, get ready."

In a half hour's time, therefore, I found myself clopping rather clumsily upon a sturdy gelding of dapple grey while Holmes rode confidently on a chestnut mare beside me. The morning sun was just peeking over the eastern horizon and the early air was fresh and cool.

We started at the L-shaped alley behind Ford's, with Holmes recalling the scene of Booth's frantic exit from it just moments after the shooting. From there, Holmes seemed to know the route in perfect detail. We took F Street eastward from the alley's opening, past the Herndon House and Patent Office to Fifth Street. We stayed on this thoroughfare past the shady trees of Judiciary Square, to the diagonal Indiana Avenue, which took us past the splendid Capitol building on its back side. We passed around its south side on Pennsylvania Avenue, entering now a district of squalid shantytowns. We were a rather odd sight to these impoverished Negro citizens, I'm sure—two properly-attired British gentlemen trotting through their district, quite obviously intent on some hidden purpose, some mysterious pursuit.

To hear Holmes relate Booth's flight through these streets, however, really did give the ride the feel of a genuine pursuit. "Now when Booth and Herold actually met up has, of course, never been determined," he said as we entered Eleventh Street. "It was almost surely not here in the Anacostia district of the city, but after they had reached the Maryland shore on the far side of the Navy Yard Bridge. Either way, as I've said, they were the only two conspirators who made the rendezvous. There were a few eyewitnesses to the early stages of the flight, when Booth was alone, but it is certain that nobody interfered with the assassin during his ride through the city. After all, why should they? Booth was riding well ahead of the news he had created at Ford's."

Before long, the massive and well-guarded Washington Navy Yard loomed to our right. We could see before us the bridge named after it, the route which had provided Booth with a successful escape from the city. It was a narrow and low structure of wooden construction, spanning the moderate expanse of the Anacostia tributary. We stopped at the very foot of the bridge, near a small grove of hungry-looking trees and a two-story frame dwelling.

"There was a guardhouse here in eighteen sixty-five," Holmes said. "It was being manned under old wartime regulations on the night of the murder, meaning that it was essentially closed and under the watch of an army sentinel. During much of the war nobody had been allowed to pass the bridge from either side after the hour of nine o'clock, but with the war several days over, these regulations were already being relaxed to a great degree.

"Booth approached the guardhouse at a gallop, alone. He was challenged by the sentry, a Sergeant Silas T. Cobb, who quite rightly asked Booth for his name and his business. Obviously, the sergeant had no idea that Lincoln had been shot just thirty minutes before. And it is at this moment, Watson, that something occurred which troubles me still. What did the assassin do when pressed for his name? He said 'Booth' very clearly! I fail to understand it. By giving his real name, Booth put his pursuers at a tremendous advantage. They learned his precise route of escape, and they were made sure of their man. He lied that he was starting out for his home in Beantown on the Maryland side, and that he'd waited for the late hour in order to ride homeward with the light of the moon. As I said, the regulations were being relaxed. Sergeant Cobb allowed Booth to pass the bridge with no further hindrance. Some ten minutes later, he would do the same for Herold, who used a similar explanation for riding past the Army curfew."

We headed our horses onto the planks of the bridge. The trek across the muddy Anacostia took but a few moments, and in no time at all we found ourselves in a small cluster of houses and trees that immediately gave way to open country to the south of us.

"When you consider that Booth had shot Lincoln less than an hour prior, you must recognize that the first leg of his escape went splendidly," Holmes said, lighting his pipe with a match scratched along his horse's harness. "He had stayed clear of his immediate pursuers and managed to leave the District of Columbia despite the curfew regulations. He must have waited here on the Maryland side for Atzerodt and Payne, at least for a period, and was likely disappointed when he realized that they wouldn't make it."

We turned our mounts around to view the narrow track which wound ahead of us into the remote country of southern Maryland. The land here was mostly open and flat, fairly well-kept in tilled fields, and marked here and there with small groves of trees, farmhouses and barns.

"This is where we leave civilization as we're accustomed to it, Watson," Holmes said. "For the next few days, we shall travel through the wilderness, just as Booth did. I've brought plenty of water and tobacco, and I'm sure we'll be able to secure proper food, if not lodging, along most of the way. Shall we commence our sojourn?"

The road, it seemed, was virtually ours, so scarce was other traffic.

It was a seldom-used track, of value really only to the local farmers and those relatively few people who lived in these environs in a scattering of small, out-of-the-way towns. We passed through the pleasant countryside at a fair trot, the only sound reaching our ears besides the hoofbeats of our horses being the droning cicadas and an occasional meadowlark's singsong in the warm morning.

"Booth and Herold, of course, would have been traveling this road at a rather faster clip," Holmes said at one point, "although certainly not at a full gallop. They knew that they had a considerable distance before them, and wouldn't have wanted to exhaust their mounts prematurely. They left the outskirts of the city at ten-thirty, perhaps eleven o'clock that night, and arrived at Surrattsville about midnight. We will make the same spot after two and a half hours, which indicates the difference in speed."

"That's a rather good pace to keep considering it was the dead of night, Holmes."

"It is, but they had a nearly full moon to help guide them, and a hearty dose of desperation to help motivate them. Still, with Booth's leg broken, the pain must have been growing steadily worse. It was no small feat, the midnight ride of John Wilkes Booth. Because of his injury, it was doomed from the very beginning, of course, but it was quite a notable effort nonetheless."

By midmorning we reached the tiny settlement of Surrattsville, surrounded by dense groves of elm trees. We had little trouble finding the simple tavern once owned by the unfortunate Mary Surratt, and no trouble in persuading the present innkeeper to let us have a quick look around the rustic old place. It was an ordinary roadhouse in all respects, with facilities to provide the traveler with food (of which we partook in lieu of the breakfast we'd missed earlier) and drink (which we declined). The building itself was of the plain "cracker box" type: two stories in a rectangular shape beneath a steep roof from which two chimneys protruded.

After breakfast the innkeeper took us to one of the upstairs rooms and showed us a tiny garret in which Booth's secretive parcel had been hidden by John Lloyd, the man who was running the inn for Mrs. Surratt. A small space had been carved out of the ceiling timbers, the chisel marks still visible.

Later, we stood outside on the pathway that wound before the inn. "Booth's parcel was duly handed over by Lloyd as Booth sat here atop his horse," Holmes told me. "It contained a compass and a field glass, valuable articles for any man on the run in the outback. They also took a carbine which John Surratt had left at the inn earlier. As Booth and Herold rapidly took a drink of whiskey, they told Lloyd—who was himself drunk—that they were 'pretty sure' they'd just assassinated the president. After a stay of no more than five minutes, they resumed their flight."

We did precisely the same thing, heading out once more into the bucolic countryside. We said little to one another as the day grew steadily warmer and the roadside no more busy. At noon we passed through a tiny crossroads village by the enigmatic name of T.B., a sleepy little settlement of four or five buildings, and once more found ourselves in the wilderness.

"You'll notice, Watson," Holmes said when we were a few miles beyond T.B., "that the escape route tends toward the southeast, not directly southwards, which I believe was the preferred direction."

"You're right, but why, Holmes?"

"The shortest route would have taken them, on a better highway, the Coach Road, almost due south to Port Tobacco on the Potomac River. That would have afforded them the quickest fording of the river and entrance into Virginia, whose people Booth believed would offer him sanctuary. I suspect that this was indeed Booth's original plan after having secured his weapons and equipment at Surrattsville. At about this point in the ride, however, they headed in a southeasterly direction along this remote course, despite its difficult backcountry terrain."

"Your point is well taken, Holmes, but still I can't imagine why he would have chosen the harder route."

"His injury, Watson. Booth's leg was growing increasingly more painful. By the time he and Herold left Surrattsville, he must have realized that he'd soon be needing medical attention. It so happened that he had had a brief acquaintance with a physician who lived along this road."

"Of course," I said. "Dr. Mudd."

"Precisely. Booth had met him on at least one of his forays into this country in previous months, and once in Washington. They had discussed horse sales, land investments, and possibly contraband work for the Confederacy, since Mudd was known to be a sympathizer, and possibly a supporter, of that cause. We should reach the doctor's house well before sunset, and I'm very much hopeful that we'll find him in."

As it turned out, we did. On the way, we spent much of the afternoon in idle conversation, with Holmes speculating on various aspects of the escape. As five o'clock approached, Holmes reined his horse to a halt. Next to us was a long and narrow drive bordered with rough birch poles for a fence. It led to a well-kept, if not particularly handsome, frame house of considerable size. Beyond it we could see the solitary church steeple of the little settlement of Beantown, a few miles due west of us.

"The home of Dr. Samuel Mudd," Holmes announced, "who joined Samuel Arnold and Michael O'Laughlin in the devilish Dry Tortugas, simply for setting the broken leg of a man who chanced to knock on his door at dawn on April fifteenth, eighteen sixty-five. We'll be unannounced, Watson, but I think we should knock on that door ourselves. Shall we?"

"What do we have to lose, Holmes?"

We rode up the drive and dismounted at the front of the dwelling. We ascended the small wooden porch and knocked upon the door. It opened almost immediately.

The man who greeted us was slender and balding, with thinning whiskers of a reddish hue on his chin and a tiny pair of gold spectacles perched over his sharply blue eyes. He wore a nicely-cut black waistcoat in the familiar style of American country doctors, and showed some of the same telltale signs of yellow fever that I had detected on the face of Samuel Arnold. His generally thin and pale appearance, in fact, convinced me that Dr. Mudd, despite his relative youth, was not at all a well man. His imprisonment had clearly taken a considerable toll of him.

"Yes?" Dr. Mudd said with a faint trace of caution in his voice. "What can I do for you gentlemen?" His accent was drawn out and elegant in the fashion of the gentleman planters from the antebellum South.

"I am Sherlock Holmes, a consulting detective from London, and this is my companion, Dr. John Watson, a physician. The purpose of our visit, to be perfectly direct, Dr. Mudd, is to seek information."

The doctor nodded knowingly and shook each of our hands in turn. "Always a pleasure to meet a colleague," he said to me. Turning to Holmes, he said, "I needn't speculate on the nature of the information you seek. You're obviously not from the vicinity. There could be but one subject of interest to you—John Wilkes Booth, of course."

Holmes seemed almost apologetic when he nodded his head in the affirmative.

"I have little problem with that, as you appear to be honourable fellows. I would like to know, however, your reasons for seeking such information. My wife has supper on the table. Why don't you join us in our repast, allow me to learn something of yourselves, and then we can discuss the unpleasant events in which you are interested?"

"We would be honoured," I told him.

He beckoned us inside, where we found a comfortable and well-appointed dwelling, kept spotlessly clean and neat, fairly filled with a complement of little children, all of whom presented as fresh and scrubbed appearance as the house itself. Dr. Mudd introduced us to his wife Frances, who smiled sweetly and seemed quite unperturbed at this unannounced intrusion of strangers into her home.

We dined on hearty country chicken at a table huge enough to allow all the children a place, answering the doctor's well-phrased questions as he sat, patriarch-like, at the head of his table. He wanted to know the purpose of our trip to the United States, the nature of our visit into the lower peninsula of Maryland and what interest we had in the Lincoln murder and Booth escape. Mudd discussed these topics with total frankness before his family, impressing me as a man with a healthy streak of caution, but of an overall generous and honest disposition.

Holmes answered forthrightly, up to a point. While he did name his client as Edwin Booth, he stated merely that his interest in Mudd's knowledge of the assassination was to help him identify a link between that crime and certain incidents that had plagued Edwin recently. Mudd seemed quite satisfied with the explanation.

"I never met Edwin Booth," he said at the conclusion of dinner, after the children had been excused, "but he does play a minor role in my own story, or at least his image does. I made the discovery, you see, that on the second visit to my house of the soldiers pursuing the fugitives through this district, that the photograph they carried was not the right one. They produced a photo and asked me whether that man had been the one who had visited my house in need of medical care. I answered that it was not, which was honest and correct, for the photograph, unbeknownst to me at the time, was one of Edwin, and not John Wilkes Booth."

This immediately caught Holmes' attention.

The doctor continued. "It seems that all the troops in the first few days after the crime were carrying pictures of Edwin Booth. Now perhaps that's understandable, since all was confusion for a while there, and it's true that it wasn't immediately clear which of the Booth brothers had been the killer. I must tell you though that I don't believe that for a minute, sir. It must have been the dirty work of Edwin Stanton. He wanted to confuse his witnesses. He wanted us to answer honestly that we didn't recognize that face so that we would appear dishonest later on, when he might be able to show that the real assassin had indeed been seen in the area among us. That's how hungry that man was for vengeance."

Holmes leaned closer to him. "You're suggesting that the Secretary of War, no less, deliberately interfered with the identification of the suspect. What a fascinating notion."

Mudd frowned. "It's not so fascinating, Mr. Holmes, when you realize that such chicanery put Mary Surratt into the noose. It's not so fascinating to me, after missing the same fate by only one vote of the military commission and gaining instead the tortures of Fort Jefferson. It's nothing less than evil, Mr. Holmes. I am told that Stanton died by his own hand, that he cut his throat because he was haunted by the vengeful wraith of Mrs. Surratt. Now I don't put much stock in ghost stories, gentlemen, and I can't honestly say I know whether the old man really put a blade to his own neck, but— Lord forgive me—I have often wished it were so. I really have."

"Do you consider it likely, Dr. Mudd, that Stanton may have had a hand in the assassination itself, and wanted to set up innocent people such as yourself as the perpetrators?"

"Oh no, not that. Stanton wouldn't have killed Lincoln. He was as loyal as a good dog to old Abe. It was all Booth's doing, plain and simple, with a little help from the others, Payne, Herold and that German fellow. Those four were as guilty as sin itself, but old Stanton, you see, wasn't satisfied with them. He wanted as many defendants as his troops could round up. He wanted to slake his own bloodlust, and that of what he felt was the nation's need for revenge and justice. He believed there had to be a show trial, something sensational, and that, Mr. Holmes, is why Mrs. Surratt was hung, that's why Mike O'Laughlin, Sam Arnold, Ned Spangler and myself went to Fort Jefferson. I grew quite close to poor O'Laughlin at Jefferson, you know. As innocent as a child he was, and he died pitifully in my arms, leaving his last words with me. And Ned Spangler, whose only crimes were to have known and worked for the Booth family and to have uttered a profanity against Lincoln's name. He came to me here, you know, after they freed him from Jefferson, an utterly broken man. Broken physically, mentally and spiritually. I gave him five acres to work behind the house, in order to give his last days some trace of dignity. It took less than two years for him to die."

The doctor rose from the table and threw his linen napkin down in a gesture of anger and frustration. "These stories, gentlemen, and my own story, are the true legacies of Edwin Stanton."

At the doctor's suggestion we retired to the lawn, where the cool of the evening was beginning to push back the steamy heat of the day. One of his daughters brought us mint juleps as we sat on comfortable wicker chairs before the house, and Mudd patiently filled his pipe with tobacco from an orange tin bearing the likeness of Sir Walter Raleigh.

"As surely as I smoke this pipe," he said, "the United States government wanted my hide, and when they couldn't get it on their gallows at Old Capitol Prison, they tried to break me as a man. Well, they've given it a good try, I must admit. I once owned five hundred acres in this county; now I own and farm but a tiny fraction of that. The rest had to be sold off during my imprisonment. The servants all had to be let go. I know my health is not good—surely you can see that too, Dr. Watson.

The Dry Tortugas do not spare one's health. And my name has been ruined in many places. There's a saying now—'Your name is Mudd'—to be used as an insult. What a legacy to leave! But for all that, gentlemen, I am not a broken man. I am alive, I am a free man living in my own home on my own land, and no matter what the rest may say, you'll not find a gentleman in this county who will disparage my good name. In that vein, I see myself as victorious over my oppressors."

Mudd smiled between the pipe clenched in his teeth. "Now there. I've made my speech. Even though I'm sure you didn't come here to discuss my hardships, that shall be the price of your questions. What do you wish to know?"

Holmes sipped thoughtfully at his drink and put his first question to the doctor. "A central issue to me," he said, "is one of identification. I am intrigued, doctor, and have long been so, by your statement that you didn't recognize Booth on the morning of his visit to your house."

"I see you get right to the heart of the matter. Fair enough. As I said, I was shown the photograph of Edwin Booth by the investigators some six days after Booth and Herold left here. I said truthfully that I didn't recognize that man as my visitor, but truth to tell, had they shown me a photograph of John Wilkes Booth instead I would have had the same answer for them. I simply did not recognize the man who visited me that morning as either of the Booths, or as anybody else for that matter."

"Yet it's well known you knew Wilkes Booth."

"That's true. I did know the man, or was at least acquainted with him, although I cannot say that I was fond of him. I had met him twice before. The first time was in November of 'sixty-four, at St. Mary's Church, perhaps a mile from here. He was introduced to me as a man interested in purchasing land in the neighborhood, and horses. He was vague on his reasons but he seemed at first to be an honest enough fellow. I even discussed the possibility of selling him some of my own holdings, but that never came to pass. On that Sunday, however, I took him home for dinner with my family. He was a gracious guest, I suppose, although he asked too many questions about the political sympathies of the local folk, about the roads and the contraband trade. It sounds absurd now, gentlemen, but I suspected him to be a Union spy seeking information on the Secesh folks in these parts. All the same, he spent the night here and I took him into Bryantown the next morning, where he purchased a horse from a friend of mine.

"I did not see him again for several weeks. It was then just before Christmas and I was in Washington to purchase presents. He hailed me on the street. On this occasion he inquired as to whether I knew a man by the name of John Surratt—which I did—and requested that I introduce the two of them. I did so, that very evening in fact, at Booth's rooms at the National Hotel. He asked of Surratt many of the same questions he'd asked of me earlier—information on the environs and Confederate activities in this part of Maryland. This must have been his motive in meeting Surratt. Although I had no way of realizing it at the time, his conspiracy must have already been underway. I regret to say that I had a hand in it, but the truth is that Surratt and Booth took to one another famously, despite my warnings to the former that Booth was possibly untrustworthy."

"So that was the last you saw of Booth until . . ."

"Until the morning of April the fifteenth, yes, although I swear to both of you, as I swore to the men who interrogated me, that I did not know the man on that occasion. Mr. Holmes, I'm not above admitting that I used terribly bad judgment in much of this matter. I handled the interrogations badly. I was dishonest even, in describing my past dealings with Booth. These were costly mistakes, and believe me, I've paid dearly for them, but on that one point—the recognition of Booth—I have told nothing but the truth. When he rode to this house at four a.m. and left here at four p.m. on the same day, I had no idea who the man was."

"He was, of course, disguised during the entire time."

"Yes. Herold knocked on the door at dawn. It was raining heavily at the time. He immediately gave me false names—Henston and Tyson, or Tyler—and he subsequently did all the talking. He said they had been traveling north to Washington when his friend's horse stumbled in a hole in the road. He feared that his leg had been broken. The stranger, who was still mounted, wore a woolen shawl up to his chin. I noticed that he had grey whiskers, and it seemed to me that they were false."

"His general appearance," Holmes said, "must have resembled Booth's in any case."

"He seemed to be a man of a hundred and fifty or a hundred and sixty pounds, well-formed physically, with black hair, worn rather long and inclined to be curly. The skin was fair, perhaps pale from his injury. Yes, the general description does fit Booth. I realize this now."

"His leg, of course, was indeed broken."

"Yes, and the swelling had grown severe. I helped the man into the house and tried to remove his boot. He groaned so loudly that I realized it would be too painful for him, so I cut the boot apart with a knife. It was obvious to me that the fibula had been fractured in a straight line, about two inches above the ankle. I devised a splint for the leg. Now Herold, or Henston as he called himself, was anxious to be off, but the stranger—the man who must have been Booth—insisted on rest. I took him upstairs to the guest room and provided him a bed. Herold had breakfast at our table and I went out to work in the fields for a spell."

"I understand they stayed on through much of the day."

"Yes, they did. The stranger remained in his bed, refusing the meals my wife brought up to him, and speaking barely a word to her. Herold, however, made a couple of requests of me. First he said he would like a razor for his friend. He said that a shave would make him feel better."

"Which must have struck you as a strange request," Holmes said.

"It did, and even more so when I saw later that the man had shaved off his moustache only, leaving the beard in place. I was indeed suspicious, but you must realize that word of the assassination had yet to reach us out in the country. This was a place, after all, where a great many suspicious characters passed in those days, a nest for Northern and Southern spies alike. I figured he must have had his reasons for doing what he did. At any rate, Herold then asked whether I could help him obtain a carriage with which to transport his companion back to the city. I had none available, but asked him to accompany me on my afternoon rounds and trip to Bryantown. Perhaps we'd find someone who could loan him a conveyance."

"Which did not happen."

"No, Mr. Holmes. We visited my father's place nearby first, but he would not part with his—he needed it for Easter services on the following day. We had no further luck so Herold left me just before we reached Bryantown. He returned to the farm and roused his companion. When I returned home later, the two of them were already mounted and on the road, ready to leave. Herold thanked me and gave me twenty-five dollars for my services. They rode away and it was the last I ever saw of them."

"By then I assume you'd heard news of the assassination?"

"I heard of it in Bryantown, yes. The town was already filled with cavalry."

"Did Herold realize this during his ride with you?"

"Oh, yes. We saw the troops from the outskirts of Bryantown. I am sure this is why he left me then."

"At this point in time, Dr. Mudd, were you still not suspicious of your visitors?"

"As I said, I was suspicious of them even before learning the dreadful news. After returning home I certainly began to suspect a connection. I wanted to report them that evening, in fact, but my wife was fearful to be left alone in the house. Some of the Confederate raiders were said to still be active in the woods. We knew them to be a bad lot, not above robbery or worse, as they were desperate men. And so I stayed with her. That was the first in my series of mistakes regarding the visitors, gentlemen. I reported their visit too late to be of any use to Booth's pursuers; I lied about the number of times I'd met Booth previously; I forgot about Booth's damnable boot, which I'd thrown beneath a bed in my house, a boot which happened to have 'J. Wilkes' written inside it. As it turned out, I nearly tied the noose around my own neck because of my fear and negligence. I have no excuses for any of it, and it's far too late to be regretting it now."

We all fell silent as the dusk descended on the farm, turning the sky to a deep bottle blue and bringing forth the mournful calls of the nightingales and whipoorwills. Mudd absolutely refused to allow us to make our camp within his barn, and virtually ordered us to take our rest in his upstairs guest room.

He wished us goodnight as we prepared to settle in the two simple beds in the sparsely furnished room. "You don't mind, I hope," he said, "that this is the very room Booth used while he stayed here?"

"Not at all," Holmes answered. "In fact, doctor, we're beginning to grow quite accustomed to such things."

We left Dr. Mudd's residence well before sunrise the next morning, after he carefully instructed us on the proper route to take, much as he had instructed two other travelers, far more desperate than us, 16 years ago. After a hearty breakfast and a warm farewell from the doctor and his wife, we rode almost immediately into the forbidding depths of a vast tract of land known as Zeckiah's Swamp.

"It stretches virtually to the end of the Maryland landmass at the Potomac River," Holmes said as the foliage began to grow dense and close around us. "It was a painfully slow route for the fugitives to have chosen since, as you can plainly see, the roads here are barely more than cart tracks. Still, they must have chosen it after careful deliberation. Their stay at Mudd's had lasted far longer than they had intended when they first arrived. Herold, don't forget, had discovered on his way into town with the doctor that Union troops were already flooding the countryside in search of them, not to mention the many investigative privateers, attracted no doubt by the fabulous monetary rewards which seemed to grow larger by the day. To resume the main turnpikes, whether the Coach Road on the eastern side of the peninsula to Port Tobacco, or the Post Road on the west to Allen's Fresh, would have been suicidal at that late hour. It was by then a full eighteen hours after the murder, and Booth had set the pursuers on his trail even before he left Washington. It was far safer for them to retreat into the shadows of this swamp, awaiting the opportunity to make a Potomac crossing, than to try to make a dash for it then. Still, the six days they spent within this wilderness certainly could not have been easy."

Indeed not. I immediately found myself contemplating with sympathy the mysterious person named Zeckiah, namesake of this place. It was as desolate and uninviting a morass as I'd ever seen, and as dangerous. Mudd had warned us not to stray from the firm ground of the sandy roads and paths, even if the assassins' route which we followed did so, since treacherous fens and quicksands were common here. It was not one continuous marsh, but rather a series of ponds, bogs and sumps of varying sizes, interspersed with sandy fingers of land. Overhead the bushes and trees, gums and dogwoods mostly, formed a cathedral-like ceiling of green which greatly diminished the light, even after sunrise, and plunged all below into deep shadow. The air was filled with the chirping of unseen birds and insects and the atmosphere redolent with the thick fragrance of vegetation.

We rode steadily through the malarial expanse, with Holmes carefully following the map he and Mudd had sketched that morning. To bide the time, we discussed the likelihood of the doctor's guilt or innocence since, to be frank, I was having my doubts on the subject. Holmes asserted that Mudd never would have taken Herold to his father's place in search of a carriage (thus exposing his own father to potential suspicion) nor would he have voluntarily proferred Booth's riding boot to the soldiers, if he had been involved in the conspiracy.

"Booth would have never seen Mudd again," Holmes said, "had he not broken his leg in the fall from the president's box. The injury forced him to depart from his chosen route, the fastest one, to a remote part of the country. It forced him as well to visit the home of a man who had seen him twice before, and who could easily have led Booth's pursuers in the right direction, as he did, albeit in a tardy fashion. The assassin wore a disguise upon arriving at Mudd's home, which is hardly the act of a man who trusts his host. You may rest easy, Watson. Mudd is purely innocent of the crime with which he was charged."

Despite the density of the swamp itself and the ever-increasing humidity and heat, we made excellent progress that day. Holmes seemed rather impatient with this portion of our trek and, characteristically, quite uncomfortable in the midst of such wild surroundings. We paused but briefly therefore at the various points of interest along the way. Holmes noted the crumbling ruins of a cabin once belonging to a Negro named Oswell Swann, who with both the promise of money and the threat of gunpoint, was persuaded to guide Booth and Herold who had soon found themselves hopelessly lost. Swann earned his money well, guiding them some ten miles through the very heart of Zeckiah Swamp, leaving them at its edge, at a spot very near the Potomac River itself.

Here the fugitives received shelter at the hands of a certain Samuel Cox, a Confederate sympathizer and smuggler, and his foster brother Thomas Jones. They would spend six damp and foggy days on Jones' property, Huckleberry Farm, while their protectors sent them food and waited for an opportunity to help them cross the river. Booth and Herold were instructed to kill their horses while at the Huckleberry Farm since the countryside was by then so filled with soldiers it was feared the neighing would give them away. We passed through the same country, taking note of the Cox and Jones farms, and trying to guess where their hideaway clearing might have been.

To the best of our ability we tried to retrace their last steps in Maryland, but since much of it was over cross country routes, we found it difficult going. Booth and Herold left the Jones farm aboard the farmer's small boat, but in eluding a Union gunboat which encountered them in the river, they found themselves washed by the flood tide back against the Maryland shore. They tried again, a day later, with the assistance of another rebel, Colonel John Hughes, and this time were successful in reaching the Virginia shore.

By the time we reached the three-mile expanse of the mighty Potomac River ourselves, it was late afternoon. We picked our way through narrow roads to the dilapidated town of Port Tobacco, and immediately rented the services of a flatboat. We crossed the river, which was very wide here so close to the sea, and as dusk arrived, finally disembarked, exhausted and dirty, in a tiny Virginia settlement called Mathias Point. We rented a shoddy room here, ate a tolerable meal, and with little further conversation between ourselves, immediately began a well-deserved rest.

Morning found both Holmes and I refreshed and eager to resume the small remainder of our trip. He knew we were but fifteen miles or so from the farm where Booth met his tragic end. Once again, therefore, we mounted early and resumed our southward journey, taking a main road which I presumed ultimately terminated in the erstwhile rebel capital of Richmond.

The morning was cool, grey and misty, a welcome relief from the blistering heat of the past few days, and the open hilly country of northern Virginia was a welcome change from the claustrophobic depths of the swamps on the Maryland side. The land was jade green in the grey light, with long open pastures interrupted pleasantly by deep stands of pines and hardwoods. The road was a good one and we made rapid progress.

"Booth and Herold were not greeted with the welcoming arms that the assassin's diary indicates he expected to find here in Virginia," Holmes said. "While nobody they met actually turned them in, nor deprived them of food, it appears that most of the Virginians were either annoyed at the intrusion or distrustful of the strangers. Some of them doubtlessly suspected who these haggard travelers were—Booth's worsening injury was a sure giveaway. It was widely reported that Lincoln's murderer was crippled in the leg and, indeed, Booth found it impossible to travel or walk without a crutch by this time.

"They stopped at the home of a Mrs. Queensberry, near Mathias Point, but when the woman glimpsed the brace of pistols and knives inside Booth's coat she refused to take them in. She sent them to a neighbor instead, William Bryant, who took them eight miles farther south, to the home of a Dr. Richard Stewart, who had apparently been recommended to them by Dr. Mudd. They were being passed from one rebel to another, most of them sufficiently wary to waste little time in palming them off on somebody else. Stewart also refused to take them in, so Bryant took them to the nearby home of a Negro, William Lucas. Booth intimidated this poor man with his weapons and commandeered his house for the night. In the morning they ordered him to drive them to Port Conway in his wagon. Lucas did so, but refused to take them any farther."

At this point in the conversation we rode into the outskirts of the little river town of Port Conway ourselves. The humble but tidy village was situated on the northern shore of the Rappahannock River, about three hundred yards across the river from the larger town of Port Royal on the southern side. As there was no bridge, Holmes and I were forced to await the return of the ferry to take us across.

"Booth faced a similar delay when he reached Port Conway," said Holmes, lighting a pipe as he contemplated the river. "The ferryman told them they would have to await the tide before crossing. While waiting, they chanced upon three men who were also heading in a southerly direction. All of them were disbanded officers of the Confederate persuasion, though still in their grey uniforms. Booth and Herold made their acquaintance, learning that the men were Captain Willie Jett, late of the Virginia Cavalry, Major Mortimer Ruggles, until recently under the command of Mosby the raider, and Lieutenant A.R. Bainbridge, also of Mosby's command. After some cajoling, the fugitives convinced the returning veterans to ferry them across with them, and then to give further assistance once on the southern shore. While they gave false names at first, they apparently trusted the Confederates to the degree that they later admitted to their real names and to their deed. It would appear the soldiers took pity on them."

Soon the ferry returned and took Holmes and me, as well as a handful of other passengers, to Port Royal on the other side. We rode quickly through the town and soon found ourselves in countryside even greener and more pleasant than that through which we had already passed.

Holmes gauged the distance by the milestones along the road, and after a distance of nearly three miles he pulled his horse to a halt.

"This must be it, Watson," he said, pointing to a narrow and overgrown lane which split away from the road. "This leads to the farm once owned by Richard Garrett, tobacco farmer and loyal Confederate. Captain Jett knew this area of Caroline County well, and was aware of Garrett's generosity toward Southerners. The soldiers gained permission from the farmer to allow the fugitives to remain here in safety, at least for a few days. Jett, Ruggles and Bainbridge then resumed their ride toward Bowling Green, a few miles to the south, where Jett had a sweetheart. Herold rode into town with them, either to check on the presence of Union troops or to seek renegade Confederate bands with whom they might gain sanctuary. In either case, he returned here to Garrett's farm the next morning with Bainbridge and Ruggles. It seems the elder Garrett might have known who the strangers really were but if so, he kept this information from his children. To them, Booth identified himself and Herold as brothers by the name of Boyd, claiming to be veterans of A.P. Hill's corps of Confederates."

I gazed at the long and serpentine drive. "Well, Holmes, now that we've arrived at last, what are we to do?"

"We shall see whether the place is still occupied, and if so, whether the Garrett family still lives here."

We had not advanced more than 30 yards up the narrow path before we were greeted by three large dogs which so accosted us with their barking and snarling that they threatened to make our horses bolt. In a moment, however, we heard a man's voice giving the hounds a sharp command to cease. They did so immediately. We then saw a thin and bearded man walking down the path toward us. He was clad in a fading red undershirt and worn denim clothing of the sort Americans call overalls. He had a wide straw hat on his head and carried a large rifle in his arms.

"Who are you and what do you want?" he demanded in a heavy drawl.

Holmes gave him our names. "We are seeking information on the visit to this farm of John Wilkes Booth," he called to the man.

"John Wilkes Booth's been dead a long time," came the drawled reply.

"I should like to speak with a member of Richard Garrett's family," Holmes countered.

"He's my pa and he's been dead a fair piece hisself. I'm Richard B. Garrett."

"Then perhaps I could ask a few questions of you."

"And perhaps you'll listen to me, mister. I don't much cotton to the idea of strangers showing up at my gate with fool questions, and the last thing on God's green earth I wish to speak of is Booth, that son of a—" The man stopped himself, and spit onto the ground. "He brought nothing but grief to my pa and to this farm. I'll have no truck with nosy folks seeking details o' what happened here. Ya'al best be on your way back to wherever you come from."

Holmes parried with him no further, but took instead a shiny half-eagle into his hand and held it aloft. "I'm willing to pay for your time, Mr. Garrett."

The farmer eyed the gold coin warily, looking first at Holmes and then at me as he struggled with the decision. At last he relented. "That'll change the picture I guess," he said. "Lately funds have been lean enough. Come on up to the house and I'll set with you for a spell."

I'm sure it was my imagination, but as we followed Garrett up the pathway into the clearing where his house stood, I immediately had a feeling of deep foreboding. There was an unwholesome air about the place, it seemed, a sensation that it had never totally cleansed itself of the death that had so violently taken place here. I shook off the feeling with effort.

The house itself was a spacious affair, a simple and common clapboard structure of two stories, a wide veranda and two tall chimneys on either side of its gabled roof. Although the fields which spread out widely from the small hill where we stood seemed green and abundant, the house itself and its handful of outbuildings looked rather decrepit. There was need of paint, and the porch had begun an awkward sag.

We joined Garrett as he sat down on the wooden porch and shouted into the house for his wife to bring coffee. A tired-looking woman in a calico apron soon appeared with a blue coffee pot and three tin cups. She poured each of us a strong brew and Garrett began expertly rolling a cigarette from a dried leaf of tobacco.

"The purpose of our visit—" Holmes began.

"I reckon I don't need to know your purposes so long as that gold is good," Garrett said.

Holmes handed him the coin. "I'd like to know—"

"John Wilkes Booth come our way on the twenty-fourth day of April, in the year of our Lord eighteen hundred and sixty-five," Garrett interrupted, lighting his makeshift cigarette. "He was brought here along with his dimwitted partner by three Southern boys, coming home after the fightin' was done. I was eleven years old at the time. My brothers had just come back from the war too—Willie, and John who'd just seen Lee sign the peace with Grant down to Appomattox. Pa took 'em in because he was a Christian soul and a Southern man. On the first night it was just Booth as his buddy rode into town with the soldiers.

"Booth had his supper with us—'course we didn't know who he was at the time—and said his wound was a'painin him something awful, so he went straight to bed up in our room. He got up late the next day and spent the morning layin' out in the grass, not sayin' much to any of us and pretty much keepin' to hisself. But we got to talkin' with him at noontime dinner and, wouldn't you know it, the subject of Abe Lincoln's killin' comes up.

"My brother John had heard from the shoemaker that day about the killing, and he came home wantin' to speak of it. He said he'd heard that the Federals was offering a hunnert an' fifty thousand for Booth. Well, Robert, who was an outspoken cuss like the rest of us, says he'd sure like to get those greenbacks. So Booth asks him if he would really turn the man in, and Robert says he sure would. Joanna, my sister, then says that the killer of Lincoln must have been paid a good price for the crime, but Booth says he figured the assassin did it for the sake of notoriety. He said he saw Booth hisself in Richmond once—imagine that! And Pa says the only Booth he ever heard of was that actor Edwin Booth. This made old John Booth smile, it seemed to me. It was the strangest chat over dinner I'm ever likely to have, I'll tell you that.

"Well, we spent the afternoon with Booth, John and Willie and me, a'shootin at the post you see right there. He was a crack shot, jim dandy. Look there, you can still see his bullet holes in the post. And a little later on, Herold comes back to the farm with a couple of those Southern boys. They all spoke for a piece, then the soldiers left, but they was back in a flash, all flush and excited. They told Booth and Herold that Yankee troops were a'comin down the road that minute, then they took off themselves, lickety-split."

"That must have been the Union detachment," Holmes said, lighting his own cigarette. "Fifty troops under the command of Lieutenant Edward Doherty, accompanied by the Secret Service officers Conger and Baker. They were put on the trail by the ferryman in Port Royal, who had recognized Jett the day before. They were bearing down on Jett in Bowling Green, where they knew he had gone."

"Well, whoever they was, they scared Booth and Herold a good fright. They run off into those woods there and didn't come out 'til supper, when they was sure the coast was clear. My brothers began to get just a little suspicious right around then. You see, Pa, he went to bed early, sayin' he was feelin' poorly, and after supper was done, Booth and Herold tried to talk John into takin' them into Orange Courthouse that night. And they'd spoke of horse thieves just that afternoon, sayin' that they figured that's who the Yankees must have been a'lookin for. Well, with all that talk, and them so anxious to leave, John and Willie took them for thieves themselves. They wouldn't let them sleep in the house or under this porch, but said they'd have to bunk in the tobacco barn. And then, once it got dark and they was asleep, John and Willie snuck out there and put a lock on the barn door. They went to sleep in the corncrib just next to the barn, so's that if there was any trouble at night they'd be able to do something about it."

"May we see it?" Holmes asked Garrett. "The tobacco barn, I mean."

"Well you can see what's left of it," the farmer said, rising. We followed him to a spot perhaps twenty yards behind the house. There was nothing there now to mark the spot but a pile of charred and broken timbers, and a heavy layer of ashes blended with the soil.

"That's all that was left after the fire," Garrett said, kicking the blackened mass with his boot. "Damned government never paid us a cent for destroying Pa's property."

"When did the troops finally get to your house that night?" Holmes asked.

"I'd reckon about two or three in the morning, in the wee hours of the night, anyways."

Holmes turned to me. "The Union detachment found Captain Jett in a hotel room in Bowling Green, Watson, and placed a number of pistols to his head. Jett was sufficiently wise to take their warnings seriously. At midnight he was leading the detachment back up the road to this very spot."

"They tore down the orchard fence and set the dogs to barkin' something awful," Garrett said, resuming the story, "and wakin' up the entire household. There was Yankees and horses runnin' just all over the place. Their officers ordered Pa to come on down and when he did they said they was a'goin' to hang him if he didn't say where the men was hidin'. Well, Pa never knew, you see, for he'd gone to bed early. That's how close those blue devils came to hangin' my Pa, but Willie and John jumped up from out of the corncrib and told the soldiers where the men was hidin'.

"Anyways, the captain of the Yankees, this Doherty fellow, he takes John by the arm and orders him to go on up to the tobacco shed and open the lock, seein's how he had the key. John says fine, but I could tell he didn't much like the notion. But he did nonetheless. Then just as he opens the lock, the captain tells him to go on inside and tell Booth to give hisself up. Well, John is really scared now but I guess he figured that old Booth couldn't have been no worse than that crazy Yankee, so he goes in the shed. I could hear Booth yellin' at him, sayin' that us Garretts had betrayed him and Herold, which was not the truth. He shouts loud enough for the captain to hear that he wouldn't be comin' out no matter what, and that they'd never be takin' him alive. He tells John to get out and I thank God to this day that he didn't put a pistol ball through poor John's head, because he struck me as the sort who could do such a thing."

"He struck you as a madman?" Holmes asked.

"Well, mister, at that moment he was mad as a hare, which is understandable enough, considerin' the predicament he was in."

"How long did the confrontation go on like this?"

"Hard for me to recollect how long it was. Half an hour, maybe more. The captain was yellin' for Booth to surrender and Booth's shoutin' back that he won't do it. He gets to soundin' crazier after a spell. He says he'll come on out if'n the soldiers will move twenty or so yards back from the barn, and that he'll fight 'em, each and every one in their turn. The captain says no way. Booth says somethin' like 'Well boys, you'd better ready up a stretcher for me then, and go on ahead and put another stain on the old banner.' He sounded real actor-like, like he was still on stage or something. Anyway, the captain says he's gettin' ready to put fire to the barn, so Booth better come on out, but Booth just says that Davey Herold wants to come out. He says Herold is innocent of any crime, and here comes Davey Herold, shuttin' the door behind him."

"How did Herold look to you, Mr. Garrett?"

"He was nervous as a cat, I'll tell you. He was all bug-eyed and stammerin' and sayin' fool things like how he used to like Mr. Lincoln's jokes and such. The Yankees got tired of listenin' to him right quick, and tied him to that tree over yonder and said if'n he didn't shut up they'd cut off his head. So he shut hisself up all right."

"What was Booth doing during this time?"

"Well he was a figurin' how to get out of his predicament, you see, because just after Herold comes out of the barn, one of them Yankees in ordinary clothes, one of the detectives, he put fire to a stack of hay upside the back of the barn. It went up right quick, I can tell you. That's when I got a good look at Booth inside, since it was all lit up with fire."

"What was he doing?"

"Well, he was a sorry sight. He was all unshaved and mussed-up lookin' with straw in his hair and all, and had a crazy look in his eyes, like he didn't know what to do. He was a'peerin' through the cracks in the barn slats and pointin' his gun like he was lookin' for someone to shoot at, so Willie and John and Robert and me, we got behind a woodpile. And then we heard the shot."

"The shot that killed Booth?"

"Yes, and then Booth went down."

Holmes stirred the old ashes with a stick and looked back to our host. "So who did it, Mr. Garrett?" he asked directly. "Did Sergeant Boston Corbett kill him or did Booth do it himself?"

"I wouldn't swear on a Bible either way, mister," Garrett said, spitting a coffee grind onto the ground, "but my gut tells me that Booth did it hisself. He had the gun in his hand the whole time, a right handsome pistol, too. Now I couldn't see quite clearly through all the smoke by then, but my guess is that the sergeant took credit for it because he figured he'd get all the reward money. Fact is, his own captain arrested him then and there, for disobeying the order not to shoot. Anyways, from where I was sittin', there's just no way that Corbett could've picked him off from the angle where he was standin'. Besides, he was carryin' a big Yankee Springfield which would've took off most of Booth's head if'n he'd fired it. That's what John told me, and he saw enough of what Springfields could do out on the battlefields."

"I take it then, that Booth's wound was not large."

"It was not. When the soldiers dragged him out of the burnin' barn and laid him over here on the grass, there was plenty of blood comin' out, but if it weren't for that, why you'd have never seen the wound. And it wasn't exactly on his head. It was on his neck, in the back, behind his right ear. The bullet went in one side and come out clean on the other."

"Pray continue, Mr. Garrett," Holmes said.

"In a minute or two the fire got too hot for them to stay so near, so they carried Booth over to the porch. Come on." We followed Garrett back to the sagging porch and sat down with him once again.

"It was comin' on dawn by then, and old Booth, he didn't live much longer. It looked to me like he was in some awful pain, and he was paralyzed, you see. He asked the captain to go ahead and shoot him but the captain says no, Booth was shot against his orders and he wants him to get better. Booth says for the captain to hold up his hands, just so's he could see 'em, and the captain holds 'em up. Seein's how he's paralyzed, Booth just says 'useless, useless.' Ma came out and washed Booth's face once or twice, and tried to give him water, but Booth couldn't take it. And finally, just as the sun's comin' up, old Booth looks up at the captain and says 'Tell mother I died for my country.' That was it. He shakes once or twice and then he's a dead man."

A soft rain began to fall over Garrett's farm and we stood back under the overhang for protection. We remained silent for several minutes, watching the rain green the pastures before our eyes. I'm quite sure that all of us were reliving the pathetic scene that had transpired here.

"What happened next, Mr. Garrett?" Holmes inquired.

"Well, there's not much left to say. My sister Joanna, who still thinks Booth was the most handsome fellow she's ever seen, she cut off a lock of his hair. I still have it in the house, framed on the wall, as a memento of that day. The captain orders the doctor to come over from Port Royal and he arrives a little while later. He certified that Booth was dead."

"How thorough was his examination?"

"The captain was in a big hurry to get the body back up to Washington, so he told the doc to go fast. All he did was check the wound and hold onto his wrist. He put a mirror up to his mouth, too. 'Hurry up!' the captain said. 'It's plain as day this man is dead as a doornail.' So that was that. They sewed the body up in an old blanket and got Ned Freeman, the nigger from down the road, to bring his wagon up. They ordered him to haul the corpse back up to the river with them. Old Ned, being a superstitious nigger, was scared to death, but he did it. He loaded it up and off they went."

Garrett spit out into the grass. "By then the barn was nothin' more than smokin' ashes, the fences was torn down and the neighbors started to thinkin' we were a bunch of traitors. That's what old John Wilkes Booth did for the Garrett family which aided him in his hour of need. He left us a curse, just like Ned Freeman said. You know, up the road a ways, after they left here with the body, Ned's king bolt snapped and he had to get out to fix the wagon. The dead man had done slipped out, and some of his blood got on poor Ned's hands. He swears to this day that it was murderer's blood, and that it'll never really wash off. Scares the daylights out of him still."

Garrett rose and pointed to a dull, rusty stain on the grey and weathered flooring of the porch. "Ned was right too," he said. "That stain's made of Booth's blood, you know. His head was a'lyin' there when he died. It shows up on days like this, when it takes to rain, like Booth hisself is comin' back in a way. Like he'll never be goin' away."

"Just as his crime will never go away," I said. "As lonely and painful as it must have been, it was a fitting death for a man such as he."

Holmes stared closely at the ghastly spot on the porch and said nothing.

—13—
The Lady in Emerald Satin

It was to my considerable relief (and that of my aching bones and muscles) that Holmes chose a more genteel form of transport for our return to Washington. After three blistering days in the saddle, over remote and isolated country, it was gratifying that we would be taking the railroad back.

After leaving the farm of Richard Garrett we rode a few miles into the farming village of Bowling Green. Holmes spent the early afternoon engaged in mercantile activity, namely, the sale of my dapple-grey gelding and his chestnut mare. He concluded the transaction quite quickly, and to the mutual satisfaction of himself and the livery man who purchased them. Thus freed of our encumberances, we were free to board the afternoon run into Washington, some 60 miles to the north of us, on the swaying cars of a backwoods railway called the Richmond, Fredericksburg & Potomac.

Although I was fairly filled with questions for Holmes concerning the nature of our findings over the past few days, my queries came to naught. As soon as the five-car train pulled away from the small siding just outside Bowling Green, its gentle rocking lulled me into a deep and comfortable sleep. I didn't awaken, in fact, until the train lurched to a halt at the Washington depot at about the dinner hour. So complete was my exhaustion, in fact, that I continued the same activity upon returning to our room at the National Hotel. (We took, once again, Booth's one-time lair.) I've no idea how Holmes spent the evening but certainly wouldn't be surprised if he immediately set off on yet another tangent of his historical investigation.

Early the next morning, after I had just emerged from a refreshing shave and bath, I returned to the room to find an utterly new figure awaiting me. It was Holmes, of that there could be no doubt, but I had to blink my eyes once or twice to be sure of that fact. He was attired as nattily as the most elegant of American gentlemen, in a new white linen suit, topped with a wide-brimmed Panama hat. He even sported a new pipe, one of those made of corncob which were so much in vogue among the Americans.

"Good day, Dr. Watson," he said, mocking the light accent of a Washingtonian.

"My but you're a sight, Holmes," I said in surprise. "One would almost think you were about to go courting a lady. If one didn't know you very well, that is."

He feigned a frown. "Don't be so quick to cancel your observations, Watson," he said. "The fact is that I do intend to call upon a lady today, although I'd hardly consider it a courting call. As for the new attire, it is only partially for her benefit. As I'm sure you've discovered by now, the tailors of Carnaby and Bond Streets do not design their wares for comfort in American climes. Besides, when one is in Rome, one is advised to do as the Romans do."

"Who might this lady be?"

"Why not come along and find out, old fellow? And do dress in your finest, would you? The lady in question is one quite accustomed to, shall we say, the finer things in life."

"Actually, Holmes, I'd rather not today. I've never been so sore in all my life. Besides, I'm growing rather weary of all this Wilkes Booth business."

"Tut, Watson," he said. "I intend to wrap up my Washington business this very day. We shall be in New York by evening, I promise you. There are but one or two details to see to, and then the retracing of old steps shall cease."

"No, Holmes, really, I—"

"If I promised you, Watson, that today will almost surely bring something to take the breath away, something highly unexpected, would you then agree to come along?"

How could I refuse? Of course I accompanied him, full in the knowledge that Holmes is the last man to make dramatic predictions without foundation. I dressed myself in my best, therefore, although I certainly did not present nearly so dazzling a figure as did Holmes in his fine white suit. We set out on foot along Pennsylvania Avenue toward the northwest, walking leisurely in the morning air, and appreciating the imposing array of neo-classical official buildings along the way.

After a dozen blocks or so, just after we'd passed the graceful White House itself, Holmes stopped and pointed at a monstrosity of a building which loomed mightily in the morning mist. "We shall begin, Watson, with a visit to the War Department, just there," he said.

The building was a massive affair, supported by what must have been a thousand doric columns, topped with an imposing number of grand mansard roofs and tall chimneys. While in reality nothing more than a large office building, the structure had an air of grandiosity about it that spoke volumes about the emerging American imperial spirit Holmes and I had discussed earlier. It seemed to be calling as much attention to itself as possible.

Its interior was just as grandiloquent, with several stories of cavernous multi-floored balconies, each safely fenced off with ornate iron railings. The labyrinthine corridors culminated in large spiral staircases. Our steps echoed loudly off the oaken and marble walls as we passed through what seemed like miles of such hallways until at last, within a shadowy corner, we found the bureau Holmes was seeking. The words "Judge Advocate General—Evidence and Archives Division" were painted in gold leaf on the frosted glass window of the door. We went inside.

Behind a tall desk sat an Army major in an immaculate tunic of deep blue and gleaming brass. His large head was balding and he seemed to have compensated for this by growing bushy muttonchop whiskers around the sides of his sallow, unsmiling face. He demanded to know the purpose of our visit without making the slightest greeting. Holmes seemed to sense his air of pomposity, for he replied with curtness uncharacteristic of him: "We are here to view the artifacts associated with John Wilkes Booth."

The major's sour face creased into a rather sardonic grin. "Ha!"

he snapped. "You are, eh? And the damned in hell want a drink of cold lemonade too, don't they? Out of the question. That material is not for public display. Why, I can't even see it myself without the permission of the Judge Advocate General himself."

"Consider yourself permitted then," Holmes said coldly, handing over the desk a folded letter. I could just barely see a gold and blue seal upon its letterhead. The major read it rapidly, his bully's grin being quickly replaced with the dyspeptic expression he had worn earlier. Without a word he nodded and turned on his heels into a back section of the office.

Holmes grinned widely at me. "It would seem my letter from the Secretary of State is more effective than I'd ever dreamed," he whispered. "It caught the attention of the Judge Advocate General's secretary immediately, and produced another letter in turn, from the Army's top barrister himself. What a wonderful lubricant influence is, Watson."

The unsmiling major returned after several minutes, struggling with a large black portfolio. He beckoned us inside to a small inner chamber where a long library table stood and placed the portfolio upon it. "You're free to look through the items inside, Mr. Holmes," he said, unfastening the cover, "so long as I'm here to supervise, of course. And do please be careful. These items of Booth's are the property of the United States government now, and constitute important pieces of American history."

"Of course, major," Holmes said warmly, seating himself at the table and rubbing his hands in anticipation. "We shall exercise ultimate care and respect. Do sit down yourself, major, as this may take several minutes."

He joined us at the long table and laid the opened portfolio before us.

The first item we saw was immediately recognizable. "Aha!" cried Holmes. "The infamous boot, ultimately useless to the assassin and nearly lethal to the physician who tried to help him." The brown riding boot, of a full knee-high cut, was wrapped around itself and secured with a cord. Dr. Mudd's knife cut along the front edge was clearly visible as was the fading ink inscription inside which read "J. Wilkes." I noticed the heel still had hardened mud clinging to it. Holmes put it aside after but a cursory look.

The portfolio also contained sundry other articles, which had either been in Booth's possession at the time of his death or had otherwise been considered to be of some value during the conspiracy trial in Washington. We saw a wad of American greenbacks totalling, according to an attached note, $175; a Canadian bill of exchange with Booth's name; a selection of weapons, including the derringer used to murder Lincoln (a surprisingly small and benign looking pistol), a larger pistol (the one used while escaping); a long hunting knife with blood stains still upon its blade (apparently Major Rathbone's) and a holster; a small compass within a leather case; a battered copy of "Perrine's New Topographical War Map of the Southern States"; and a small signal whistle carved of wood.

Holmes glanced knowingly at me, but said nothing, when he next handled a shiny object which appeared to be a badge. The complex design upon it—a Maltese cross with an eight-pointed star and the word "Bickley" in its center—was immediately recognized by me as the grand seal of the Knights of the Golden Circle.

At last Holmes found an object of particular interest to him. It was a small datebook for the year 1864, bound in red morocco leather, of the sort easily available at any stationer's. The slender volume had served as John Wilkes Booth's diary during his desperate last days as a fugitive. Holmes opened it cautiously and, taking his own notebook from his pocket, began rapidly copying the diary's words, reading them aloud as he did so. Written in a shaky hand in fading pencil, it began, strangely enough in Italian, with the enigmatic inscription "*Ti Amo*" (I love you):

> *April 13, 14, Friday, The Ides*
> *Until today nothing was ever thought of sacrific-*
> *ing to our country's wrongs. For six months we have*
> *worked to capture. But our cause being almost lost,*
> *something decisive and great must be done. But its failure*
> *was owing to others who did not strike for their country*
> *with a heart. I struck boldly, and not as the papers say. I*
> *walked with a firm step through a thousand of his friends;*
> *was stopped but pushed on. A colonel was at his side. I*

*shouted Sic semper before I fired. In jumping I broke my
leg. I passed all his pickets. Rode sixty miles that night,
with the bone of my leg tearing the flesh at every jump.*

*I can never repent it, though we hated to kill. Our
country owed all our troubles to him, and God simply
made me the instrument of his punishment.*

*The country is not what it was. This forced union
is not what I had wanted. I care not what becomes of me.
I have no desire to outlive my country. This night (before
the deed) I wrote a long article and left it for one of the
editors of the "National Intelligencer," in which I fully set
forth our reasons for our proceedings. He or the Gov't—*

Friday 21

*After being hunted like a dog through swamps,
woods and last night being chased by gunboats till I was
forced to return wet, cold, and starving, with every man's
hand against me, I am here in despair. And why? For
doing what Brutus was honoured for—what made Tell a
hero. And yet I, for striking down a greater tyrant than
they ever knew, am looked upon as a common cut-throat.
My action was purer than either of theirs. One hoped to be
great. The other had not only his country's, but his own,
wrongs to avenge. I hoped for no gain. I knew no private
wrong. I struck
for my country and that alone. A country that groaned
beneath this tyranny, and prayed for this end, and yet now
behold the cold hand they extend me. God cannot pardon
me if I have done wrong. Yet I cannot see my wrong,
except in serving a degenerate people. The little, the very
little, I left behind to clear my name, the government will
not allow to be printed. So ends all. For my country I
have given up all that makes life sweet and holy, brought
misery upon my family, and am sure there is no pardon in
Heaven for me, since man condemns me so. I have only
heard of what has been done (except for what I did myself)*

*and it fills me with horror. God, try and forgive me, and
bless my mother.*

*Tonight I will once more try the river with the
intent to cross. Though I have a greater desire and almost
a mind to return to Washington, and in a measure clear
my name—which I feel I can do. I do not repent the blow I
struck. I may before my God, but not to man. I think I
have done well.*

*Though I am abandoned, with the curse of Cain
upon me, when, if the world knew my heart, that one
blow would have made me great, though I did desire no
greatness.*

*Tonight I try to escape these bloodhounds once
more. Who, who can read his fate? God's will be done. I
have too great a soul to die like a criminal. O, may He,
may He spare me that, and let me die bravely.*

*I bless the entire world. Have never hated or
wronged anyone.*

*This last was not a wrong, unless God deems it so,
and it's with Him to damn or bless me. And for this
brave boy with me, who often prays (yes, before and since)
with a true and sincere heart —was it crime in him? If so,
why can he pray the same?*

*I do not wish to shed a drop of blood, but 'I must
fight the course.'*

Tis all that's left me.

Holmes sighed and put his own notebook away when he was
finished. "An understandably rambling, fanatical account, wouldn't
you say, Watson?"

"Indeed," I replied. "He compares himself to Brutus and William
Tell, no less, which suggests he saw himself in rather a glorious and
patriotic light. Still, it seems he was trying hard to justify to himself
something he clearly knew was terribly wrong."

"Quite, and there's no real explanation for the murder itself. His
love of country is clear enough, but still somehow insufficient as a

motive. Was it a desire to somehow rekindle the embers of the rebellion? A chance at cementing his name in the history books? Booth never quite says. He alludes to them all, but he never comes out and says it. And what do you make of the fascinating remark that he thought he could clear his name by going back to Washington?"

"Frankly, it puzzles me, Holmes."

"It indicates either the demented illusion that he felt he could somehow justify the act, or that he knew something else which might extenuate his position. If that's the case, it's tragic that he didn't go into more detail."

Holmes turned to the major, who was clearly growing impatient at our leisurely speculations. "Or did he?" he asked. "The words 'Tis all that's left to me,' appear to conclude the diary, don't they major, but that's really not the case. For here we come to the famous missing eighteen pages of the diary, do we not? What do you think, major? Did Stanton tear them out once it came into his possession, fearful of some dangerous secret Booth had committed to writing? What happened to those pages while the War Department, while this very office, had them?"

The officer cleared his throat. "You're a detective, Mr. Holmes," he said rather sarcastically. "It oughtn't be so hard to figure. A man is running for his life for nearly two weeks in the wilderness. It's April, still cold at night, so he needs a fire to keep warm. Perhaps a few pages of the diary come in handy for tinder. Or maybe he needs to pass a message along to one of the rebels who's helping him out on the way. He tears out another page or two. Maybe he'd like to roll himself a smoke. There's a page or two. Before you know it, there's eighteen pages or so missing. Where's the wonder in that?"

"Bravo major!" Holmes rejoined. "A decent analysis, yours, except for this."

Holmes held out the opened diary where the torn remnants of the missing pages came into contact with the binding. He handed the major his magnifying lens and asked him to study the remnants. "What do you see?" he asked.

"Why, nothing but torn paper," the major replied.

"Torn paper yes, but with the tiniest remains of pencil writing,"

Holmes corrected. He handed the glass to me and I saw them as well—practically invisible pencil markings left in the margin after their pages had been torn away.

"Proof that Booth had fully covered most of these eighteen pages with his writing, before he tore them out," Holmes said. The major merely raised his eyebrows and shrugged his shoulders.

Holmes continued with the portfolio. He came upon a small envelope, bound with a lavender silk ribbon, and opened it. He gave a cry of dismay as its contents—a handful of old photographs—slid out of his hand and onto the floor.

"Be careful, sir!" the major barked sharply in rebuke, joining Holmes on his hands and knees in gathering the pictures. "These are the property of the United—"

"The United States government, yes I know," Holmes said. "Believe me major, I'm terribly sorry. I promise to be much more careful." He spread the photos out over the table, ignoring the indignant nodding of the major, which fairly shook his bushy whiskers. There were five photographs—all of women, and all daguerrotypes in a fading sepia tint.

"You may recall, Watson, that I once described Booth as something of a libertine," he said.

I nodded in response.

"Well, here is the photographic evidence of that fact. These were found in the pocket inside Booth's diary cover, an obviously important place, probably kept in his inside pocket, close to his heart. It's more than a safe bet to say that each of these women were, at differing times and to different degrees, lovers of Booth's."

"Who are they, Holmes?"

"There names are written on the back. I came across them in one of the official reports of the Military Commission. Four of them are actresses, and these photos are, in fact, professional *cartes de visite*."

He separated four of them from the last one. All were of comely young ladies with dark hair. "Fanny Brown," he said, holding the first one up, and then in succession: "Effie German, Alice Grey, Helen Western."

"And the fifth?" I asked, eyeing the final photograph, a side profile of a young woman of a slightly buxom figure with long hair neatly done up in the braids popular in the period of the Civil War.

"Ah, Watson. Remember the face on the fifth photograph. There's no name written on the back, and the Commission referred to the fifth young lady simply as 'a Washington society woman.' I have reason to believe that she was the most important of them all to Booth. There can be little doubt that she is Miss Bessie Hale, daughter of one of the most influential senators of the eighteen-sixties, John P. Hale of New Hampshire, and one of Washington's, shall we say, most sought-after young ladies at the time of the assassination. There were even rumours that Robert Lincoln, the president's son, was among her early suitors."

"What exactly was her relationship with Booth?"

"Nothing less than his fiancée, Watson, if the rumours of the day are to be believed, and in this case I choose to believe them fully. The engagement was quite secretive, albeit with the permission of the Hales and Mrs. Booth. It was never formally announced, but Booth was Miss Hale's escort at the Inaugural Ball—Lincoln's Inaugural Ball, mind you—a few weeks before the crime. Once the murder took place, of course, all mention of the courtship ceased immediately. Probably owing to Senator Hale's considerable influence on Capitol Hill, a terrible public scandal was adroitly avoided. It now remains a taboo area of local history, strictly not to be mentioned."

Holmes put the photographs carefully back into their envelope and rose from the table, stretching himself as he did so. The major and I followed suit. We had gone through the portfolio's entire contents.

"Major," he said with a smile, "it has been a rare pleasure to be supervised by one as efficient as yourself. We really must do this again sometime." The unsmiling, mutton-chopped major gave us but a "harumph!" as a farewell.

When we returned to 17th Street, the quiet morning had been transformed into the busy activity of noontide. A gusty summer thunderstorm had moved in over the city, sending the clerks, secretaries and bureaucrats on the street scurrying for shelter under the awnings and *porte cochères* of the buildings. Like most of them we carried no umbrella.

"One more stop, Watson," Holmes said, hailing a cab from the busy thoroughfare, "and then we may consider our business in the capital completed."

"I can't say I'll regret it," I responded, joining Holmes in the welcome shelter of the landau. "I must confess to a certain weariness of this business of old conspiracies."

Holmes gave the driver an address of 1421 I Street (usually denoted as 'Eye Street' by Washingtonians). It was unfamiliar to me. He turned to me as the cab joined the traffic heading north on 17th.

"Come now, Watson," he said. "I find the whole business immensely fascinating. I thought it would be of great interest to you as well, what with your passion for history and your love of all things American."

"It's quite interesting indeed," I told him. "I find it fascinating to meet such men as Arnold and Mudd—people who were witnesses to great historical events and so on. My only objection is the apparent aimlessness of it all. It's all well and good to be exploring the momentous events of the distant past, Holmes, but what of the present? I can't for the life of me see what any of this old business has to do with Edwin. Forgive me, Holmes, but it almost seems to me as if we are neglecting our real client in this matter."

Holmes opened the window so as to allow the cool, rain-scented air into the cab. "Your point is well taken, old fellow," he said, "if slightly misguided. Rest assured, Watson, I would never have begun my examination into the deeds of John Wilkes Booth if I did not feel strongly that it would, in some indirect way, shed light on the calamities facing his older brother. It has most certainly done so, although my theories remain incomplete, my grand picture only partially composed, which is why I am less than comfortable in discussing it at this moment."

He reached into his pocket. "As for our neglect of Edwin, Watson, it rather seems that he relishes the opportunity to be away from us for a time. I received this telegram from Long Branch last evening, while you were asleep. He tells us that he is fine, that he is relieved to find his mother's health better than he expected, that Edwina shall remain there, and that he expects to be back in New York on the morrow. He asks not a word of the investigation, which indicates the level of his interest in such matters. Read it for yourself. I'm sure you'll agree that he sounds more lighthearted than we've yet to find him in person."

I read Edwin's message and could but agree with Holmes. It sounded fairly effervescent in tone, and surprisingly carefree for such a melancholy man as the actor. "I concede Holmes," I told him. "I withdraw my comment. Now tell me, what is our imminent destination?"

"The home of a prominent, if not highly visible political man, Watson," he replied. "The home of a certain William Eaton Chandler, influential New Hampshire attorney, powerful figure in the politics of the Republican Party, and reputedly the man who caused the disputed eighteen seventy-six presidential elections to fall in favor of Rutherford B. Hayes over Samuel Tilden. Current gossip on Capitol Hill predicts his appointment as Secretary of the Navy within months, if not weeks. He wants the gargantuan job of transforming the U.S. Navy from a wooden fleet into an iron one."

"Sounds like an ambitious fellow, Holmes, but where lies our interest in him?"

"We have utterly no interest in him," he said as the cab pulled up to the curb. "It's his wife I seek. Mrs. William Eaton Chandler, you see, has the maiden name of Bessie Hale. Had Abraham Lincoln not been assassinated, she might well be today the happy wife of John Wilkes Booth." Holmes winked, noticing my annoyance at his mild deception.

We alighted in the rain to behold a handsome and well-kept residence, one of a long row of townhouses fronting directly on I Street. Painted a cool and somber grey, which well matched the weather, it was crowned with an artful cupola with finial. We ascended the steps after Holmes had directed the hack to await us under the shelter of the house's narrow, brick-paved breezeway.

A maid greeted us at the door, dressed in formal black and white livery, and quietly bade us enter. We were directed to wait in the parlor, a gracious room of silken upholstery and velvet curtains, well filled with exotic and beautiful plants. The silence of the room, and of the entire house, was broken only by the steady ticking of a delicate mantel clock and an occasional trill from a canary residing alone within an ornate cage.

Mrs. Chandler entered at last. She was a highly attractive woman, one of those rare females who become gracefully slender at middle age after a youth of capaciousness, and more fetching of face. She had a creamy complexion, and hair of a deep auburn shade, adorned lightly with grey, which she wore high. Her eyes were bluish grey, and were set off perfectly by a long flowing dress of emerald satin. For all her beauty, however, no trace of a smile appeared on that face as she greeted us with a courteous nod.

"I'm deeply grateful," said Holmes, taking his seat only after she had taken hers, "that you have agreed to meet with us over so delicate a matter."

She allowed the barest ghost of a smile. "To be perfectly frank with you, Mr. Holmes," she said quietly, "when I received your message last night I immediately threw it into the fire. I could not imagine how any gentleman would dare broach this subject with me. It was only later, after I pondered your statement that Edwin Booth's life might be in danger, that I changed my mind. No soul was kinder to me during that nightmare, no individual better understood my own tragedy, than he. His letters were more than soothing to me after everything that happened, and this from a man whom I had never met. At least I owe him this much, to assist a detective working to protect him."

She rose and went to the window, where the faint glow from the fanlight made her delicate features even more lovely. "You must understand, however, Mr. Holmes, and Dr. Watson as well, that anything I say to you here must be kept in the strictest of confidence—the confidence of a confessor priest and no less. My husband is away on Navy business in Boston. I've just sent the maid home, so you see I am very careful about being overheard. I have discussed John . . . I have discussed this matter with no-one in more than fifteen years, and I had hoped never to discuss it again. I do so now, I caution you, only with great pain and sadness." When she turned to us again and took her seat, I saw that Mrs. Chandler's eyes glistened slightly.

"Where would you like me to begin, Mr. Holmes?" she asked.

"At the beginning, Mrs. Chandler. How did you meet John Wilkes Booth?"

Though she had obviously tried to prepare herself for this unpleasant conversation, Mrs. Chandler had not sufficiently steeled herself for the mention of that name. When Holmes uttered it, she winced visibly and looked quickly to the carpeted floor.

"In December of eighteen sixty-four," she said at last, "at Grover's Theater in Washington. It was just before Christmas, I remember, and the city was lovely with decorations and carols. He performed the role of Pescara in *The Marble Heart*—John considered it his best role, you know. I was immediately taken with the man—forgive my blushing, gentlemen—for his portrayal was so overwhelming to me. He had such grace, such a physical presence upon the stage, such command over his audience. It was foolish, yes, it was girlish infatuation with the eloquent player and all, but it was very real at the time. Very real and very rapid in its progress. I think I was in love with him before the fall of the final curtain that night."

Mrs. Chandler's wincing and blushing seemed now to be over. A certain calmness seemed to settle over her comely features as she continued with her account.

"I did something very unlike me that night, gentlemen. I requested an audience with him, backstage, at Grover's. My father, poor father, was aghast. It was scandalous enough for him that I insisted on one night per month to visit the theater, mind you, and now to request to meet the actor! But father was as dear as he was old-fashioned. He allowed me to meet John. A fateful mistake is how I recognize his permissiveness now, of course.

"I shan't discuss the details of our romance. Suffice to say that we found ourselves strongly attracted to one another, or at least I so believed. After our first meeting that night he began to make steady calls upon me, for walks in the park or for evenings at the theater. He was always the perfect gentleman in all respects, gracious and courteous to me almost to a fault—the epitome of Southern manners. My attraction for him, no, my love for him, grew very quickly.

"And I believed that his love for me grew in turn, lovesick fool that I was. Now I see what it was all about for him. It is difficult for me to admit, even painful, but I must face the fact that he used me purely because of my father's position. He must have known that Senator Hale was one of President Lincoln's closest confidantes and that some connection to Senator Hale would likely avail him of fine opportunities to pursue his murderous intentions against the president."

"You are convinced that he harboured no amorous affections for yourself at all?" Holmes asked cooly.

"I am absolutely convinced of it, even though I wished it were otherwise."

"Yet, when he was— Pardon me, madam. When he was overtaken in Virginia, he carried your photograph within his diary. We've glimpsed that photograph this very morning."

"Yes, Mr. Holmes, I know of that. I presume then that you likely saw the other photographs as well—the actresses? And in your thoroughness surely you've learned of the famous Ella Starr as well. She's the woman who took chloroform unsuccessfully on the day after the president's murder. She loved John enough to try killing herself over his deed. A prostitute! He was courting me, a fine and delicate society flower, while he spent his nights with a harlot. That's where his amorous affections were directed, Mr. Holmes. What a magnificent actor he was. I am no longer confused by any of it—it is all as clear as day— but I am very bitter, believe me. I am very angry, ashamed and humiliated that it all took place. If only I could turn back the clock!" She looked quickly away from us.

Holmes and I both felt the virile anger which emanated from Mrs. Chandler, yet despite her harsh tone and expression, the tremendous pain of her experience clearly lingered. I suspected strongly that her feelings for Booth had yet to be totally erased by the waves of tragedy which had befallen her.

"He proposed to me in early March," she resumed, "and I accepted his proposal immediately. Father hesitated but, realizing the depth of my feelings, finally gave his approval. He was simply distrustful of actors in general, I believe, and knew nothing of John's sympathy with the Secessionists. For that matter, I knew little of this aspect of John myself. We never discussed politics between us. I had heard rumours from my friends that he was a rebel in civilian's clothing but I paid them little heed. Besides, by then the war was nearly over. I thought that such feelings would grow softer with time. How I underestimated him!"

"The engagement was never formally announced as I understand," Holmes commented.

"Father wanted us to wait for several more weeks. He told us not to rush things. It pains me to say it, but I believe he was hoping that the affair would somehow end before any announcements were made."

"You did, however, allow yourself to be seen publicly with Booth."

"Of course. We were together at the president's Inaugural Ball just a week or so before our engagement. We were the talk of the town for days. I loved it at the time, and I shudder now to think that my position allowed the assassin to walk within a few feet of Mr. Lincoln himself. I still believe he would have murdered him then and there if he had found the chance."

"It is widely believed that Booth was also in attendance at Lincoln's Inaugural speech."

"He was, and once again through my good offices. I gave him my tickets to the speech at the Capitol. I'm sure he carried his gun along that day, too. It was but another failed opportunity for him."

Holmes crossed his legs and put his fingertips together thoughtfully. He stared intently into Mrs. Chandler's eyes. "When did you see him last?" he asked.

"It was the day before the crime, Mr. Holmes," she said after a moment's hesitation. "On April the thirteenth, which was an appropriate number for the occasion. He visited me at home in the afternoon and stayed but briefly, saying that he was busy that day. Now I know with what he was so busy! We walked in the yard and spoke near the rose trellis we had there."

"What did you discuss with him?" Holmes asked.

"It was trivial, almost funny in retrospect. I've not thought about that since it happened. He was worried about which church we should use for the wedding. John was leaning toward the Roman Catholic faith at that time—I believe it was because he somehow associated Catholicism with the South—and my family is Episcopalian. I told him not to worry, that we would reach a suitable solution. I told him, Mr. Holmes, that our love would conquer all. Those were my last words to him." Mrs. Chandler laughed softly but bitterly at this memory of irony.

Holmes then rose from his chair and began slowly pacing the opulent parlor, much (I thought) in the style of a prosecutor in court. The gentleness and consideration of his earlier manner seemed to have suddenly dissipated. "You still love him, do you not, Mrs. Chandler?"

I saw her body stiffen at Holmes' insolent question. She looked at him with those fetching grey eyes with an expression of surprise and hurt.

"How dare you ask me such a question?" she demanded sharply.

"You detest John Wilkes Booth for his disloyalty to you, for his dishonesty in deceiving you, for the terrible violence of his deed. All this, and still you love him with all your heart, do you not?"

She rose to face him. "If I do, Mr. Holmes," she said in a low, almost hissing voice, "you may be assured that such a secret will never leave the locks of my own heart. And you may be further assured that I am insulted by your demeanor!"

I joined the two of them in standing. "I'm afraid I must agree with the lady, Holmes," I said angrily. "I think she deserves an apology for this outrageous—"

"I admire your chivalry, Watson," he said sharply, "but quite the opposite is true. It is I who deserves the apology, and it is I who ought to feel insulted."

"Whatever on earth do you mean?" Mrs. Chandler asked him in a breaking voice.

Holmes approached her closely, until his face was but a few inches from her own. "I refer to your dishonesty, madam," he said softly.

"My dishonesty!" she said incredulously.

"You see, Mrs. Chandler," he continued in a soft voice, "I know everything, the whole story, with nothing intentionally left out."

She took a step back away from him and clutched the coral cameo at her throat. An expression of total shock now dominated her face. There was no longer any trace of defiance or anger in her voice.

"What do you know?" she asked shakily.

"Everything," Holmes repeated, raising his eyebrow.

"How could you— Where did you—"

"It matters not where I obtained the information, madam. What matters greatly is your confirmation of the fact."

For a moment I thought Mrs. Chandler was about to faint, so close did she come to collapsing. Holmes and I helped her to a chair and I presented my handkerchief to her. I began to protest to Holmes once more but he hushed me silently with a finger to his lips.

"I repeat," he said after she had regained a measure of composure, "that your confirmation will make a great difference in this investigation."

She began crying then, softly at first, and gradually allowing herself to sob pitifully. Her weeping went on for several minutes as I paced uncomfortably through the room. Holmes waited patiently by the window. At last she wiped her eyes for the last time and regarded us with an exhausted appearance.

"It's true, Mr. Holmes," she muttered in a hushed and tired voice. "I beg your forgiveness for not revealing the whole truth, but surely you can understand the seriousness of an oath. John begged me to swear to absolute secrecy. What choice did I have? It would have meant his life. It still may."

Holmes could barely conceal his elation. "Then he is alive!" he exclaimed.

"Yes," said Mrs. Chandler with resignation. "John Wilkes Booth, as far as I know, is alive today."

I was much too dumbfounded to speak. The potent implications of her statement—that a man I had fully regarded as dead, a man believed to be long in his grave by an entire world, was today walking the earth alive—were far too much for the brain to absorb in one moment. I looked silently at Holmes and beheld on his face the supreme satisfaction of a successful hunter.

"How is it possible?" I finally managed to blurt out to Mrs. Chandler. "How can this be?"

She returned my handkerchief to me and somehow managed a weak smile through her drawn and drained appearance. "Poor Dr. Watson," she said with sympathy. "It seems you're the only one in this room to be surprised by all of this. Really, Mr. Holmes, you should keep your partner better informed. I rather think the shock was severe to him. I know how he feels. I confess myself utterly shocked as well. How did you know about John, Mr. Holmes? Who told you? Who besides me could have known?"

Holmes resumed his seat and Mrs. Chandler and I followed suit. "I won't belabor you with the details, madam," he said graciously. "Suffice to say that my intimacy with the fine points of the Lincoln case, coupled with simple deductive science, led me to an inexorable conclusion. I was correct in my analysis that you were probably the only available person who could confirm my theory. That you have done so is valuable to me, and I am grateful to you for it. Permit me also to apologize for what I fully recognize as my brutish behavior just now. I really could think of no other way than to force the secret from you. I should like to hear the rest, of course, but not before you know that your secret shall remain sound with Dr. Watson and I, save the possibility that we may have to inform Edwin of it. Is that acceptable?"

"The secret is out," Mrs. Chandler said weakly. "What harm can come from my elaboration of it?" While still clearly upset, she seemed to be shaking off the effects of her surprise. A trace of colour was returning to her cheeks.

"I beg your pardon for the expression, madam," Holmes said, "but where did your previous story begin to part from the truth?"

"I was less than honest on only one point," she said, "and that was my claim that my meeting with John on the thirteenth, the day before, was our last. Surely I thought it was, of course. I heard the news on Friday night, just an hour or two after it happened. Father had heard it downtown, and he came home shaken, pale as a ghost. It would be morning before I read in the newspaper who was suspected of the crime."

Tears began to form, once again, in her grey eyes. "I haven't words to describe the horror, the shame, the guilt, the shock of that news, Mr. Holmes. It was every terrible emotion all at once, and more than that. It was pain as well—the dreadful pain of a starry-eyed lover coming to the realization that her love was utterly in vain. Loss, that was it. I suffered the loss of John even as I had to force myself to hate him for what he had done. And, of course, there was the humiliation. We hadn't announced our betrothal, but it was well enough known. Father did all he could to keep the newspapermen away from the story, and I bless him for that, but it was years before I went to a social gathering, Mr. Holmes. Years! To this day I hesitate to be seen in public. The mark of Cain remains part of me wherever I go." She began again to softly weep.

"At any rate," she resumed, "this was the condition in which I found myself. Every day the newspapers brought more terrible news. I discovered that John had been in league with those terrible men. I learned of his other loves. I heard how close they thought they were getting to him in those dreadful swamps. It was a nightmare. That is the only word for that spring, gentlemen."

"And the nightmare became something else indeed, did it not?" Holmes asked quietly.

"It was two weeks after the assassination. The eve of May Day—I remember the date. The Germans call it *Walpurgis Nacht*, a night for witch's sabbaths. Four days before, we had read the news of John's death at that farm in Virginia. I had cried for nearly the whole time, and was just beginning to come out of it, I think. I was awakened in my room by the slightest of sounds, a pebble being thrown against the windowpane. It was late, past midnight. I looked down to see a figure in the dark and, growing frightened, nearly went to waken father. And then I heard him whispering my name—'Bessie! Bessie!'— so very quietly. I nearly fainted then and there! It was John! I was so happy for a moment, and then so terrified, and then so angry. I was so confused it was five minutes before I made up my mind to go down to him."

"You decided, I presume, to offer him help," Holmes said matter-of-factly.

"What else could I do?" Mrs. Chandler implored. "I saw his face, that Adonis face of his, and my heart melted with the joy of finding him alive. No, Mr. Holmes, I was not blind to what he had done. I was not blind to his infidelity to me with his harlots and actresses. I hated him at that moment just as I hate him today. But, all the same, I loved him, too. To answer your brutish question of a few minutes ago, Mr. Holmes, I do still love him today. I cannot help being a woman of strong passions, and I could not help but offer him assistance. He begged me. He dropped to his knees and implored me to help him. He asked how I would feel to see him swing from a gallows, knowing I had turned him away. He expressed his love for me time and time again. I could not turn him away from my door. I secreted him in the attic, far from the rest of the household. I brought him food and water and newspapers every day. All he wanted was a week, two weeks perhaps, until things grew quiet once more."

Holmes rose once again and looked at the sullen skies through the window. "Did he admit to his crime, Mrs. Chandler?"

"No," she said thoughtfully, "but I never allowed him to. On the first night, before I'd even agreed to take him in, he said he could explain. He said there was an explanation for everything, but I shook my head to him. 'Don't ask for my forgiveness, John, and don't try to explain what you did. Don't insult me so, or I shall call the authorities this moment.' That's what I said to him and he protested but once or twice and then grew quiet and somber. He said only that he had heard the bells of all the churches during the president's funeral at the White House, and that the sound filled him with dread. I hardly spoke to him further about anything. It would have been too dangerous with him hiding in my father's house. It was just as well. Whatever demons drove him to do what he did were better left unseen by me."

"You were committing, of course, a potential capital offense by shielding him from the law," Holmes informed her.

"Do you really think I didn't know that, Mr. Holmes?" Mrs. Chandler replied sharply. "I did what I did because I had no choice, not because I was anxious to disobey the law, or to shield a killer. I knew the risks."

"And the question must have come up about who died at Garrett's farm in Virginia, since it was obviously not he."

"All he told me, Mr. Holmes, was that he'd been hiding in Washington. He said that they had somehow killed the wrong man, and that he had no idea who this man could have been. He didn't gloat over the fact, but seemed as puzzled as I was. Still, both of us realized that for him it was a stroke of uncommon fortune. So long as the government believed him dead, of course, his escape would be far easier to manage."

"Did you observe that he had an injury to his leg?"

"He was carrying some sort of stick, as I recall, and his general appearance was quite ragged and disheveled, as if he'd been having a rough time of it, but I cannot be sure whether he was injured. If he was, he made no mention of it to me."

Mrs. Chandler dried her eyes once more. "He left after ten days. He left the same way he arrived, in the dead of night with nothing but the clothes on his back. He pleaded for my forgiveness, which I did not grant him. He asked again to give his side of the story, as he put it, and I refused to hear him out. He told me that he loved me and I said the same to him. We kissed, and that was the end. He left without telling me in which direction he was heading, if he even knew it himself. I wouldn't have wanted to know in any case. I've not seen nor heard from him since. I remember that it was his birthday, the tenth of May. He turned twenty-seven on the day we parted."

"And quite literally was reborn on that day as a new man," Holmes said rather cryptically, rising from his chair. "Who knows where, or who, John Wilkes Booth might be today."

"I don't wish to know that, either. Life must go on, Mr. Holmes," she said quietly. "I've worked hard to put the entire episode behind me. A few weeks after John left, our family embarked for Madrid. Father had been appointed to the ambassadorship in Spain by President Johnson. Being so far away from home, from all the people who knew about John and I, was the best possible elixir for me."

"I hope we haven't reversed its effects with our intrusion today," I told her.

"You're very kind, Dr. Watson," she said with a gentle smile. "You have done what you had to do."

"Mrs. Chandler, we've taken entirely too much of your time and have been entirely too careless with your emotions," Holmes said. "I cannot thank you enough for your confidence in us. You have been as gracious as you have been helpful."

Mrs. Chandler, beautiful even in her distraught state, rose gracefully, and showed us to the door. "Be careful with your newfound information, Mr. Holmes," she said as we parted. "The world doesn't always react kindly to those who take it upon themselves to rewrite history." We left the house to find the rain diminished, and the storm clouds rapidly giving way to sunlight.

I was naturally overwhelmed with Mrs. Chandler's revelations, and quite consumed with newly considered questions. "Holmes, those were the most incredible words I've ever heard," I said as our carriage was brought around. "But the whole thing is impossible! How in the world could they have thought they'd killed him at Garrett's farm? And how did David Herold happen to be traveling with that poor fellow, whoever he was? And, if—"

Holmes chuckled as we stood on the steps. "How many times have I told you Watson, that when you have eliminated the impossible, whatever remains, however improbable, must be the truth? Don't worry, my friend. I shall soon tell you all, for our work is far from finished and nothing clears up a case like discussing it with my Boswell. For now, Watson, behold the heavens." He pointed to the sky where a glorious rainbow was arching itself against the menacing clouds to the east, brightly illuminated with the new sunlight from the west.

"There is our rainbow, Watson, and we have just found our pot of gold!"

—14—
Of Theory and Speculation

The Pennsylvania countryside was aglow with the warm golden light of late afternoon as our train sped northwards to New York, but I paid the idyllic scene scant attention.

Holmes was discussing the means by which he obtained his recent and dramatic discovery from Mrs. Chandler and I was eager to learn the details. We had packed our bags and left Washington hastily earlier in the afternoon, and were now well on our way back to New York.

"You must have suspected that Booth was alive when you determined to visit Mrs. Chandler," I said to him. "That was your sole intention in speaking to her, wasn't it?"

"Of course," Holmes said casually, throwing down his newspaper, "but it was much more than a suspicion or a hypothesis as I had already obtained factual evidence of Booth's survival by then. I knew Wilkes Booth to be alive, but I wasn't sure if it had been Bessie Hale who had assisted him, nor did I know other pertinent details of the story. She was most helpful to me in those areas."

"But how did you perceive it, Holmes? What alerted you to the notion that Booth might have survived?"

Holmes leaned back into the velvet seat. "I'm far from being the first to entertain such a notion, Watson," he said. "The corpse of the man killed at Garrett's farm was hardly cool, the funeral train of Abraham Lincoln had yet to complete its black-shrouded journey to Springfield, when the first such rumours appeared. I daresay there are a good many Americans to this day who refuse to surrender their belief that Booth escaped both death and justice. What we heard earlier today confirms the fact that they've been correct all along.

"My studies of the Lincoln case have always left me suspicious on the subject of the disposal of Booth's body. The entire affair was handled in a strange, almost melodramatic manner, Watson. The troops hauled the body via wagon from the Garrett's to the Rappahannock River. They waited briefly on the shore and transferred it to a steamer sent down from Washington for the purpose. Near Washington, at Alexandria, the alleged body of Booth was taken on a tugboat to the naval ironclad *Montauk*, which lay off Washington. David Herold had accompanied the corpse along its final journey. He was imprisoned in the bowels of the warship along with most of the other conspirators, Mudd and Arnold included, while the body lay alone upon the deck. It is here, Watson, that the story veers into the comic-operatic."

Holmes closed the curtain against the brightening sunset to the west. "An autopsy committee of sorts was summoned to the *Montauk* on the afternoon after the body and Herold had arrived there. It consisted of several government officials, the clerk at Booth's National Hotel and Dr. John Frederick May, a former physician of Booth's. The physician had performed minor surgery on Booth's neck some two years before and it was his familiarity with the incision marks that was considered valuable. Now, while Dr. May said the scar looked familiar to him, he later said something else of a rather surprising nature. "Never in a human being had a greater change taken place,' I believe he wrote, 'from the man in whom I had seen the vigor of health and life to that of the haggard corpse before me.'"

"Such a difference between the appearance of the living and the dead is fairly common, Holmes," I said. "I saw plentiful evidence of that in Afghanistan."

"Ah, but Watson, Dr. May also claimed that the corpse aboard the *Montauk* appeared to have a broken right leg. That's highly puzzling, of course, because it's well known that Booth broke his *left* leg in the fall at the theater. Nevertheless, despite these doubts, Dr. May formally concluded that the body was indeed that of the assassin, as did several of the other committee members. It was noted that the initials J. W. B. were tattooed on the corpse's right hand. The hotel clerk remembered seeing such initials on the hand of the living man. The government report provided no evidence of Booth's identity beyond these highly questionable findings, yet the official judgment was that the dead man was indeed John Wilkes Booth."

"Well, the initials certainly appeared to confirm that conclusion," I said.

"Tattoos are easily made with ink-pens, Watson, even beneath the skin of dead men. I recall a case concerning a warrior from a primitive tribe in Sumatra in which tattoos played a significant role, but never mind, that is another story entirely."

"But Holmes, all the same, the people at the autopsy did conclude after all that the body was that of just whom the government was claiming it to be."

"Suborned witnesses, Watson, are really not such a fantastic notion, especially when considering the powers of persuasion possessed by Edwin Stanton. It could have been bribery or threats or both, but Stanton probably had little difficulty in convincing the autopsy members to see things his way. And remember, they were the only people allowed to view the corpse for at least four years."

I remained unconvinced. "Forgive me, Holmes," I said, "but it all sounds a bit theoretical to me nevertheless."

He smiled patiently. "The concealment did not stop with the autopsy, old fellow. It appears that Secretary of War Stanton also feared that Booth's body might become some sort of sacred relic to the vanquished Confederates, or so he claimed later. He claimed to believe, of course, that the South had been behind the assassination to begin with. He attempted, therefore, to deceive the public into believing that the corpse of the rebel assassin had been cursed with a wretched resting place indeed."

The detective laughed with ironic humour. "The public quickly discovered on the morning of April twenty-seventh that Booth's body had been returned to Washington. A crowd gathered near the USS *Montauk*, therefore, and waited in morbid anticipation of catching a glimpse of the body. The government gave them such a glimpse, in the form of Booth's coffin being lowered from the ironclad at dusk into a waiting rowboat. Inside were two Army officers who were careful to allow the crowd to see a heavy ball and chain which they lowered into their boat along with the coffin. They rowed into an impenetrable swamp nearby as the heartier members of the crowd tried to keep up along the shore. At last the rowboat with its deathly cargo fell out of sight. The crowd went home, convinced that Booth's body had been sunk into a dark and lonely morass, a horrific place where the Army had been prone to discard its dead livestock. The papers agreed that it was a fitting grave for a villain as vile as Booth.

"In other words, Watson, the ruse worked. What really happened, it is now widely known, is that the rowers waited in the swamp until midnight and then furtively stole into the nearby penitentiary grounds through a hole in its masonry fortification. The coffin was taken by a handful of soldiers to a deserted warehouse and buried beneath the floorboards. Stanton's wishes were followed to the letter—Booth's place of interment had been kept utterly secret. The assassin would find no posthumous opportunity to ignite the passions of the Confederacy. Nor, for that matter, could any stranger's corpse be used to disprove the claim of Booth's death at Garrett's farm—a death, we now know, which never occurred."

I reopened the curtain to view the farmlands now basking in the pleasant light of early dusk. "Was the body never returned to the family, Holmes?"

"It was released eventually, through Edwin's longstanding efforts. It was disinterred from the penitentiary warehouse, taken to an undertaker in Washington, and put on display before several members of the Booth family. Edwin was along but never went inside to take a look. It is said he couldn't bear that thought."

"What was the conclusion of this examination?"

"The family agreed to take the body, which at least implies that they felt the body may have been that of their son and brother. But remember, Watson, the disinterment took place in eighteen sixty-nine, nearly four years after Booth's supposed death. I hardly need tell you, doctor, that four years of deterioration has a rather significant impact on the non-scientist's ability to identify a body."

"Well then, Holmes," I said, "I'll concede that the whole matter concerning the body was highly suspicious but still, how did these suspicions prove to you that Booth had never been killed in Virginia?"

"They did not, in fact, prove it, Watson. They merely convinced me that something quite crucial was amiss in the official version of the assassin's fate. I had no material proof of that fact until this very morning. This is what convinced me beyond all doubt that I was correct."

Holmes drew something from his inside pocket and handed it to me. It was an old tintype photograph, badly illuminated and somewhat blurry. There could be no doubt, however, as to what it portrayed. I gasped when I saw it.

It was clearly the image of a corpse, lying stiffly upon what appeared to be boards or planks. The face was swollen in death and bore a hideously blank rictus. It was the body of a large and powerfully-built man of perhaps 35 years, with prominent cheekbones and dark, matted hair. A bushy moustache appeared over his lip. The area around the neck was covered with a dark stain that might have been blood..

"My God, Holmes!" I muttered. "Whose body is this?"

"Read the inscription on the back," he replied.

I did so. In fading red ink it read:

BODY OF J.W. BOOTH. APR. 27, '65. ABOARD THE USS MONTAUK, WASH. D.C.

I gazed at the morbid portrait once again. "I realize, Holmes, that I just said that the differences in appearance between the living and the dead can be striking, but Lord help me, this cannot be the body of John Wilkes Booth!"

He smiled and tamped shag into his cherrywood. "I concur entirely, Watson. Here, view this *carte de visite* of Booth and compare the two."

He handed me another photograph, this one a popular view of the assassin-actor as a young man, showing him in a dark suit and holding a silver-headed cane. While the features of Booth on the *carte de visite* were graceful and well-defined, those of the cadaver were irregular and thick. While the eyes of Booth were dark and sharp, those of the corpse (which were open in the photograph) were light-coloured and small. The difference in weight between the two men must have been at least 40 pounds, I calculated. It was impossible for these two photographs to be of the same person.

"Where in the world did you find this photograph, Holmes?"

"Just this morning, old fellow, at the War Department. Do you remember when I dropped the packet of photographs onto the floor? The major nearly had a fit. Imagine his reaction now if he were to discover that, by sleight of hand, I had pocketed this very item."

"Good Lord!" I exclaimed. "You've stolen evidence from the War Department itself, Holmes! That's a crime by any definition!"

Holmes waved my indignation aside as he put a match to his pipe. "Tut," he said. "I shall return it to them in due time. Besides, what need have they of it now? As far as the government is concerned, this case is long closed. Perhaps that explains their carelessness in not destroying this photograph, Watson. I have long read rumours that the corpse aboard the *Montauk* had been photographed before its ghoulish interment. I could scarcely believe my good fortune this morning to discover that very piece of evidence."

I looked once more at the dead man's expressionless face. It gave me a chill as the twilight began to spread over the countryside outside. I hurriedly palmed the photo when the conductor came in to turn on the gas in our Pullman and returned it to Holmes when he'd left.

"If this man isn't Booth," I said, "then who do you suppose he is, Holmes, or was, rather."

"That will likely never be known by anyone, Watson," he replied. "I can only conjecture as to whether he was the man killed at Garrett's. I have serious doubts that he was, considering his strikingly different appearance from Booth. I can safely say that he is the one, however, who provided the corpse at the so-called identification of Booth's body on the *Montauk*, and that this body lies today under the tombstone of John Wilkes Booth. As to his actual identity, who knows? A war casualty, perhaps? An executed criminal? It doesn't really matter, Watson. What matters is that it proves that the government did not have the body of Booth at a time when it was telling the public that it did. It proves also that Booth had neither been killed nor captured. If he had been, rest assured that Stanton would have made the most of it. We know the government botched its supposed capture of Booth and did so badly. A corpse was needed to provide at least some degree of authority to the story concocted by Stanton. The details of this cover-up, of course, remain unknown to us."

I put a hand to my forehead. A few hours ago the entire case had all seemed simple enough to me. Holmes' revelations of today, however, had thrown the entire thing out of kilter. Now, the contradictions and paradoxes seemed endless. I found myself totally confused.

"Let me try to understand this," I said at last. "The photograph proved to you that Booth was not killed by the soldiers in Virginia. How then, Holmes, did you conclude that the assassin went to Bessie Hale's home after the crime?"

Holmes smiled and puffed contentedly. "I confess to taking a gamble on that one, Watson. When we visited Mrs. Chandler this afternoon I was far from sure that she knew anything at all. I risked insulting her gravely in confronting her in the hopes that my gamble might pay off. I'm more than grateful that it did, of course, but it began on shaky ground. It began with something I hate to deploy in an investigation—an assumption—and that assumption was that Booth had been in Washington in the days after the crime. Until Mrs. Chandler's confirmation of that fact today I was unsure on that point."

"And so?"

"The pressing question then became where Booth would likely have sought shelter from the law. I decided on Bessie Hale, first of all because Booth was surely aware of her powerful love for him. He most certainly wouldn't have expected her forgiveness, but he might well have expected enough loyalty to prevent her from betraying him. She was also a member of an influential and respected Washington family, one well above the potential of suspicion. Such a home, therefore, presented the perfect hiding place. Finally, where else could he go in the city? He had no family there, and no friends whom he could trust with such a dangerous undertaking as hiding him, with the exception of his fellow conspirators, most of whom were rounded up in short order. The logical conclusion, therefore, even though it was speculative, was that Booth sought the protection of his fiancée."

"Very well," I said. "That all makes enough sense on the surface of it, but by proving your theory with Mrs. Chandler, of course, you must realize that you have turned the entire case on its head. If Booth's was not the body aboard the ironclad, and if instead he was hiding in the attic of the Hales' house, who in the world were the troops chasing so fervently through those swamps?"

Holmes propped his feet upon the cushion opposite from him and regarded the darkening sky outside our coach. "Perhaps you recall that I predicted this case would be a particularly difficult one, Watson. With each passing day I find that more to be the truth. The entire episode of the manhunt presents an amazing deductive challenge. I've still not explored that thicket to my satisfaction. Let us look at the hard evidence we've gathered so far, basing all of it on the new findings that Booth's body was never obtained by the authorities and that he was in Washington after the crime."

He enumerated his points of logic by holding up a finger for each one. "We know, firstly, that somebody fled Washington shortly after the assassination and gained passage over the Navy Yard Bridge after telling the sentry there that his name was Booth. We know that this person was followed shortly by David Herold, a known member of Booth's conspiracy. We know further that this person, along with Herold, appeared at Lloyd's Tavern in Surrattsville around midnight, that the pair took certain weapons and articles that had been left there earlier in the day by Mary Surratt, and that our mystery man took credit for murdering Abraham Lincoln while speaking to Lloyd.

"As the flight progresses," said Holmes, holding up another finger, "we can be certain that this person knew, or at least knew of, Dr. Samuel Mudd, and that he sought him out to treat an injured leg which would have been compatible with the injury suffered by the assassin at Ford's Theater. We also know that this person attempted to disguise himself while at Mudd's.

"We know that at the Rappahannock River, this man, who was still traveling with Herold, told a trio of Confederate officers that he was John Wilkes Booth and acknowledged being Lincoln's killer. From there the story continues on to Garrett's farm. We have no doubt that Herold was captured there and that a man was killed there by Union troops. We know that a body was taken to Washington and officially identified, however wrongly, as being that of Booth. We do not know who this man was."

Holmes knocked his pipe against the side of the car, allowing the ashes to fall outside. I could see the dimly-lit outskirts of New York City gathering around us.

"The plot continues to thicken, Watson," he said. "We know that various personal effects of Booth's were taken from the body of the man supposedly killed at Garrett's, including photographs of his sweethearts and a diary in which the writer took credit for the Lincoln assassination. We know that the escaping man was identified as being Booth by a virtual host of persons along the escape route, excepting Dr. Mudd, for whom a disguise was effected. Finally, we must confront the fact that Herold, an admitted member of the kidnapping and assassination conspiracies, never hinted that his companion in Maryland and Virginia might have been anyone other than Booth. He maintained this posture throughout his interrogations, during his entire trial and up to the time of his execution."

Holmes straightened himself in his seat. "And that, Watson," he said, "is the evidence with which we are now forced to contend. What do you make of it all?"

"I'm as helpless, Holmes, as a sailor in a gale without a compass. I have no idea where to begin making sense out of this mess."

"Come now, Watson," he said chidingly. "Roll out a general theory or two, just for exercise. Let us mull the matter over a bit."

"All right then," I said. "What of the possibility that the entire escape story was an invention, part of the government's coverup of the fact that they somehow lost Booth?"

"Impossible, considering the number of eyewitnesses to the flight itself, two of whom—Mudd and Garrett—we've spoken with ourselves. There must be a dozen other people who saw Herold and his companion at some point or another between Surrattsville and Garrett's farm. The flight was no invention, surely."

"But isn't it possible, Holmes, that they simply assumed this man to have been Booth? Couldn't they have identified the wrong man all along?"

"Highly unlikely, old fellow. This person not only resembled Booth greatly, but claimed in fact to be him on at least two occasions. He also took credit twice for murdering Lincoln, not counting the admission in the diary. He may well have told others the same thing."

I shifted uncomfortably in my seat. "Well then, he must have been a hireling of Booth's, paid a high price for taking the assassin's

place along the roads leading southwards. He was serving intentionally as a decoy, to give the real assassin the time to escape."

"Absurd, Watson," Holmes said curtly. "No price could ever be
high enough to compel someone to undertake such an enterprise. Consider the consequences. Escape for the decoy would have been as difficult as escape for the true assassin under those circumstances. If the
hireling weren't killed in the course of the pursuit itself, he would
almost surely be hung as a conspirator after capture. The assassination
of a president is no insignificant matter, even without a civil war. Only
an utter fool would have accepted so suicidal an assignment."

Holmes' methodical demolition of my ideas was raising my ire.
"Well drat it, Holmes!" I snapped. "What is your conclusion then, if
all of mine are so wrong-headed?"

He smiled patiently. "Don't be upset, Watson. You should know
that your analyses are invaluable to me, that through them I see the
paths of my own thinking much more clearly. Have patience with my
methods. I strongly suspect there is at least one valuable idea left
unexpressed in that brain of yours. Come, let's have it."

I shook my head and sank back into my seat, watching the
streetlights of New York that now flashed past our train. I closed my
eyes and concentrated my utmost and realized in a moment or two
that Holmes had been right about my idea. The notion struck me
with all the suddenness and clarity of a thunderbolt.

"Of course!" I said. "It all makes perfect sense! Holmes, consider
this: Consider that we were correct in our original thinking, that it had
been Booth all along. He murders the president, escapes the city over
the bridge, and commences his flight with Herold through Maryland
and Virginia. Assume that all of this is correct as is widely believed."

"Very well," he said, leaning forward. "Pray continue."

"The man on the escape route with Herold is Booth himself, all
the way up to, and including, Garrett's farm. There, at the very last
moment, Booth somehow manages to put another man in his place
in the tobacco barn and effects his own escape. When the troops
arrive, they wrongly kill this innocent man, who has been compelled
to take Booth's place. The detachment realizes its mistake too late and
substitutes a stranger's body for Booth's. Stanton manages to keep the

whole affair quiet. As for Herold, either he remains silent about the switch out of sheer loyalty to Booth, or his version of events is suppressed by the authorities. Are you still with me?"

"Still with you, Watson," Holmes said.

"The man at Garrett's dies in the early morning of the twenty-sixth of April. We may conclude then, that Booth has no less than four days to reach Washington in time to pay his unexpected call on Bessie Hale on the night of April thirtieth. It would have been a manageable journey to make, although not particularly easy, since the manhunt, at least covertly, likely continued for a period. Booth may have discovered that the government had reported his death and capture, and gambled that they had lost his trail. Therefore, likely in disguise, he returns to that place to which few would suspect him of going, the very scene of the crime, and enlists the aid of his lady love. It all adds up, Holmes! It explains each and every contradiction in the story."

Holmes allowed his face to crease into a wide and enthusiastic smile. "Bravo, Watson!" he cried, slapping me on the shoulder. "Did I not tell you that a brilliant idea was lying in wait? And what an intriguing theory it is, Watson."

"You agree with it then?" I asked, basking in the warmth of Holmes' approval.

He rose from his seat and peered out the window. "We're well into Manhattan already," he said, ignoring my question altogether. "We have an item or two to discuss before we greet Edwin in the morning, Watson. I feel it's quite important. We have made dramatic discoveries in the last few hours—our trip to Washington was surely no failure—but I fear that the effect of such news might well be staggering, if not devastating, to poor Edwin. We must use care. After all, the news we're carrying is that his brother, Lincoln's assassin, long believed dead, is very much alive somewhere. As abhorrent as I find the idea of denying information to a client, I must insist that we remain mum on the news of Wilkes Booth for the present. I am not prepared to let Edwin in on our shocking secret."

"But Holmes," I protested, "it's his brother we're talking about."

"We will have to tell him in time, Watson, but not until I have furthered the case and not until I have determined his ability to absorb such news. I implore you to indulge me on this."

I nodded somewhat reluctantly. "Of course. You know that your secrets are safe with me."

"There's another consideration to ponder," he said as the whistle announced the imminent approach of our station, "and a rather disturbing one at that."

"What's that, Holmes?"

"Some of the evidence we gathered here in New York—the Golden Circle ring from the hand of the man who killed Oglesby and attacked you, the pamphlet on the assassination, the walking stick left behind in Mulberry Bend—now take on a new sheen when viewed with the knowledge that Wilkes Booth remains alive, do they not? The fact that we know our attacker walks with a decided limp on his left leg, the one injured by Booth and treated by Mudd, carries a new fascination in light of our recent findings, don't you think, Watson?"

I must confess that this dreadful prospect hadn't occurred to me at all. "Surely, Holmes, you're not suggesting that Edwin's attacker is his own brother? You are suggesting fratricide! That would be monstrous!"

"That's exactly what I'm suggesting, Watson, and I can only hope that I am dead wrong." Holmes paused, extending his fingers and pressing them together. An enigmatic expression appeared on his gaunt face.

"There is one puzzle that disturbs me, Watson. Consider this: A man has his leg broken. He is in need of medical attention, gives his name to an Army corporal who will surely be questioned shortly, and does so at a place which will clearly mark his path. It's a singular puzzle—most singular indeed, Watson. And what of the motive? Why, with his escape secure and his death assumed, should John Wilkes Booth contemplate anything like fratricide?"

—15—
Old Secrets Unveiled

It was entirely illogical, of course, but somehow our return to New York felt much like a homecoming to me. We had been away for only a few days, but the amount of territory Holmes and I had covered, the variety of people we had met, and the great portent of our discoveries in Washington all made the trip seem like a much longer one. Indeed, America itself, in all its vastness and surprise, was still new and a little overwhelming to me, I confess. Our cheerful, homey rooms at the Windsor Hotel, therefore, seemed to provide some sort of stability for this Englishman so far from home.

Our reunion with Edwin Booth on the morning after our return was warm and pleasant. He seemed a considerably more relaxed and contented man than the one we had left some days before.

The report he gave us was, in general, a positive one, marred only by the fact that Booth had no good news to relate regarding his stricken wife. She remained at her parents' home here in New York, quite ill, and vehemently opposed to even seeing her husband. Booth's mother, however, was faring considerably better than he had expected. He was also obviously relieved that his daughter would be temporarily staying with her. He was, however, quite rightly still concerned over the prospect of another attack.

That prospect was driven home to me when I saw the two burly Pinkerton men who patiently stood watch at Edwin's door. They had accompanied him on his recent visits with family and friends, Booth told us, just as Holmes had advised him. Booth, however, wouldn't permit the guards to enter the homes of his hosts. He bade them instead to keep their watch from a nearby distance. In this way he was not forced to explain to an aging and easily worried mother why her son would need to travel with armed bodyguards. He told neither his friends nor his relatives about the dangers he was facing.

"So now you know all about my little journey," Booth said. "Tell me, gentlemen, how did yours go? Did you scare up any old ghosts in Washington?"

Holmes glanced quickly in my direction before replying. "One or two, Edwin," he said, "although I'm not entirely sure that you'd like to hear about them, at least for now."

Booth regarded the detective with an expression of sudden concern.

"However," Holmes continued, "if you do wish to hear of it, I can only comply with your desires."

Booth pondered this offer. "I'm assuming," he said after a pause, "that you have confirmed some tie between the Lincoln affair and the attempts on my life."

"That is correct."

"And may I also assume that the information you've gotten in Washington will be of some assistance in tracking down the man on my trail?"

"You may safely assume that, yes."

"Then I do not wish to hear the details, Holmes, and thank you for not trotting them out. My trip has left me in splendid spirits, I must say, and the last thing I want to think about now is the whole Lincoln business. If you're on the trail of the culprit, Holmes, then I'll gladly take your word for it. I've no doubt that you'll run him down in time. We'll leave it at that."

"Splendid," said Holmes, rising from Booth's sofa and approaching the actor, "although, regretfully, there is one last shred of old Lincoln business that I must bring up. I promise you it shall be the last."

A cloud seemed to pass over Booth's face as he heard this. "What then?" he asked quietly.

"I must know whether or not you have in your possession any personal effects that once belonged to your brother."

Booth reflected for a moment or two. "There once were such things," he said at last. "Until eight years ago, that is. There was a trunk that belonged to John. He'd left it in his hotel in Montreal and eventually, through a long and tiresome trail, it found its way back to me. By that time, of course, the government had removed anything of pertinence to the Lincoln case."

"What happened eight years ago?" Holmes asked.

"I could no longer bear its presence," the actor said quietly, gazing thoughtfully out the window. "I burned its entire contents in the furnace beneath my theater here in New York."

An expression of vexation appeared on the detective's face, but he made no cross remark. "What was in the trunk when you burned it, Edwin?" he asked calmly.

"John's theatrical costumes mostly," Booth said, "some of which had once belonged to my father. There was also a handful of letters from . . . from somebody who was once quite important to him."

"Bessie Hale, perhaps?"

Booth turned quickly to Holmes. "You know about her too, then? Yes, they were her letters, Holmes. I read one or two of them before tossing them into the fire. Pitiful, heartwrenching things to read, you know, with hindsight and all. And that was all. There was nothing else in the trunk."

Holmes began to pace restlessly through the parlor. "Think hard, Edwin," he commanded. "Is there nothing else, no other relic that once belonged to him?"

"I can think of none."

"What about a second trunk? Was there not also a trunk found in your brother's room at the National? It seems possible that this trunk might have been given to you as well."

At this, Booth stood up suddenly. "Of course!" he exclaimed. "You're right, Holmes! Another trunk did come, perhaps two years after I'd destroyed the first. I believe it did come from the National Hotel. A large steamer trunk, I think, with a lock. I put it in the basement at the theater with plans to burn it like the other. Somehow I've forgotten entirely about the thing. The trip to Europe, poor Mary, everything else—I've just plain forgotten it existed. As far as I know, it's still there."

"Have you any idea what this one contains?" Holmes' grey eyes were burning brightly.

"None at all," Booth replied. "I've only opened it once, shortly after receiving it. I had a handful of letters from strangers, you know, from insane people, who wrote me after the Lincoln killing. I kept them in case they might one day be requested by the police or something, and it only seemed proper to store them in John's trunk. At the time I didn't bother to look through the rest of the contents."

"Excellent, Edwin!" Holmes exclaimed. "And can we see this trunk?"

"If it's still there, I cannot see why not. Garrie Davidson was the caretaker while I owned the theater and I understand he's still there. Here, I'll write a note authorizing you to look at it."

"Which theater are you referring to, Edwin?" I interjected.

"Why the Booth Theater, of course," he replied. "Haven't you heard of it?"

"I must admit ignorance."

"That's probably a fitting measure of its fame," Booth sighed as he penned the note. "I worked like the devil to raise the capital—a million dollars, no less—and to organize the project, and it opened under my ownership in 'sixty-nine. There were perhaps two good years in the place. I put on some of the finest presentations of Shakespeare ever undertaken, Dr. Watson, and I say this with modesty. My Hamlets there were the best of my career, but I'm an actor, not a businessman. After two seasons the debts were mounting at a far greater pace than were the revenues. When the Crash of 'seventy-three hit, the project was doomed. I lost it shortly thereafter and it has since gone through a handful of owners who have at least enough skills at legal chicanery to keep me from having my name removed from the place."

Booth handed his note to Holmes. "When you see old Davidson," he said, "remember me to him, will you?"

Early that evening, after an uneventful afternoon, we did just that. The theater was unused that night, and it was the dark of the moon, so the facade of the theater at 23rd Street and Sixth Avenue was particularly gloomy. Despite this, the building's character was an imposing and impressive one, with twin mansard rooftops and seven high arches, all attesting to the hopes Booth once attached to it.

Garrie Davidson, the caretaker, cautiously opened the large door and politely asked us our business. Holmes tipped his hat and handed over Booth's note. In a moment or two the door was opened and Davidson admitted us cheerily.

"Why it's been a coon's age since I've seen old Edwin Booth!" said Davidson, a well-groomed man with a trim moustache and an impeccable suit. "Tell me how he's faring these days."

"I'm happy to report that he's fit as a fiddle," said Holmes. "Are you aware of the trunk he refers to in the note, Mr. Davidson?"

"Oh yes, it's in the furnace room, just where the other one was, the one I helped him burn."

"You helped him?" Holmes inquired.

"My, yes. I remember the night well. It was very late, and snowing like the devil. It was the saddest thing, gentlemen. It was only costumes, but such costumes! Silks, satins, velvets! And Edwin looked so forlorn as we threw each of them into the furnace, like he was burning his last memories of his brother. You know, he even had me break up the trunk with the fire-axe and throw the boards in. It was a pitiful thing. Ah well, but you're here for the other one, so come on, follow me down."

We followed Davidson, a rapid walker, through the empty theater, lit only with the few gaslights allowed to glow dimly here and there. In the spacious foyer I glimpsed an imposing bust of the Booths' father, the celebrated Junius Brutus Booth, Sr. The face of the sculpture was a striking one, displaying prominent brows and a powerful chin. It was clearly the face of an artistic genius, it seemed, but there lurked something else in that face. There was a disturbing essence of restless madness there, and a profound sadness, somehow not fully understood by its own bearer. I did not linger for long before the haunting likeness of the patriarch Booth.

In the large and elegant auditorium I saw a wonderful scenic curtain and three handsome galleries. As we walked, our footsteps echoed clearly throughout the cavernous room, attesting to its superb acoustic properties.

"What an impressive building," I said to Davidson as we ascended the stage.

"Isn't it, though?" the caretaker said a bit sadly. "It's so unfortunate that Mr. Booth wasn't able to keep it going. He was a wonderful man to work for, let me tell you. These people now, ah, they wouldn't know drama if it struck them on the head. I think they're getting ready to close it down, you know. Not enough money in the old place. It will be the wrecking ball by next year, I suppose. And I'll rue the day, gentlemen, I'll rue the day. Here, down the stairs. Watch your step."

We followed him down a narrow staircase behind the stage into a massive cellar. Davidson held a kerosene lamp to light the way as we entered a large room of vaulted brick, in the center of which stood a monstrous coal furnace.

"There," said Davidson, lighting a single gas-jet and pointing to the corner. A large trunk of black leather bound in brass stood under a heavy coating of dust.

Holmes procured a convenient axe and with one sturdy stroke broke off the lock.

"I'll see to my duties upstairs, gentlemen," said Davidson. "Take as much time as you need."

Holmes looked quickly—hopefully, I thought—in my direction as he lifted the lid of the trunk. The hinges creaked loudly and a faint odor of cedar and camphor issued forth from its long unseen interior. Something that appeared to be a bundle of grey cloth lay upon the top of the contents.

As Holmes unfolded the fabric, however, I saw what it really was—a woolen uniform of the Confederate army, with trousers bearing an officer's gold stripe along the sides and a tunic with silver buttons. I saw the insignia upon the collar, an oak leaf, and recognized the rank as that of colonel.

Holmes held the unfolded tunic at arm's length. "It would seem to be a proper fit for a man of Booth's general size, wouldn't you say, Watson?"

I nodded in agreement.

"We can only speculate, of course, as there are no nametags within the uniform. Still, it poses rather interesting questions about the assassin's possible ties to the Confederate army, more specifically its Secret Service. Most obviously, it is a dress uniform, for formal occasions or parades, and would unlikely ever be taken into battle. So why would a man like Booth, whose only likely ties to the C. S. A. were that of secret agent or contraband smuggler, be issued such a uniform? Well, we'll have our answer in time, I'm sure. Let us see what else our treasure chest holds, shall we?"

Holmes proceeded to extract from the trunk a series of rather ordinary and banal articles, things one would expect a young man taking his room and board within a hotel to have in his possession. Among these were a finely tailored pair of black mohair trousers, a tortoiseshell comb, an ivory toothbrush, a disheveled white shirt along with black pearl buttons and paper collars, a tin of apple-scented hair pomade, a pair of dress boots much in need of a bootblack's attention, a packet of very dry tobacco labelled "Killikinick," and an unopened bottle of lilac cologne.

Finally, near the bottom of the trunk, Holmes found the last item—a tied bundle of letters and cards, all addressed to Edwin Booth, all dated in eighteen sixty-five or 'sixty-six, and not one with a return address. They had been marked with a single piece of torn paper upon which was written, apparently in Edwin's hand: "Crank Letters."

Holmes divided the small stack in two and handed half of them to me. "Read them aloud, Watson," he asked, "and we shall save time. We don't wish to be here all night."

The letters, I'm afraid, were nothing less than shocking. Never have I seen such a vile and vicious collection of writings. Fueled by grief and anger at the assassination of President Lincoln, and obviously inspired by an indiscriminate, vengeful hatred for any person related or connected to the assassin, the anonymous writers had chosen Edwin as the undeserving target of their venomous epistles.

"Dear Edwin Booth," I read from one letter dated April 23, 1865. "'That man was right to say that all the damn Booths was crazy. I hope your happy now that your kin has had his day. Just as he was put a ball through the head, and just as his wretched and lifeless bones was sunk into those bogs, I hope your hole family shares the fate of this Judas.'" It was signed simply "A Lincoln Man."

Another letter, dated just three days after the crime, and mailed from Providence, was only slightly more literate: "Like a viper he lived—like a dog he died, and like a dog was buried—J.W. Booth, the Accursed. May he rest warmly within the breast of Lucifer in Hell."

Less clear in its motivation was the message penned upon a postcard dated April 30, 1865, and postmarked in Washington. "Dear Ned (Hamlet)," it began. "If I could but convince you, but no, there is no point in this. What must be, must be in the end. But if there be but one spark of recognition within your tortured soul, please recognize the hand of your brother. I am off to the Cloud City now. Far away from all of this. And, God willing, to be at peace. I pray for the chance to see you once more, and to tell you all." It was signed "Your brother John (Pescara)." To the side of the message had been drawn a tall mountain peak, in the upper reaches of which appeared a Latin cross.

"It almost sounds like some sort of reference to Heaven," I said. "How awfully morbid!"

"Listen to this one," Holmes rejoined. "'John Wilkes Booth did not murder Abraham Lincoln. The man sitting next to him did it. I know, for I am that man!' It is signed 'Rathbone.'"

Holmes sighed and rose from his kneeling position beside the trunk. We had made it through all the letters.

"A national tragedy, Watson, just as any sensational crime, provides much grist for the lunatic mill, it would seem," he said. "I pity poor Edwin for having had to bear this burden. I am beginning to understand his attitude much better as time goes on. Come, let's depart."

"I take it you're disappointed with what we found here, Holmes."

"Time will tell," he said quietly. As he closed the ponderous lid of the trunk, however, I noticed that Holmes had taken one of the letters from the stack marked "Crank" and placed it unobtrusively into his inner pocket.

We thanked Davidson the caretaker for his time and courtesy and walked once more through the ghostly emptiness of the Booth Theater. As we returned to the dark streets of the city, my mind was once again filled with the phantoms of Abraham Lincoln and the shadowy man who took his life.

Morning brought a brilliant sunrise and a surprise from Holmes. I rose to find him standing fully dressed at the door. Two suitcases, apparently packed, stood next to his feet as he adjusted his necktie in the mirror.

"What's this, Holmes?" I inquired.

"Another journey old fellow," he said nonchalantly.

"Another journey?" I was utterly confused.

"You needn't trouble yourself about accompanying me on this one, Watson. I'll be fine on my own and besides, I think the bulk of this trip would bore you frightfully. I should be back in ten days, less perhaps. I'll feel much better about Edwin if my stalwart Watson is residing next door, Pinkerton men notwithstanding."

"Ten days, Holmes? Where in the world . . ."

"You needn't trouble yourself about that either, old friend," he said. And with a wink and a grin, Holmes was out the door.

As characteristic as this was of Holmes, and as accustomed to such impulsive decisions as I was growing, I was still a trifle perturbed at being thus left to my own devices. Nevertheless, for the next two weeks I endeavored to make the best of my protracted time of idleness in New York.

I resumed my habit of walking throughout and exploring various sections of the metropolis, and managed to acquaint myself with many more New Yorkers of all stripes. I made a point of taking at least two hours every morning with my newspaper (three hours, if I could find a copy of London's *Telegraph*) and spent most of the evenings quietly reading on the hotel's veranda, taking advantage of the respite from the day's heat.

Booth and I saw one another frequently and it was during this period that my friendship with him was firmly cemented. We spoke about many things—his family, excepting a certain brother, of course; his love for the theater; my love for medicine; the advent of electricity. Through the course of these talks I found him to be an intelligent and kind individual, not at all morose nor aloof, as many people (including myself) tended to perceive him after one or two meetings. He was in possession of a fine sense of humour and an ironic wit, almost rural in its simplicity and tone. As strange as it might seem, I found him almost Lincolnesque in this regard. Stranger still, I discovered Booth to be a profoundly shy individual with most strangers, a puzzling trait in light of the fact that he was accustomed to performing before full houses the world over.

We played numerous games of closely contested checkers and chess, and made occasional forays to the homes of various friends of his. One evening, after a particularly hot day, we decided to attend the theater, a recreation which I considered something of a novelty in that my fellow spectator was himself one of the profession's great actors. I was disappointed that neither of my favorite heroines, Sarah Bernhardt nor Lillie Langtry, were to be found on any New York playbills—the former had left New York a few weeks earlier after a prolonged and successful run of *La Dame*; the latter was at her home in London, spending time with her newborn baby. (Holmes and I, of course, would have dealings of some import with the notorious "Jersey Lily" a few years hence.)

Edwin and I settled instead on a new and largely unknown actress by the name of Elise McKenna playing in an new drama in an equally obscure venue. Despite her lack of experience before the footlights, she impressed both Booth and me with her skills and charm.

Upon our return to the Windsor that night, I was pleased to receive a letter from Holmes, delivered exactly five days after his departure. I was surprised to see that it had been posted from the city of Chicago.

"Dear Watson," it began. "I am, as you can see, here in the fair city of Chicago, an absolutely fascinating place, not only for its hustle-bustle and energy, but for the fact that it lies at the edge of the great American frontier. That fact is why I am here, to be frank, and I am hopeful that its location will be of some value to our investigation. Time will bear me out on that hope.

"All seems busy here, with much of the city engaged in shipping goods into the adventuresome West, or in receiving them in return—livestock and minerals pour into the city in profusion, and many new immigrants are engaged in turning these resources into saleable commodities. As I sit here upon a bench, I see before me the blue expanse of Lake Michigan, fairly dotted with cargo ships carrying these goods to the far reaches of the north or through the straits into Lake Huron and on to the lower Great Lakes and the large cities to the east. It really is fascinating, old fellow, to catch this glimpse of the American interior—so much newer and more raw than what we've seen there on the coast.

"But enough of geography. In one significant respect, Watson, the trip has already borne fruit. Yesterday I took the stagecoach to the town of Elgin, a trip of perhaps forty miles from the city. There, I paid a visit to the massive state asylum for the insane. I managed to secure a brief interview with a certain Mark Lyon Gray—do you remember the name? He is the man who fired a pistol at Edwin while he was performing in Chicago a few years ago, and was ultimately declared criminally insane. His act was the first link, albeit an indirect one, in the series of attacks on Edwin.

"Mr. Gray is outwardly quite calm and normal in appearance. This condition deteriorates quite rapidly, however, as he speaks of Edwin. I asked him why he fired the shot that landed him in Elgin. His reply, if I remember his words exactly, was: 'Edwin Booth attempted to take license with my dear sister, to besmirch her honour in a most villainous manner.' When asked for further details, Gray admitted that he had never seen Edwin with his sister, that his sister had denied ever having met Edwin Booth, and that he had no other personal knowledge of the purported offense.

"'How then,' I asked him, 'did you know of Booth's villainous deed?' He replied, quite nervously, that he had been told of it. When asked by whom, he answered after some moments: 'By John Wilkes Booth!'"

"The orderly who was in the visiting room with us, Watson, had himself a good chuckle over this. Needless to say, Gray's answer caused me precious little mirth. I showed him a *carte de visite* of Wilkes Booth—the same one I showed you in Washington—and Gray seemed positive in identifying him as the one. He claimed that 'Wilkes' paid him a personal visit about a week before Edwin's performance in Chicago was scheduled. In their one meeting together (which 'Wilkes' had requested), Gray told me, the 'living assassin' informed Gray of Edwin's alleged offense and suggested he set matters right. Gray said that 'Wilkes' was quite explicit in suggesting that he shoot Edwin during his upcoming performance. Gray then requested a Bible upon which to swear to the veracity of his claims. The orderly laughingly brought him one, and the madman dutifully swore an oath over it.

"In closing, Watson, I shall state the obvious. None of this is for Edwin's ears, first of all, and secondly, let me request that you remain on your top vigilance. I am, as you know, adverse to following hunches, but I have an uneasy feeling. Keep your eyes and ears open. Re-enlist McPheeters and the rest of the Irregulars, and keep them watchful. There are a few details remaining here for me to conclude. I shall return post haste when I have my answers, or when I am convinced that they shall not be forthcoming. Until then, I remain, Respectfully Yours, Holmes."

Needless to say, this disturbing letter from Holmes jolted me from the idle apathy in which I had spent the last several days. I spoke to young McPheeters early the next morning, and he was only too eager to put himself and his fellow street Arabs back onto their watches. He reported regularly to me in the mornings, but had little of worth to report. There certainly appeared no sign of the attacker.

As for me, I found myself unable to rest well. I stirred from my slumbers at the slightest noises in the middle of the night, dreading to hear sounds of violence from the suite next door. I had certainly not forgotten my one close encounter with the attacker and my misgivings about him were only increased with the new intimations of his true identity. I was increasingly grateful for the two strong and silent body-guards, and much more tolerant of their intrusive presence.

In this tense fashion, a second week passed since Holmes' sudden departure for Chicago. I hadn't told Booth of Holmes' correspondence to me, but I sensed an increased anxiety in him all the same. When he knocked on my door after midnight one evening, I wasn't surprised that, like me, he was suffering from insomnia. He walked into the room in a long crimson robe, clutching his box of chessmen.

"Up to a game despite the hour, doctor?" he inquired.

I was relieved to see him. "By all means," I replied.

Booth's two guards began to take their positions inside my door but Booth waved them away.

"Take a break my vigilant friends," he said. "Go back to my suite and have a drink. Take a nap if you like."

"Our orders from Mr. Pinkerton are quite clear, Mr. Booth," one of the guards said. "We are not to let you out of our sight."

"Yes, yes, I know. But remember that the good Mr. Pinkerton was hired by me, which makes me the boss. Go on, we need a respite from each other. I promise you that Dr. Watson here shall keep his revolver handy. He'll put it right on the table in fact, so there's no need to worry. He's saved me once, you know, which proves him capable of the challenge."

With a shrug of their shoulders, the guards reluctantly left us alone. I wasted no time, however. I took my service revolver from its drawer, checked the chamber for cartridges, and placed it next to the chessboard. Booth merely gave me a rather tired grin, and we began to set up the board.

We played for more than an hour, winning a game apiece, and spoke little, allowing the steady ticking of the clock to serve as the room's only sound. We decided on one more game, a rubber to settle the series, and began to set the board one last time.

The soft sound of footsteps in the carpeted hall was unmistakable. Booth and I regarded each other silently. When I heard—and saw—the doorknob slowly turning, I felt chills go rapidly up my spine. I grasped the revolver and turned in my seat to face the door.

As the shadows in the doorway drew back to reveal the face of the man who stood there, I heard the sound of a chessman clatter to the floor after falling from Booth's hand. I rose rapidly from the table and pointed the pistol at the intruder, but found my finger frozen upon its trigger.

An awful silence filled the room.

The man who stood before us was John Wilkes Booth.

—16—
Mr. John Wilkes Booth

What words exist to describe such a moment?

Even now, I recall it as an instant which seemed suspended in time, and strangely surreal.

I stared silently at the man I took to be John Wilkes Booth, still holding my revolver level with his chest. He regarded me, in turn, with an expression not of fear but of total surprise. He appeared to be unarmed.

There could be no doubt as to his identity. The man was strikingly handsome, with long curly black hair, which revealed but a few strands of grey. The face seemed almost feminine with its fine lines and ivory complexion, and was made to appear more masculine by a full pendent moustache—identical to the one once worn by the infamous assassin. He was dressed in what I assumed to be a Western fashion—a knee-length coat of grey flannel worn open, a black string tie and a wide-brimmed, low-crowned hat. I saw that his riding boots sported engraved silver spurs.

I took my eyes from him for just an instant and turned to Edwin. I shall never forget the confused expression I saw upon his face, a wrenching combination of horrified shock, incomprehension, joy at seeing a loved one long assumed dead, and utter rage. His lips and hands trembled. I knew that he had recognized the intruder much more quickly than I.

All of this took place within a moment lasting less than three or four seconds, until the strange spell was broken by the sound of a voice no less surprising to hear than the face of Wilkes Booth was to see.

"Put down the gun, Watson," came the calm, measured tones of Sherlock Holmes. He stepped slowly from behind Wilkes and walked into the room. "Trust me, old friend. There is no danger here."

Slowly, and not without hesitation, I uncocked the revolver and placed it gently back onto the table. As I did so, Wilkes Booth took one tentative step farther into the room. His eyes were now fixed on those of his older brother. They stared at one another with an almost feverish intensity.

"Ned?" Wilkes asked in a low and timid voice.

Edwin took a step back away from him. "No!" he cried, his face pale with shock.

He turned sharply in the direction of Holmes. "My God!" he cried. "What have you done?"

Holmes looked calm despite the extraordinary moment. "I am terribly sorry," he said softly. "I had no idea I would find you in this room at this hour. I had no wish to surprise you in this—"

"Have you robbed a grave?" Edwin interrupted him in a shaky voice. "Don't you realize that this man is dead?" As he pointed toward his brother, though still not looking at him, I saw the unmistakable signs of approaching hysteria in Edwin's eyes.

Wilkes then addressed Edwin again, speaking in a calm tone that belied the pained expression on his face. "No, Ned," he said. "You see, I'm not dead at all. I am alive and well. I've come back at last."

Edwin coldly turned his back on his brother and stared into the dark night outside our window. "You are dead to me," he muttered in a near-whisper that gave me a chill.

Wilkes turned to Holmes, an expression of helplessness on his face. "Holmes?" he pleaded. "Say something to him. Please."

The detective approached Edwin and placed a hand gently upon his shoulder. "I really do apologize," he said. "I knew fully what a shock this would be to you. I wanted to break such news to you gently."

Edwin turned slowly to face him. "What gentle way could there be?" he asked in disbelief. "You appear at my hotel, utterly without warning, with a president's assassin in your company—my own brother, whom we've believed dead for sixteen years—and you expected to break this news gently?"

Holmes looked directly into Edwin's eyes and grasped his shoulders firmly. "Sit down, Edwin," he commanded. The actor took his chair without protest. Holmes positioned himself directly before him. "Yes, I did," he said. "I expected to tell you that Wilkes was still living, and that I had located him and brought him back, only after I had informed you of something else beforehand."

Edwin looked at Holmes doubtfully, and then glanced quickly in my direction. "What else would you have said?"

Holmes took a deep breath. Time seemed momentarily suspended as he appeared to search for the right words. "That your brother did not murder Abraham Lincoln."

We must have gasped, Edwin and I both. We must have gone pale, we must have done something, upon hearing these words, but I honestly do not remember. I do remember that all of us focused our eyes at that moment on Wilkes Booth, as if we were testing the truth of Holmes' claim by looking at its subject. Wilkes held his hat in his hand and stood before us like a prisoner in the dock. Could that face, so long equated with a shameful and catastrophic crime, actually belong to an innocent man? Could so many people have been so wrong for so long? Could history itself have allowed an error of such titanic proportions? I was silently asking myself these questions, and could only guess at what was going through Edwin's mind at that moment.

His eyes sharpened as he turned to Holmes and then he cocked his head, as if his mind were having trouble accepting such news.

"You are telling me that John—" Edwin began.

"That your brother is not the man who took Lincoln's life."

Edwin finally glanced at his brother, still standing silently a few feet away.

"For the love of God, Holmes, this had better not be some sort of awful joke. This had better be no mistake."

"You have my personal guarantee that it is neither, and that what I say is the absolute truth, Edwin. Make no mistake. This man is no assassin."

Edwin rose from his seat and turned at last to face his long-lost brother. After a painfully long pause, he slowly held out his hand in a tentative greeting. Wilkes grasped it.

The icy expression on Edwin's face began to gradually transform, as did the fearful one on Wilkes'. It was as if years of bitterness were melting away, as if the warmth of a spring thaw was at hand after a long and cruel winter. Their apprehensive handshake soon became a powerful embrace and I saw tears in the eyes of both brothers. When at last they separated they looked at each other and smiled. It was a moment in which no words had any place, and they stood that way for at least three full minutes.

Edwin was the first to speak. "You have indeed come back from the grave," he said to his brother, "and you have come back redeemed. I feel like two thousand pounds have been lifted from my back after years and years, John. I can't believe all this is true. I can imagine no greater gift than this moment."

"Nor can I, Ned," Wilkes managed to say through a sob which he had tried very hard not to allow. "We have traveled long and tragic roads, haven't we? Who would have thought that two backwoods boys would ever come to know such things?"

There followed an emotional exchange between them on the sort of things one would expect two brothers, meeting under such circumstances, to wish to speak of. Edwin assured Wilkes of their mother's health, updated him on his daughter's progress in school, spoke of their sister in London and elicited a sympathetic response when he reported on the hardships he had recently been facing with his wife. They joked about each other's grey hairs and remarked, despite them, how little they had each seemed to change in the course of their years of separation. It was quite bizarre, it seemed to me, precisely because the reunion seemed so very awkward and normal.

At length, Wilkes turned to me and extended his hand. "My apologies, Dr. Watson, if I've seemed impolite," he said courteously. "I'm sure you can understand in light of the suddenness of this meeting. I am pleased to meet you."

I took his hand, but—and I am still loath to admit it—I did so at first with a powerful feeling of repulsion. It had nothing to do with the living man who stood before me; he was a perfect gentleman in every respect. It was, I am sure, a reaction to my long-held pre-conceptions about the historical figure he had come to represent. I simply could not remove from my mind the image of Wilkes Booth stealing through the narrow passageway leading to Lincoln's box at Ford's, a crazed look in his eyes, and uttering his profane oath as he fired the derringer into the president's skull. This was despite the fact that I believed in Holmes' claim implicitly. I hoped that Wilkes did not notice my reaction.

He certainly seemed not to have. "Holmes and I enjoyed a long train ride to New York from Chicago," he said to me, "and he spoke of you often, and in highly complimentary terms, doctor. Allow me to express my personal gratitude for your courageous act in saving Ned's life here in this hotel. I consider myself in your personal debt for it, sir."

At a loss for words, I merely nodded in acknowledgment of his kind remarks.

Wilkes turned once again to Edwin. His voice had lost its shaky quality and now came forth boldly and with confidence. "And Holmes told me a great deal more than that, Ned. He informed me straightaway that he is our cousin, which is fascinating in itself. But he also told me about the madman who has been stalking you. To be honest, this was one of my main reasons for deciding to come back. I'm worried sick over it all, Ned, even though I think you couldn't have possibly picked a better man for the job." Wilkes turned appreciatively to Holmes as he said these words.

"Indeed," said Edwin, "and the sheer fact of your presence in this room is powerful testimony to that. Holmes, I think a supernaculum is very much in order. I do not ordinarily partake of spirits, as you know, but in honour of this occasion I shall break my own law. Dr. Watson, is there something stronger than seltzer in your cabinet there?"

I procured brandy and served a hearty portion to each of us. "To a man who is not only the world's only consulting detective," Edwin proclaimed in his clarion actor's voice, "but who is without doubt, the world's greatest detective of all time."

"And to the courageous Dr. Watson," chimed Wilkes in a voice as powerful and as clear as his brother's.

We all drank the contents of our glasses and smiled warmly at one another. Wilkes, however, seized the bottle and poured everyone yet another drink. "And to the celebrated Edwin Booth," he said, "whose skills at tragedy are unsurpassed by any living soul. Ned, I've read of your performances often. I heard of your triumphs in England with Irving. I cannot tell you how many times I've wanted to tell somebody 'That's my brother, you fool! The man who taught me everything I know!' That would have been impossible, of course, and so I want to tell you now, face to face."

I saw that Edwin was blushing at this praise—his legendary modesty had once again gotten the better of him. "Enough of me, John," he said, returning his empty glass to the table. "My life is a paltry dime novel compared to the one you must have been living. This entire thing, your being here, even your being alive, is a total mystery to me. I feel giddy with all this good news, like Scrooge on Christmas morning, but I am so baffled, bewildered beyond words. Tell me what happened. Tell me what you have been—who you have been—since eighteen sixty-five."

Wilkes returned again to the brandy bottle and held it up with a questioning expression. Holmes and I indicated that we would partake of more. He filled our glasses and handed out cigars. Then, with a dramatic flourish and a smile that did much to explain why Wilkes' audiences once loved him so passionately, he took a seat before the three of us. "I shall tell my story with pleasure, my friends," he said, looking at each of us in turn, "for it is a story I have never before confided to another soul."

—17—
A Fugitive's Tale

"I am a Southern man through and through, as loyal to its land and to its cause as I was when Lee still rode at the head of his columns. Neither Appomattox nor the death of Abraham Lincoln, for whose murder I have been blamed, did anything to change that. On those rare occasions when I happen to hear the strains of Dixie, or to see the Stars and Bars, my friends, it swells my heart with pride."

Wilkes Booth was a riveting speaker, possessed of a fine dramatic flair and powerful, emphatic gestures. As he sat across from us in that strange late night session at the Windsor, I realized how different he was from his brother Edwin, notwithstanding the striking physical similarities between the two. While Edwin was modest and shy, almost to a fault, Wilkes was outgoing and confident, in a manner that one might easily have mistaken for arrogance. He was a man of style and self-possession, despite the traumatic circumstances of his life, and was not the least bit ashamed of his vanity.

"My feelings about the South and the Confederacy certainly did not come from my family—Ned knows this well. I was impassioned about it, and certainly overbearing at times, during the war itself. Ned, you haven't forgotten how you forbade me to speak of it while in your house? I was the only Secessionist among the Booths, I'm afraid. Neither did it come from being a Marylander, although many of my fellow Marylanders fought bravely for the South. I wished fervently that I had been born a Virginian. I still regard it as my true homeland, deep within my heart. I did not, nor do I to this day, hate the black man nor wish hardships upon him. The South would have surrendered slavery on its own terms, in its own time, and when the consequences would have been less dire to her.

"Honour is the thing, my friends! Honour was the heart of the South, before Grant and Sherman ripped it out, before the carpetbaggers sullied it with their poisonous greed. The South had the right to determine its own destiny and its own fate, yes, but it had the absolute and sacred duty to defend its honour when the North challenged it. That it did, my friends, that it did, and it has paid the price. And that is the only reason for the actions I undertook in eighteen sixty-five."

Wilkes rose and strode before us, one hand held behind his back and his chin held high. I was amazed at how similar he looked to the engraved portrait of him we had seen on the assassination pamphlet in Mulberry Bend. It seemed to me he relished the opportunity to pose, to grandstand if you will, as if he had been longing for the chance for sixteen years.

"I am, however," he resumed, "not enough of a romantic to resist reality forever. The war is long over, the sacred cause long lost. What was left of the South's honour at the end of the war has been worn away by now. Those issues are for the historians today, and they call for no further tears from any man."

Wilkes put his hands upon the arms of his brother's chair and leaned closely to him. "But that was not the case in eighteen sixty-four, was it Ned? You remember those days as well as I. That's when I hatched the kidnapping plan. I can say today that it was foolhardy—it probably was. I can look back and blame it all on the passions and adventurous nature of my own youth, but I can never say that my heart was not in it entirely. I can never say that I was not ready to give my very life for its success!"

He stood straight and regarded Holmes and I. "And nobody can say, gentlemen, that the plan was an impossible one, can they? No indeed, for I know—just as John Surratt knows, and Sam Arnold knows—how close we really came to success. And with Abe Lincoln in chains in Richmond, who knows what might have been the result? Who knows how history might have been changed? Who can say for certain that Lee, and not Grant, would have been today's hero had the fates been kinder to us?"

Wilkes returned to his seat and seemed to gather his thoughts as he sipped his brandy. "But alas, the fates were not kind to us. We were partly to blame ourselves. We toyed with foolish plans for too long a time. We tarried over details. We took too long to muster our courage, and when we had found both a workable plan and the courage to act, it was too late. Our one chance to grab Lincoln before the end of the war, our single opportunity, came to naught on that miserable afternoon near the Soldier's Home. It was the wrong man! Lincoln had changed his plans at the last moment! The old rail-splitter had outfoxed his foes again, and this time he did it without even knowing about it." Wilkes grinned sardonically and shook his head as if the frustration of that long past moment had yet to leave him.

"We would gain no further chances and, even if we had, the conspiracy was torn asunder by that one failure. John Surratt was a busy man with the C. S. A. Secret Service; he had other pressing matters to attend to. Arnold and O'Laughlin were stout fellows but had no stomach for persistence in such matters. They feared Union spies even before we acted that day. Atzerodt was useless under any circumstances and Herold, loyal pup that he was, was no good on his own. Lewis Payne, of course, would have done anything asked of him, but with the first three men out of the picture and Grant closing in on Lee by the day, I had nowhere to turn. My moment had flown. I gave up the plan. Within three weeks Appomattox took place. Even before then, Lincoln had made it to Richmond on his own, in the company of his own generals. He patted the heads of the Negroes who came to greet their liberator, and he put his boots upon the desk of Jefferson Davis. In other words, my friends, all was lost. We had missed our chance and would be granted no others."

Wilkes cleared his throat and grew more somber as he continued, his voice losing its sense of passion as he did so. "Would but that the story had ended there for me, indeed, for all of us in the conspiracy. My friends, I can state with certainty what took place up to this point but my knowledge is limited when I approach the week of April seventh of 'sixty-five. I was quite despondent over the failure of the plan and was made no more happy with the news of Lee. Washington, meanwhile, celebrated with a vengeance. I shall never forget the grand Illumination, with thousands upon thousands of lights and lamps and candles blazing everywhere. It felt like they were burning my very soul, my friends. I gave up my contacts with Herold, Payne and Atzerodt entirely. I don't think I even told them that the plan was off. To see their bland faces was nothing but a reminder of my dismal failure. I believe I spent the entire week, up to the afternoon of the thirteenth, either in the saloons with a drink in my hand or in the brothels, with a woman in my arms. Forgive me, Ned, but I must acknowledge what you already know, what the world already knows about me. I have neither excuses nor apologies. I have never claimed sainthood for myself.

"Finally, on the afternoon of the thirteenth, my friends, I sobered up enough to visit Bessie, the girl I was to marry. We had a trivial little conversation—the sort of talk a man has with his sweetheart." Wilkes' face took on a sudden melancholy cast before he resumed.

"And let me clear up the record for all of you on the subject of Miss Hale," he said a trifle nervously. "I was a scoundrel in more ways than one, I confess, but as to Bessie, my intentions were never dishonest or criminal. I saw other women, yes, but they meant nothing to me, I swear it. I did use her family's connections to gain entry into the Inaugural, yes. The plan was still active at that time, but I swear to you all that this was not the reason for my courtship of her. I loved this woman like I've loved no other, before or since, and I regret losing her to this very day." The actor looked disconsolately at the floor for a moment.

"Be that as it may, that day, the thirteenth day of April, was the last normal day of my life. It can honestly be said as well that it was the last day on which the man once known as John Wilkes Booth walked the face of this earth.

"On the next day, the fatal day, I slept for hours in my hotel room. I did very few of the things the newspapers credited to me. I did visit Ford's Theater to get my mail, but I did not meet with John Matthews and hand him any sort of letter; I left no messages for Vice President Johnson at his hotel; I rented no horses; I did not meet with Payne, Atzerodt or Herold; I did not spy on General and Mrs. Grant; I carved no niche in the plaster of the presidential box at Ford's. The only thing they got right was my remark to the clerk at the National

Hotel when I departed in the evening. I did indeed tell him to expect fine acting at Ford's that night. I meant it literally! I knew Laura Keene and Harry Hawke as friends and colleagues and I expected *Our American Cousin* to be a fine performance. That is all.

"I did not drink at Taltavul's Saloon that evening. In fact, I avoided the area around Ford's entirely, simply because I had no wish to witness Lincoln and Grant enjoying their moment of glory before an adoring public. It would have been a humiliation for me, you see. Instead I visited a tavern where I was utterly unknown, a dark and quiet place in Georgetown—I forget the name if ever I knew it. I drank, slowly but steadily, until eleven o'clock in the evening, and then I went out into the street, intending only to return to my room at the hotel."

Wilkes rose from his chair and poured himself another brandy. He looked out the window where we could see the faint discolourations of false dawn spreading over the sleeping city.

"It was the strangest thing, my friends. I gained my warning through a man's curse of my own name. There was a commotion in the street before the saloon, a small throng of men speaking excitedly and passionately, apparently about something terrible which had just occurred. I heard bits and pieces of their conversation—things like 'he's not dead yet, but they say he won't last 'til the morning' and 'it happened at Ford's.' And then I heard one of them say: 'Well, they know who did it. It was that damned actor Wilkes Booth who shot the president! There's soldiers all over the city looking for him at this very moment!'

"What could I do? I began to walk back towards Ford's, fully intending to stride right in and clear up such a terrible mistake. I was outraged that they would associate something like this with me! Kidnapping the president? Yes, I had attempted it, and considered it an honourable act of patriotism. Assassination? Never! It was a cowardly thing to do, and a pointless one with the war over. Such an act would have worked only in the South's disfavor. I knew this as plain as day! Any fool would have told you so! How dare they even think that John Wilkes Booth, the actor, would shoot a man in the back of the head?

"It did not take very long, however, for my outrage to fade. As I walked along M Street I encountered a few more groups of people, and heard their talk as well. More than once I heard my name mentioned again. I realized at last that something was more than wrong. I could understand a single mistake perhaps, but three or four of them? It made no sense! These people were convinced that I had shot the president! There were troops, at that moment, scouring the city for me! And then I remembered the kidnapping conspiracy. Of that, surely, I was easily guilty, and there were plenty of witnesses to it. How would that look when coupled with the widespread belief that I had shot Lincoln, too? With amazing speed, my friends, my anger turned to apprehension and then to utter dread. I quickly chose a less traveled street and even here, I walked on the far side of the street lamps. I grew desperate and fearful. I headed for a warehouse district which was dark and found an opportune hiding place—a small storage shed adjacent to a vegetable cannery. There were plenty of dark and little used passageways here, and plenty of food nearby. I determined to lay low for a period, to try to follow the tragic events through whatever sources I could find, and from whatever conversations I might overhear.

"With no more ceremony than that, my friends, and no more preparation, this is how my life changed. I am glad, obviously, that I chose to hide rather than to face and try to rebut the charges against me. With the benefit of hindsight, the desperate decision surely saved my life. Had I walked into the chaos at Ford's Theater instead, I've no doubt that I would have been hung with all the others before the summer was out.

"I remained in the shed for two weeks and two days, lying low or sleeping during the days, and venturing out for scraps of food and water by night. I made an effort each night to venture into the offices of the cannery nearby. The place was unguarded and usually left unlocked, and one of the workers there had a habit of leaving his newspaper behind. I scoured these for details of the crime and the pursuit of those being held responsible. Through these accounts, I learned how Lincoln had been murdered, as well as the fact that an entire theater of people had claimed to see me jumping from the presidential box. I learned how they quickly uncovered the kidnapping plot and my accomplices in that ill-fated venture, and how Lewis Payne was being blamed for the attempted murder of William Seward. Obviously, the entire thing was a maze of contradictions to me, but I had plenty of time to contemplate the matter in those dark and lonely hours in the shed. There could be but one possible conclusion—that I had been carefully, and very successfully, framed for the murder by a sophisticated plotter who was familiar not only with my personal history but must have had personal contact and influence with Payne and Herold at the very least. It seemed to me then, as it still does today, the utterly perfect crime, and I have nobody but myself to blame for putting myself in such a vulnerable position. I was the perfect scapegoat! I had done little to hide my Southern sympathies from many people in Washington. I was known to be a little rash from time to time. It was easily established that I had not only plotted, but actually attempted, to kidnap Lincoln. The true assassin could not have possibly wished for more.

"It was also in that shed, my friends, that I heard the mournful bells of the churches of all Washington at the president's funeral. It must be said that I was no friend of Abraham Lincoln's and even though I do not admire a cold-blooded murder such as his, I would be dishonest to say that I shed a tear for the old man. The bells, rather, filled me with dread because I knew that they tolled not only for Lincoln, but for me as well. If captured, I had no chance at survival, not with Stanton running the show. I knew this. And if I managed somehow to make good an escape, John Wilkes Booth—or at least the identity attached to that name—would have to die in any case. My life could never go back to the way it was. It is, my friends, a frightening reality to have to face.

"But suddenly, as events would have it, my luck changed. One night, in my foray into the office to fetch a newspaper, I read of the government's killing of the man in Virginia. They claimed it was me! There seemed little doubt of it, to read the official accounts. I pondered this long and hard, of course, and concluded that the entire thing must have been a mistake. Somehow, the troopers pursued and shot the wrong man, possibly Davey Herold's traveling companion. They must have realized their mistake, and discovered also that they had never had my trail at all. Old Edwin Stanton, fearful vulture that he was, must have decided to invent an elaborate lie in order to salvage some sort of dignity from the mess they had made of their investigation. They went ahead and buried the poor man they'd shot by mistake, whomever he may have been, and then proceeded to hang three innocent people and imprison several others. I still feel guilty over Sam Arnold, you know. He was implicated because I failed to destroy his letter, but what could I do? I could not return to the hotel to retrieve it!

"I say that three innocent people were hanged, my friends, because I feel Lewis Payne was never an innocent man. I am convinced that the key to it all died with him on the gallows. Only Payne knew of the true killer's identity—he worked with him, I'm sure—and infiltrated my group in order to gather the information needed to frame me.

"Be that as it may," Wilkes continued with a sigh, "the events in Virginia suddenly made the prospects for my own escape much more favorable. I realized the government might continue to search for me, secretly of course, but at least the public would have been assuaged by Stanton's hoax. I ran much less a risk of being spotted on a street somewhere and being revealed to the authorities or, worse, being handed over to a lynch mob. I waited for four more days, and checked the news daily, before I felt confident enough to try to run for it. Even then, my condition was poor. I'd had little nutrition during my stay in the shed and very little sleep because of the constant fear of discovery. I risked going to Bessie for help in order to gather my strength for what I knew would be a long and arduous trek. I cannot thank God sufficiently, my friends, for the act of kindness she performed for me, despite the fact that she'd discovered my disloyalties to her (for which I have absolutely no excuses) and that she firmly believed me to be a cold-blooded and merciless assassin."

Wilkes spent several minutes discussing his brief stay in Bessie Hale's attic and the recuperative benefits this stay bestowed upon his health and condition. When he spoke of his former fiancée, the actor's face revealed tremendous regret at the manner in which his betrothal to her was broken, and eternal gratitude for the way in which Miss Hale had risen above her emotions and given him the chance to escape and survive.

"I left Washington, at last, on my birthday, the tenth of May," Wilkes resumed. "No man in history, I am sure, was ever as glad to leave a place as I was to leave that cursed city. It had been nearly a month since Lincoln's death and I had spent the entire time living in fear, in dark and hidden quarters, cursing my fate for having brought me so wrongly, and yet so inevitably, toward this unjust crossroads. My life, for all practical purposes, was ruined. My marriage, my family, my career, my wealth, my reputation, my very name—all of it was torn asunder in a matter of a few seconds at Ford's Theater. But I was alive, and not so indignant even then to be unaware of my good fortune in that regard. If Wilkes Booth had to die, then so be it, I concluded. I shall become a new person and rebuild my life from scratch."

Wilkes rose and opened the windows to admit the cool and fragrant air of dawn. He adopted once more his cocky stance as he regarded his small but attentive audience. "And I have successfully done this, my friends, against all the odds that the assassin stacked against me. That remains, of course, my one and final victory over him. He never had the chance to laugh as Wilkes Booth was led, wrongfully, toward the gallows, and I shall see to it that he will never have that chance.

"I left Washington in a boxcar, my friends, in a freight train heading westward. I had forty dollars in gold in my pocket before I went into hiding, and so I had some limited resources. I had allowed my beard to grow in fully during my period in hiding, and had managed to steal a pair of spectacles from the cannery office, and so my appearance was considerably changed. I didn't ride the train for long. When it began to climb into the Allegheny Mountains I jumped off, convinced that my chances were better within the wilderness of these old hills.

"As it turns out, I was correct. The Alleghenies were safe enough, and quite remote over the backroads and old trails I chose to travel. I walked for three days and finally, near the town of Covington in Virginia, I purchased a sturdy old mare from a hillbilly fellow for ten dollars. My progress, of course, was considerably quickened after this. I lived a rustic life at first, avoiding inns at all cost, and sleeping out under the stars with nothing but a blanket to keep me warm. I purchased my food from farmers when I could find them, and stole it from barns and orchards when I could not. Most of my travel was done at night. For two weeks I journeyed in this manner, and was fortunate that nary a soul along my way stopped to ask me a question or to give me a second glance as we passed.

"In those two weeks, I made my way into the heart of Kentucky and was beginning to feel myself safe at last, knowing that with each mile I traveled in a westerly direction, the chances of my being spotted by somebody who knew me, or who had once glimpsed my face on a stage, grew less.

"I was perhaps forty miles from the Missouri border early one evening, however, when my luck seemed to change for the worse. I had made a makeshift supper with a small campfire and was preparing to ride on, when I suddenly found myself surrounded by a dozen or so armed and mounted men. I drew my pistol and had it immediately shot from my grasp by one of the riders. I despaired for a moment that it was a lucky Union patrol, which were known to still be operating in the area, but then I saw in the gloom that the riders wore no uniforms. I was then convinced that they were highwaymen out for plunder, and quickly bemoaned the irony of my arduous escape, only to die at the hands of backwoods pirates.

"As it happened, neither was the case. My luck had not changed for the worse, but for the better! The men were fleeing Confederate raiders, they told me, stragglers of the fierce Missouri guerrilla Billy Quantrill, who had been gunned down a few weeks before by Yankees not far from there. They were finished as far as the war was concerned, but were still being hunted by the local Yanks, and intended to make it back into Missouri and safety themselves. I was so relieved I shook their hands, one by one, but remained distrustful enough not to tell them the truth of who I really was. Thousands of dollars had been promised to the man who brought me in, I knew, and nobody could be trusted to pass up such a temptation. I told them instead that I was a fugitive rebel myself, a former member of Mosby's raiders, and used the knowledge that Lewis Payne had shared with me of Mosby to convince them that I was telling the truth. They treated me like a comrade in arms, and asked me to ride with them. I was overjoyed! No longer would I have to skulk like a hunted fox through the woods at night. I could travel in the company of an armed and courageous band of experienced guerrillas, a force that would likely deter many Union patrols, and outgun many of those brave enough to challenge them. And they were heading in the precise direction that I was. In truth, my chance meeting with the Quantrill boys may well have saved my life. I rode with them for three full weeks, often riding day and night, and became fast friends with the lot of them. It was an easy time of it, too. Not once were we challenged by a soul, nor hardly glimpsed by one, so elusive and clever were these horsemen. We lost the riders one by one as we passed through Missouri—the men took different roads to head back to their homes and farms—and it was a sad sight each time. It is a touching moment, my friends, to see soldiers part from one another for good, after having survived the horrors and terrors of war as brothers in arms. Mind you, I know of Quantrill's reputation. They say he was a blood-thirsty maniac, as much a pox to the South as he was to the Union, and it can't be denied that these men rode by his side. But to me they were the kindest and truest hearts I've ever known. I only wonder how they would have treated me had they realized that they spent three weeks riding in the company of John Wilkes Booth.

"I left the last of my fellow riders at a tiny place called Adrian, just shy of the Kansas line. The beginning of the Great Plains lay before me at last, my friends, and for the first time since my misfortune began that spring, I felt like a free man. It was well into summer by then, and the winds were hot and brutal out on the prairies, but it felt like the balm of Gilead to me after what I'd been through."

Wilkes rubbed his forehead in exhaustion as the hour was late. Indeed, the grey luminescence of dawn now appeared over the streets of New York and the first city birds were beginning to trill. Neither Holmes nor Edwin nor I, however, seemed the least bit tired, so fascinated were we with the tale of Wilkes' dramatic escape. I rang the kitchen for coffee and with a steaming cup in everyone's hands, Wilkes continued.

"The journey through Kansas was not a perilous one," he said. "By then my beard had grown in long and full and the common wisdom among most folk was that John Wilkes Booth was safely dead. I had few problems, therefore, in circulating among the people and even in finding work. I spent two or three months as a common laborer, working on the railway bed for the Kansas Pacific Railroad, which was at that time not extended far from Kansas City. In August, after having heard the news of the dreadful executions of Herold, Atzerodt and Mrs. Surratt (and the just one of Payne) I grew tired of the back-breaking work in the hot sun. I hired on as a scout with a small wagon train bound for the Rocky Mountains. It was fine work, easy enough for an experienced horseman such as myself, and of a solitary nature for the most part, which contributed to my safety. Other than one or two frightening run-ins with local Indian bands—Kiowas and Comanches, I believe—the ride was uneventful. I arrived in Denver in early October with silver and gold in my pocket and well over a thousand miles behind me.

"I was by then very close to my destination. Yes, my friends, there was a specific direction to my flight from the very beginning. My reasons for heading out West are obvious enough. In the 'sixties, you see, Colorado was the land of unequalled opportunity because of the precious metals finds in the Rockies. The major finds occurred in the late 'fifties and early 'sixties, just when there was a large and adventurous transient population looking for such opportunity—veterans of the war, both North and South, freed slaves, various scofflaws and flotsam from any number of places. Law and order were scarce commodities in places like Colorado. I realized, therefore, that no easily accessible location would offer me greater anonymity, and greater refuge, than the Colorado gold camps. Even an attempt to go overseas would have carried a greater risk, I am sure, since I've no doubt that Stanton was still keeping a sharp eye on the major ship runs to Europe and elsewhere. Canada, I knew, was less than safe, since U.S. agents infiltrated its borders with impunity. I knew this from my own Secret Service days, and I knew that they had done so in search of John Surratt shortly after Lincoln's murder. Colorado, therefore, was a logical location, and in this, I am glad to say, I have been proven correct.

"In 'sixty or 'sixty-one, you see, I had read of the fantastic gold finds in a place that came to be known as Leadville, high in the mountains and perhaps a hundred-mile ride from Denver. In the gloomy attic of Bessie Hale's house I had decided that this camp, so far from civilization and yet offering such opportunity, would be my destination. I spent no more than two or three days in Denver after my arrival before I set out for the camp.

"I shall never forget my first impressions of it that autumn—the sudden appearance of streets and buildings amidst the majestic glory of peaks of staggering height, blanketed already with a dusting of snow among the golden aspens and deeply green pines and spruces. My friends, they say a man knows he is home only when he finds it, and on that October day, despite my birthright as a Marylander and my love for Dixie, I knew that this place was to be my home.

"It was not yet called Leadville in eighteen sixty-five—it still used the old name of Oro City—but there were several hundred souls who called it home even then. I rented a poor log cabin in a little area known as Jacktown and soon realized that the chances for quick riches were well gone by the time of my arrival. There was, however, enough placer gold still left in the creeks and runs to furnish a frugal means of life, and in my desperate condition, I considered this sufficient. It was a period of decline there—men were leaving Oro City for greener pastures by the day. I had a sense, however, that things weren't through and so, with the few dollars I managed to save from the little gold I panned and sluiced from the streams, I began to purchase claims. I have always been interested in mineral speculation, as Ned knows from my oil days in Pennsylvania, and there were bountiful deals to be had for the taking. I bought more than one claim for nothing more than a dollar.

"I shan't belabor you, my friends, with a telling of the twelve years I worked and lived in Oro City, and later Leadville, other than to say that I grew into quite a reclusive soul. I was bearded and dirty and used foul language like most of the other stout souls who lived in Leadville all year round. I was known to my fellow miners by an assumed name, and nary a suspicion was voiced about my true identity, nor a question asked about my past. In fact, now I realize how crude this life really was, but I grew into the role so well, my friends, that after two or three years, I was no longer playing any role at all. I had become the grizzled mountain man whose identity I had intentionally created.

"In eighteen seventy-seven, two things took place that forever changed the life into which I had fallen. The first was the rather sudden discovery of silver in the Leadville hills—to be found in the very slag and tailings that we had rejected in our gold mining days. No man had predicted that Leadville's greatest days lay still ahead of her, but there we were. I found myself in ownership of more than a dozen claims, all boasting ore fairly bursting with silver. With new processing methods available, and better transportation in place, they were suddenly worth thousands upon thousands of dollars, my friends. I had become, overnight, a very wealthy man.

"I would not have sold my claims, however, had not something else occurred that year. I chanced to meet a man one dreadfully cold and snowy night in one of the town's saloons. He was a man of about my height and weight and, in more ways than one, bore a considerable resemblance to me. I sat next to him at the bar and we began to speak of various ordinary and simple things. He gave his name as John St. Helen, and told me that he considered Oklahoma to be his home state.

"As the night wore on, however, and his consumption of cheap whiskey increased, he began to tell a tale that chilled my very soul. He said that his real name was John Wilkes Booth! He claimed to be Lincoln's murderer, and told a bizarre and obviously false tale of his escape. A good number of miners gathered around him as he boasted of such dishonest infamy and I could see that more than one of them believed him.

"Now, the man was either drunk or mad, or perhaps both at once, but somehow, after twelve years of my solitary and rustic life in Leadville, his claims reminded me of my own, very real, vulnerability. I grew defensive as some of the miners looked at me that night, as if somehow even the suggestion that Wilkes Booth might yet be living, even if uttered by a madman, might well cause some man, some day, to suspect me. The feeling was there the next morning and the next and the next, long after St. Helen had moved on. My dread of discovery only grew. Any sense of safety I may have established during my long stay in Leadville, I'm afraid, was utterly shattered by St. Helen that night. In the fall of eighteen seventy-seven, therefore, I sold my claims, made an astronomical profit, and I quietly left Leadville, leaving behind forever my days as a miner.

"I went only so far as Denver. I found that in my absence the city had grown to an astonishing degree, yet still it held for me the essence of a foreign city—a place where I could comfortably continue to exist as a stranger and, therefore, be able to establish myself as a new man. I shaved my beard, purchased a fine wardrobe, and with my silver earnings, had constructed a fine home on High Street, in the city's new and fashionable Capitol Hill district. I took a new name and invented an entirely new background, claiming to be a teacher of English and history and, yes, of drama, whose hometown was Detroit. It worked splendidly, my friends. Within weeks I was teaching these very subjects in a small school for boys, earning the loyalty and obedience of my charges, and the admiration and respect of their parents. In two years' time, I was well enough known to receive invitations to the homes of some of Denver's leading citizens, including the mayor. In one more year, I remain happy to report, I took a beautiful and wonderful woman as my wife. She bore me a son, your beautiful little nephew Ned, just three months ago."

Edwin rose and silently embraced his brother to congratulate him on this warm news, and the two brothers once again fell prey to tears and smiles.

"There is not a great deal more to tell," Wilkes resumed, "other than to say that my life continues now in this way. Not a soul, including my wife, has any idea as to who I really am. I am now comfortable enough with my assumed identity that my only attempt at disguise is a pair of spectacles. I once met a man in Denver, the father of a student of mine, whom I had earlier regarded as an acquaintance in Baltimore. We spoke at length, he and I, yet he never showed the slightest hint of recognition. It's not that I have changed so much—Ned, you can see that—it's simply that when the world regards one as a dead man, it simply does not occur to them to recognize that person any longer. One ceases to exist, in mind if not in fact.

"My stature in the community continues to grow. Just last year I accepted a position at a prestigious new girl's academy—the Brinker Collegiate Institute—and I already have offers from Denver's finest institute of learning, Wolf Hall. I am wealthy, true, but continue to work daily, not only because it tends to stifle any suspicion that might be caused by an idle style of living, but because it actually gives me great satisfaction to teach the young."

Wilkes rose tiredly from his chair and stretched with a yawn. He strode again to the window and threw the curtains widely open, allowing the rising sun's brilliant rays to flood the room.

"My greatest regret, of course, is that I will never come to know how great an actor I might have been," he said. "I shall never know, Ned, whether or not I could have matched your skill upon the stage. You shall forever be the star among the Booths, as I must remain the villain. And yet, I also know that few actors have faced as enormous a dramatic challenge as I must face each and every day. To have put John Wilkes Booth quietly and invisibly into his grave of obscurity, and to have resurrected a new man with an utterly new life from his dust, is the most demanding role that any actor has ever attempted."

—18—
A Mystery Within A Mystery

"Do you remember the gypsy fortune teller who read your hand, John, that crazy old crone who came by when you were at the Quaker school in Cockeysville?"

This seemingly bizarre question was asked by Edwin Booth of his younger brother beneath the shade of a quiet and deserted rustic arbor in the far reaches of Central Park. The advent of dusk was marked by the deepening of the heavens to the east. We sat amidst a host of twinkling fireflies which Wilkes fondly called "bearers of sacred torches." It was a fine and pleasant summer's eve in New York City.

Wilkes nodded. "You mean the one who said I was born under an unlucky star, that I'd have a 'thundering crowd of enemies' or some such?"

"That's the one. How did she put it? Your hand was 'full enough of sorrow, full of trouble, trouble in plenty,' I think it was. She advised you to become a missionary or a priest in order to escape such a fate."

Wilkes smiled wanly at his older brother. "She also said I'd die young, if I recollect properly, and that I'd leave many to mourn me. And who can say she was wrong, in a way? Not me. You must remember, Ned, Mama's vision too, when I was just a babe. She dreamed she asked the flames in the grate for a foretelling of her infant's destiny, and out came the words 'Country' and 'Impatient Love.' There's a certain truth to all of it, it seems to me, my friends, old wives' tales though they may be. And what of your caul, Ned? Do you deny that it has bestowed luck on you?"

Edwin ran a hand through his hair. "Not for one moment, John. I'm as superstitious as they come, you know."

Holmes sighed loudly as he tapped his pipe against the wooden bench of the arbor. "If you ask me, it's absolutely amazing that grown men of the late nineteenth century could still entertain such outlandish notions," he sneered. "No amount of progress in the scientific arts, no quantity of industrial advancement, can divorce mankind from his morbid preoccupations with black cats, four-leaf clovers and other such drivel. Really, gentlemen, I'm aghast at such talk."

Wilkes, Edwin and I—all superstitious fellows to varying degrees—smiled knowingly at one another. Even Wilkes, the newest of Holmes' acquaintances, seemed well aware of the detective's disdain for all things metaphysical. Holmes was likely the world's foremost champion of the rational approach to all things, and the inevitability of a scientific and rational solution to every possible problem.

It was, in fact, the earnest request of the Booth brothers to hear such a scientific solution from Holmes' lips that had brought us to this remote quarter of the great metropolitan park. It was the evening following our all-night encounter with Wilkes at the Windsor, and Holmes had directed the cabman to drive us here to the area of 72nd Street and leave us off. There were highly secret details to discuss, Holmes informed us, and he wished to eliminate any chance of our being overheard. I would later discover that we sat directly across from the site of the Dakota Flats apartment building which, when it was constructed some three years later, would be considered so remote from the central city that "it might as well be in the Dakota Territory."

Earlier that day, after a brief slumber, Holmes had honestly informed the omnipresent Pinkerton guards in Edwin's suite that the actor's brother would be staying for an indefinite period. He informed them, falsely, that this brother was Joseph Booth, and the simple ruse seemed to have succeeded entirely in allaying any suspicions they might have had. I noticed that when we left the Windsor after dinner, Wilkes donned a pair of silver spectacles that lent his dramatic features a decidedly scholarly and bookish air. Here in Central Park, in an environment so peaceful and quiet we might as well have been in the countryside, Wilkes removed them and replaced them in his pocket.

"As is obvious to all by now," Holmes began, blowing blue smoke into the still air, "we have been dealing with a mystery within a mystery. I began my investigation on the simple level of tracking down a stranger, who, for reasons unknown, wished to cause Edwin harm. I've arrived at a point where we know that Edwin's brother is not only among the living, but is innocent of the crime with which history has charged him. It is a surprising state of affairs, I must confess. I have found this case to be much like a telescope. Every time one section is pulled away and exposed, another appears to extend the case even further. We have yet to reach the final stage of that telescope, gentlemen, for though we have revealed much that is striking and have made dramatic progress indeed, we are still left without the very objective for which we began searching—the attacker."

Holmes explained for Wilkes and Edwin how the pursuit of the attacker soon became intertwined with the old assassination case, and the process by which he concluded that Wilkes had never been killed as the official version of events stated. He related the words *Sic Semper Tyrannis* as uttered by the attacker as he murdered poor Oglesby in Edwin's apartment; he described finding the assassination pamphlet with its strange inscription in Five Points; he reviewed in detail the highly suspicious manner in which the government disposed of and concealed the corpse of the man they claimed to be John Wilkes Booth. Holmes also explained how he determined that the former Bessie Hale would be a likely person for Wilkes to seek for assistance in the wake of the assassination. Wilkes muttered "Remarkable!" more than once as Holmes unraveled and traced his actual footsteps, sixteen years after the fact.

"My visit to Bessie Chandler with Watson so recently," Holmes said, "was based on my confidence that Wilkes had never left Washington in the aftermath of the crime. This confidence, in turn, was based on the suspicion that the man who accompanied David Herold in escaping across the Navy Yard Bridge was not Wilkes Booth to begin with. We can thank Dr. Samuel Mudd, who was kind enough to permit me to interview him a few weeks ago, for shedding light on this hidden fact.

"Mudd, as you know, Wilkes, was a personal acquaintance of yours.

He had met you several times and, in fact, had entertained and lodged you in his very house in the autumn prior to Lincoln's death. Still, despite the fact that on the morning of April fifteenth he knew his mysterious visitor to be trying with little success to affect a disguise, Mudd has always insisted that he did not recognize this man as Wilkes Booth. It struck me as very puzzling indeed that the one man along the escape route who knew John Wilkes Booth personally did not recognize the fleeing man with the broken leg as being him. As to Mudd's dishonesty on the matter, it is understandable that he might have lied during the original investigation, out of fear of the dire consequences. After all, he did originally deny even that he had met you more than once, Wilkes. Yet, in his discussion with Watson and me, during which he admitted the gross mistake of his earlier dishonesty, Mudd did not change the aspect of his story relating to his failure to recognize you on that morning. What motive could he have for lying now, in eighteen eighty-one, since he has received a full presidential pardon for his role in the affair?"

None of us could think of an intelligent answer to Holmes' question and the detective took advantage of the moment to leisurely relight his briar. He leaned back against the trunk of the massive sycamore, whose limbs arched over us within the arbor, and resumed his discourse.

"Intrigued, though not yet convinced, that Wilkes never showed up at Mudd's place that fateful morning, I sought Bessie Chandler in order to confirm my theory. She did so splendidly, did she not, Watson? She confirmed both the theory that Wilkes was alive and that he had never left Washington. You see, gentlemen, Watson formulated an interesting theory, one that I entertained myself for a brief period—that Wilkes had indeed shot Lincoln, fled through Maryland into Virginia, somehow switched places with some unfortunate soul at Garrett's farm and then returned to Washington by the thirtieth of April to seek Mrs. Chandler's help in furthering his escape. It seemed to explain many of the paradoxes we were facing in the case at the moment, but the theory was demolished by Mrs. Chandler's statement that you, Wilkes, told her of hearing the sound of the bells of Lincoln's funeral. You repeated the same story to us just last night. Since the Washington funeral for the slain president took place on Wednesday, the nineteenth of April, it meant that it would have been impossible for you to have been the fleeing man. The fugitive, in the company of Herold, was known to have spent the nineteenth of April hiding on Huckleberry Farm, Thomas Jones' property, awaiting a chance to cross the nearby Potomac.

"This was an important development because it led me, unfailingly, to the next length of the telescope," said Holmes, rising to walk among us as he revealed his train of logic. "I had, however, suspected for a long time—many years in fact—that you were not, in reality, the assassin of Abraham Lincoln, Wilkes. I had problems with a potential motive, to begin with. Would you actively support a Confederate conspiracy against Lincoln and, if so, what could possibly be the reason for an official plot out of Richmond, especially after the government had fallen? Would you accept the murderer's role in a plot of the Radical Republicans, when you were a known Southern patriot and the Radicals' stated aims were to plunder the South and render it politically and economically impotent? Would you act purely on your own when you had demonstrated no overt signs of madness, when you had much to lose in the way of fame and fortune, and when you—forgive me, Wilkes—were not known as a man of exceptional daring or bravery? You see? Even a sterile examination of motive steered me away from the conclusion that you pulled the trigger."

"Your logic is perfectly sound," Wilkes said. "All of the reasons you state about my having no clear motive were, in fact, true. I stayed away from a murder plot for exactly those reasons, in addition to the demands of my own morality."

"And then there was the question of the fall from the stage," Holmes resumed. "Watson saw me make the very leap from the box at Ford's that the assassin made, with no more injury than a stung foot. But you, Wilkes? You were known as the 'gymnast actor,' praised and reviled alike for your athletic approach to the stage. It never made sense to me that you would have made that leap in such a clumsy manner.

"The blundered leap, of course, proved nothing. It was entirely, if remotely, possible that your spur simply caught the flag as you made the jump. No, Wilkes, what proved your innocence to me beyond a doubt was the unavoidable fact of the escaping man. Traveling as he was with David Herold, an admitted member of your kidnapping conspiracy and a confessed accomplice in Lewis Payne's failed attempt to murder Seward, who else could he have been but the assassin? He fled Washington within minutes of the crime and managed to stay ahead of the pursuing troops for twelve days. At Mudd's place, he showed injuries totally compatible with the fall from the presidential box. He even took credit for the crime, both orally and in a diary. So, to put it in the simplest of terms, if *he* was the assassin, it meant that you could not have been."

Holmes paced methodically through our little assemblage, itemizing his continuing deductions upon his long and narrow fingertips. "So," he said, taking a breath, "I knew Wilkes to be alive." He looked directly at the man about whom he was speaking. "And I knew, or at least had fairly positive indications, that he was innocent of the aptly-named 'Crime of the Century.' It only made sense, therefore, that I should make an effort to locate this man himself. I had no idea at the start whether or not finding Wilkes would at all influence the investigation into Edwin's assailant, but I will say more on that in a moment.

"How did I find him, then? On the surface, such a challenge seemed insurmountable, since Wilkes Booth is but one tiny needle in the great haystack that is America—a needle which, no doubt, had long endeavored to appear as invisible as possible. I concluded first of all that America was indeed the hiding place. Wilkes has spoken of his fears of trying to make passage to Europe or to another location overseas. I considered that very difficulty myself, as well as the fact that few men are willing to pitch their fortunes—no matter how desperate their situation—in a land to which they've never journeyed, and where quite likely they do not speak the native tongue. John Surratt attempted such an escape, remember, with fairly predictable results. It was his very foreign nature, his obvious standing as an alien, that drew official attention to him in the Vatican. With America being such a vast place, and one with so many prime opportunities for hiding, it seemed almost certain that Wilkes would have sought refuge within his own country.

"But where? Certainly he could not stay in the East—either in the

North or the South, where his face was a familiar one to thousands of theater-goers and millions more who had seen the wanted posters bearing his likeness. That leaves the West, of course, which for a multitude of reasons, presented an attractive choice for a fugitive. So, while convinced that Wilkes had made his way westward, the region itself is a vast one. Where in the West would he have gone? I decided that Colorado, or perhaps Montana, presented the most likely choices because of the heavy mining activity which took place in those regions during the eighteen sixties—operations whose bustling activity and populations of newcomers by the thousands offered superb cloaks for a man seeking to escape attention.

"Ultimately," said Holmes with a smile of satisfaction on his face, "I did not have to narrow my search any more than that. Wilkes did that for me, with this short and seemingly insignificant piece of correspondence." Holmes produced from his pocket a postal card. Upon its obverse I saw that it bore a crude mountain penned in ink, with a cross drawn within it. I recognized the card immediately as one of those Holmes and I had found within Edwin's trunk in the cellar of the Booth Theater.

"'Dear Ned (Hamlet),'" Holmes read aloud from the card. "'If I could but convince you, but no, there is no point in this. What must be, must be in the end. But if there be but one spark of recognition within your tortured soul, please recognize the hand of your brother. I am off to the Cloud City now. Far away from all of this. And, God willing, to be at peace. I pray for the chance to see you once more, and to tell you all.' The card is signed 'Your brother, John (Pescara).'"

Holmes handed the card to each of us. Wilkes smiled as he viewed his own writing. Edwin's expression was one of blank surprise. He brought his palm forcefully to his forehead.

"This was from you?" he asked his brother in a tone of astonishment. "I remember this card! It arrived shortly after your death . . . your disappearance, excuse me! I took it as just another crank letter. I got so many for a while there. John, really, I had no idea . . ."

"I intended for the message to be obscure, so that it might well be taken as the writing of a deranged mind, or gallows humour, as it were," Wilkes said. "I could not risk the government somehow deter-

mining my true destination from what I'd written. I was desperate
when I mailed it—just before I left Bessie's place to go west. I wanted
this tiny chance, Ned, this one clue that you might understand, so
that perhaps you could have told mother that I was safe. God, how I
worried about her! All the same, it's not your fault. I knew it was but
a tiny chance that you would know it was from me."

"But what is here to prove anything, Holmes?" Edwin asked, holding the card up to close scrutiny. "What do you see here that I did not?"

"Any number of things," Holmes replied laconically. "It is addressed to you by the nickname 'Ned' for one. I know from my
research into your family that Wilkes preferred to use this name for
you. This is but a little-known fact, however. How could any common
counterfeiter have known that? Note secondly the theatrical character
names written after the real ones—Hamlet after Ned and Pescara after
John. It indicated that the writer of this card somehow knew that
these were the two roles which you and Wilkes respectively considered
your very best. Again, this seems an intimate bit of detail for a stranger
to possess, don't you think?

"Finally, the card indicated Wilkes' intended place of refuge in
two references. The first is the term 'Cloud City,' and the second is
the drawing of a mountain bearing a cross, both of which Watson
took to be morbid references to heaven or to death. It did not take
extensive research, however, to discover that Cloud City was a popular
nickname for the high-country Colorado mining camp officially
known as Oro City, and later Leadville. Eastern newspapers were fairly
filled with references to Cloud City, or the City in the Clouds, as the
town's fame grew. As for the cross in the mountains, a casual check of
an atlas revealed that Colorado's famous Mountain of the Holy Cross,
so named for a geological feature that greatly resembles the Christian
symbol, lies only fifteen or so miles by crow's flight from Leadville.
Wilkes, then, was not only trying to inform you that he was alive, but
to provide information as to where he intended to go."

"You read it all perfectly!" Wilkes exclaimed.

"My God," Edwin muttered, looking again at the card. "I am so
sorry, John. To think that I had the answer in my own hand sixteen
years ago and did absolutely nothing about it!" He shook his head at the

irony represented by the yellowed piece of paper, still bearing its cerulean Washington postage stamp. "To think that your effort was in vain because of me . . ."

"Not in vain, Ned," Wilkes said gently, "just delayed. The card was late in serving its purpose, but thanks to Holmes and yes, thanks to you for keeping it all these years, it has done its duty at last. It provided the direction which led Holmes to me."

"Which, of course," Holmes rejoined, "was the next portion of the telescope. In traveling to Chicago so recently, my objective was not merely to meet with the unfortunate and deranged Mark Gray, but to put the relative Western location of that city to use in trying to find Wilkes. I confess, gentlemen, that luck had some role in my locating the needle in the haystack. I composed a simple advertisement and had it telegraphed for publication in a number of Colorado newspapers, including those in Leadville and Denver, in hopes that Wilkes might happen across it. It was a strategy designed to save time, my first salvo so to speak, and it paid off handsomely.

"It read simply: 'Dear John (Pescara). The truth is known by me. I am working for Ned (Hamlet) and am trying to remove a great danger to him. Have made discoveries concerning the fourteenth of April. You can assist your brother and I, in turn, can work to clear your name, if you so desire. Would you care to make contact? If so, please wire S. Holmes at the Belmont Hotel, Chicago, at your earliest convenience."

"It was the word 'Pescara' that attracted my eye to the advertisement," Wilkes said. "I was at my breakfast table and the sight of it nearly stopped my heart. My wife asked what was the matter. She said it looked as though I'd seen a ghost! I knew without a doubt that it was intended for me. The mysterious S. Holmes must have finally deciphered my long-forgotten card to Ned. Still, I admit, it took me days to gather the courage to wire Holmes in Chicago. I dreaded a sophisticated trap, even after Holmes and I had exchanged several telegrams discussing the circumstances of a meeting. Finally, I invented an excuse to travel east, in order not to alarm my wife, and I boarded a train for Chicago. Holmes explained everything to me upon my arrival there."

Wilkes glanced around at our small group and smiled warmly. "And here I am!"

"And here we are," echoed Holmes. "We have extended the telescope as far as we can for the moment, I daresay, although the final portions remain hidden from view."

"Bravo, Holmes!" I cried. "You've solved the Lincoln mystery! Why, you've changed history itself!"

"Here, here!" chimed in Edwin and Wilkes, raising imaginary glasses in Holmes' direction.

"Tut," said the detective modestly. "It was nothing more than studying hard and visible evidence with keen observation. But let us leave the accolades for the genuine conclusion of the case, shall we? For the moment, since explanation seems to be the purpose and spirit of the evening, allow me to clear up one or two nagging questions while Wilkes is present."

"Ask away," Wilkes said cheerily.

"I remain unclear, for one thing, on the roles played in the conspiracy by Samuel Chester and John Matthews."

"What about them?"

"Both men testified during the military commission that you approached them to join the kidnapping plot."

"Quite true. They were old friends of mine, both actors, and I made the mistake of misjudging their political sympathies or their courage—or perhaps both at the same time. Both Sam and John turned me down. I'm afraid I was a little rough on them afterwards. I couldn't risk the breach in security, you see, so I told them that if they breathed a word of the plot to a soul that I would implicate them in the conspiracy. It was a dastardly threat to use, I know, and I lost them as friends, but I saw no other means to keep them quiet once I had shown my cards."

"Chester also testified that you once remarked to him that you had been close enough to Lincoln on Inauguration Day to have easily killed him. He saw it as proof of your murderous intent."

"Who can blame him for thinking thusly, in light of what happened?" Wilkes replied. "I may have said such a thing, Holmes, but it was hardly a serious comment. Perhaps I mentioned it to illustrate the irony of Lincoln being within a few feet of the man who once wished to kidnap him. I honestly meant nothing by the remark, if indeed I made it."

"And Matthews, of course, is the one who claimed that you handed him a letter on the day of the assassination, with instructions to deliver it to a newspaper on the following morning. He claimed to have read it after Lincoln had been shot, and remembered seeing your signature along with the names of Payne, Atzerodt and Herold, but recalled clearly only the final words: 'The moment has at length arrived when my plans must be changed. The world may censure me for what I am about to do, but I am sure that posterity will justify me.' He said he grew alarmed and burned the letter at once, out of the fear of implication."

"That remains a great mystery to me, Holmes. I did not see Matthews once during the day of April fourteenth and I certainly handed him no letter. We had not spoken since my last attempt to recruit him."

"Interesting," Holmes said, puffing leisurely on his pipe. "And what about visiting with Mary Surratt on the fourteenth? She claimed that you asked her to deliver a few articles down to Surrattsville. She enlisted the help of one of her boarders in Washington, a Louis Wiechmann, who later testified that he rented a buggy for the trip on Mrs. Surratt's behalf, that he personally saw you handing over these articles to her, and that he drove her down to Surrattsville himself."

Wilkes shrugged his shoulders and held out his hands in a gesture of ignorance. "It must have been the same man who took my place later that day at Ford's," he said. "It was very likely the same man who handed Matthews the letter. I did not ask Mrs. Surratt to take anything down to Surrattsville that day, nor did I see or speak with Wiechmann. These are among the many things which I am believed to have done on the fourteenth, none of which actually happened, at least not to me. For example, a number of stagehands at Ford's claimed that I took them in a group for drinks in the afternoon at Taltavul's. I swear on my life that I did not do so. A number of stable managers in the city also claimed to have seen me. I went to no stables on that day. I rented no horses. Somebody was obviously taking my place that day, and perhaps before, without my knowledge of it."

"Is it also not true, Wilkes, that you had reserved a box at Grover's Theater for the night of April fourteenth? There are records indicating such a reservation in your name."

"That is true," he replied. "I had reserved the box, intending to invite Miss Hale to attend with me; *Aladdin* was being performed that night. But as I said, I was in particularly low spirits during the illumination spectacle, and I changed my mind, preferring to spend the evening alone, with only brandy to keep me company."

"Indeed," said Holmes, clearly fascinated with Wilkes' answers and intrigued with the new mysteries they presented in turn. "Quite recently, Wilkes, Watson and I came across an old Confederate uniform in the trunk your brother has kept—the trunk you used in eighteen sixty-five while staying at the National Hotel. Is the uniform yours?"

A rather sheepish look now seemed to come across Wilkes' face. "It was," he said at last. "I held a brevet colonel's rank in the Confederate Secret Service, you see. If the truth be told, the rank was mostly an honourary one. I wore the uniform on one or two of my trips to Montreal on Confederate business—trips to purchase quinine supplies. It was purely for the sake of my self-esteem, my friends. Ned knows how I promised our mother that I would never fight in the war—she begged me to make such a promise—and this is the only reason, I swear on my honour, why I did not serve more directly. So, as it turned out, my Secret Service duties and the rank, such as it was, were about as close as I could come to being a real soldier."

"But what about the kidnapping plot? If you were a C. S. A. colonel, even an honourary one, you must have informed Richmond of your intentions."

"Oh, but I did, Holmes!" Wilkes said forcefully. "I tried for months to convince them of the plan's value, but my superiors in Richmond refused to get officially involved. Nor would they give me a dime toward financing the plan. I don't believe they ever took it, or me, very seriously. The final response from my superiors was: 'If you suddenly show up in Richmond with Abe Lincoln in tow, let us know, and then we shall see what to do about it.' They said this with a laugh, my friends. I decided to act without their help. They were timid old fools, I'm afraid, men without vision or imagination, which is likely why they ended up as they did."

Wilkes then rose and strolled around the arbor bench, stroking his moustache as if in deep thought. "Either that," he said, looking at Holmes, "or I was most terribly and shamefully used by my supervisors in espionage. It has occurred to me more than once that perhaps the Richmond government, or at least a fanatical cell within it, took advantage of my kidnapping effort in order to provide cover for their own plan to assassinate Lincoln. They had the means to carry out such a sophisticated plot, and the inside knowledge of my own plans. What their reasons might have been, though, I can hardly guess."

"A fascinating theory," said Holmes in a tone of barely perceptible condescension—a tone which I knew from my own experience indicated that he put little stock in the idea. "But let us veer away from speculation for the moment, into the realm of what we know to be undeniably true, based on the evidence we have collected at this juncture."

Holmes paused as a lone carriage rattled past on the nearby road, carrying elegantly-clad passengers out for an evening's ride. He nodded in response to the driver's courteous tip of his silk hat.

"There can be no doubt as to one thing," he said, turning back to us, "and that is that we are dealing with some sort of simulacrum for Wilkes, a man who is so naturally similar to him in appearance, or so adept at adopting a disguise in his image, that he was highly successful in convincing a virtual host of people that he was, in fact, Wilkes. On the day of April the fourteenth alone, we know that he hoodwinked both Mary Surratt and Louis Wiechmann, both of whom had known Wilkes for weeks at least; he convinced a small platoon of Ford's stagehands that he was so; he raised no apparent suspicions in speaking at close quarters with John Matthews, an old friend of Wilkes' no less, and in gaining his personal trust for an important letter. He was also recognized as Wilkes at Taltavul's Saloon on the afternoon and the evening of the fourteenth. As far as I know, however, I am the only one to note the telling fact that he ordered whiskey on those visits, instead of Wilkes' usual brandy. His *coup-de-grâce*, of course, took place in Ford's Theater, where he managed to convince the entire house that he was John Wilkes Booth. And, with the notable exception of Samuel Mudd, a fair number of people along the escape route made the same mistake.

"This simulacrum, or surrogate assassin if you will, had also pen-etrated your inner circle of kidnapping conspirators, Wilkes, and worked at least to some degree with their help and cooperation. It is virtually certain that Lewis Payne was in his employ; I consider it likely that David Herold also had some knowledge of him; it is pos-sible, at least, that Atzerodt was involved. He knew of every step you made for several weeks at least, and used this knowledge to construct his well-conceived frame. The obvious program was to murder Lin-coln, and to escape justice for the crime by weaving an ironclad web of apparent evidence against yourself. As you've noted, Wilkes, to this degree our surrogate was utterly successful. The frame-up was bril-liant, both in concept and in execution. Its secrets, and hence the surrogate's own identity, remained safe even as Payne, Herold and Atzerodt went to the hangman. If they knew otherwise, and Payne almost surely did, they took this knowledge to the grave with them. None of them would make the slightest contradiction of the government's version of the events. It comes as close to being the proverbial perfect crime as I have seen thus far in my career."

"But Holmes," I protested, "if the true assassin fled southward with Herold, I cannot imagine why he did so. If he had so perfectly set up Wilkes to take the blame, why did he flee so suddenly, and with such apparent desperation?"

"Excellent point, Watson, but I'm afraid I haven't quite pondered that problem to my full satisfaction. I conjecture that the move might have been one of prudent caution. In other words, he fled on the odd chance that somehow the pursuers might somehow get on his own trail in Washington instead of Wilkes', or that Wilkes might some-how manage to escape the trap he'd set for him. As it turned out, of course, he was half right; Wilkes was sufficiently cautious, as well as lucky, to avoid capture."

"Well, if that's the case," I countered, "I can imagine no reason for his giving the name 'Booth' when questioned by the sentry at the bridge."

"Ah, Watson," said Holmes, clapping his hands. "You do impress me with your gaining skills at logic. You are right, of course. The problem is an immensely baffling one. By giving Booth's name, he did nothing less than set the entire Union army upon his very own trail. It makes little obvious sense. Neither does the fact that, to some degree, the surrogate kept up the ruse of being Wilkes at various points along the escape route. He disguised himself at Mudd's, yet told the Confederate officers at the Rappahannock River that he was Wilkes. I'm sorry to fail you, Watson. I simply have yet to gain the answers to these."

Holmes knocked the ashes from his pipe onto his heel and began refilling the bowl. When he struck a match I realized how dark the dusk had grown since we'd stopped here. The nearest street lamps must have been a quarter of a mile away and the gloom was growing pervasive.

"Another piece of the puzzle which eludes me," said Holmes between puffs, "is how the surrogate managed to survive the showdown at Garrett's."

"Well how do you know that he *did* survive it?" Wilkes asked.

"The government's cover-up, of course, raises many suspicions. Being aware of it yourself, Wilkes, you surmised it to be merely an attempt to conceal their bungling of their own manhunt. I surmised something worse, indeed. Not only did they fail to track down John Wilkes Booth, they somehow failed to capture the surrogate, the true assassin, although they must have come within mere inches of it. There is no doubt in my mind that the surrogate was at Garrett's, and little doubt that he was literally cornered in that dismal tobacco shed. Yet somehow, he slipped past them all. Somehow he escaped the irony of being captured for the very crime he worked so hard to have blamed on you."

Holmes pulled something from his pocket and struck a match to illuminate it for us all. It was the ghastly photograph of a bloated corpse which he had pilfered from the War Department's archives. Edwin and Wilkes gasped in unison as they viewed the gruesome visage which stared out at them in the glow of the lucifer match.

"The very best that the United States Army had to show for their pursuit of Abraham Lincoln's murderer was this corpse," said Holmes. "I can only imagine where they found it. What is significant, of course, is that this War Department photograph proved to me not only that they failed to capture Wilkes, but that they failed to capture your surro-

gate as well. There is absolutely no way that this body could have belonged to Lincoln's assassin, is there? Not with hundreds of people
ready to swear they saw Wilkes himself committing the crime. Under
no circumstances could this man have substituted for you."

"Which further proves . . ." Wilkes began.

"That the surrogate assassin may well remain among the living
himself," Holmes said.

"And," said Edwin, raising a finger for emphasis, "that this so-
called surrogate, Holmes, might easily be the same man who's trying
so hard to do me in!"

"Quite."

"Wait a moment," I said. "I've followed quite well until this moment. Now I am confused again. Didn't you believe, and not so very
long ago, Holmes, that Wilkes himself might be the man who was
tracking Edwin? Didn't Mark Gray help convince you of this?"

"Excellent point once again, Watson!" the detective exclaimed. "When
I left Washington the last time, after you and I had been to Garrett's farm
and already met with Bessie Chandler, I admit that I considered the
possibility—and I beg your forgiveness for it, Wilkes—that Wilkes might
be the attacker who so persistently wished to murder Edwin. We had
found articles in the attacker's Mulberry Bend hideout that pointed in
your direction, after all, and I had learned that the mysterious man
walked with a detectable limp on his left leg, which only now can we see
that Wilkes does not have. The simple knowledge that you were not killed
in Virginia as the government claimed at least raised the possibility that
it could have been you.

"A paradox, however, immediately reared its head. If you were not
the man who fled Washington with Herold on the night of April
fourteenth, how likely was it that you were, in fact, Lincoln's assassin?
As I've already noted, this struck me as highly unlikely. And if you
were not Lincoln's assassin, how likely would it be that you were
Edwin's attacker? Again, highly unlikely. If you are innocent of the
madness that inspired Lincoln's murderer, in other words, I could see
no reason to assume that you harbour the madness which drives
Edwin's attacker. I traveled to Chicago, therefore, not with the conviction that I was pursuing a nefarious assassin, or a madman bent on

murdering his own brother, but a wronged man—a fugitive, yes, but an innocent one."

"But what about Mark Gray?" I asked. "Didn't he tell you that the man who caused him to murder Edwin in Chicago was in fact John Wilkes Booth?"

"He did indeed, Watson," the detective replied, "and I have no doubt that he believed every word of it, even though I am convinced that he must be wrong. The man who persuaded him to fire at Edwin in the Chicago theater must have assumed Wilkes' identity for Gray's benefit. Not only that, but he too must have borne a striking physical similarity in order to so convince him. Gray identified him quite positively, remember, from the photograph I carried. This points powerfully, gentlemen, in the direction of the surrogate—the man who seems to have no trouble at all in taking Wilkes' place.

"All of which leads inexorably to yet another portion of the telescope. The assassin of Abraham Lincoln is almost surely the same man who hired Gray, who stalked Edwin through Oberammergau, who pursued him through the hallways of the Lyceum, who killed Agent Oglesby here in New York, and who nearly did the same to Watson. The attacker and the assassin, in other words, must be the same man."

"Then both of us, John and I alike, are victims of the same man?" Edwin asked with a tone of strong wonder and discovery evident in his voice.

"Precisely."

"But why, Holmes? Where is the reason to it?"

"I confess that I have yet to vanquish the problem of motive which is, without doubt, a three-pipe problem if I've ever seen one. I plan to ponder it this very night."

The four of us then began to stroll leisurely back toward our hotel, as the night had grown quite dark. None of us spoke more than a word or two, with each man seemingly lost in his own contemplations of Holmes' abstruse but utterly logical path through the twists and turns of this remarkable case.

It was Wilkes who broke the silence. "What you've said so far makes perfect sense," he said to Holmes, "but all of your conclusions are based on theories and logic. I accept the logic of what you say,

Holmes, and I find it remarkable that you've put it all together as well as you have, but what sort of proof is there? I suppose I am a doubting Thomas when all is said and done, and I'd feel a lot better if you could show me something tangible to prove it all."

"Well, that is no problem," the detective replied in a casual air. "Here's a street lamp at last. Stop here for a moment, will you, and hold out your hand."

With a puzzled look in my direction, Wilkes did as he was told. Holmes took something from his waistcoat pocket and placed it upon Wilkes' finger. In the illumination of the gaslight, I saw at once that it was the ring which had been lost by the attacker in struggling with me.

"A perfect fit, is it not?" the detective queried.

"It is not only that," replied the startled Wilkes. "It is undoubtedly my own ring! I know it well, for I had it made especially for me in Philadelphia. There is no other like it."

"You were once a member of the Knights of the Golden Circle, I understand."

"Yes, Holmes. I joined with them in 'fifty-eight or 'fifty-nine, and remained active for a year or two."

"I assume the Knights then had nothing to do with the kidnapping plan?"

"Nothing at all, quite correct. I realized early on that they were but a bunch of strutting fools, not at all serious about their stated aims. But the ring, Holmes. Where did you get it? It must be fifteen years since I've seen it."

"Sixteen, to be precise. I assume it left your possession sometime in the spring of eighteen sixty-five, probably along with a number of other personal things of yours."

"Well yes, that's about right! I did miss a few things—some photographs, a compass, a handkerchief—which the Army later claimed to have found on the man they had killed. It only made sense that Lewis Payne was the thief. He was in my rooms a great deal, of course. Still, I've heard no mention of this ring."

"I propose that you are correct, Wilkes. The items stolen from your room were doubtlessly intended to help buttress the frame-up in one way or another. Payne probably stole the articles you mention, and the ring as well, although that was not left behind at Garrett's place. It turned up much more recently, in fact, in Edwin's apartment at the Windsor after the attacker's combat with our sturdy Watson."

"Yes! I see!" Wilkes exclaimed, examining his ring closely. "So this is the proof! It means we are dealing with the very same man after all."

"Quite right," said Holmes as we crossed 57th Street, "although none of us, least of all Edwin, should take much consolation from this simple fact of clarification. We have made great strides in the past few weeks, it is true, and your return to Edwin is a cause for celebration, but we must remember that the surrogate remains at large, waiting with his terrible patience and daunting cunning. We must remember that until I can expose the telescope's next portion, we have one important fact in common with him."

"What is that?" I asked.

"That we consider our work unfinished."

—19—
Baltimore

Virtually every historian, biographer and journalist who has attempted to describe the historical figure of John Wilkes Booth has done so by attributing to him the traits of madness, loose morality and a passionate, headstrong nature.

In having the chance to know the man personally, of course, I gained a considerable advantage over those who have sought to depict him through whatever meager sources were available to them. I found that I both disagreed and agreed with the popular notions of who Wilkes Booth really was.

First of all, I am positive that madness was never among his traits. The historians, naturally enough, base this conclusion upon the belief that Wilkes was Lincoln's assassin, but since I discovered otherwise, I found the charge utterly fallacious and without foundation. As to Wilkes' disdain for morality, I assume that this may have been an accurate description of the man in his youth. He admitted as much to Edwin, Holmes and I—more than once—even while giving every indication that as he matured in years and in mind, he became a man of unimpeachable integrity and sound moral foundation in every respect. He is not the only man, surely, regretful of the transgressions of his younger days.

I am, however, forced to agree with the chroniclers as to the passionate and headstrong dimensions of Wilkes' personality. He had hardly been reunited with his brother in New York for three days when he'd already started and conducted two arguments with Edwin, and another with Holmes himself.

In the case of Holmes, Wilkes immediately and angrily rejected the detective's suggestion that he stay as quiet and hidden, and as far from the investigation, as possible. The actor would have none of it. The case had even more to do with him than with Edwin, Wilkes insisted, and had already affected his life profoundly. In coming back east, his sole determination had been to resolve the mystery of the frame-up in one way or another, no matter the cost. He was not dissuaded by Holmes' arguments that such involvement could well result in bodily harm to him, nor that it might lead to his public exposure at a premature moment—with equally dangerous implications. Even the detective's urging to think of his new family in the Rocky Mountains had no effect on Wilkes. He would be a part of the case regardless, he insisted, and Holmes reluctantly resigned himself to that fact. In an rare instance of apparent surrender, Holmes agreed to keep Wilkes abreast of his progress in the case, and to include him in any endeavor that might result in an encounter with the shadowy surrogate.

The first quarrel with Edwin was ignited by Wilkes' expression of indignation at comments he had made in 1865, in the wake of the assassination, in which Edwin publicly revealed his belief that Wilkes had been mentally deranged. The statement had "stuck in my craw since I first read of it," Wilkes said, and even the passage of time could not erase the offense he took at the remark.

Edwin defended himself stoutly, chiding Wilkes for not understanding the position into which the crime had placed him. "How could I possibly have known otherwise," he asked, "when every man in the country believed you to be guilty, including myself?" Until this very week, Edwin said, he had received no indication whatsoever of his brother's innocence, and madness seemed the only explanation for such an act. If Wilkes had wished to inform him otherwise, Edwin angrily chastised him, he had had 16 years in which to do so, and yet he had apparently thought so little of his own family that he let them go for this long with no word of his survival nor of his innocence.

Subdued, Wilkes replied that he had desperately longed to do so, but feared that such a move might lead to his capture, and end in even more tragedy and heartbreak for his long-suffering family.

This spat, however, was tame in comparison to the one between them when the war came up as a subject of discussion. I went so far as to ask the guards to leave the suite, for fear that the brothers' raised voices would reveal far too much. In Wilkes' passionate oratory of the rightness of the Confederate cause and the savagery of the Union army, and in Edwin's equally impassioned condemnation of slavery and treason, it seemed to me as if the war had never really ended at all. It brought home to me very vividly why the Americans tend to remember this war as one in which brother was pitted against brother. In the case of the brothers Booth, this was very literally true.

The Booths were, however, brothers after all, and their disputes tended to end peacefully and amicably when all was said and done. Their differences certainly did not prevent them from attending to a most important piece of family business. Some five days after his arrival in New York, Wilkes joined Edwin in a joyous, but extremely clandestine, reunion with their mother, brother Joseph and sister Rosalie in nearby Long Branch. Edwin had informed them all of the imminent meeting beforehand, in order to save them the shock and surprise which he had had to endure, and had made similar notification by post to the other Booths—the eldest Junius, Jr., and sister Asia—who resided in distant places.

The reunion lasted three days, as it turned out, and both brothers reported that it seemed to rapidly bring their mother back from the state of gloomy despair into which she had fallen, and from which never really arisen, 16 years ago. It evidently did much to elevate the spirits of the entire family, not surprisingly, and obviously had such an effect on the actor brothers themselves, despite the fact that it was held under conditions of the utmost secrecy.

As soon as I was able to overcome my prejudices about Wilkes' false historical role as an assassin, which was not terribly long, he and I became fast friends. We spent several enjoyable afternoons riding about New York in Edwin's handsome surrey, as Wilkes wished to see many sights which were once familiar to him—theaters, saloons, houses and the like—and through his scholarly spectacles his eyes lit up repeatedly as one landmark or another inspired a pleasant and nostalgic memory from his younger days. His pain was evident too, as

Wilkes was quite aware of the fact that this entire world of the past was now utterly closed to him.

We held long and interesting conversations about his experiences in Leadville and Denver. For his part, Wilkes wanted to know my impressions of people Holmes and I had met during the investigation. He was quite interested in hearing of our conversations with his old friend Samuel Arnold and his acquaintance Dr. Mudd, who came to play such an important role in the case. More than anything else, however, Wilkes wanted to hear every word uttered to us by Bessie Chandler. He wiped his eyes when I told him that she had admitted to Holmes that she loved Wilkes to this day, and it was clear to me that in spite of everything that had happened in the interim, he continued to feel the same way.

"It's no less a tragedy than Romeo and Juliet," Wilkes said sadly one day as we smoked and watched the workers at the Brooklyn Bridge. "It was truly a glorious love, Watson, the love of a lifetime, yet never meant to be."

During this period, we saw very little of Holmes. He was once again working alone, in his furtive and ferret-like way, doubtlessly examining new angles of the case, but (despite his promise to Wilkes) informing us of none of his progress. "I am not without my resources, Watson," he said in reply to my one request for information, and there I let the matter drop. He was often away for most of a night, and sometimes its entirety, and bore a manner of nervous excitement and anticipation which I took to be a sure sign that his efforts were reaping some sort of fruit.

Finally, on a sunny Saturday morning, I discovered that I was correct. It came in the form of a telegram from Holmes—he had been away for the past two days—which had been wired from Baltimore. "May need your help," the telegram read. "Be in Baltimore, armed and ready, by this evening. Have rooms at the Carrollton. Come alone."

Sensing both danger and adventure in Holmes' brief missive, I packed hurriedly, cleaned my revolver, and left a message for Edwin and Wilkes. By noon I was aboard a train speeding southward from Pennsylvania Station, eager to join Holmes once again and to do something to further the case.

The trip to Baltimore took most of a warm and brilliant after-noon. I reached the city by teatime and, finding nobody to greet me at the bustling depot, hired a cab for the short ride to the hotel. I was in such a rush that I hardly paid any heed to the pleasant old port town in which I suddenly found myself, and through which my coach was hurriedly passing.

The Carrollton Hotel, in its outward aspect, was a typically bulky and imposing structure, bedecked with American flags of huge di-mensions, and located within the very heart of the city's close and hilly commercial district. It boasted, however, a fair share of interior innovations. The place was illuminated by something called "galvanic fluid," which I took to be electricity, and it boasted as well a smooth and efficient elevator for its five floors, powered by the same energy. I marvelled at the progress reflected in the new establishment as I ascended briskly to the top floor, bellhop in tow.

I had to let myself into the assigned room as the door was locked. As I entered, I was immediately met with a powerful blast of noxious tobacco fumes—obviously the effluvium of Holmes' cherrywood—and saw that all the shades had been drawn. Holmes sat in a chair near the corner, eyes closed, fingers pressing thoughtfully against his temples, a great stream of blue smoke issuing from his pipe. He opened his eyes halfway when he heard me enter and waited to speak until the bellhop had taken his gratuity and departed.

"My gratitude for your coming on such short notice," he said languidly. "Was the trip a pleasant one?"

"It was fine, Holmes."

"You are alone then?"

"Quite."

"And armed?"

I pulled away my coat to reveal the stock of my weapon.

"Excellent, Watson. Now you may relax. I realize the trip is a long one."

"Relax?" I asked. "But I gathered from your wire some sense of urgency."

"Oh there is urgency aplenty, old fellow, don't fret about that, but we have at least one night's respite before things will, shall we say, commence. I wanted you here tonight for we have an important meeting to make in the early morning."

"A meeting with whom?"

The detective smiled faintly and yawned. "We shall rise at five," he announced, "and I confess to being exhausted, with not a wink since Thursday. I suggest you catch a good night's rest yourself."

Holmes curled up in his chair, cat-like, and promptly went to sleep without another word.

Dawn found Baltimore beneath the blanket of a chilly and pervasive fog which had silently snaked its way up the Chesapeake Bay and Patapsco River during the night. The weather gave the deserted streets a spectral and mystical air as it encircled and obscured the tops of the taller buildings and church spires. Nary a pedestrian nor a milk wagon violated the quietude on that early Sunday morning as Holmes and I walked steadily toward the east, our footsteps barely making a sound on the peculiar Belgian blocks with which the street was paved.

We had arisen, on schedule, at five o'clock, with barely time for coffee before Holmes rushed on his way, with me hurrying behind him. Holmes maintained his mysterious air about our duties this morning, but I persisted in pressing him for details. In all frankness, I was growing quite weary of heading off on yet another unknown pursuit, with an equally unknown factor of danger, provided only with the scant information Holmes was willing to divulge.

He paused, scratched a match against the solemn face of a wooden Indian chieftan guarding a closed tobacco shop, and lit his pipe. "Impatience does not become you, Watson," he said irritably.

"And your refusal to illuminate me does not become *you*," I fired back.

"Very well," he sighed, resuming his pace. "If you must know, we are bound for one of the city's more obscure cemeteries, the precise location of which took me no less than two days to determine. I daresay I have visited each and every churchyard in Baltimore in search of one particular grave."

"Grave?" I asked. "We're to have a meeting with the dead, then?"

The detective shot me an ill-amused glance. Holmes was never fond of my occasional habit of making light of his work.

"Hardly," he sniffed. "I am interested, rather, in one particular person who is likely to be visiting that certain grave. On virtually every Sunday for the past decade and a half, the sexton has informed me, this individual pays a proper and fitting visit to this particular grave, and sees to its upkeep. It is he who interests me."

I tipped my bowler to two passing ladies in white crinoline, early risers, apparently on their way to church.

"Do you feel that this man might be . . ."

"The surrogate?" Holmes interrupted. "Quite likely, I'd say. The sexton at the cemetery did note that the grave went unvisited and unattended for several months earlier in the year, a period of time which coincides nicely with Edwin's recent tour of Europe as well as the surrogate's presence in London."

"Well then," I persisted, "who is he?"

"I cannot say for certain at this juncture."

"Come now, Holmes, if you know whose grave he's taking care of, you must have a vague idea of who he is."

"That is elementary, my dear Watson," he said with a smile, "but what if I'm wrong? I am not closed to the possibility, remote as it is. I should never like to place my cards upon the table before a player as astute, and as eager to record, as yourself."

We walked on in silence for the better part of an hour, watching the close quarters of Baltimore's mercantile district slowly transform into a neighborhood of residential dwellings, composed mostly of seemingly endless lines of neat rowhouses, each fronted by ornate railings and spotless marble stoops. We had walked to a quiet and orderly section of eastern Baltimore.

There was still hardly a soul upon the foggy streets when at last we came to the high spiked gates of a tiny and nearly invisible cemetery on Eden Street, virtually shrouded in dense trees. I detected from the statuary within the old necropolis that the cemetery was likely a Catholic one, noting as well the battered sign reading "Cathedral Cemetery." From where I stood, most of the tombs and graves seemed rather neglected. Beneath its trees, the place was covered with a heavy growth of underbrush and rose bushes left to their own devices, and with the heavy mist weaving its way in and out of the tombstones and stone figures, the atmosphere was nothing less than sinister.

Holmes gently rattled the gate until a wizened little old man emerged from a tiny shed nearby. The white-haired sexton seemed to recognize Holmes immediately, and with nothing more than a nod of his wispy head, he opened the heavy gate and let us in. I noticed that Holmes placed a silver coin into the man's hand as we passed.

We walked along the path until Holmes found what he must have considered a favorable vantage. It was near the corner of the grave-yard, beneath the cover of a massive spruce. Holmes squatted beside a grave whose occupant was identified by a rounded marble tombstone reading:

Here Lies Elias Barth

1775-1849

Beloved husband of Hepzibah

beloved father of

Jedediah, Jonathan, Abigail and Zachariah

"This is it, then?" I inquired, joining Holmes in kneeling next to the overgrown, half-sunken grave.

"Not at all," Holmes whispered, "and keep your voice down Watson, please. Our grave is just over there." He pointed to a spot some 30 yards distant, beneath a Normandy poplar, marked with a Celtic cross that had gone slightly awry. At this distance, I could not even see its epitaph, let alone read it.

"That's the one. We must keep our eyes upon it, even as we appear to be mourning the late Mr. Barth here. Our visitor mustn't have the slightest indication that he is being watched."

I found it difficult to appear as if I were mourning a loved one when I knelt by this stranger's grave, and found the damp grass un-comfortable, but fortunately Holmes had timed our arrival with some precision. We waited less than 30 minutes in the misty cemetery, amidst a few other scattered mourners who had trickled in, when Holmes spotted his prey.

He gave a stifled cry when we saw a lone man walking from the gate toward the grave Holmes had pointed out. He walked directly to his objective, paying no heed at all to the pebbled footpath nor to the fact that he was treading atop others' graves. Holmes gave me a slight nudge when he realized I was staring at the man, and I quickly reassumed the false pose of praying we had been maintaining.

I had, however, gotten à fair glimpse of the stranger, though insufficient to gain a clear look at his face. He was not tall, several inches at least below six feet, but he walked erect and straight, as if he were in good health. The exception, I saw with considerable excitement, was a slight but still noticeable limp in his left leg. He was carrying a walking stick in his right hand in order to compensate for it. He wore a long black cloak, rather old-fashioned in style, and tall dress boots. He was without a hat.

The hair on top of his head was snowy white, long and thick. A moustache of similar colour adorned his face. This surprised me, as I had been expecting a younger man. There was, despite the distance, an unsettling and vague familiarity to the figure.

We took quick and furtive glances in his direction as we knelt. The stranger did indeed halt at the specific grave, and he stood reverently beside it. From our distance, I could not tell if he was praying, or speaking aloud, but I think I was able to detect movement of his lips. He remained in that posture for some minutes before he wiped something away from his eye.

The man then knelt beside the grave, despite the heavy dew, and began methodically removing the weeds and leaves from its surface. He went about this work almost lovingly, it seemed, and with great care and patience. At last, he produced from the inner folds of his cloak a single red rose and, leaning near the tombstone, injected its stem into the earth. He gazed upon it for a moment or two, and then rose, and began striding with rapid steps back toward the gate.

Holmes nudged me again, more forcefully this time. "It is he!" he whispered. "We mustn't tarry! We'll follow, but carefully. Come!"

We followed the man out of the graveyard at a distance roughly equal to that from which we had observed him inside, and tried not to appear suspicious in any way. The stranger, at any rate, seemed utterly ignorant of our presence as he continued to walk purposefully through the streets. He was indeed a fast walker, and apparently a courteous fellow as well. He nodded pleasantly to the gentlemen who passed his way and bowed his head graciously whenever a lady came by. He once patted a little girl upon the head.

He led us southward, through more neighborhoods filled with neat rowhouses, and then turned east on the busy thoroughfare that was Fayette Street. It was past seven o'clock by now, and a fair number of people were walking about the sidewalks or riding by in their carriages, but we had little trouble keeping sight of him because of his starkly white head of hair. I counted two blocks southward and another seven blocks eastward along Fayette before he turned to the north.

By this time, it appeared he was close to home. As the stranger turned into a quiet and narrow residential lane, Holmes casually stopped and leaned against an iron lamp-post, invisible from the stranger's position, signalling for me to do the same. The man approached his domicile, one of a long phalanx of handsome brick townhouses, pausing only to take the rolled newspaper that had been placed in his gate. He glanced first to one side and then the other, taking in the entire street's worth of houses, but it was clear that he could not see us at all. Holmes was an exquisite tracker! I realized only by the sound of the man's key and the opening of his door that he had let himself in.

Holmes and I waited by the lamp-post at the corner for several minutes before we approached the house for a closer look. I made a motion of reaching for my revolver but Holmes silently bade me to disregard the notion. We passed by the stranger's front door in a casual manner, appearing to discuss something with one another, but both of us glanced at the place.

Every drape had been drawn tightly shut, along with the door. I noticed, as did Holmes, a small rectangular wooden sign which had been attached to the iron railing surrounding the tiny dooryard. In simple Roman letters it announced: "Samson Morrissey—Solicitor-at-Law."

We walked steadily past the residence until we reached the end of the block. Holmes turned to me. "I would imagine this street to be a pretty place in autumn," he said.

"What do you mean, Holmes?"

"These trees, Watson, southern red oaks, which line the lane so neatly, must bear a striking scarlet colour when the weather turns."

"Yes, I suppose they would," I replied, confused. "And so?"

"You might notice that their acorns are just beginning to bud, old fellow, see?" He pointed to a small clump of greenish spheres nestled high in one of the oaks. His meaning suddenly became clear.

"The acorns!" I said. "Of course! He takes them from his very own street." Holmes merely regarded me with a raised eyebrow.

"What now, Holmes?" I inquired.

"Now we must wait."

"But Holmes, if this is our man, he is firmly within our grasp!" I protested. "We can take him this very moment!"

"I daresay it's not quite so simple," he said with an ironic grimace. "He *is* the man, Watson, entertain no doubts about it, but I think I should like to prepare a rather better trap for him. There are, in addition, one or two mitigating circumstances we must consider regarding our client brothers. In any case, the wait shan't be long, and we know that he works and lives here, so he won't be a difficult fellow to find. Come, we've had a busy morning with all this walking and lurking about graves, and with no breakfast to fortify us! Let us hire a cab and return to the hotel."

I was, of course, disappointed by Holmes' decision not to corner the scoundrel that minute, but stood by his decision, fully trusting his wisdom in the matter. We hailed a cab within a block or two and cut through the fog with considerably greater ease than we had enjoyed while walking.

Near the hotel, Holmes ordered the driver to stop. He leapt to the curb, where I saw the familiar blue and white sign of a Western Union telegraph office. I heard Holmes dictate his message from where I sat.

"To Mr. Edwin Booth, Windsor Hotel, New York," he told the clerk at the streetside window. "Please be in Baltimore, at the Carrollton, by Monday noon. Bring your companion but no guards. The time has come. Holmes."

When he was back in the cab I asked Holmes about the telegram.

"On the morrow, my dear fellow, the elusive Samson Morrissey, Esquire, shall experience a harsh encounter with justice and destiny," he said with a satisfied smile, "and a long-delayed one at that. I think it's only fitting that Edwin and Wilkes, the principal victims of his villainous work, be present for the occasion."

–20–
The Simulacrum

It is a rare man indeed who has the chance to gaze upon his own grave, and I can say from experience that it is a strange occasion when it occurs.

"Rest in peace, nameless one," Wilkes said aloud as he stood before the tall obelisk bearing the name of Booth upon its base. He was referring not only to the utterly unknown man whose bones, resting here, were universally believed to be his, but to the fact that his own name appeared nowhere in this family plot which contained the graves of his father and siblings who had perished in their infancy. The state of Maryland, it seemed, had forbidden the detested name of the assassin to be displayed in any public place, even at the site of his supposed grave.

Wilkes shook his head slowly, a haunted look on his ivory features. "It reminds me of an ancient Hebrew curse I read about somewhere," he said quietly to Edwin and I, who stood beside him. "Something like: 'May your name be forever erased from the book of life.' I understand it is supposed to represent the gravest of insults, as Jews believe that the souls of the departed live on only through the memories of the living. I think they selected their curse well. It *is* insulting. It is worse than that; it is a damnation."

The three of us stood, virtually alone, within the sprawling expanse of Baltimore's Greenmount Cemetery, the second graveyard I had visited in as many days. The brothers had arrived on Monday morning, in response to Holmes' telegram, and joined me at the hotel. Holmes, not surprisingly, had left the hotel at daybreak, well before their arrival, and instructed me to keep them occupied until we should hear further from him.

We hired a brougham, therefore, and spent a few hours riding easily through the city which the Booths had long considered their hometown. Fortunately, the fog of the previous day had lifted, but the skies over Baltimore remained sullen and dark, stubbornly threatening rain. We rode past the Booths' former house on High Street, a plain and ordinary dwelling which the family had occupied primarily in the wintertime. We looked in vain for the once magnificent manor of Belvedere, long a personal fascination of Wilkes', and were disappointed to discover that the estate had been demolished some five years past. We strolled about the harbour streets and feasted on crab cakes for lunch; we rode through the lush greenery of Druid Hill Park. And, of course, we visited the cemetery.

That was Wilkes' idea entirely. Edwin felt that a visit to Greenmount would be a morbid pursuit at best, but Wilkes, fully in character, would not be talked out of it. He wished to pay his respects to his father, he stated. "And besides, no man should miss the opportunity to view his own resting place," he added, laughing at his own dark humour while Edwin grimaced at it.

What we were really doing, of course, was trying to while away the time as we awaited word from Holmes. I had brought Edwin and Wilkes as up to date on our findings in Baltimore as possible, and all three of us were in a state of nervous anxiety. We had a sense that some form of resolution was imminent, that a long festering sore was about to be lanced. Within that prospect, there was the expectation both of release and of danger. I saw this restlessness most clearly in Wilkes, whose entire demeanor seemed one of tension and readiness. His movements were sharp and animalistic in their quickness, his eyes constantly darting this way and that, as if visually seeking his foe. Edwin was dark and quiet as usual, but even he bore a decided edge of wariness about him.

We returned to the Carrollton in the midafternoon, just in time to avoid the downpour which then began to descend upon the city, and to receive a crosstown telegram from Holmes. Like most of the detective's messages, it was succinct and to the point:

"Gentlemen. At seven-thirty this evening, I shall appear in our rooms with a special guest. Be ready for him, and for anything. Holmes."

With but these words as our guide, the three of us spent a maddening afternoon in the hotel as thunder and lightning raged outside. We made attempts at conversation, traded tobaccos and attempted to read the magazines scattered about, but always returned to a state of restless and impatient silence, broken only by the steady rhythm of the clock pendulum. Despite the constant reminder of time passage which the clock provided, the hours seemed to stand utterly still during that long afternoon.

Seven o'clock, however, came and went at last and was duly marked by the sonorous chimes. Several minutes later, a terrific bolt of lightning struck somewhere near the hotel, knocking out the electricity and plunging our room into near darkness.

"So much for the wonders of galvanic fluid," Edwin remarked as he lit a glass kerosene lamp which had been thoughtfully provided. I believe we all felt more comfortable in the warm and familiar glow of the flame.

And then there came a quiet knock upon the door.

Not one of us made a move toward it. Edwin and Wilkes seemed to have frozen in their tracks. I grasped the butt of my revolver and quickly brought its barrel to the fore. The door opened.

"And these gentlemen," came the familiar voice of Holmes, "are the associates about whom I was telling you."

I remember a macabre feeling of *déjà vu* swept over me. It was precisely in this manner—through the simple opening of a door—that I had unexpectedly first glimpsed the faces of Edwin and John Wilkes Booth not so very long before. There was much more, however, that was disturbingly familiar about the man who now crossed our threshold.

The detective held the door open wide to admit a man who stood by his side. He was a stranger, of that I was sure, yet somehow, he was unlike a stranger. Somehow I recognized him. Instantly I felt the disorienting sensation of gazing into a mirror that reflected the images of those of us who stood within the room.

It took the man a moment or two to accept the reality which confronted him. The businesslike expression upon his face—that strangely familiar face—instantly grew into one of horror as he stared at the three men who awaited him. He saw my gun, I am sure, but the focus of that horrified gaze was upon the two brothers who flanked me.

His eyes were suddenly wide and staring orbs. His mouth gaped open. A slight raspy cry issued from his throat.

The expressions on the faces of Wilkes, Edwin and I must have been no less striking as we stared back. We saw before us a virtual copy of John Wilkes Booth, a chillingly accurate simulacrum as Holmes had forecast, with the only apparent difference being one of age. The sharply chiseled features, the jet black eyes, the graceful chin and forehead—all made up a visage so like that of Wilkes it might have been his death mask. Only the hair, of a lustrous silvery white, distinguished one man from the other.

"What in the name of God—!" I heard Wilkes utter behind my back.

The surrogate was surprisingly quick in his movement. He reached inside the black cloak he wore and grasped the handle of a long and formidable dagger he had tucked into his belt. He had nearly exposed its deadly blade when I cocked my trigger.

"I will shoot you on the spot," I said to him, "if that weapon isn't upon the floor this instant!"

The man grinned ever so slightly as he looked first at me, and then at the muzzle of my revolver. With his hand upon the twisted handle of the dagger, he seemed to contemplate his next move carefully. At last, he took the dagger gingerly between two fingers and dropped it harmlessly to the carpeted floor. Holmes closed the door behind him, retrieved the surrendered weapon, and walked over to our side in order to face him.

"The man is every bit as dangerous as he looks, Watson," Holmes said. "Don't waver for an instant in shooting him if you think it necessary."

The surrogate grinned his awful grin once more.

"A thousand apologies for the deception, my good man," Holmes said to the stranger in an almost normal tone, "but under the circumstances I'm sure you will understand. How else could I lure you to meet these particular gentlemen, if not under the pretense of offering you potential clients? And other than my friend and associate here, the able Dr. Watson, I am sure you shall need no further introductions."

The man then spoke, in a low and malicious whisper that revealed no trace of fear or surprise. "Oh, heavens no, sir. Not at all! Why, there's darling Eddie there! Him I know well, indeed. And what a bonanza! It seems that Johnny's come marching home, too! Why you've brought the whole damn family, my dishonest but clever Mr. Holmes."

Holmes regarded the three of us. "Allow me to introduce our visitor, then. Mr. Samson Morrissey, Solicitor-at-Law in the city of Baltimore. Better, and more truthfully, known as Richard Booth."

A terrible silence, borne of confusion and disbelief, filled the room, along with a tension that seemed to crackle in the very air around us. Not a man among us, the newly-unmasked Richard Booth included, could think of a thing to say.

It was Edwin, so often the shy and withdrawn of the brothers, who finally made a move. He walked directly before Richard, the stranger, and peered intently into his eyes. He stepped back from him and appraised the man's full face with careful scrutiny. He rubbed his own chin thoughtfully.

"The man is a Booth all right," he said at last, in a strangely matter-of-fact tone. "He is related to us closely, John, without a doubt. Look at the resemblance. It is remarkable. He could be your twin."

"Believe me," Wilkes said timorously, "I can see the resemblance."

"The only question," Edwin continued, turning to Holmes, "is exactly *how* he is related to us."

Richard Booth smirked and gazed disdainfully at the ceiling.

"He is your brother," said Holmes in a flat monotone that belied the moment of his words. "To be more precise, he is your half-brother."

Wilkes took a sudden step closer to Richard. "Impossible!" he cried, staring intently at his double. "How dare you insult the honour of our mother in this way? I'll not have it, Holmes!"

Holmes spoke plainly in reply. "He has nothing whatsoever to do with your mother," he said. "Richard Booth, rather, has the same father as yourself, but a different mother entirely. He is, in fact, your father's first-born son."

Wilkes gasped. "Now you insult my father!" he cried, stepping back with a confused expression on his features.

"It is true, John," Edwin said quietly. "Holmes is perfectly correct. I knew of the other family years ago. I had heard the rumours at school, and backstage, and then I discovered the truth myself. It was in father's trunk, in the attic at Tudor Hall, remember the one? There was a portrait of father as a young man, with a woman by his side whom I did not recognize, and . . . and, a little son upon his knee."

He looked back to the impassive face of Richard. "It must have been him as a boy."

Wilkes put his hand to his brow. "I can't believe it!" he cried. "It's too much to take in! Why have you never told me of this, Ned?"

Edwin sighed. "It was a pact with mother. She was aware of it too, of course, as there was an awful scandal and a divorce. There were confrontations in the street between father and that woman, John, when you were just a boy. Mother made me promise, and Junius too, not to speak of it to the younger children. I was silent at her wishes, so as not to hurt you. We knew how much father meant to you."

Wilkes turned his back and, shaking his head, walked toward the window. He stared silently at Richard, muttering something inaudible beneath his breath.

"But Holmes," I interjected, still training my weapon at the half-brother. "You told me clearly, while we aboard the *Bothnia*, that you had discovered that Richard Booth had died in London many years ago. Yet here you are, telling us that this is he."

"I believe that what I said," the detective replied, "was that I had located Richard Booth's death certificate in London, which was indeed the case. I may not have mentioned, Watson, that I was never able to locate his grave in London. It was only recently, during this investigation, that it occurred to me that a forged certificate of death would not have been such a difficult matter, especially for a man as clever and as daring as this one is."

"Bully!" exclaimed Richard in a voice that had suddenly grown clear and loud. "You certainly are talented, Mr. Holmes!" He laughed heartily over something that only he found humourous in the conversation. His voice, much like his appearance, was strangely similar to Wilkes', and like his, carried the trace of a Southern accent.

Wilkes returned to our side and addressed Edwin. "And this man, this madman who stands before us, is father's son, the same as we are?" His voice was shaking, enraged.

"Father married even before he left England for America," Edwin returned, "and had a son born to him—this man—in London. Adelaide was his wife's name. There was a daughter too, who died when young."

At this, I saw the captive man flinch slightly.

"And then, and then came the disgrace," resumed Edwin. "Father was, as you know, intemperate in some things, John, less than modest and proper in some ways. He did something, something not quite . . . he . . ."

"Spit it out, man!" Wilkes barked angrily. "What in God's name did he do?"

"He abandoned his London family," Holmes said quietly, relieving Edwin of the burden. "He took as his mistress Mary Ann Holmes, your mother, my aunt, and embarked with her for America."

At this, the captive man flinched again. Much more visibly this time.

"Your father, Junius Brutus Booth, never reassumed responsibility for his first family," Holmes continued. "He sent a few dollars their way to England, and to Brussels where they also resided for a period. He even made the effort of visiting England twice, primarily for the sake of keeping up the illusion that he had remained faithful to them. The fact is that it was during this time that his new family—you and your brothers and sisters—were born and raised in Maryland. When Richard finally came to Baltimore to greet his father in eighteen forty-two—already a young man of twenty-three years—Junius took him under his wing for some months. The idea was to apprentice Richard as an actor and he took him along on one or two of his tours for this purpose. It was a rather hushed arrangement, of course, in order to avoid a scandal among his fellow actors. Rumours, however, surfaced regardless. Perhaps for this reason, the apprenticeship did not work out. He abandoned his son once more, but this time, things would not go neglected for two decades. Richard sent for his mother, who soon joined him in Baltimore. They confronted your father—they pleaded with him to take them back—and he refused their entreaties. There was an ugly divorce trial, and a scandal, which has been a skeleton well-closeted ever since, Wilkes, as evidenced by the fact that you knew nothing whatsoever of it until now. As for the unfortunate Adelaide Booth, she died penniless in Baltimore in eighteen fifty-eight, a lonely and broken woman."

At this, Richard did not flinch, but moaned softly instead.

Wilkes stared blankly at Holmes. I'm sure he didn't yet believe a word of the outrageous story, still it was painful to watch him wrest with the awful truth of his own father's long-hidden disgrace.

Holmes turned at last to Richard, who had grown quite pale in the past few moments, and lost all of his arrogant bearing. "Is my brief history not correct?" he asked.

Richard remained silent, a look of cold malevolence in his eyes.

Wilkes took another step closer to him, a look of gaining rage upon his features. "And this," he said menacingly, "this is the man you have brought to us." It was an odd sensation to see these two men, so remarkably alike in appearance, standing face-to-face.

"Yes, for this is the man we have sought," said Holmes. "You are gazing upon the face of the surrogate assassin himself, Wilkes, the man who ended Abraham Lincoln's life and convinced the world that it was you, and not he, who committed the crime. This is the man, Edwin, who tried four times to murder you."

Wilkes slowly clenched and unclenched his fists as he glared at his half-brother, unknown to him throughout an entire lifetime, yet so deadly an influence in his life. I felt certain that he would strike him then and there, but he held himself back. At any rate, his threatening gaze did nothing to visibly intimidate the other. Richard met the stare of his near-twin steadily and without blinking.

"You bastard!" Wilkes finally shouted at him.

"No!" shouted Richard in turn. "No sir! It is *you* who are the bastard! You and your brother here, and all the rest of the brute's ill-gotten brood! Do not forget, Johnny Boy, that I am his only proper scion! The rest of you are illegitimate! That is the fact of it!"

Wilkes drew back his first in rage and charged Richard, but Edwin caught him by the elbow, breaking the blow. For a perilous moment, Wilkes and Edwin struggled with one another while Richard watched the distraction anxiously, and began slowly to inch his way toward the door behind him. My warning stopped him, as well as the other brothers, in their tracks.

"One more step and I'll fire!" I cried. He ceased his movement immediately and regarded me with that maddening grin once again upon his face. "I believe you would, Dr. Watson," he said smoothly.

I ordered him to sit on a chair in the corner where I could keep a sharper eye on his movements. He did so immediately. Wilkes and Edwin, meanwhile, had composed themselves, and were straightening their coats, slightly embarassed from their scuffle. I could tell by the flushed appearance of Wilkes' face, however, that his anger had certainly not subsided.

Holmes nonchalantly put a match to his pipe and took a chair himself. He crossed his legs and looked thoughtfully into space. "Now that we have the villain, of course," he said to nobody in particular, "the immediate problem becomes what to do with him. Any suggestions, gentlemen?"

"Why, we must inform the police at once," I offered. "We've collared the criminal of the century, I'd say. That's quite a catch, Holmes."

"I think Watson is correct," Edwin added.

Wilkes nervously stroked his moustache and paced between us. "If only it were that simple," he said.

"What's so difficult about it?" I asked.

"My identity, Watson, is what is so difficult about it," he replied. "If we take this . . . this man, into the police, what shall I do? Remain in the shadows until the case is cleared up? Should I acknowledge who I am? I still have a death warrant out for me, surely, whether it be a secret one or not. That would have to be cleared up. It would take a long trial at least. I would have to face the public. I would have to tell my wife that I am John Wilkes Booth, for God's sake!"

"And for any of that to succeed," Holmes said, "we would have to prove our case against Richard. We would have to be certain indeed of our evidence before we dragged him into a precinct station with the outrageous claim that he is Lincoln's assassin."

"I had no idea it would be this complicated," Wilkes muttered. "Perhaps I never really believed that we could actually track him down. Now that we have, it poses a thousand problems."

From Richard's corner, we then heard a low muttering which grew slowly but steadily into a chuckle, and finally erupted into a crescendo of raucous, hysterical laughter. He rolled his head back and roared for all he was worth, and when he was through at last, he cleared his eyes of the tears it had brought. I lost at that moment any doubts I may have entertained that Richard Booth was insane.

"Oh, my poor, stupid Johnny Boy!" he gasped. "You're every bit the impulsive idiot today that you were sixteen years ago! Never giving a thought to the consequences of your actions. That suits you pretty, I'd say. God, what a jackanapes you are!"

Enraged anew, Wilkes moved toward Richard with clenched fists once more. Both Holmes and Edwin halted him this time, however, and forcefully sat him down on a chair. Obviously, Holmes did not want anything to ruin his opportunity to hear Richard speak, now that he appeared willing to do so. We still had a great deal to learn.

After more beserk laughter, Richard glanced at Wilkes with a malicious smile. "Yes indeedy, little brother, you were easy meat for me," he said contemptuously. "You were an easy trout to hook all right."

After a nervous glance at Wilkes, Holmes turned once more to Richard. "An easy trout you say? Tell me about it."

"What, and pull the noose even tighter around my neck?" he replied. A concerned look on Richard's face was suddenly and inexplicably replaced with one of secure confidence, as if he had reached a sudden and impulsive decision. His emotions, changing as quickly as unsettled weather, only convinced me further of his derangement.

"That settles it then," he said as if in response to a question he had asked of himself. He looked directly at Holmes. "Why yes, Mr. Holmes, I suppose I really have nothing to lose in telling you about it at this point," he said. "It was such a marvelous success in so many ways, you know, that I've longed for years to speak of it, to brag of it, as it were. It really was the accomplishment of a lifetime, quite truly, and now is as good a time to speak of it as any. You see, you'll never be taking me alive, you know, despite your obvious advantage of the moment. I shall not be taken alive! You've heard that before, haven't you Johnny Boy? That's what the people seem to remember *you* saying!"

The laughter returned briefly. "Ah, well," Richard said after his hilarity seemed to have finally left him, "you see, it was something like this. Our dear, kind-hearted father, the brute, kicked the bucket on a Mississippi steamboat, as all of us know. Well, who could be sorry about that? But I was! Yes, truly I was, you see, because the act of dying kept me from putting a bullet square between the brute's bleary old eyes, which had been my design for years. It is a terribly frustrating thing to have one's target taken away, I'll tell you. It's like being cheated in a high stakes game of cards. I thought at first that maybe this was for the better after all—vengeance is mine, sayeth the Lord, and all that rubbish—but that didn't last for long. No, you see, because the demands of justice against the hateful old man became something of a life's passion for me, and grew so strong that not even my wife's lovely presence could wash them away. Not even the war could fade them; not Antietam, not Shiloh, not Gettysburg, none of the places where I fought. And so, quite simply, I decided that the sins of the father must be visited upon the son. And which son would it be? Why, who else but you, Johnny Boy! Of course! The Apollo, the rich one, the handsome one—see how your face is like mine?—the darling of all the ladies! The celebrated actor!" Richard's voice had gone rapidly from that of a deranged storyteller into one of clearly visible rage.

"It had to be you!" Richard cried, pointing at Wilkes. "You stole away my birthright! Did you know that? Did you ever stop once to consider that? You seem to have stolen my very face! All of your fame, all of your wealth—don't you see?—it was supposed to be mine! It belonged to me, and it was only because of the brute that all of it went to you!"

The force of Richard's tirade struck all of us silent, including Wilkes, who seemed to have lost much of his earlier anger. The crazed hatred within the surrogate's words took all of us utterly aback. Richard composed himself for a moment and continued in a milder tone.

"The idea of vengeance," he said, "is but a crude emotional force, in need of much refinement. I could have killed you outright, easily enough, with a simple gun or knife, but where is the glory in that? I saw enough men die that way in the war, many at my own hand it is true, and I realize the anguish of pain and fear that they felt. But that is a physical anguish, not a suffering of the soul, and that, Johnny Boy, that is what I wished for you."

Wilkes squirmed uncomfortably in his seat.

"And you made it easy enough for me, little brother. Yes indeedy. I rode with the rebel cavalry, you see, up until Spotsylvania, that is. Unlike you, I fought for what I believed in. I took a ball in the shoulder during that scrap, and was sent home for good. I returned to Baltimore, only to discover that my wife had died during my absence. Sarah dead! You wouldn't have known that she was the only person besides my mother who ever showed me an ounce of affection. I was left with nothing then, and with nothing to lose. I had no purpose to my life until the day I saw your pretty face upon a theatrical poster, Johnny Boy, and that's when lightning struck! I would have a lark for myself!

"That is when I began to study you. I had long made my living in the instruction of languages to young boys and girls in Baltimore—I had a studio near Franklin Square—and it was easy enough to transfer my trade into Washington. I set up shop, lived modestly, and found plenty of time to study you. It was the fall of 'sixty-four, by then, and I found your movements at the time very intriguing.

"Never have I seen as furtive a man as you were during those days! Secret meetings! Mysterious trips down to southern Maryland! Train rides up to Montreal! Yes, I knew about all of it, and I knew that you must have been up to something dark and seditious, something that might well fit in with my own plans. And then luck struck. Lewis Payne paid me a visit one fine afternoon during that autumn. Yes, I'd known Lewis well before. I saved his life, in fact, at Gettysburg. Five Yankees were set to string him up, just for the fun of it I suppose, when my patrol caught sight of them. We blew the Yanks to bits and cut poor Lewis down from the tree. He looked at me like a faithful dog looks upon a master who has just taken a thorn from its paw, and promised he would do anything—he emphasized the word 'anything,' Johnny Boy—in order to repay his debt to me. More than a year later, in the Yankee capital itself, I found a way to take him up on the fine offer he'd made to me in his hour of gratitude.

"'Meet the actor named John Wilkes Booth,' I told him. 'Introduce yourself to him. Become his friend. Make yourself available to him.' And he did! Yes indeedy, he did. Lewis was a dull fellow in most regards, but in loyalty he will never be bested. And what a specimen of manhood! An animal! A titan! Did you know he was half-Apache? He succeeded beyond my wildest dreams, didn't he, Johnny Boy? You never expected a thing when he introduced himself to you backstage one evening, and declared himself an ardent fan of yours, did you? Your vanity got the best of you again. And so you allowed him into your little circus, recognizing that every ringmaster needs a lion or a tiger or a wolf in order to give the show some teeth, some muscle.

"And Lewis—dear Lewis—he told me everything about you. He told me of the grandiose kidnapping scheme, the glorious plot to drag old Abe, kicking and screaming, into Richmond. I met Lewis nightly, and each night he had more to tell. We laughed about you, Johnny Boy, we laughed and we plotted, even as you plotted yourself. Had you succeeded in taking Lincoln that day on the road to the Soldier's Home, you would have met with a most unpleasant surprise. You would have found dozens of soldiers and sailors waiting for you, well armed, at the Benning Bridge. They would have been expecting you because I would have told them all about your heroic little plan. Yes, it was all organized beforehand. Had you taken Abe from his carriage that day, Lewis would have signaled me along the route of escape. I would have dispatched a telegraph message to the sentries well before you would have reached their position. And, Johnny Boy, if they didn't kill you on the spot, they would have done it soon enough, don't you know. They would have had you swinging soon enough, yes indeedy!"

Wilkes glared back at his mocking half-brother, once again slowly clenching and unclenching his fists, but he remained silent and did not move from his chair.

"Luck was on your side that time, although you thought the opposite was true, didn't you? You were the winner that day and I was foiled, and so, as your opportunity to kidnap the president passed away, and as your little circus of clowns folded up their tents and left, I plotted on. I realized how well you had set yourself up for my next step. And we all know, of course, what that step was."

"You decided to murder Lincoln, and to use Wilkes' history in the kidnapping conspiracy as a frame-up for the crime," Holmes said.

"Of course, my clever Mr. Holmes," Richard replied. "And also, I was only too aware of my uncanny resemblance to Johnny Boy. It was an asset I knew should not be wasted. So Lewis and I worked for a few more weeks, studying more of the details of your life, Johnny Boy. Lewis stole things from your room, things to help make you appear guilty. He even took notes about the people you knew, the places you liked to frequent, the things you had said. For my part, I slowly transformed myself into your very image. I combed my hair in your fashion, cut my moustache to the length you preferred, purchased clothing identical to your own, even labelled them with your name. I practiced copying your handwriting for hours on end, and grew able to make an excellent facsimile of it. Lewis told me of your manner of speaking, your gestures and expressions, and I practiced these things. It was not such an arduous transition to make, Johnny Boy. Within ten days or so, I can say with confidence, I was enough like you to convince even your close friends that I was, in fact, John Wilkes Booth, so long as the conversations were brief, and did not go into great detail. I went so far as to test it once, by meeting and conversing with John Taltavul, the keeper of your favorite saloon. We spoke for fifteen minutes at least and he never suspected a thing. It was mid-April by then, Richmond had only just fallen, and I knew that I was ready."

Holmes leaned forward with interest. "You spent the entire day of April the fourteenth in the guise of Wilkes Booth, did you not? You went to great lengths to create a trail of evidence leading directly to him."

"Oh yes, Mr. Holmes, and it was such a lark! It went so smoothly! Mrs. Surratt, that humourless old widow, and her boarder, the timid Wiechmann—how well I remember them saying 'Yes, Mr. Booth, of course we'll take your things down to Surrattsville for you.' Anything for Mr. Booth! And Matthews. He never gave me a second glance as I handed him that incriminating letter. The boys down at Ford's Theater—they drank with me, and toasted me, thinking all the while that I was somebody else entirely. I left a note at the vice president's hotel, signed of course, with your name. It was jolly fun being John Wilkes Booth for a day, I'll tell you that. It was nice to be loved for one's fame and influence. Yes, Johnny Boy, now I know that you once led a pleasurable life indeed."

Holmes leaned forward and asked of him: "How did you manage to convince Atzerodt and Herold of your identity? You met them, too, that evening, did you not?"

"Oh, but they were even easier than the others. The idea, you see, was to finish off as many Yankee leaders as possible, to make the crime as horrendous as it could be. I assigned Lewis therefore to go after Seward, after I learned that Grant had skipped town, and I give him credit for trying manfully. Of course, I would have liked to kill the vice president too, and so I decided to gamble on Atzerodt. I had Lewis convene a little meeting that night for this purpose at the Kirkwood. He made sure that the lights were kept low and that my chair sat well in the shadows of the room, but I hardly felt it was necessary. Neither Herold nor Atzerodt had two cents' worth of brains in their heads anyhow. Atzerodt was already staggering from drink at the time, so I had no worries about him. Herold, who was really just a boy you know, and a rather dull boy at that, mentioned that I looked a little peaked that evening. I nearly laughed at that one! I gave Atzerodt his assignment really just for the ritual of it. I never believed that he'd find the courage to make the first move against Johnson. And Herold I ordered to accompany Lewis, as he was not yet very familiar with Washington."

"Had you no compulsion about enlisting these men into a plot that was sure to bring about their executions in the event of capture?" Holmes asked sharply.

"I was willing to dispatch Abraham Lincoln himself, wasn't I, Mr. Holmes?" came the assassin's reply. "Why in the world should I worry about a dull boy and a drunken carriage-maker? Yes, yes, they hung for it, all right. I know that, but consider the excitement I brought them. Think of the drama that their encounter with me brought into their ordinary little lives. It was a moment of glory for them—they shall live on in history! It was well worth the final resolution."

"You took it a step further though, did you not? In your letter to Matthews, you signed their names along with Wilkes' and Payne's, thus sealing their fate."

Richard's face grew suddenly serious. "They were *his* friends," he said, pointing at Wilkes. "Why shouldn't they have gone down with him? It was all just a part of the lark for me."

"What of the murder of Lincoln?" Edwin asked, his own voice now growing angry. "Did you find that a lark as well?"

"Oh, but murder is such an inappropriate word—don't you think, Eddie?—considering the true nature of what I did. I prefer the term sacrifice. Yes, I sacrificed the old pioneer in order to put your brother, the poppinjay here, into his proper place. My aim was never just to kill Lincoln. Political assassination for its own sake, why that's the dullest of crimes, the work of the most horizontal minds. I had no bone to pick with Lincoln. What did it matter to me, after all? The war was done, there was much rebuilding to do, let us bear malice toward none, all of that. Yes, Lincoln was a noble enough fellow, I suppose, for an enemy at least. But what of that? He had to be sacrificed. It was the only way. He was the only target whose death, whose sacrifice, would guarantee that Johnny Boy's graceful nape would meet the rope. That was the goal! And oh, how I envisioned that moment! There he is, high upon the scaffold, facing the horrible prospect of his own death moving closer, ever closer, and as he looks at the sun, the clouds, the leaves, the soil, for one last bitter moment, he realizes for the millionth time the gnawing irony of his fate and of this injustice. Yes, that would have been suffering of the soul indeed! That is why Lincoln had to die, and that alone. It was the pinnacle of my ambition, and I am grieved to this day that misfortune thwarted its realization."

Richard flashed his mocking grin at Wilkes, whose fists were again clenching and unclenching in growing rage, and then he returned his gaze to Edwin.

"And as for the act itself, Eddie, well I suppose it really *was* a lark, at least up to a certain point. I took a drink at Taltavul's beforehand, and admonished a man in his cups by telling him that before I was through, Booth would be the most famous name in America. Did I lie? It was an easy matter to get into the theater, and to find a boy to hold my horse. I was John Wilkes Booth, after all! Who within any theater would deny entry to such a star? I strolled past the dress circle, I presented my card—your card, Johnny Boy—to some functionary, and I proceeded. A bonus! There was no guard at the inner chamber! I would not have to use my blade after all. The door, of course, was ready. I had prepared the plaster earlier in the day, and my jam would hold it fast against any outside intruder. The box was open too—careless fools!—and there sat the old man himself. It was as easy as pie, I tell you. Easy as pie."

Richard paused, as if to catch his breath, and regarded his three horrified but utterly spell-bound listeners. He was speaking rapidly and enthusiastically now, in a strange voice, as if the open admission of his deed after this great passage of time were a great catharsis for him. He seemed unwilling or unable to hesitate or slow down. His eyes reflected the excitement he was feeling, and the sweat upon his brow indicated that he was reliving those terrible moments with considerable, and obscene, pleasure.

"Never have I seen a man expire so peacefully and so gently," he continued. "I was almost disappointed in the very ease of Lincoln's death. He never heard my approach, never detected my movements, never realized just how near the Grim Reaper had come to his shoulder. He barely stirred when the bullet entered his head. I had timed the shot perfectly to coincide with the laughter of the house—a nice touch, eh, Johnny Boy?—just the sort of thing an experienced man of the stage would be expected to know! Even his wife didn't know what had really happened at first. Nor did the soldier who was in there with him, although he at least sensed that something had gone quite wrong. He resisted me, or tried to, but my blade took care of him nicely. He went down in a bloody heap after the second thrust.

"I took the stage itself! I brandished my blade as I beheld the entire stupefied house. I glared openly at their uncomprehending faces, making sure that they beheld my own face, and would recognize it immediately as the actor they had seen perform dozens of times themselves—John Wilkes Booth—the cowardly, infamous, dastardly assassin of Abraham Lincoln! Ah, what a moment of crystalline clarity! What an instant of glory it was!"

"It was, in fact," said Holmes, casually putting a match to his cherrywood, "your very last moment of so-called glory, the end of your enjoyable lark, was it not, Mr. Booth?" He regarded the assassin through the smoke of his shag, a slightly sarcastic eyebrow raised in expectation of reply.

Richard met his stare with a cold and humourless eye, as Holmes had apparently knocked his frolicsome mood utterly away. He stirred uneasily in his chair and lost his grin entirely.

"As in the old nursery rhyme," Holmes continued, "in which the kingdom is lost for the want of a nail, so was your kingdom lost—so were all your dark ambitions shattered—by the presence of a simple spur upon your heel. Had your spur not caught the Treasury flag decorating the presidential box, things would have gone a great deal smoother for you, would they have not?"

Richard made a feeble attempt to grin. "Ah yes, the cursed spur. Well, yes, of course, my fall from the box changed the picture of things a great deal, my clever Mr. Holmes."

"Wilkes Booth, the real Wilkes Booth, would have made that simple leap with far more grace than you displayed," said Holmes, continuing to chide him.

"Wilkes Booth may now take advantage of his opportunity to gloat," came the disheartened reply.

"The fall broke your ankle bone, yet you still managed to flee Ford's untouched. That's no small feat in itself."

"I should say it isn't! You cannot imagine the pain, the wrenching agony of walking—let alone running—on a shattered ankle bone. I thrust aside any fool who stood in my way. I kicked away the Negro who held my horse. I galloped into the night, as the historians are fond of saying these days. Yes, Mr. Holmes, it was a fine enough escape."

"And yet your injury altered your very strategy of escape. I believe you had no intention of leaving Washington after the crime. You must have been smarter than that."

Richard was silent for a few moments, as if deciding whether or not to continue with his confessional narrative. He must have determined that by this time he had nothing whatsoever to lose by finishing. He had, after all, already confessed to the murder itself, and without a scintilla of guilt.

"I was indeed smarter than that," he resumed. "The plan, you see, was for Lewis and me to meet near the Navy Yard Bridge—after Lewis had successfully killed Seward and lost Herold—and not to cross the bridge into Maryland, but to secure ourselves in a hideaway I had prepared in a small bungalow in Anacostia. I never intended to go into Maryland at all, never planned on actually stopping at Surrattsville. That was only a part of the ruse. The plan went wrong from the start.

It was Lewis who got lost, not Herold. It was Herold who somehow managed to meet me at the point of rendezvous near the bridge, suspecting nothing in his boyish way of my assumed identity. I never saw Lewis again, of course.

"I was badly injured, of course. I knew I would have to have treatment soon, but how could I remain in Washington to get it? A patient with a broken leg? A man who so greatly resembled John Wilkes Booth that only a simpleton would fail to note the resemblance? To seek help in Washington would have meant my certain capture."

"And so Herold suggested a certain Dr. Mudd who resided safely away in southern Maryland, well ahead of the news of Lincoln's murder."

"Very clever, Mr. Holmes. Very clever indeed. Yes, it was Herold who suggested Mudd. I made the decision to try to cross the border to see him, aware that he had recently met Johnny Boy, and felt that a disguise would be of help in case he should mistake me for him and so inform others of that. I felt that within a day or two, Johnny Boy would surely have been caught in Stanton's web. At that point, I could safely return to the city."

"You were, of course, wrong in assuming the capture of Wilkes."

"All I know," said Richard, casting a malevolent glance at Wilkes, "is that luck played into his hands, giving him enough warning to seek cover before Stanton ran him down."

"You are, of course," Holmes continued, blowing a great puff of blue smoke into the air, "also aware that your gravest, your most fatal, error took place at the Navy Yard Bridge."

At this, Richard looked dejectedly at the floor. "Yes," he answered quietly.

"When the sentry asked for your name, you replied quite honestly that it was Booth, not giving pause to the critical fact that Booth also happens to be the surname of the very man you had so carefully set up for the crime. Your relation to your victim was the irony that so nearly finished you, was it not? You set the whole pack of hounds directly onto your own tail, with no way to take back the one word that brought it all about—your own name."

Richard kept his gaze away from all of our eyes, and remained utterly silent.

"And still you managed to elude those persistent hounds for twelve days."

"Twelve days of hell!" he suddenly started, looking up. "Twelve days of pain—God, what pain it was!—of privation, of starvation and thirst, of humiliation! Oh, don't tell me that I haven't paid for my crimes, Mr. Holmes. Oh no! I paid in eights for my crime during those days, but I made my way through it! I came out of it alive, and free to boot! There's few men in this world who could have managed that, I tell you."

"I'm quite sure of it," said Holmes, "but I am curious as to why you bothered to maintain the Wilkes identity—off and on, as it were—during your escape."

"That's simple," Richard said, apparently having gained back some of his confidence. "With Mudd, I worried that he might take me for Wilkes, since he'd known him, and so I wore false whiskers. It must have worked. He went to Jefferson Island, didn't he, claiming all the while that the man at his doorstep was never Wilkes Booth. He was not lying! As for the other times, well there were rebels down there whom I felt might treat me better if they knew me to be Lincoln's assassin. What did I know? That was a mistake, too. They were more cowards than they were Confederates, and their knowledge of my deed only hastened the Yankees on my trail."

"And the diary? Whatever motivated you to keep up the ruse in the diary, of all places?"

Richard looked directly at Edwin, his sinister grin now fully back in place. "That was to be my ultimate revenge," he said. "By the end of the trail I realized from the newspapers I'd read that Johnny Boy had somehow eluded capture. Of course he had, or why else would they still be after me and poor, stupid Herold? But I had another weapon all the same. I would compose a diary, fill it with all the nonsensical patriotic sort of rambling people would expect from the pen of John Wilkes Booth, and then, as my *coup de grâce*, I would implicate the entire family in the murder plot—mother, brothers, sisters, lock stock and barrel. Yes, and Mr. Stanton would have gone for them too, you know, for he was a hungry avenger, yes indeed! It took very little proof for him to hang three innocent people and imprison who knows how many others. Johnny Boy might have escaped me, in other words, but the rest of the brute's family would not. I intended to leave the diary in a place where the Yanks would be sure to find it."

"I suspect you never had that chance," said Holmes quietly.

"I wrote the entire forgery during my stay at the Garrett farm," Richard said, "when I was attempting to rest and recover from my pain. As history has noted, I was rudely interrupted while there."

"Then it really was you who was there!" said Wilkes, suddenly breaking his long silence. "And yet, here you are! How did you manage it all?" In his curiosity to learn of the man who had supposedly died in his place, Wilkes seemed to have momentarily lost his rage toward his half-brother.

"I died for you, Johnny Boy! That's how I did it!" Richard broke into a high-pitched, awful laughter.

"No, I mean it! I died then and there, on the Garretts' porch, just as the newspapers said, with the morning sun coming over the horizon and the mysterious words 'Tell mother I died for my country' upon my lips. Yes, it all happened that way.

"Except, of course, that I was not dead at all. Herold and I, as you know, were trapped in the shed during the night. There would be no way out, of course. I knew that. I could see the Yankees had come in strength, and that they meant business. And so I stalled for time. Poor Herold. He never knew that he was not fleeing with Johnny Boy, you know, right up to his own death! He was so God-awful gullible and loyal to boot. He wanted to stay in the shed with me, to die by my side, but I used his surrender to stall the soldiers for time as I pondered a way out of my fix. Finally I let him go. Then one of the Garrett boys was sent in, to try to talk me out of the shed. I stalled further while speaking to him. At last, I parried and dealt with the Yank commander, challenging each of them to a fistfight. Oh, it was a comedy, I tell you! Of course, they grew impatient at last, and threatened to fire the barn. But by then I knew exactly what to do."

"And what *did* you do?" I asked, literally on the edge of my seat.

Richard pulled the cloak away from his neck and held it open for all of us to see. "This," he said, pointing to well-healed but still quite visible scars upon either side of the neck. The wounds had obviously been neat ones, round in shape, and quite like the entry and exit wounds of a pistol ball.

"Gunshot wounds?" I asked.

"Exactly what the Yankees thought," said Richard triumphantly. "They greatly resembled pistol wounds when fresh, and looked for all the world as if a ball had been fired through one side of my neck and out the other, severing the spinal column. In fact, I made them rather easily with a baling hook I'd discovered in the shed. Oh, it hurt a great deal, but it was well worth it! I punctured the flesh, you see, skewed them around a little in order to bring forth the blood, and then fired my own pistol into the dirt, just before falling prone. The perfect suicide! I tell you, it looked absolutely like the genuine article!"

"And they believed that?" Wilkes asked incredulously.

"Well, why shouldn't they have?" Richard laughed once more. "I am a great actor, too, you know. Greater than either of you boys, and the proof was to be had at Garrett's farm. I lingered for an hour or two at least, feigning paralysis, moaning a few deathly words for effect, deliberately appearing to die in great agony."

"But a doctor was called to confirm death," I protested. "He pronounced you dead on the spot."

"And what of it? He held a mirror to my lips. I held my breath for a few moments. He felt my wrist, for ten seconds perhaps. Again, I held my breath to slow my heartbeat. He put his finger into the wound. Now that was not quite so easy, I'll tell you. There was great pain—yes indeedy!—but I steeled myself against flinching. His wretched hand was gone in a moment, thank God! I lay as still as any corpse, and the morning was cold. I've no doubt I looked and felt the part! Besides, the doctor was hurried. The Yank commander was in a rush to get me back to Washington, you know. There was big money to be had for the man who ran me down, so he pushed the doctor to move quickly. And then I was rolled into a blanket. It was easy from then on. I could breathe normally and nobody could see."

"Your actual escape, therefore, must have taken place between the Garrett's farm and the Rappahannock River, where the troops were met by a boat," Holmes ventured.

"Correct once more, Mr. Holmes. You see, they placed me in a wagon—some old darkie from the vicinity had the misfortune to be so commandeered—and the buckboard broke down a few miles up the road. I actually slipped out! I wish to God I had seen the expression on that poor darkie's face! It took the old fool the better part of an hour to fix the contraption, and the soldiers were tired. I heard them complaining that they'd had no sleep for two nights straight, so as soon as our little procession was halted, the whole lot of them laid down on the grass for a well-deserved nap. I simply rolled out of the blanket when the Negro was away with his tools and, very quietly of course, slipped away into the brush."

"But they must have been after you in minutes," Edwin said.

"Oh, of course they were, Eddie! Why they were petrified, and for good reasons. They must have thought at first that they were tracking some sort of living dead man! Secondly, they just might have become dead men themselves, if they showed up empty-handed in Washington, after having telegraphed Stanton with the news of my capture and death. Oh yes, they were after me all right. But I had hardly traveled a mile—and it was no easy feat with my leg—before I found myself in an eminently appropriate location. A cemetery! It was a quiet, mostly forgotten, country sort of cemetery, with graves going back to the colonial days. Within it was a crypt, its slab having been pushed slightly ajar. I pushed it farther open, drew myself into its depths, and managed to bring the lid back into place."

"A crypt!" I cried.

"Ah well, good doctor, it was not a very pleasant abode, I'll tell you, not with the ancient remains of its occupants sharing it with me. No, it was quite a horrible place really, but quite preferable to Stanton's gallows! I heard the squadron ride through the cemetery in their frenzy. I heard them cursing, and I bit my lip so as not to laugh at them. I stayed there for three days and three nights, venturing out only during the darkest depths of the night for water. Had anyone been out there to see me, I'm sure I presented quite the ghoulish sight."

Holmes regarded Richard with an air that carried a trace of begrudging respect. "A remarkable escape indeed," he said. "Your survival instincts are impressive, Mr. Booth. But tell me, how did you get out of the cemetery? How did you make it to safety in the end?"

"I am afraid my story loses much of its drama after that point," Richard sighed. "During my evenings out, so to speak, I did a little checking on the local inhabitants. There was one woman in particular who interested me, a thin and ragged old lady. She lived all by herself, in a broken-down little cabin deep in the woods, perhaps a mile from the cemetery. She raised a pitiful little patch of crops out back and, to all appearances, lived as a genuine hermit. I presented myself to her one quiet night, around ten o'clock or so, claiming to be an injured Confederate who was being sought by Union patrols for having escaped a prison camp. I looked the part, yes indeedy! In fact, I was close to death from hunger, from exposure, and from the injury to my leg. She took pity on me, acknowledging that the Yankees had indeed been to her cabin some days before and had treated her most harshly. I'd hardly call her an ardent rebel, but she had some knowledge of the war. Still, she had never even heard of Abraham Lincoln! Imagine it! I could not have prayed for a more perfect shelter.

"During the whole of the summer of eighteen sixty-five, she slowly nursed me back to health. I was fortunate in two particulars. First, the leg had somehow avoided going gangrenous, although its long neglect did cause a deformation of the bone, as you can see to this day. Also, the Yankees never once came back to her place, although I did hear cavalry in the vicinity on several occasions during the first few days. By two weeks' time, I was confident that the search had been abandoned. It would only be that autumn, when I had safely sailed for England, that I read of the supposed capture of John Wilkes Booth at Garrett's farm, and concluded that the entire story had been a fabrication."

"In London, of course, you forged a death certificate for Richard Booth," Holmes commented.

"Yes, and for obvious reasons. One could never be too confident that someday, someone might not somehow connect my name to the crime. If they did, of course, they would have found Richard Booth to be a dead man."

"How long did your stay in London last?"

"For eleven years, until eighteen seventy-six, when I sailed back for the States. I resided in Philadelphia for a year perhaps, and was able there to amass a considerable fortune in, shall we say, certain pursuits. Since my return to Baltimore, this has provided me with the sustenance of life's necessities."

"Wait a moment!" Edwin interjected suddenly, as if an old memory had just struck him. "That means you would have been in London in eighteeen seventy. I was there that summer to visit Asia, my sister—it was the summer I heard Dickens give a reading."

"So?" Richard returned.

"I met someone on the street there—we were in the carriage—he looked so much like John . . . so much like you, that I halted the carriage and went to speak with him. Even at close quarters the resemblance was shocking."

"And do you remember what I said, Eddie?"

"Then it was you!"

"Yours truly," Richard said with his grin. "You're right. This is not our first meeting."

"You told me that you'd never heard of John Wilkes Booth," Edwin said, "that the resemblance must have been coincidental."

"Forgive the lie, Eddie, but consider yourself lucky that I didn't kill you on the spot. If I'd not been taken so aback at the chance meeting, I might well have done so! As it was, I felt the meeting was one of destiny, don't you agree? For it was at that happenstance encounter, Eddie, that I began thinking of you. Somehow I just couldn't get you out of my mind."

"Was that why you returned to America?" Holmes demanded.

"Why I should think that to be obvious, Mr. Holmes! In my long stay in dreary London, you see, I came to regard my triumph over Johnny Boy as but a Pyrrhic victory. His career had been ruined, yes, but so had mine. He had been forced to flee in terror, yes, but still he survived somewhere. Were my own travails any less than his? Somehow he had preserved himself and, since I'd been cheated of the chance to implicate the family in the assassination, I began to feel once more the old stirrings. In time this . . . need, as it were, grew so great that I had no choice but to return."

"And this renewed sense of vengeance," Edwin said to him, "could be no better satisfied by any Booth than it could by me?"

"Of course, Eddie. Seeing you in London reminded me that you've always been the most beloved member of the brood, after all. You were so good, on the stage and off, that the people even forgave you your brother's act. You would have to be my second choice."

"And you began with Mark Gray in Chicago," Holmes stated.

"A mistake, I admit. I convinced Gray, a nervous, quite unstable fellow I happened to meet in a Chicago saloon, of Eddie's liberties with his sister. I told the fellow that I was the shade of Wilkes Booth come back to avenge himself upon my living brother! Oh how the idiot went for it! I'd come to Chicago expressly for this purpose—to create once more a sophisticated crime in order to punish a Booth—and I thought Gray would handle things well for me. I should have known how dismally he would fail in the end, but he came pretty close all the same, didn't he, Eddie?

"Thereafter, I determined to do the job myself, and the devil with the sophistication or the cleverness of it. All I sought was to finish off the great and beloved Booth, and to let him know in his dying moments why he was killed, and by whom."

Holmes poked carelessly into his pipe with his tamper. "Did you discover in the process, Mr. Booth, that your knack for creative crime had somehow deserted you in the intervening years?"

Richard grimaced at this challenging remark and responded rancorously. "Fortune has failed me," he said defensively.

"Without a doubt it has," said Holmes leaning closer to him, "but so have your very skills as an assassin—your sense of illusion, your cunning, your simple aim, perhaps your very courage. In Germany, in London and in New York, Mr. Booth, your attempts to kill Edwin have been consistent flops, have they not?"

Richard refused, however, to be so easily mocked. "Well, my clever Mr. Holmes, you must admit that I had you going in London, at least. I left you little to work with there."

"The false French accent was a nice subterfuge, I admit," said Holmes. "You did, I presume, escape by way of France?"

The assassin nodded.

"And yet in America, you provided me with a great deal," the detective continued. "You left me strange passages from Shakespeare in an old pamphlet. You lost the Knights ring you'd stolen from Wilkes, and did so in Watson's presence. You foolishly kept up the melodramatic business of acorns. Why, in New York, Mr. Booth, you even played so poorly that you murdered the wrong man, did you not, uttering so famous a line as you did so that it could not fail to prove valuable to me." Holmes was clearly enjoying this taunting parry with his captured prey.

Richard's face was twisted. "I am an old man!" he cried. "I am more than sixty years old, for God's sake! Nineteen years older than this poppinjay here! If I were but ten years younger, Eddie Booth would have been long buried by now, be sure of it!" He shook his head, obviously in frustration over the failures about which Holmes was prodding him. The irony of the moment, that his main regret over his own aging was the diminishing of his skills as a cold-blooded murderer, would have been comic had not the results of this man's lunacy already proven so terribly tragic.

A long silence then ensued between the five of us gathered in the room, a silence that seemed to hover over each man's deliberations as to what the next move should be, and which, more importantly, seemed to focus on the most fundamental question of all.

It was Wilkes who addressed the unspoken issue at last. He rose and stood before his half-brother and, looking into his near-twin's jet black eyes with his own equally as black, he asked: "Why?"

Richard squirmed in his chair. "It is a foolish question."

"Why do you hate us?" Wilkes persisted.

Richard suddenly found words. "It is not hatred, Johnny Boy, dear God no! It is something far worse than that, something much more profound, something ungodly which I feel for you and your kin. It is loathing, it is detestation . . . no! No, such words fail the test. There are no words to describe how I feel toward you!"

"But why?" interjected Edwin, who now joined Wilkes in standing directly before Richard. "Why have you murdered a president, ruined our lives, attempted to kill *us*? We have done absolutely nothing to you! Before this day, John did not even know you existed!"

"It is not what you have done, but what you are that plagues me."

"But we are absolutely innocent!" Wilkes shouted into his face.

Richard then rose quickly and firmly from his seated position, causing me to tighten my grip upon the trigger of the revolver. He faced his two half-brothers squarely, looking one and then the other, directly in the eye. His face bore a ghastly contortion of expressions which reflected the chaotic ebb and flow of emotions that must have been raging within his breast.

"There is," he hissed, "no such thing as innocence!"

None of us were prepared for what happened next. Richard was so quick in his movement, and so surprisingly agile, that an instant reaction would have been impossible.

His arm thrust out at the glass kerosene lamp which had been burning upon a small table near him. The lamp flew onto the hearth directly at our feet where it shattered easily upon the tiles. A bright plume of kerosene-fed flame erupted on the spot, and then followed a deadly trail of the spilled fuel as it moved unerringly over the carpeting toward the curtains. The delicate lace fabric of which they were made was immediately caught up in the fire, rapidly encircling the window in a bright halo of raging flame. In a matter of seconds, the entire room seemed engulfed in the conflagration.

Our first reaction, of course, was to step back away from the orange fireball at our feet, which threatened our very clothing. The second was the shocked awareness of the flame's rapid progress toward the window. Both reactions were automatic—instinctive—and unfortunately, our reaction to Richard Booth's move to escape came in third. By the time we noticed him, he had streaked to the door, opened it and raced into the corridor, slamming the door behind him.

"Edwin!" barked Holmes, "get us a blanket or a sheet, and be quick about it! We've but moments before the fire takes hold of the woodwork! Watson! Wilkes! Get after him! Go! We shall see to the fire!"

The detective's commands spurred us into action. Wilkes and I bolted for the door but, to our horror, it held fast, refusing to budge. "He must have taken a key on his way out!" Wilkes shouted. "Who has another key? Watson, where is your key?" We heard the hungry crackling of the flames behind us.

"Damn the key!" I cried. "Stand back!" I leveled my revolver at the doorknob and put a bullet neatly through its center. The door swung violently open on its own, allowing Wilkes and me to dash from the room into the hall. We left Holmes and Edwin, and the angry flames, behind us as we went.

—21—
The Chase

My memory of our first few frantic moments in that long hotel corridor still bears a distinctly nightmarish cast. Wilkes and I ran through the door as fast as our legs could carry us, but our progress seemed dreadfully slow, our steps sluggish and futile, even as we saw our prey before us.

As we gained the hall, Richard's cloak was still in view, just turning into an opening on the left wall at the far side. The elevator! We sprinted as we heard a brief scuffle within the lift itself. Wilkes pulled from his belt a deadly Navy Colt pistol of large caliber and raised its long barrel into the air. We saw the operator, in his gaudy crimson jacket, fly from within his cage-like quarters and tumble against the opposite wall. We heard Richard's curse as he fumbled with the steel grating that formed the elevator's inner door.

As we reached the opening of the shaft, Richard had secured the grating and pulled the lever which controlled the conveyance. It came to life with a muffled groan and began to descend with a loud creaking sound—the electrical failure within the hotel had somehow spared the elevator's source of power. We tugged at the ornate iron gate as we watched Richard rapidly hurtle downward, but it had locked automatically with his departure. For a maddening second or two, we saw his mocking grin as he glared back at us.

"Damn!" cried Wilkes. "Come on, Watson! The stairs!"

We practically flew down those five flights of stairs, Wilkes and I, colliding frequently with one another and with the walls of the narrow staircase itself. Both of us were thoroughly winded when we reached the lobby at last. There we found nothing out of the ordinary, and absolutely no sign of Richard. A few solitary men lounged about with books or newspapers. Not one of them seemed the least bit alarmed about anything, until Wilkes and I approached one portly gentleman in evening attire, enjoying his cigar from within the depths of a burgundy chair. He saw our raised pistols and his face became at once a mask of fear.

"Did you see a man, about my height, white hair, just dash through?" Wilkes demanded through his labored breathing. The unfortunate gentleman wordlessly shook his head that he had not. Obviously, Richard had proceeded through the lobby at a leisurely pace, so as not to attract undue attention.

We raced through the main door and out into the street. We stood there, glancing from side to side against the failing sky of twilight, and saw nothing.

"Are you looking for the white-haired man?" came a tiny voice.

A lad of no more than seven years, dressed precociously in a little sailor's suit, stood at our knees next to the hitching posts.

"Yes!" I replied. "Where did he go?"

"He took his horse, not three minutes ago, from this post sir! He rode that way!" The little boy pointed due north, along Light Street.

"God bless you, lad!" Wilkes said to the boy, ruffling his hair. "Now, how would you like to earn this dollar?" The boy looked in wonder upon the silver coin Wilkes held up. "All you need do is inform the gentlemen who own these two fine geldings here—whoever they may be—that their horses were taken for reasons of a dire emergency, and that they will be returned unharmed post haste. Do you think you can do that?"

The little boy eagerly nodded.

"Good for you! Then we shall immediately take them." He turned to me as he began untying the two healthy-looking horses. "Now is not the time for propriety, Watson! Let us ride!"

Fortunately, the mounts were well saddled and had recently been fed. They responded smartly as we turned them into the street, and began to eagerly gallop as if their very owners were riding them. At the moment I had absolutely no compunctions about the fact that Wilkes and I had just become horse thieves in the eyes of the law. The only thing on my mind was our pursuit.

According to the boy, Richard had gained some three minutes on us, which was considerable in light of the fact that he was on horseback. The streets were occupied with only light traffic, however, which made our progress easier. We rode rapidly northwards on Light Street, even though we had no glimpse of our quarry, in hopes that something would turn up.

Some eight or nine blocks along the way we met with an unexpected delay. We were forced to rein in our mounts suddenly to avoid striking the frenzied team of a dreadfully long fire engine, whose bells we had not heard due to the heavy sound of our own horses on the pavement. The fire wagon hurried past us on Orleans Street, a clanging blur of white horses, brass boilers and red helmets, and was followed by two lesser, but still persistent pieces of apparatus. It did not occur to me until later that they might have been on their way toward a certain hotel behind us.

"We have lost him!" Wilkes cried in despair after the commotion had passed. "We'll not find him now!" He looked hopelessly all around him.

"Perhaps not," I rejoined, "but it won't be for lack of effort. I'm riding on for a piece. Do what you will!" I kicked my gelding into action and soon had him at full gallop once more. Our earlier ride down to Virginia seemed to have done wonders for my horsemanship. I was really not surprised to see that, within moments, Wilkes was riding immediately beside me.

In short order we received our first indication that we were on the right trail. Before us loomed in the dusk the wooden frame of an impressive bridge which spanned the narrow tributary known locally as Jones Falls. I noticed that a number of people were milling about its entrance, speaking in what appeared to be animated tones with one another, and pointing in the direction of the bridge itself.

"Hello!" I cried to one of them as we approached. "What's all the fuss about?"

"Why, there was a crazy man in the Belvedere Bridge!" a young

306   The Surrogate Assassin

woman called back to me. "Just a moment ago, he rode through like nothing I've ever seen, knocking carts down, making the walking folks take cover!"

"A white-haired man, with a black cloak?" Wilkes asked her.

"That's the very one!" the woman replied indignantly.

With a quick look at one another we bolted for the bridge ourselves, albeit with more caution than Richard must have shown. Within the single-arched structure, feebly lit with torches, we saw two angry tradesmen righting their carts and placing their contents back into them, and one elderly gentleman along the footway nursing what appeared to be a bruised shin. It had clearly not been long since Richard had roared through here, upsetting the unwary traffic.

Once out on the other side Richard still remained invisible from view, but Wilkes had the presence of mind to halt both of our horses. "Listen," he ordered. We remained still and silent for a moment and heard clearly the unmistakable sounds of galloping hoofbeats, moving at a desperate pace.

"He's changed directions on us!" I cried. "He's heading due east now!"

"You're right! Come on!"

Our well-paved street now became a neglected roadbed of dirt and brush, as we had apparently reached the more remote quarters of the city. Once past Jones Falls, the houses grew farther apart, the lots interspersed with small fields cultivated with crops, and the street lamps non-existent.

The latter fact, however, proved more a boon than a bane, for the moon had risen full, a bright orange sphere in the eastern sky which had cleared totally since the afternoon. The wind was up as well, a brisk breeze that carried within it, despite the fact that it was only mid-August, the wild promise of the autumn to come.

It was the moon that finally allowed us a glimpse of him. As we passed, with considerable irony, the southern boundaries of the same cemetery we had visited earlier in the day, we caught sight of him upon a rise perhaps a half-mile ahead of us. His cloak fluttered cape-like as he drove his mount mercilessly eastward. His silhouette was a spectral sight as it passed by the stark outlines of the cemetery bearing the remains of his own father.

A few moments later, when we had virtually left the city behind us, he turned into a well-traveled track which ran directly toward the northeast, and once more spurred his horse into a deadly pace. We could barely hear the hoofbeats ahead of us now, dull but rapid thumps upon the earthen road that indicated that he was showing the horse no quarter in his flight. Wilkes and I soon lost sight of him again as the roadway before us grew obscured by the great and ancient trees that clustered around its sides, throwing an impenetrable shadow upon it.

"His mount runs like lightning!" Wilkes shouted as we turned onto the well-traveled highway ourselves. "But I don't think it can keep it up, not for very long. If he keeps riding like that, the horse will be dead within five miles. Slow down a bit, Watson, slow down!"

Wilkes' obvious skills as an equestrian were proving valuable indeed. In my excitement, I would surely have driven my own horse to utter exhaustion, if not worse. Wilkes realized that the geldings had already had a long sprint of it, and that the road ahead, for all we knew, might be a long one. We drew them back, therefore, to a steady trot and I could tell by the relaxing muscles on my gelding's back and his easier breathing, that the move had been a wise one. After ten minutes, we resumed our former gallop, held it for five minutes, and then reined them in once more.

"His steed is powerful" Wilkes shouted over to me, "a stallion without doubt, but don't worry that he'll get too far ahead of us. I don't think it will be very long before the horse is forced to slow down with fatigue. By then it will be too late to take him back up to a gallop."

The northeasterly road led us farther into the remote countryside which now seemed composed of endless tracts of tall corn, waving crazily in the intermittent wind, and occasional lines of tall trees. In the distance here and there we could spot the yellow glow of a window, revealing the locations of the scattered farmhouses. The road itself was a fine one, with only shallow ruts and few holes. Its borders, however, were fairly lined with large old sycamores, oaks and maples which, despite the road's good share of bends and short hills, effectively prevented us from gaining a vantage point of the roadway ahead of us. The moon had lost its golden hue and exaggerated size, and was now climbing the ebony heavens as a silvery white disk. Its pervasive half-light, while it might prove useful to us, gave the landscape an eerie cast.

We rode on like this for the better part of an hour, alternately galloping and trotting the geldings, all the while trying to keep a sharp eye on the roadsides and farm tracks in case Richard, in the manner of a fox, had decided to try letting his pursuers unknowingly overtake him, allowing him to slip in behind us and head off in the opposite direction. I worried also at the junctions, in fear that he might have chosen another road. We opted silently, however, to retain the main road, convinced somehow that he would stay upon it, too.

It occurred to me, also, that he must have had a particular desti-nation in mind. Why else would he put himself to such a disadvan-tage? He was now heading into ever more remote country, steadily eliminating the sort of hiding with which the city had provided him. Had he so desired, it seemed to me, he could have veered off the main streets into the alleyways at any number of places in Baltimore, with-out our knowing it, but he either scorned or was oblivious to these opportunities. Instead he was playing well into our hands, it appeared, by isolating himself out here in the country.

Indeed, when we caught another glimpse of him at last, this seemed to be true. We fin1ally entered a portion of the roadway which curved a long way ahead of us, and gently toward the right. It ran through a rather wild and uncultivated section of the countryside, which is perhaps why there had never been any trees planted by its sides. In the long clearing, we spotted Richard's profile easily in the moonlight. He still seemed to be flying along at a good clip, but there could be no doubt that we were gaining rapidly upon him. He was less than a quarter mile ahead of us.

"Back to a gallop, Watson!" Wilkes cried. "We'll try to close in on him!"

We gained steadily on the fleeing horseman, growing so near that we now kept sight of him constantly. This was fortunate indeed, since Richard now left the main road and headed abruptly north on a narrow and treacherous farm track. The difficulty of the new route slowed down our horses considerably, but had the same effect on his.

We spurred the geldings as fast as we felt safe, and they responded stoutly, having preserved much of their strength during the paced run. At the heightened sound of their gait, I clearly saw Richard turn behind him and gaze upon us. Though the distance was still considerable, I thought I could detect only an impassive face crowned with flying white hair. There was not the slightest indication of surprise or panic upon Richard's obscure features. In a moment he turned away from us once more, and regarded the moon-lit road before him.

I suspect that Richard had no more warning of the disaster that then befell him than we did, riding steadily perhaps 200 yards to his rear. We saw his horse lurch suddenly, as if its hoof had fallen badly into a pothole or a leg had suddenly begun to cramp. I heard its startled neighing as it pitched headlong off the road, just where a gentle curve turned more sharply into a bend toward the left. We saw its flaying hooves kick aimlessly into the air as it tumbled, head over heels, into a field, and over it all, we saw the black shadow of Richard's cloaked figure fly like some monstrous bat ahead of his fallen stallion.

In less than a minute we were on the spot ourselves. Richard's stallion lay on its knees by the side of the road, sides heaving with its labored breathing, eyes staring in animal fear, but otherwise apparently unharmed from his fall. A fine glint of sweat covering his taut black body testified to his heroic run. There was, however, no sign of Richard as we dismounted warily, pistols at the ready, and cautiously walked off the road.

The horse had stumbled into a large cornfield which appeared to have been recently harvested. The early corn had been put up in long, neat rows of shocks which seemed to stretch endlessly ahead and to the sides of us, like assembled soldiers upon a nocturnal parade ground. The spot was fortuitous for Richard in two respects—the rustling of the infinite cornstalks in the restless wind effectively covered any sound of footsteps and, more importantly, the six-foot shocks presented a virtually endless supply of hiding places and vantages for ambush.

Wilkes took a long look at the full moon and regarded me. "We'll have to split up," he whispered. "I'll head for the left; you take the right. Search every one, Watson, and for God's sake stay in the shadows of the corn. With this moon, he'll have a clear shot at you should he happen to have kept a gun with the horse, which would not surprise me at all." I nodded in reply and we headed off—very stealthily—in two directions.

I walked with my legs in a half crouch position, so as to lower my profile, and soon found myself utterly alone in the strange geometric straightaways formed by the harvested corn. The task of finding him within such a field was daunting enough, and was made only more difficult by the sheer nature of the place. I could glance to one direction and see for perhaps a full half-acre along the illuminated rows, but could see nothing within the shadows cast by each shock. The fact that there were rows both ahead of me, and to both sides, began to disorient my senses. Within five minutes, I realized that I had lost all sense of direction. I knew not whether I was continuing to head in a direction away from my starting point, back toward it, or in some unknown diagonal angle. The moon had by then risen to its very zenith, obscuring Polaris in the starry sky, and was thus rendered useless as a navigational aid. It felt as if I had stumbled into one of the great mazes at Kew Gardens back in England, and I sensed the early gripping sensation of instinctive panic. I heard nothing but the steady wind and unsettling sound of the dry stalks rustling against one another.

One sound, however, one tiny and barely distinguishable noise, was different from the rest, and by the time I realized its difference, it was too late. I turned sharply to face the sound and found myself staring into the eyes of Richard Booth, standing next to a shock no more than ten feet away from me. His white hair and black cloak flowed with the wind, and his face was set in a pale grimace. Both of his hands gripped a fearfully large pistol, holding it at steady aim in my direction.

There was no time, I knew, to bring my revolver up into firing position. Instead, I leaped to the side, hearing as I did so the sharp report of his gun, and feeling its bullet slam into my leg even before I reached the stubbly ground. The force of the shot hurled me neatly on my back, throwing my gun off into the darkness. It took a moment before my body relayed to my mind the hideous pain of my wound. I gasped as it seared through my entire body, momentarily blotting out my vision and replacing my hearing with a loud hissing noise. The visual and aural chaos was gone in a moment—the pain remained in place.

Richard walked triumphantly to within a few feet of me, the pistol still gripped tightly in both hands. He pointed it directly at my forehead and pulled back the hammer.

I cannot testify that my entire life flashed before my eyes; I cannot say whether I mentally uttered a prayer at that moment. I can only say in honesty that I knew at that moment, with absolute certainty, that my own death was at hand. Those who have stood at such a crossroads will understand when I say that the experience is inexplicable beyond that.

Yet my death was not to be. For some reason—some reason which mystifies me to this day—Richard did not fire his weapon. He did not fire even as his face reflected a frightening sort of confused rage, and began slowly to soften into an expression of tired resignation. He did not fire even as I saw above my head the blue steel of Wilkes' Colt glinting in the moonlight; even as the half-brothers briefly faced one another, as if combatants in a duel from a century before.

Although as deadly as the duels of yore, this one witnessed only one gun's firing. Wilkes hesitated but a moment before the roar of his pistol rent the chilly night air. His aim was true. Richard was literally knocked off his feet by the shot striking him, and thrown backwards into a cornshock which collapsed from the impact.

Calmly, Wilkes returned the Colt to his belt. He placed his arm beneath my shoulder and lifted me to my feet where I managed to remain standing on one leg, albeit quite shakily. Together, with Wilkes supporting my weight, we trudged the few yards to where Richard lay.

I could tell immediately that the bullet had entered the heart. A bright scarlet stain was spreading rapidly over the snowy whiteness of Richard's linen shirt, and his face had already gone deadly pale. He lay upon his back, spread-eagle, upon the broken cornstalks, and stared at us, unblinking. The expression now was not one of pain, or of rage, or of confusion, but of a strange sort of melancholy wonderment—an expression of realization.

Wilkes stared upon his victim with a hard and angry stare—an expression that carried no hint of regret or pity, and I could not blame him for any of this.

But then Richard held out his hand to his half-brother, trembling with the exertion of extending it to Wilkes, who remained standing by my side. Wilkes' face did not change in the slightest. Still, the hand of the assassin remained stubbornly extended—whether in fear, in friendship, or as a plea for forgiveness it was impossible to say—even though Richard could not have been more than moments away from death. I was stricken with the thought that Richard was deliberately holding death away with that hand—that he would not yield to its persistent tug until it was taken.

Somehow I think Wilkes sensed this too, for he began to slowly lose his unfaltering expression of hatred. He looked briefly at me, and in the dim light I could see the emotional wavering and debate taking place within his mind. There was a look upon his face as if he were seeking confirmation, or approval, from myself, and I gave it to him. I nodded my head, and Wilkes once again regarded the stricken man upon the ground. At last, and with nearly as much effort as it took for his dying half-brother to extend his hand, Wilkes knelt down beside him and took the pale hand into his own. The two men regarded one another silently.

Richard Booth was unable to utter any dramatic soliloquys on this night—unable to repeat the bravura performance he gave before a troop of Union soldiers 16 long years ago upon the porch of the Garrett farmhouse as the cold Virginia sun rose in the east. That had been a performance, after all, a dramatic and well-performed imitation of death. The encore would be very much the real thing.

All he managed to say, as Wilkes gripped his hand, were the whispered words: "My brother."

And then, with a final breath, the assassin closed his eyes against the night and died.

—22—
Ḥome at Last

It may have been nothing more than the imperfect light emanating from the moon; it may have been that the nightwind had blown something into the eye of John Wilkes Booth, but I could have sworn that he wiped a tear from from his cheek as he finally released the dead hand of his half-brother and rose to his feet.

"It is over," he said to me in a low voice. "All of it is over now."

Wilkes' face bore a dejected expression, it seemed, and a downcast slump weighed heavily upon his shoulders, as he uttered these words. Another man might have been celebrating his victory over the evil that was, until moments ago, personified in the form of Richard Booth. I sensed no trace of elation in this victor.

"You saved my life," I said, grasping my bleeding leg.

"Perhaps," said Wilkes. "If so, it is only what you are owed, my friend, having saved Ned. I said that I would not forget that, Watson, and I have not, but I am not sure that I saved you at all. I am not sure that he really intended to kill you. We both saw that he had his chance. For that matter, he could have easily taken me down, as well. I was none too quiet in reaching you after I'd heard the shot. He just stood there. Did you see how he just stood there and looked at us, Watson?"

"What are you suggesting?"

"We can never know for sure, of course, but I saw the look in his eyes. It was not surrender, nor defiance, that I saw within them, but despair. He wanted to die. He was waiting for it. He forced me to do it. I will always believe it."

"That amounts to suicide, Wilkes."

"Suicide by another's hand. By my hand to be exact. It is a major distinction to me. Now I really have killed a man. Now I have . . . never mind. You are wounded. Here, take my arm again. We'll get back to the city to have you looked after." He leaned against me to provide support and placed my arm around his back. We began to walk clumsily through the cornshocks back to the road.

"What about him?" I asked, nodding in the direction of the corpse.

"It will have to wait. We will see to it later."

All was quiet, save the wind, when we regained the road. The gunshots, it seemed, had not disturbed the peace of the farmers in the vicinity. Nobody but us was about. The horses had thoroughly rested themselves during our absence, and were calmly grazing in the tall grasses that grew by the wayside. Wilkes tethered Richard's fine stallion to his own gelding and was preparing to assist me into the saddle when he paused.

"What's that?" he said, straining to hear something.

In a moment, I heard it too—the distinct sound of carriage wheels rolling over the hard track of the roadway, surely less than a half-mile from where we stood. We waited in the shadows until we saw its approach in the moonlight. It was an elegant cabriolet, topped with black satin, and drawn up by a fine palomino mare, moving along the road at a fair clip. Two men appeared to be sharing its driver seat.

As it came near I immediately recognized the face of the man who held the reins in his hands.

"Holmes!" I cried.

The detective lurched the buggy to a halt and leaped down, dressed in his customary cap. He held out a hand and Edwin clambered down after him.

"How in blazes did you find . . ." Wilkes began to say.

"Oh, you are injured, Watson, just as I feared. Is it bad, old fellow?"

"It's a flesh wound, Holmes, still bleeding, but—"

"Edwin, if you please, the doctor's bag is inside the carriage. We shall treat him presently, under his own expert guidance, of course." He glanced quickly down the road. "I take it that he has escaped you then?"

"Hardly," said Wilkes, indicating the tethered stallion in the shadows.

Holmes looked sharply into my eyes, silently demanding an explanation.

"He is dead, Holmes," I told him. "Over there, in the cornfield. Not more than ten minutes ago."

Holmes glanced into the dark field and, for just a moment, I thought I saw cross his face a pained look—not one of pity, but of regret that circumstance had prevented him from glimpsing the final scene of the drama he had so expertly directed. The look was gone in an instant.

"So Richard meant what he said when he promised never to be taken alive," the detective said, rolling up my trouser leg and examining my wound.

"I am certain that he meant it very literally," Wilkes replied.

"Perhaps it is just as well," Holmes said without elaboration.

We entered the buggy and Holmes followed my instructions in cleaning and sanitizing my wound. The injury was painful enough, and deep, but the bullet had passed through mostly muscle tissue and the bleeding had not been extensive. As he worked and I winced, we discussed the details of the pursuit and final combat with Richard. Holmes and Edwin, in turn, explained how they had rapidly extinguished the fire in the hotel and, in the same manner Wilkes and I had used, quickly purloined the cabriolet from the street.

With the wound heavily bandaged, I began to feel considerably better. Holmes put away the tools and tinctures from my medical bag and jumped back to the ground, helping me descend in turn. "Take me to the body," he commanded, offering his shoulder as a crutch. The four of us soon formed a strange and solemn procession back to the spot.

In the cold air, Richard's features now appeared stiff and waxen. His white hair flowed in the wind. Everyone looked upon the body for a moment and then quickly turned away to look at one another. Holmes, apparently unaffected by the scene, sat himself down upon the earth in his Indian fashion and began carelessly filling the cherrywood with shag with a devil-may-care attitude.

"He who lives by the sword—" the detective began.

"Dies by the sword," finished Edwin quietly, looking once again with muted terror and fascination upon the corpse. He quickly turned to Holmes. "You've known about him for some time, haven't you? How did you know so certainly that it was he?"

Holmes pulled his jacket tighter against the growing chill and puffed into the air. "The motive for the assassination, first of all, set me off on that trail," he said, gazing thoughtfully at the brilliant stars. "Once I realized that Wilkes was innocent of the crime itself, I realized that the man who really did murder Lincoln could never have acted out of a primary ambition of putting the president out of the way, but of implicating Wilkes in the crime. This had to be true, or why else would he undergo the elaborate preparations, and incur the extra risks, to imply Wilkes' guilt—the contact with his kidnapping conspirators, the possession of his personal articles, the obvious attempt to resemble him, the impersonations so successfully portrayed? Would it not have been far easier to shoot Lincoln on one of his many rides through the countryside, or one of his nightly walks upon the Washington streets? Lincoln was never careful in protecting himself—he fully expected an assassin to strike eventually, it is well known— and an expert assassin would have learned this. These would have been the methods of a political assassin, and these were not deployed."

The rest of us soon joined Holmes in sitting or crouching on the cool ground. We were a macabre sight, I am sure—four men sitting, by all appearances, with complete ease next to the corpse of a fifth—but none of us seemed to give it a thought. Holmes pointed his amber pipe stem at Wilkes.

"You, Wilkes, were the assassin's true target and victim, not Abraham Lincoln. That is the ultimate irony of the crime. Therefore, I had to develop a motive for such an act against you. To some degree, Richard himself assisted me in this. He left clues, you see, for me to follow, either subconsciously symbolic of his torments or consciously so, which maintained a certain pattern. To you, Edwin, he spoke the line about oaks and acorns as he fired on you in the Lyceum corridor. He also made a practice of sending acorns to you in the wake of his attacks. Oaks and acorns, of course, are the most obvious symbols of fathers and sons, of sire and seed, if you will. And in the pamphlet on the assassination, found in his New York hideaway, he had written the passage from *Cymbeline*. Do you remember the words? 'I love thee brotherly, but envy much. Thou hast robbed me of this deed.'

"In each of these clues, these little talismans, one finds the strain of paternal or fraternal reference. Clearly, the attacker was obsessed with the ideas of 'father,' 'brother' and 'son,' in some aspect then unknown to us. The symbolic pattern is consistent, whether it was an unconscious effort to communicate his true reasons for acting so violently or a partly conscious effort to eventually ensure his capture. Either scenario is possible. At any rate, when I reviewed the history of the Booth family, particularly that chapter which deals with your father's hidden first family, the theory of vengeance against two brothers, in return for a father's negligence and abandonment, originally led me to suspect Richard. There indeed I glimpsed a potential motive, and a potent one at that.

"There were, of course, other indications as well. The unavoidable fact of an uncanny resemblance to Wilkes suggested the possibility of a blood relative. The fact that the attacker occasionally affected a French accent coincided nicely with my knowledge that Richard had worked as a French instructor. But the clincher, as they say here in America; the true coup-de-grâce, if you will, came to me as Watson and I rode over the Navy Yard Bridge."

"Aha!" exclaimed Wilkes. "His reply to the sentry's challenge!"

"Precisely, cousin. I knew at some point that it had not been you who faced the sentry on the night of the assassination, Wilkes, and that even if it had been you, you would have answered differently. I could imagine no other reason for the solitary rider to give his name as Booth unless his real name—the name with which he had grown up—was in fact Booth. He had worked desperately to create the illusion that Wilkes Booth had murdered the president. Under no circumstance would such a meticulous plotter as the assassin have risked his own neck, and the integrity of his entire plot, by giving this answer unless, in fact, the answer was a disastrous but honest slip of the tongue. He wanted them to hunt for, to catch and to punish John Wilkes Booth for the crime he had committed, in other words, so the last thing he would have wanted would be to steer the soldiers onto his own trail. And yet, this is precisely what he did and it was this very same trail, sixteen years later, that led me unerringly to him. A case of double jeopardy."

I took the detective's hand and shook it vigorously with my own. "It is brilliant, Holmes!" I said. "Absolutely brilliant!"

Edwin and Wilkes could only shake their heads in admiration of the detective's skills.

"It was nothing more than observation, my friends," the detective replied with a bow of his head. Typically, he was less interested in resting upon his laurels than in completing his explanation. "My location of Richard Booth, of course, involved the same strategy—that of eliminating the impossible in order to isolate the truth. I knew first of all that he had declared himself dead years ago in London, and that surely he had long ago abandoned the name of Richard Booth. I chose therefore to pursue his likely choice of location instead of his name. Baltimore, at least in America, had been his traditional home and so I began there. I made a check of all the foreign language instructors capable of teaching French in the city, and came up with no individual who even remotely matched Richard's general description.

"It struck me at last that a man whose motive of revenge stems from a childhood deprived of a father's love and attention, may well have tried to offset that lack with great love for his mother. She, of course, has been dead for many years, and so I headed for the cemeteries of Baltimore, searching them one by one until I located the grave of Adelaide Booth—your father's first spouse, and Richard's mother. I learned in short order that the symbiotic bond had indeed survived past her death. The grave of Adelaide had been well cared for since her burial twenty-three years ago, and the caretaker, my friends, could have been none other than Richard himself, Adelaide's only child.

"Watson and I confirmed this during our spectral vigil two days ago, when we saw the caretaker and followed him to a residence marked Samson Morrissey. We had come to the final portion of our telescope, gentlemen, and the figure of Richard Booth at last stood sharply within its lens. Just this morning I visited with the ersatz Mr. Morrissey in his office and convinced him to accompany me to the Carrollton Hotel, on the pretense that there were certain British clients waiting there who were involved in a potentially lengthy litigation over probate matters, and that his involvement in the case as a solicitor was being sought. He suspected nothing, quite obviously, and met me at the entrance of the hotel precisely on schedule, having ridden there upon his own horse. The rest of the drama, gentlemen, is well known to yourselves."

The four of us then grew silent as we sat in the wind-tossed cornfield with the body of Richard Booth. A great sense of peace seemed to have descended upon our small band—a powerful feeling of relief at having finally arrived at the end of a dangerous and very tangled trail.

Holmes broke the silence at last. "We have arrived, obviously, at a time of great decision," he said, regarding Wilkes, "and that decision, Wilkes, is purely your own. If you wish to clear your name of the terrible blot placed upon it, if you wish to resume your former name and identity, you must decide now to do so. It is the moment of truth. I do believe that with the details we have learned, and with the witnesses who have heard his confession, we stand a good chance in the courts of doing so."

Wilkes rose and began restlessly pacing around our strange little circle, hands in his pockets, a perplexed expression on his face. He pondered his weighty decision for several minutes before taking a stance directly before Holmes.

"It may sound absolutely absurd to you," he said deliberately. "It may sound like nonsense, Holmes, but I feel I have no choice but to let things go on as they are. I will let sleeping dogs lie. Justice has been done in this cornfield tonight, hasn't it? My pistol did the work that Edwin Stanton's purges and commissions failed to do—it avenged the death of Lincoln, even if the fact must remain a secret. And what would I have to gain by becoming John Wilkes Booth once more? Do you think that the hatred of an entire nation would simply cease of a moment? Do you think that their curiosity would not grow ever more morbid; that my life would not become a carnival? I would not impose such a humiliation on myself, let alone my wife and child. No, I cannot do it. I will not do it. And I implore each of you to hold this secret within your breast for the rest of your lives. It is a great deal to ask, my friends, but I am asking it because I must."

Holmes stood before Wilkes and solemnly took his hand. "I will honour your secret, cousin," he said softly. Edwin and I, after but a moment's glance at one another, rose ourselves. We placed our hands atop those of Wilkes and Holmes and together, over the body of

Richard Booth, the four of us made a solemn and silent pact to keep within ourselves a story that, if told, would shatter the very foundations of history.

The detective approached the prone body upon the ground. "Then we have work to do, gentlemen," he said. He leaned next to the body and began to remove Richard's cloak in order to make a form of shroud from it. Suddenly, with a start, he ceased his work.

"Hello," he said, taking something from the cloak's inner pocket. "What have we here?" He held a small packet of paper, folded neatly in half, upon which writing appeared. Holmes unfolded the pages and tried to study them in the dim light.

"We will need a light in order to read this," he said. "Let us return to the carriage. Unless I am mistaken, we have a lantern there."

"There are nine leaves here," he said as we walked back to the road. "Nine leaves with writing on both sides, which makes eighteen pages. Is the figure familiar, gentlemen?"

I pondered the question for but a moment. "Eighteen pages!" I cried. "Why, the missing diary pages, Holmes!"

"We shall shortly see," he replied, unable to hide his excitement.

We gained the cabriolet and quickly lit its kerosene lantern. Holmes scrutinized the tiny documents with his powerful lens. "Yes," he said. "Do you see? The pages are identical to those of Richard's forged diary, likewise written with pencil, and they have clearly been torn away from a binding. The writing is different from that in the diary, much larger and in a much finer hand, but I am sure the hand is Richard's all the same. It perfectly matches his inscription in the pamphlet. I suspect that within these pages he was writing strictly for himself, with no attempt to make the words appear to be someone else's. Surely this is why he tore them out, probably at the last moment available to him in the shed at Garrett's farm. From their patina, I suspect that Richard had carried them on his person for a good many years. He must have attached great importance to them."

"Either that," I said, "or he made sure to bring them tonight, somhow knowing that he was going to meet his doom." This dark possibility elicited no comment from my companions.

Holmes read the first few lines silently and then stopped. He handed the pages to Edwin. "I think it is better that you read this," he said.

The elder brother took the sheaf of papers with some hesitation and beheld the words upon them. With a troubled look at Wilkes, he began reading them in his fine, clarion voice. With Edwin's narrative skills at work, it soon felt as if I were hearing Richard himself recite the words rather than his half-brother.

With a glance at all of us, Edwin read the date: "'April seventeen, eighteen sixty-five'":

Dear Father, the passage began.

Can you hear me, Father, as I write these words to you? Can your ears still hear, there in that mysterious place of death, or your soul still sense, passions upon the earth? Somehow I am convinced that you can—that despite your place within the citadel of the afterlife, you may still hear the words, and feel the pain, of your eldest son.

I am cold, Father. I am hungry and I am in pain. Tonight I lie beneath a great tree, in the midst of a terrible and gloomy swamp, far from the warmth of humankind. Every man's hand, it is true, is turned against me on this night. I glimpse faint lights in the swamps, and I cannot tell if they are will-o'-the-wisps lurking there, or the torches of the soldiers. Thousands of men ride through this forsaken wilderness—I can hear their thundering horses even now—in search of me, and with a terrible vengeance within their hearts. I am not surprised. I have brought this down upon myself in order to settle a score with you. Yes, Father, with you. Even though the intended beneficiary of my recent and shocking act is another of your sons, you, Father, were on my mind when I pulled the trigger and changed forever the course of the river of history. I understand the minds of those who pursue me and who, in every likelihood, will take me in the end. I think I even understand the mind of your other son—he who, like me, must be hiding in fear of his life on this dark night. But your mind, Father, remains the deepest of mysteries to me. I cannot understand how you failed to see so very much.

Did you never picture in your mind's eye, Father, from the vantage point of your new American home, the sight of your son—a lad of five or six years—standing alone upon the shores of Belgium watching the ships sail slowly past him? And yet I stood there, Father, hoping against hope that one of those majestic ships was carrying you back to me. I would wait and wait, hour after hour, day after day, rejoicing when my spyglass offered me a view of the American flag upon their masts. Yes, rejoicing, and crying bitterly when my mother told me, yet again, that no, Richard, your father was not aboard that vessel either, but perhaps he may be on the next one. Did you not hear the weeping, or see the tears, of your own little boy as he laid awake in his bed by night?

Did you never contemplate how your two visits—two short visits in more than twenty years Father!—brought such happiness to your son? How I rejoiced to see you! How my

heart jumped with childish joy! I remember
one afternoon in October—this was in England—when we walked, just you and I,
through that great grove of oak trees. They
were so golden on that afternoon, and so
tall against the blue sky, that I felt we were
walking through the woods of the gods
themselves. It was a golden day, Father, one
of precious few among many grey ones. Do
you remember it? Do you remember also
how you departed the very next day, with
hardly a kiss for good luck—and the promise, your dark and dishonest promise, that
soon you would return once more, and that
this time Mother and I would go to America
with you? I remember it, Father. I remember
it well.

No less do I recall the look upon your face
in Baltimore—was it just shock or was there
guilt upon your features?—when I approached you unbidden and unexpected. A
young man already, able to make his own
way in the world, I gave you one more
chance to be a father to me. And for a few
weeks, I believed in you. You would make of
me an actor, like yourself. I would be a student of one of the greatest stars of the
stage—yourself—and we would travel
together in road shows, and share the applause of the audience side by side. This
you told me, Father, and this I believed. I
believed it until one of the other actors told
me what you had said to him—that I was a
great burden to you, and that you would be

rid of me as soon as the right opportunity
came along.

And then Father, your son discovered the
truth. You were embarrassed by my company, and fearful of it, because you knew
that a scandal might ensue. The scandal, of
course, was your ill-begotten family—the
American Booths!—and the knowledge of it,
father, drove a stake through my very heart
which bleeds to this day and, I fear, forever
will.

When one discovers that one's entire life
has been a cruel illusion, Father, when one
finally realizes that he has been abandoned upon a distant shore and replaced—
replaced!—with others, the sense of one's
self undergoes a change. It is a bitter
change, rest assured, and a demeaning
one. It is a change that makes one grow
hateful of his own company, and distrustful of anyone else's. I saw it in myself, and
I saw it in Mother—your forgotten wife who
soon joined me in order to make matters
right.

You rejected us, Father! You rejected us to
our faces, and forced my dear mother—a
woman who once walked with pride in the
knowledge that she was the chosen wife of
the great Booth—to endure the humiliation
of a public scandal. Piece by piece, Father,
the episode tore her very soul to shreds.

You could never have pictured, I know, the
scene of that tired and prematurely old
woman, thin and ill, lonely and despair-

ing, as she spent her final days. Only I
came to see her, Father, lying there in the
cold room of a miserable tenement in the
city. Only I held her trembling hand as she
died. Only I know that even then, even after
all her losses and humiliations, she wished
to be known as the wife of the great Booth,
and that she made me pledge to mark her
gravestone in this way.

If things had gone the honourable way,
she would have lived many more years. We—
the three of us—would have spent our years
together basking in the warmth of family
love, caring for one another. I know that you
enjoyed such a life, Father, for I came to
Tudor Hall to witness it myself. Did you
never know? I stood by the window upon a
cold Christmas Eve, and watched you dote
upon your new sons and daughters. I saw
the smiles upon their faces, and upon
yours, as you sang caroles around the tree.
I felt the love and the devotion of your home,
even as I felt that this home, this entire life,
had been stolen from your true family and
given to another. I understood then the
travesty of our poverty and the iniquity of
your comfort, Father, and I remember this
feeling well indeed.

So now perhaps your shade understands
something of the bitter harvest your little
boy has reaped. I have taken away the rewards bestowed upon your bastard son, but
never earned by him. If he does not die a
shameful and fearful death for it, surely

his life shall become a harsh and desperate one, such as I have known. But I have done more than this, my father. I have shaken the very heavens with my rage! I have cast a pall over an entire nation—I have wreathed its skies in black—so that mother shall now have plentiful mourners indeed. And I have done even more than this. I have taken your name—your beloved name—and given it to history dripping with indelible blood! Never again shall the name of Booth be uttered in this nation lest it be with anger and outrage and hatred and regret. You see, Father, I have given you the legacy you deserve.

My hatred of you knows no bounds. My contempt for you is infinite. Even with this act, I fear I shall be unable to fully express how bitterly I curse you. And yet, somehow, I am confused on this dreadful night. I am wondering about whether or not I have acted rightly. I am thinking about his own little son, grieving for his father within that great white house, and I am reminded of another little boy who grieved for his missing father as well. Have I erred? Was it unjust to punish your other son so? These are fearful questions, and in the darkness of this night and the darkness of my own soul, I am unable to find answers. I am lost, Father, in this dreadful wood and within myself. I am lost in untold ways.

I must hasten. I have told you everything—of the son you never knew, of the son who hates you still, of the son who has placed an everlasting curse upon your name. All of this is true, Father. There is but one last thing to say, words which my lips never said to your living ears. It is as true as everything else, and is but two words:

Edwin was ashen-faced and somber as he finished the document, and his hands trembled slightly. He regarded the rest of us sitting silently in a circle around him. "It is the end of the page," he said quietly, in a bewildered tone. "The last two words are missing."

"I believe that I know," Holmes said softly, "what the words are."

All of our eyes were upon him.

"If one recalls the mysterious first two words written upon the diary pages the government seized, those which are believed to be in Wilkes' writing, one cannot fail to speculate that Richard wrote them there, intending them to end the narrative we have just heard, but later forgot them in his haste, and began his false narrative immediately below them."

"What are the words?" I asked.

"*Ti amo*," Holmes replied. "Italian for 'I love you.'"

None of us could find a word of response to those final words, but I thought that I saw Wilkes shake his head sadly as he contemplated their ironic and awful portent. I thought too, that within that lamplit coach out on the lonely country road, there took place a certain departure of hatred for Richard, on the part of each of us, and a replacement of that with a profound sense of sadness. This case, in a manner unlike all cases before it and after, had proven far deeper than anyone might have imagined.

"All of our questions then," said Holmes, alighting from the coach, "are answered."

We followed him back out to the road. "Except for one," I said. Holmes turned to face me.

"How did you and Edwin know where to find us, Holmes? We were far ahead of you, heading out into the countryside, and yet you followed us to the very spot."

"We asked pedestrians if they had seen the two of you," the detective replied, "and their directions led us to the edge of the city. From there, I confess, the path was illuminated solely by Edwin's intuition."

Edwin regarded us modestly. "The road upon which we traveled is the Belair Road," he said. "Did you not recognize it, John?"

"For mercy's sake, I did not!" Wilkes exclaimed. "The pursuit was so feverish and I have been away for so long that the fact did not dawn upon me until this minute."

"The Belair Road, gentlemen," Edwin resumed, "is a familiar route to our family. If you did not notice the road, Wilkes, you must have also missed seeing the house, just there in the distance to the northwest. See the big woods, off to the side?"

Wilkes peered into the moonlit terrain and soon spotted, as did I, the black outline of a square farmhouse, topped with high peaked gables. The house stood perhaps a quarter mile away from us, situated well back from the roadway.

"My God, Ned! It's Tudor Hall! We played in this field as boys!"

Edwin smiled sadly as he spoke. "Tudor Hall was our boyhood home. We grew up here. Our father built the original cabin on the spot shortly after arriving in America, and later built a new house all around and over the original. It's been out of the family's hands for years."

"And somehow you knew—" I began.

"When Richard chose the Belair Road," Edwin replied, "I knew that he could have but one destination in mind. Why else would he head this way unless he wished to come to Tudor Hall?"

"He wanted to come to the place he considered home," added Wilkes softly.

We gazed at the dark and forlorn house once so familiar to these two brothers, and then regarded the shadowy shape of the man who chose this spot to die. The restless wind pushed a great and melancholy sigh through the cornfield.

"So the surrogate assassin," said Holmes, "has come home at last."

—Epilogue—

As August waned into September, and as the last warmth of summertime gave way to the early frosts and changing hues of autumn, Holmes and I finished up what little business was left to us in America.

Before we left the city of Baltimore to return to New York, Holmes and I paid a clandestine visit to the erstwhile quarters of the late Samson Morrissey, better known, at least to us, as Richard Booth. His townhouse in eastern Baltimore was remarkably humble, nearly Spartan in its absence of luxuries and almost military in its neatness. Holmes determined that Richard had indeed been engaged in solicitor's work, although the detective never found any evidence that Richard had in fact ever been licensed in the practice of law in any of its forms. He had apparently occupied himself with fairly pedestrian and low-profile cases, in order to keep up the appearance of gainful employment. In fact, we soon discovered, Richard had no pressing necessity to work for his upkeep at all. In a strongbox beneath his bed, we found a substantial sum, more than twenty thousand dollars, all of it in gold—in American eagles, British guineas and other, more exotic, coinages. It was Holmes' conclusion that this wealth stemmed from the shady enterprises in which Richard had briefly engaged during his stay in Philadelphia, and to which he obliquely referred during his remarkable discourse with us. Holmes felt that the enterprise may in some way have been connected with sophisticated fraud schemes perpetrated on unwary, but wealthy, European immigrants to the United States. If so, it would have been a scam for which Richard was eminently qualified in more ways than one. However gained, the treasure trove had surely underwritten Richard's determined if unsuccessful campaign to do away with Edwin which, with its travel expenses, must have been a fairly costly undertaking.

In Richard's parlor, above a plain mantle, we also found a touching portrait encircled within an aging oval frame. The painting was of a young family—a youthful and dashing Junius Brutus Booth, a pale but smiling woman we knew to be Adelaide Booth, and a handsome lad of perhaps six years dressed in children's fashions of perhaps five decades past. The elfin face of the youthful Richard Booth was immeasurably more innocent than the face of the man with whom we had so recently dealt, but unmistakably, and heartbreakingly, a young version of the very same person. We concluded that the portrait must have been painted during one of the elder Booth's two visits to his original family—probably the same portrait Edwin had once glimpsed in his father's trunk—although it remains a mystery as to how Richard managed to come into possession of it.

We took the portrait as we left the dead man's house, as well as the fortune in gold. Holmes presented the portrait, along with the eighteen "missing" pages of the diary, to Edwin shortly thereafter. What has become of them since I haven't a clue, although in truth I wouldn't be at all surprised if Edwin wasted little time in throwing them all into the fire—much in the way he had once disposed of another brother's personal articles.

As for the money, it was Holmes' idea to distribute it evenly, and anonymously, to a dozen or so orphanages in Baltimore and several other American cities. He accomplished this through a series of bank drafts. I found the gesture not only appropriate, considering the nature of Richard's inner torment, but extremely virtuous and noble of Holmes.

Holmes followed the Baltimore newspapers for some time after our adventure near Tudor Hall, even after our return home, but never found the slightest reference to a missing person by the name of Samson Morrissey. Richard had been so successful in living the life of an utter stranger to all men that his disappearance went utterly unheeded. One assumes his landlord simply concluded that his tenant had left without notice, and didn't think to report it. To this day, I get a chill in contemplating the fearsome anonymity of Richard's death. I find it a profoundly sad way for any person to leave the company of the living.

An additional task in Baltimore, of course, was the return of the geldings and cabriolet we had temporarily taken from their owners. This went remarkably well, as it turned out, and was undoubtedly smoothed by Holmes' timely offer of generous compensation. No charges of thievery, thankfully, were ever brought against us.

Once back in New York, it fell to Holmes to somehow explain things to Allan Pinkerton, whose agent, Titus Oglesby, had perished in the line of duty by Richard's hand. I am not sure how he accomplished this without revealing the details of our secret pact, but Holmes informed me that he had assured Pinkerton that justice had indeed been served, and that the details of its facilitation could not be broached. There the matter apparently ended. Pinkerton, at any rate, was far more interested that summer in his pursuit of the Western outlaw Jesse James than in our particular case, according to Holmes, and that may have made matters easier for the younger detective.

Less than two weeks after our departure, Edwin returned to the American stage at last, opening in the first week of October in his beloved Booth Theatre supported by a large and expensive company. His performances there received rave reviews from an American public which had been highly impressed with Edwin's triumphs earlier that year in England. It marked the return of the elder brother to prominence upon the American stage—a prominence he would retain for several more fruitful years.

Edwin, we would later learn, was overjoyed that his brother Wilkes—suitably disguised—was among his audience that night in New York. We would later hear as well that Wilkes had been powerfully impressed with his brother's performance, even as he could barely contain his urge to rush upon the stage himself and begin to recite the lines he had never forgotten. The two brothers, according to a letter from Wilkes, performed an entire act from *Hamlet* with one another, in the solitude of Edwin's apartment at the Windsor, before Wilkes' own departure. The recital, if I can remember Wilkes' words accurately, "lit up a great many old sparks between us."

By mid-October, Wilkes, eager to rejoin his young family, bid
Edwin an emotional farewell upon the platform of the Pennsylvania
Station. Since I was not there to view the scene personally, I cannot
describe it. I can speculate, however, that after their long and tortuous
absence from one another, and the startling events of that remarkable
summer, the separation must have been a dramatic one indeed.

Edwin's second engagement that fall was at Philadelphia, and it was
while he was here that he learned of the death in New York of his
unfortunate wife. While I am sure that his grief at her loss was great, I
cannot help but believe that her passing, after a dreadfully long and
emotionally destructive illness, must have come as a tremendous relief.

We were to learn of yet another death in the wake of our departure. President Garfield, wounded by another assassin's bullet within
days of our arrival, died within days of our farewell, in Elberon,
New Jersey, after painfully lingering through the summer. It was
sadly ironic that one assassination was culminated just as another
had been avenged at last.

Holmes and I were back in London before September was out,
having steamed over leaden and chilly seas aboard the *Great Eastern*.
Our departure from Edwin and Wilkes was a melancholy one for
both of us, but more so for Holmes, I am sure, because of the close
relationship he had established with his American cousins. On shaking each of their hands in turn, I saw the barest glint of a tear in
Holmes' eye—it was to be the only time during my entire association
with him that I witnessed such a thing.

Not very long after we had re-established ourselves in our Baker
Street lodgings, Holmes was back at work again. Within a few weeks,
I accompanied him to Dartmoor on his investigation into the death
of John Straker and the disappearance of the racehorse Silver Blaze,
widely believed to be a shoo-in for that autumn's Wessex Cup. The
case, as many of my readers know, was a fascinating one, and its
complexities did much to remove the Booth affair from the forefront
of Holmes' mind.

The story of the surrogate assassin, however, certainly did not escape my mind. Before the winter was out I had, after much difficult
debate, persuaded Holmes to allow me to compose the story from start

to finish, while my memory of the actual events was still clear. In a dinner at the Northumberland Hotel, Holmes predicated this on the condition that the story would, in the manner of a tontine, be withheld as agreed to in our pact with the Booths, for as long as each of us lived. Holmes' demands, however, did not cease there. The sealing of the manuscript, as I have noted in the Prologue, would have to continue for at least 50 years following the death of the last survivor, whomever that may be. I calculated that the period would amount to roughly a century, give or take a decade. Only then, Holmes said to me, would we be assured that no living person could have any connection with the events or individuals described in the story. The conditions were stringent indeed, I felt, but in the interest of historical accuracy, and of granting Wilkes at least a posthumous acquittal in the eyes of future generations, I agreed to them. Holmes' permission to allow me to write the story at all was quite a victory, after all.

Although Holmes and I would never again work with the Booths in an investigative capacity, we did maintain some contact with both of the brothers over the years. A year after our American adventure, Edwin was back in London, in an engagement that brought him only greater praise and more ovations than his previous trips. He paid us a call that summer, of course, and we shared many enjoyable moments discussing the events of the previous year. He returned to London later that year, at Christmas-time, and hosted us in a lavish banquet in his rooms at Morley's Hotel. It was to be our last glimpse of him.

The remaining nine years of Edwin's life were plentiful ones, during which he achieved greater heights upon the stage than his career had yet witnessed. He worked regularly, earned ovation upon ovation, and gained a reputation among young and old alike as an outstanding and compassionate gentleman. He passed away in his rooms at the Players, a club for actors he had established in New York's Gramercy Park, on the seventh of June, 1893, with his beloved daughter by his side. Through his art, his manner and the many good deeds he performed throughout his life, Edwin did much to counter the damage done to his family name by the assassin of Abraham Lincoln.

Two days after his death, as he was being buried in Boston, a chilling event took place, at the very moment, they say, that his casket was being lowered into the ground. Hundreds of miles away, in Washington, the foundations of the old Ford Theater finally gave way, collapsing most of the interior of the accursed old house, and killing dozens of government workers. I recall that Holmes winced painfully when I mentioned the macabre coincidence of the two happenings, but said nothing.

Over the years, Wilkes maintained a long and steady correspondence with us, writing us of his daughter's progress, and that of the other three children he came to father. He became a distinguished teacher and respected citizen in Denver, arousing no suspicion whatsoever as to his former identity, despite the fact that ghostly legends of the assassin's survival persisted for decades. He wrote twice, in 1887 and 1889, to tell us of Edwin's visits to Denver and his triumphant performances there during his great Western tours of that period. Wilkes visited with him on both occasions, he wrote us, adding that his solitary regret over their warm reunions was that he could not introduce his brother to his wife, for fear that her suspicions might thus be aroused.

He wrote with considerable relish to tell us of one of Edwin's performances at Denver's Tabor Grand Opera House, the very pride of the city, and the creation of the legendary mineral baron H.A.W. Tabor. The powerful Mr. Tabor, and his beautiful wife Baby Doe, Wilkes wrote, customarily arrived in their venue only after the performance was well underway, a tactic by which the audience's attention was naturally diverted to their entrance. They followed this custom as Edwin was at work on *Richelieu* and immediately earned the actor's ire. "The performance will progress for those who have the taste to appreciate it!" Edwin barked to his distracted audience. Wilkes watched the Tabors leave in a huff, he reported, as he sat uncomfortably in his chair, trying not to break out into hysterical laughter at his brother's assertiveness. The incident, Wilkes wrote, illustrated "how Ned is much less the shrinking violet he used to be, and is now quite capable, thank you, of taking difficult matters into his own hands. You two would have been very proud of him."

Wilkes finally retired as a pedagogue at the age of 70, in 1908. He lived subsequently near the small Iowan town of Polk City, where his son had years before established a productive farm. To judge by his letters, the old age of John Wilkes Booth was a pleasant and rewarding time. He doted on his grandchildren, read many of the books he had never found the time for earlier, and managed to change with the times. He wrote once, in 1925 or so, to tell me of the new Stutz Bearcat motor car he had purchased, and was learning to drive over the country roads.

Wilkes was always aware that, after the death of Edwin, the only bearers of his secret were Holmes and I. Surely this is why, in November of 1927, I received a telegram from an attorney in Des Moines, informing me of the death of an individual I knew to be John Wilkes Booth. A codicil in his will had required both Holmes and I to be notified of his death when it took place. "Mr. R——," the telegram stated, "succumbed on Thursday last, while sitting upon the porch of his son's farmhouse in Polk County. He was 89 years of age."

It was, of course, a sad message to receive, yet somehow I was heartened by the sheer simplicity of the attorney's description of Wilkes' passing. To die upon a friendly porch, perhaps while watching the setting of the sun over the verdant fields, perhaps while reflecting upon a life wisely spent, is really not such a terrible way to go. The life of John Wilkes Booth, I realize, was not without its regrets. I don't believe he ever recovered fully from the loss of his first true love, Bessie Hale, for example. He referred to her in a letter decades after the case was settled, commenting that he had read a news article somewhere that mentioned her name, or that of her husband, in connection with their later home in West Point, New York. He wondered if she ever thought of him at that late date. In reply, I wrote him that I was confident indeed that she did.

The loss of his acting career remained a great burden for Wilkes throughout his life. With the exception of Edwin's performances, he wrote, he had never again entered a theater. The agony of being so close to the stage, and yet so maddeningly distant from it, was more than he could bear.

Despite these travails, however, Wilkes led the life of a decent and upright man, working hard in his chosen field and reaping the rewards of having raised a fine family. Like Edwin, he lived to see a peaceful time in his life, and to die in a peaceful and honourable way.

That fact alone represents the ultimate victory of Edwin and John Wilkes Booth over their demented and tormented half-brother, who had far more terrible designs in mind for both of them. An unlikely combination of luck, circumstance, and the work of Sherlock Holmes was all that prevented the spider from consuming the various victims he had so cleverly trapped within his webs. There had been no luck, no circumstance and no Holmes—alas—to keep Abraham Lincoln from falling victim to him.

It would be easy to hate Richard Booth for his villainous deeds against his own kin, easier still to hate him for his crime of assassination, which had such a devastating and lasting impact upon America that I am sure its aftershocks will linger still when these words are finally read by a generation yet unborn.

For all that, I cannot bring myself to say that I hate the man. I may still feel rage over his deeds, but I cannot hold him fully responsible for them. I have never been able to erase from my mind the image of that little boy awaiting his father's homecoming—a homecoming that was never to be—and to shake my head in helpless sadness at the monster that arose from that innocent boy's mind.

Of those who are living, only Sherlock Holmes and myself know of Richard Booth's terrible role in history and of his ultimate fate. Only we know that beneath the tilled fields of a Maryland farm, within a stone's throw of the home he had once so desperately wanted to call his own, his bones lie unnoticed and undisturbed within a grave that has no marker.

I can only hope that here at last, where he has but the nightbirds to sing his requiem, his troubled soul rests in peace.